THE BEACH
OF ATONEMENT

ARTHUR W. UPFIELD

ETT IMPRINT, SYDNEY

Exile Bay

ETT IMPRINT
PO Box R1906
Royal Exchange NSW 1225
Australia

First published by Hutchinson, London 1930

First published by ETT Imprint in 2016. Reprinted 2017, 2019.

ISBN 978-1-922698-59-9 (paper)

ISBN 978-1-875892-50-3 (ebook)

The publisher would like to thank Rosemary King for her help.
Design by Hanna Gotlieb

TO

the many courageous women dwelling in the depths of the Australian Bush, each helping to add to the British Empire a further need of greatness, and each at the same time flinging back the lie that the youth of Great Britain are lacking in the spirit of adventure, I dedicate this book.
A. W. U.

150 miles from nearest town,
Western Australia.

CONTENTS

CHAPTER I

"ELLEN AND TRACY"

ARNOLD DUDLEY mechanically lifted the telephone receiver from its hook in the early morning of the day that was to witness the beginning of his exile from the world of men. The voice at the other end of the wire was masculine, slow, and distinct. He did not recognize it. He never heard it again.

"Is that Dudley—Arnold Dudley?" inquired the voice.

"Yes."

"Are you alone?"

"No. My stenographer is with me. Why?"

Dudley heard a slight cough, the speaker evidently desiring to clear his throat. Then:

"I am about to say something very unpleasant. It is entirely for your benefit that I suggest that you are better alone when you hear it."

Frowning, Dudley motioned to the stenographer to withdraw, and, when the office door had closed behind her, he said shortly :

"Well ? I am alone. What is it?"

"You are acquainted, I think, with Edmund Tracy, the stock and station agent, of Geraldton?"

"Yes ; he is an acquaintance of mine. Who are you?"

"In the circumstances I cannot divulge my name," replied the unseen man with finality. "I am commissioned by a mutual friend to inform you that for the last five Saturday afternoons Mrs. Dudley has given your servants a holiday as from one to seven o'clock, and that shortly after they have left the house she is visited by Edmund Tracy, who remains with her until about six: Whilst our mutual friend trusts that nothing dishonourable is going on, he has decided that it is only right and proper you should know."

"I think you are a liar," Dudley said distinctly.

"I expected that you would think that," came the clear voice. "Your cook, however, spends her pleasant Saturday afternoons with her mother at No. 7, Hyland Road, North Perth. No. 5 is occupied by a Mr. Smith, whose telephone number is A 2778. I suggest you ring him up at two o'clock and ask him to call Miss Merrill, your cook. She will undoubtedly substantiate my statement regarding her extra half-holidays. Good-bye!"

"A-two-seven-seven-eight," Dudley repeated. "Is that right?"

He received no answer and, realizing that the man at the other end of the wire had broken the connection, replaced his own receiver on its hook and gazed vacantly at the figures he had noted on his paper block.

Arnold Dudley was not yet thirty-five. Clear hazel eyes regarded the world with penetrating keenness; straight dark eyebrows almost met above the well-defined, slightly Roman nose ; whilst above the broad low forehead wavy dark brown hair with a tinge of copper in it was brushed back in a manner that denoted pride. Altogether Dudley's face was a strong one, but withal a likeable one. It was his mouth that attracted. Kindliness and tolerance were it on the lines about it.

On this day he was a wholly successful business-man. From a rabbit-trapper he had become a skin-buyer, and his early struggles as a buyer of rabbit-skins, kangaroo-skins, sheep-skins and hides had been shared by Ellen, his wife. They had met and loved and married when he was touring the pastoral districts of Western Australia, driving his own truck and buying in person the furred skins from the trappers, and the sheep-skins and hides from the squatters.

Now he occupied a suite of offices on St. George's Terrace, and owned a warehouse in Fremantle, and his name was a household one all over the back country. He was famed as an honest dealer, and no longer did he have to "scout" for sellers. They sent him their combined produce in tons, and after it was graded and weighed, and promptly paid for, his bales of rabbit-skins, kangaroo fur, and hides, were shipped to America. And his wife, who had heartened and helped him in his struggles and disappointments, and now shared his success, occupied one of the most magnificent homes in Perth.

To listen to that slanderous swine on the telephone was to insult his wife. The mere thought of her being unfaithful to him was criminal. Ellen, the girl he had married, was a vision of winsome loveliness. Ellen, still in her twenties, the wife of a successful businessman, was just a wonderful, brave, sweet woman. Unfaithful! It was impossible.

No—improbable, not impossible.

There was the affair between a friend of his and a woman in Smith Street some nine years before-an affair that had stamped itself on his mind. It had been arranged that he should call for his friend in a car at nine o'clock one evening. Slightly disgusted with his friend's intrigue, he had stopped his car a little further along the street. At the appointed time the friend had joined him, and not twenty seconds after he had left the house the woman's husband walked up to the door. And the woman, fresh from the embraces of her lover, had said loud enough for them to hear:

"Why, Harold ! you are home early. Ted has only just gone."

In the light shining out through the open door they had seen the woman draw her husband to her and kiss him before leading the way indoors. Dudley's friend had said, with a sigh of relief:

"That was a narrow shave. Can you beat a woman for slyness? The Ted she spoke of is her brother."

It was the Judas kiss which had shocked Arnold Dudley far more than the woman's betrayal of her husband's honour. And even worse was the cynical laugh of his then companion at the expense of the poor blind trusting fool of a husband.

But Ellen—no! a thousand times no ! She and he had become so bound together by their intimate life, their reliance each on the other, that the mere thought of unfaithfulness in her was an outrage. Yet—! That other man—the man betrayed—would then have thought of his wife precisely as he was thinking—or trying to think.

Then there was Tracy. He and Edmund Tracy had risen to success at about the same time. Their acquaintanceship had dated back to those far-off years when he had been a skin scout. There were many traits in Tracy's character which were to be admired, but his attitude towards women was not one of them. Tracy would be about thirty years old. He was good-looking in his dark, pale way, unmarried, and judging by reports of his feminine conquests, alive with what has been termed "sex appeal".

But Ellen! Ellen, the fresh and the beautiful, who had waved him good-bye that very morning when he drove off in his car to business! Ellen and Tracy! And Tracy three hundred miles north in Geraldton! Ridiculous!

A girl came in with a sheaf of letters for his signature, and Dudley forced his mind to concentrate on them. Yet at the back of his mind, as though an imp dwelt there constantly shrieking, came the reiterated phrase:

"Ellen and Tracy—Ellen and Tracy—Ellen and Tracy!"

The girl having gone, he rose and paced the room, a tall, lithe figure in a grey suit, yet supple and athletic. The poison of doubt had been inserted in his brain, and only proof, certainty, of his wife's fidelity, would remove it. The voice over the telephone line, clear and incisive, had sounded top grade incoming fur, without blemish. There was no doubt, no hesitancy, no blundering, in that now hateful voice.

"I can't believe it—I simply can't believe it," Dudley moaned, sinking into his chair and burying his face in his arms over the littered desk. "But proof! I must have proof!"

When he looked up, his face was drawn, his eyes wide, and in them a strange glitter. He pressed the buzzer on his desk, and when his stenographer entered he was writing a message on an Urgent Telegram Form, to be dispatched to Tracy's chief clerk. The message asked for Tracy's whereabouts.

The telegram was sent at ten-fifteen, and precisely one hour later 'the reply was handed to him. Quite calmly he tore open the buff envelope and read:

"Mr. Tracy left for Perth last night's express.—

"MILLER"

The stenographer, who had waited whilst he read the telegram, was amazed to see blood on his nether lip, and alarmed by his colour-drained face and staring eyes. She was about to leave hurriedly; when he reassured her by saying quietly:

"Put me through to the warehouse, please. Then draw a cheque to self on my No. 2 account for a thousand pounds. Ask Mr. Thomas to come here."

There was no hint of emotion, no hint of panic, when he directed the manager of his warehouse to dispatch in a car an employe named George Finlay to the office. Then entered Mr. Thomas, Dudley's chief clerk, who was requested to be seated on the further side of the table.

For Arnold Dudley had decided to kill Tracy if he were. engaged in an intrigue with his wife. Since the law is incapable of protecting a man from dishonour, since the law will not punish a seducer of married women, he must then be a law unto himself. But on no account must he suffer the law's punishment for punishing the wrecker of a man's life, "happiness, and home; for such retribution would defeat the injured and not the injuring party. He was his own man when he spoke.

"It is quite possible, Thomas, that I shall be absent from business for some time," he said. "I intend making you the manager of it, and giving you a power of attorney to act for me. I can trust you, Thomas, to give me a fair deal in my absence. You know my principles and my methods. Adopt them as your own, and you'll keep the old ship sailing. Go at once and get the necessary papers drawn up. I want the matter fixed before we close at twelve. When Finlay arrives, show him in."

"It may be needless to say it, Mr. Dudley, but I am surprised," Thomas answered, rising. "You may be sure, though, that I shall do my best."

"I know you will," Dudley returned rapidly. "Remember that we have a hundred and thirty people on our pay sheets, and if you let the business down they go down with it. Now, hurry off for those documents."

The chief clerk's place was taken by the stenographer, who laid the cheque before him for signature. After signing it, he told her to get it cashed in one pound notes, and added:

"I may have to take a long journey, Miss Sawyers. During my absence Mr. Thomas will manage the business. I trust that you, as well as the staff, will serve him as loyally as you have served me. Always remember that personal honour is your greatest possession."

"I will always do my best, sir," was her reply, before hastening to the bank.

Ten minutes later she returned with twenty wads of one pound Treasury notes in a black bag, and found him counting the money that had been in the safe. When she had again withdrawn he replaced the amount taken from the safe with the new notes obtained from the bank, an operation assuring him several hundreds in untraceable currency. The black bag containing this money he set down beside his chair, and from a drawer in his desk he took a small-calibre automatic pistol, which he dropped also in the bag before finally closing it.

Then it was he sat slumped in his chair, his body hot with fever, his brain as though encased in ice, and deep within his mind the voice of the imp:

"Ellen and Tracy—Ellen and Tracy—Ellen and Tracy!"

He heard sounds beyond his door denoting the departure of his staff, and then Thomas entered, followed by the stenographer dressed for out-of-doors.

"Here are the documents you asked for, Mr. Dudley," Thomas said, laying before Dudley several papers. "I have asked Miss Sawyers to please witness your signature."

Dudley signed without speaking, and passed the documents across to the manager, who pointed out the places for the witness's signature. The girl, glancing at her employer before turning to the door, wondered at Dudley's strained expression. Thomas said:

"Is that all, sir? I trust your journey will be a pleasant one. Finlay is waiting outside. Shall I tell him to come in?"

"Yes, do. I am not absolutely certain that I shall have to go away, Thomas. You will know either way on Monday morning."

"Very well, Mr. Dudley" And when Thomas left he did not wonder so much at his employer's haggard appearance. He had heard an ugly rumour about Mrs. Dudley.

Finlay came in. He was a stocky, powerful man of fifty or thereabouts. Dressed in a rough suit of tweed, his many years of outdoor life evidenced by his reddish complexion, Finlay looked what he was, or what for years he had been before he entered Dudley's warehouse as a skin-classer.

"Sit down, George," he was told. "Till and light your pipe. I want no one to hear what I am going to talk about."

Dudley lit a cigarette, and for several minutes the two smoked in silence. Each understood the other; for many a year they had been partners in rabbit-trapping and kangaroo-shooting. At last Dudley rose and passed into the outer office. It was clear of workers, and he locked the main door before returning to his own office and reseating himself.

"Have you still got your old ton truck, George?" he asked.

"Yes, Arnold. Why?" Finlay replied with old-time familiarity.

"Is it in going order?"

"Yes. Me and the missus went up Moora way last week-end, and we got a couple of foxes."

A further silence fell between them. Then:

"I am facing a lot of trouble, George," Dudley said. "I am told that Ellen is carrying on with Tracy.   You remember Tracy?"

"Tracy! Ellen carrying on with Tracy!" gasped Finlay, the pipe sagging from his mouth, his body suddenly bent forward. "Like hell, she is!"

"Precisely. It may be like hell she is," Dudley said with sudden, surging anger. "I am going to make sure this afternoon. It has been my custom to spend Saturday afternoons on the golf links. We play till it is too dark to play, and it is generally eight o'clock when I reach home. I have been informed that the servants have been sent out on Saturday afternoons, and that Tracy goes to my house and remains there several hours. If he is there this afternoon I am going to shoot him."

"And get yourself hanged," stated the now calm George, adding: "I don't believe Ellen is carrying on with Tracy. I've known her ever since

10

was she a little dot. As for Tracy-well, I never liked him. He's too flash. Anyway, he ain't worth getting hanged for."

"I am not going to get hanged for him, Dudley said quietly. "That is why I want to buy your truck. What's it worth?"

"About eighty quid. But look here, it is —."

"Have you still got your trapping-gear?" Dudley cut in. "Yes. Six dozen rabbit-traps, rifles, and loading outfit, a tent, and tucker utensils. But why — ?"

"How much do you want for the gear?"

"Twenty quid would cover all that, Arnold. But what is the idea?"

From the black bag now on his knees Dudley took out notes to the value of a hundred and fifty pounds, which he slid along the desk towards his old partner. Then he said:

"I do not believe that Ellen is dishonouring me, but from what I have been told this morning the maggot of doubt has been created in my brain. I have simply got to kill that maggot. If I find Tracy with my wife I am going to shoot him, and you are not going to prevent me.

"I am not going to get hanged either, if I can help it. There are a hundred and fifty pounds for your truck and all the gear. Go home and tell your wife you are going out with a friend for the day. Get her to fill the tucker-box to last a couple of days. Then about three o'clock leave with the truck and drive to Midland Junction, where take the north road to Geraldton, and stop about two miles beyond the Junction. Wait there for me. Is that plain?"

"Yes, it is. But don't be a fool, Arnold," Finlay said earnestly. "They ain't worth it. Even Ellen ain't worth it. No bloomin' woman is worth hell and damnation."

"You're, a good sort, George," Dudley said after a short silence: "We've been pals a long time. You won't fail me now, will you?"

"I might be doing good by failing you."

"You won't. You will be assuring me a hempen rope."

It did not enter Finlay's mind that when he consented he became accessory to the contemplated crime, nor did it then occur to Dudley that he was placing his old partner in that unenviable position. It was sufficient for Finlay that he was asked for help by one who had always been a friend in fair weather; and a stauncher friend in foul weather. He could never forget how Dudley had engaged specialists regardless of expense when his youngest boy almost died.

"Very well, Arnold; I'll be there," he said slowly.

CHAPTER II

"THE MOVING FINGER WRITES—"

WHEN Finlay had gone, Arnold Dudley sat alone in his office. It occurred to him how utterly strange it was that during the morning of that ordinary. Saturday he should have planned a murder and elaborated means to escape the legal punishment of the crime. He had left his home thinking happily of his wonderful Ellen and of the golf tournament in which he was to play that afternoon. Now he was not merely contemplating killing another man, but was absolutely resolved to kill if he found that man with his wife.

If Tracy had dared to seduce Ellen's allegiance from him, then it was probable that others knew of it also, more than probable that others as well as Tracy were laughing, sneering at' him, at Arnold Dudley. He would be the butt of coarse jokes, the man with bull's wool over his eyes, the simpleton, the easy-going poor silly fool.

Mentally, Dudley squirmed in his chair, Physically, his body twitched as though each muscle strove inde-pendently to kill the beast who tortured it. Tracy—the laughing, good-looking peacock, conscious of power over women, to whom no woman's virtue was sacred! The powerful hands lying on the office table clenched and unclenched to the sound of rubbing fingers and snapping tendons.

The mood vanished. The expression of agony and hate working the features of his strong face was wiped away as writing on a slate is wiped off with a damp sponge.

"Ellen! Ellen! God! it is unbelievable, was the cry wrenched from him. Ellen of the starry eyes, Ellen of the adorable red lips, Ellen of the soft entwining arms! Ellen who had been his, was his! Yes, damn it! was his.

Springing to his feet, he paced the room, his hands locked behind him, his head thrown back, his eyes seeing not the ceiling but the pictures, the flashing pictures of Ellen, as she had appeared to him through the years.

"She'll be alone. She'll be alone. I'll bet a million she will be alone," Dudley muttered.

Of course she would be alone. It was to insult her, to wrong her past forgiveness, to even think, let alone believe that she would be with Tracy. Why, her loyalty, her goodness and freshness and beauty, had proved themselves a thousand times—a thousand times. That lying devil on the 'phone! It was he who deserved a pistol bullet. And—

"Ellen and Tracy—Ellen and Tracy—Ellen and Tracy!" screamed the imp in his mind.

He beat his forehead with his open hands, as though to smash the shrieking, lying imp. He was in the Garden of Gethsemane. The mental agony, not less than his bodily exertion, brought to his forehead beads of perspira-tion that streamed down his face, trickled into his eyes and burned them. The room seemed hot, suffocating. Lurching to the con-necting-door, he passed into the bigger office without, and gazed stupidly at the desks, the covered typewriters, the safe, the press. Hanging on the wall was a large cheap mirror. He almost ran to it, there to stare and stare at the ghastly face it reflected, the unnaturally wide, unwinking eyes.

"You're the mug ! You're the fool! You are the poor fool who plays golf, whilst Tracy plays with your wife and laughs, and laughs, and laughs ! Handsome, eh? A man! A thing of no account, a thing in pants to raise a laugh among real men."

"Ellen and Tracy—Ellen and Tracy—Ellen and Tracy!" screamed the imp.

It was then that Nature made one tremendous effort to assert itself and stave off the menace of insanity. The heat of his body and within his brain subsided, vanished. He became cool, almost cold. His eyelids winked as though with threatening tears, and wearily he rubbed them with the back of his hand.

Yes. He must keep calm. He must not let himself go like that again. There was nothing he could do till about four o'clock. It was no use worrying, for worrying would not put back the finger of Fate. What was it that wise old Persian had said ? "The moving finger 'writes?" Yes, that was it. "The moving finger writes and having writ-having writ-moves on." Of course! Worrying would not mend matters. Whatever the moving finger had written could never be wiped out.

His body made its wants known. He became sensible that he was hungry and thirsty. Yet to go out to a restaurant meant meeting people, and perhaps someone of them would notice him, and, knowing, smile when he had passed. They would smile, laugh, jeer. They —

There! He was off again. That must not be. That was dangerous. He would get Jones, the hall-porter, to fetch him some sandwiches and a bottle of wine. Let it be champagne. He needed bucking up.

When Jones brought the wine and the sandwiches, Arnold Dudley was emerging from the lavatory refreshed by a wash and a brisk towel-rubbing. Again within his office, he poured himself a water-tumbler of the wine, and drank as a man drinks whisky when he is seeing strange, non-existent things. It was then five minutes past two. He was feeling much better; in fact, his brain was so clear that the thoughts raced through it. He must not allow that, mental storm to arise again.

For a while he cogitated the advisability of ringing up A 2778, and finding out if Ellen's cook was then with her mother. But that would prove nothing. And Ellen would hear of it and want to know his reason, and if Ellen was innocent he would be unable to confess the terror of his suspicions. Some day he would tell her. He would have to. He would never again feel clean in her presence until he did.

Presently he began to wonder why he was being tortured, why he was being punished. He had never committed any crime, legal or moral.

Always had he striven to give his fellow-man a "square deal". It was his very honesty that had made him successful in the world of business, wherein honesty was as rare as a jewel in muck. Was it payment exacted for his years of happiness and prosperity? But he had earned them in previous struggling years !

It was a quarter after three when he rose to his feet and, picking up the black bag, opened it and took out the evil-looking black automatic pistol. Dudley handled it like one well accustomed to firearms, as indeed he was. Of latter years he never used that automatic, but in the old days he had shot with it many, many kangaroos from the seat of his truck. He knew well that if Tracy was in his house he, Dudley, would not miss.

Slipping it into his right-hand coat-pocket, he shut the bag, secured his hat and gloves, passed out into the hall, and hung the keys of the doors on their nail in the porter's office. At the kerb was waiting his single-seater, a beautiful Southern Cross super-six.

The "Terrace" was deserted; the workers in the blocks of offices and the banks were scattered over the beaches, the recreation grounds, the far-flung roads among the eastern range of hills. Leisurely he drove east, the black bag. beside him, the automatic weighting the right side of his coat. Crossing the Causeway; he idly noted the shags drying themselves on marking piles or diving down into the sun-bronzed water, and wondered why men could not be as they were, without emotions, without the pain and the strife pounding at a man's life.

Coming to the Sandringham Hotel at Belmont, he felt tempted to stop and have more champagne. The urge demanded that he should drink and drink until he became insensible to feeling, insensible to hearing that vile imp in his brain with its everlasting scream : "Ellen and Tracy—Ellen and Tracy—Ellen and Tracy !"

It was because he knew, if he did get drunk, there would be an inevitable awakening, when the imp would revive and go on shrieking, that Dudley resisted and drove on till he came to the cross-road leading to his house.

There he pulled into the kerb of the newly-made sidewalk, and, leaving the car, walked slowly along the road until he came to a narrow lane that would lead him past the rear of the houses adjoining his own. They were mansions rather than houses, each set within its three acres of tree and shrub-covered grounds.

He paused when he came to two high wooden gates admitting to the short gravel path that ended at the kitchen and offices. Passing on, for the gates being opened would make their familiar creaking noise, Dudley finally scaled the wall where the branches of a great almond-tree spread above it.

Now in his own grounds, as a thief in the night he walked circumspectly towards the house, keeping always to the concealing shrubs and ornamental trees, until he came opposite a never-used side-door. To reach the door he had to cross an open space, asphalted and gently inclined, whereon he always hosed his car on Sunday mornings. Listening, no sound of human activity within the house reached his ears, and, whilst thus he listened, a tabby-cat rubbed itself against his leg, purring, its back arched, its tail erect. It was the kitchen cat. And the kitchen cat was locked out.

So the servants were away.

Crossing to the door, he produced his bunch of keys, fitted one into the Yale lock, and slowly, very slowly, pushed the door inward. It creaked softly once—twice. It creaked again when he slowly closed it after him and stood in a short passage that debouched into a longer one running the length of the house.

The house was as still as though it were deserted.

He put down the bag against the wall, and, unlacing his shoes, took them off his feet and set them beside the bag. When he moved forward along the passage the automatic was in his hand, his finger within the trigger-guard. At the angle of the passage he stopped to listen again. At that point he could hear the ticking of the grandfather clock in the morning-room. He thought he could hear another sound besides. He held his breath. Very low, as though coming from a great distance, he could hear the murmur of voices.

Soundlessly; he edged along the main passage towards the hall. Several doors opening into the passage were open. A cross-passage which he passed revealed a conservatory at its further end and a splash of green and brilliant reds and yellows. And just beyond it he halted outside a closed door.

It was from within this room that the voices came. It was his wife's room—Ellen's room.

"Ellen and Tracy—Ellen and Tracy—Ellen and Tracy !" shrieked the triumphant imp.

The truth struck Dudley as a blow from an iron fist. He rocked, on his feet, his eyes closed, his face drained of blood. For a moment he remained there, a man on fire with hate, rage, and madness. His left hand sprang to the handle of the door, but stopped its movement, poised above it. On the verge of flinging it open and rushing within to press and press and again press the trigger of the automatic, Arnold Dudley heard another voice, a voice that whispered fatefully down the ages:

"The Moving Finger writes; and, having writ, Moves on:...."

He was too late. Too late to save his honour, too late to save Ellen's virtue. Too late for all things worth while in life to be saved. Think ! He must—he must think.

Opposite the door, its back against the wall, was a chair. Dudley seated himself on it, unconsciously taking care to make no noise and there, his wide feverish eyes fixed on that fatal closed door, and the automatic in his right hand resting on his knees, he waited.

It seemed that his mind no longer dwelt in his body, as though it was an entirely separate entity, a separate thing that fought and strove to get through the door, to gain the room beyond. It urged and coaxed and swore at his inert body for refusing to rise and do its bidding. The struggle went on for a long time, but presently his mind came under a peculiarly soothing influence. It was going back into the months and the years which had gone, and the happiness contained therein became some-thing real, a material thing that welcomed it and showed it pictures as a mother will show the pictures in a play-book to a child that has awakened from a nightmare.

He found Ellen just a girl, a lovely winsome girl, a governess teaching a squatter's young children. He had found her in a squatter's garden, and the blue of her eyes rivalled the plumage of the "forty-eights" screeching in a near-by gum-tree. Loving her, he knew she loved him. They drove together one evening in his truck whilst the setting sun tipped the leaves of the mulgas and the jam-woods with tiny points of gold. And she had leaned against him, and he had suddenly brought the heavy truck to a stop, and, turning, had looked into those blue pools, looming ever larger the closer he drew her face to his, closer until her parted lips lay beneath his own, and her scented breath fanned his face.

Ellen! The shackles of mortality fell from him. The touch of her lips made him a God.

And their wedding ! Just a quiet personal affair in a little old church in Fremantle which had been built, stone by stone, by haggard, hopeless hulks of men deported from a country across the world, and now blessed and redeemed by Ellen's happiness.

Frightened, shy, elfin Ellen! Ellen who wanted to run away from him! Ellen who had stayed and worked and saved his money and urged him up, up, till he gained the pinnacle of success.

It was a wonder woman, lovely, alluring, and tender, who always ran out of the house to the garage when he was putting away the car on his return from the city. Who took his arm and led him within the house, led him within their marvellous paradise, and insisted on being kissed and kissing him again and again, before they went in to dinner. There was a green gown she wore, a gown that did not criminally hide her white arms when they slid up and around his neck boy, and would not let him finish his dinner, but insisted, demanded, entreated to be taken at once to Mrs. Finlay; and then, whilst she and the mother watched beside the cot, sent him rushing about Perth to find and dispatch to the bedside West Australian's greatest doctors.

"Ellen and Tracy—Ellen and Tracy—Ellen and Tracy!"

Curse that clamouring devil! What had Ellen to do with Tracy, or Tracy with Ellen? And why was he seated in that chair in that long passage and facing that closed door?

Dudley's body shuddered. His face was as though he were dead, as white as the back of a dead cuttlefish; but when he opened his eyes the pupils were expanded, surrounded by white, emitting light, a jade-green light, a light that springs from hell.

To him came the sound of movement beyond the door. Someone was walking across the floor, nearing the door. Footsteps paused, hesitated on the further side. The handle of polished bronze turned, ceased to turn, then turned a full quarter of a circle.

Slowly the door was drawn inward. Dudley saw a splash of pale blue. It was the colour of a silk wrapper, and through the opening door he saw the wrapper was about his wife. How slowly that door was opening! Ellen was turned sideways to him. A man's arm, dark blue-coated, and white-cuffed, encircled her shoulders. She was looking upward, an astonishing expression of loathing on her face, and into Dudley's vision, when the door opened still further, came the pale handsome face of Edmund Tracy.

Tracy's head sank down towards Dudley's wife's upturned face. When he kissed her Arnold Dudley's body shivered. There was neither fire nor passion in that embrace. And after the kiss Tracy straightened up, and, swinging back the door to its full extent, took half a step forward.

Dudley saw the satisfied, triumphant smile fade from Tracy's face. He watched with peculiar incuriousness the dawning of an expression of horror, of terror. With icy calmness he regarded Tracy's high white forehead, which bore a faint vertical line above the bridge of the straight, delicately-moulded nose. He heard, when he raised the automatic, his wife take in her breath with a sharp hiss.

The automatic roared.

Comical surprise leapt into Tracy's face the instant he sagged and collapsed.

CHAPTER III

THE JUSTICE OF MAN

TWO days and two awful nights had dragged out their leaden minutes, and towards noon of the third day Arnold Dudley drove his old tone truck towards the old-fashioned village of Dongara, on the west coast of the Sunset State.

The period of mental excitability had passed and was followed by a lethargy of mind which caused him to live far more in the immediate past than in the present. The truck was driven by a robot rather than a man.

His wife's shrieks immediately after the collapse of Tracy were more real than the warbling of a magpie high on a box-tree limb beneath which he passed. Nor did he see the tree or the glittering sheet of water in the bed of the valley below the road. He was again in that fateful passage, looking down on the still form of his wife's seducer, and then at his wife beyond the body, cowering, the twitching muscles of her face drawing horrible marring lines.

His following actions were but dimly remembered. He retained the idea of a memory that he had levelled the automatic at Ellen, and that when he was about to pull the trigger the thought occurred that to shoot would be only to waste a good cartridge. Ellen was like a dream of loveliness painted on a vase, and the vase had fallen and broken, and the lovely face was lined by tiny cracks. It was a vase, a broken vase, he looked at so gravely; and what was the use of smashing a vase already broken?

How he left the house, whether by the front, the back, or the side door, he never remembered. The next picture in the sequence of the past he was living through and through again in the present, was of his passing over the bridge spanning the Swan river at Guildford. There remained nothing tangible or visible of Midland Junction; the next picture showing his car drawn up behind a dilapidated ton truck and George Finlay standing beside him. Finlay's red face was serious to the verge of blankness; Finlay's eyes, grey and shrewd, searched every feature of his, Dudley's, face, and Finlay said ;

"He was there—you've done him in?"

Dudley nodded.

"Ellen–by Gawd ! You didn't do 'er in, too?"

"No. Ellen is a vase—a broken vase. It was no use breaking a broken vase, was it?"

"If yer 'ad of done Ellen in, I ain't sure but wot I'd 'ave bashed you, Arnold, and 'anded you over to the police," Finlay whispered hoarsely. "She may 'ave come 'er thud, but it wasn't 'er fault. That there Tracy mesmerized 'er—must 'ave done. Anyway, things being as they are, the sooner you do a get the better. Do you know where you're headed for?"

"Yes."

"Well, you'd better get on and get there. But, first of all, slide out of them clothes and climb into this old suit of dungarees. Come on, now! Here they are on the seat of the truck. There's no one about and I'll keep nit. Spark up, Arnold, old lad! Killing Tracy ain't nothing to worry about, exceptin' that you were such a crimson fool as not to liven me up to 'is little game and leave the killing to me. Yes, off with them shoes! Put on them old boots. You're dopy, man! You wouldn't make a real murderer's shadow, dinkum you wouldn't! And that flash 'at! Here, shove on this old felt. This good clobber I'll take 'ome and burn in the copper. Your car I'll leave on the river-bank below Guildford, and heave your flash hat into the water. The police'll think you've drownded yourself—with luck. Avoid talking to people as much as possible, and keep yery old felt down over yer eyes. Now—are you right? Good! Let me know if you want anything. Away you go! Jam both feet on that blasted accelerator, and keep 'em down hard. So long!"

Conscious of nothing but the present, Dudley had driven north, finding his way along the main road with the sureness of a somnambulist. His driving was perfect. At Three Springs and Mingenew he filled the petrol tank, and early on the day he reached Dongara he stopped to remove the plugs and clean them and readjust the points, because the engine was missing on one cylinder; but of that he remembered nothing whatever.

The road he was following lay along a valley leading to the sea. He was passing paddocks fenced, in places, by the old method of posts and rails—paddocks wherein enormously fat lazy market cattle were wallowing knee-deep in a rippling sea of emerald-green lupins. Away on his right rose the steep slopes forming the edge of a great breakaway worn back ages ago, when the ocean swept up this wide inlet. Here and there the slopes were covered by short bush trees, but on the flats below grew giant boxes and gums, set here and there like grand ancestral oaks in an English park. Above the ridge; in mighty sweeps, circled eagles of seven-foot wing-span, watching, incessantly watching, the scurrying, gambolling rabbits below.

In the rattling, roaring old truck, Dudley passed across the three-mile bridge, but had no eyes for the old pise-built hut erected by some dauntless settler in years when the State was young. One of the richest valleys in the Commonwealth, one of the fairest that early summer morn, was lost on Dudley, who saw beyond the radiator nothing but Tracy's face wearing its comical expression of surprise.

Presently he arrived at the eastern end of the long straggling village, where the houses were typically English in their walls and chimneys, but crowned with modern Australian ugliness in their cheap corrugated iron roofs. Two cottages there were, before which a British exile would have paused, and which might have been transplanted from a Hampshire countryside by Aladdin's genie. The yellow-washed walls, the squat wide chimneys, so suggestive of an open hearth and great wood logs a-blazing, the neat little gardens filled with homely hollyhocks, wallflowers, and geraniums—all were there in that transplantation of England to Western Australia.

He stopped the truck outside the main store. The whole village was more English than Australian. Even the newly-built hotel, its name and date lettered on the cement beneath the eaves—"Dongara Hotel 19—"—was less of Australia and far more of England in its architecture. Placid peacefulness reigned here, the peaceful placidity that had caused men contentedly to omit to add the figures after "19" to indicate the precise year when the hotel had been built.

At the store, where grocery was sold on one side, drapery on the other, and kitchenware at the farther end, Dudley waited whilst a man wearing blue dungaree trousers and a navy-blue woollen guernsey examined a mass of fish-lines and boxes of fish-hook lying on the counter. The task of selection was deliberate, unhurried, as though the fisherman had lost many a fine jew-fish through faulty tackle.

When Dudley's turn came to be served he told the storekeeper he wanted to leave an order which he would call back for the next day. Without surprise the man behind the counter made out the list—a case of tinned milk, a case of tinned meat, a case of assorted jam, a dozen this and two dozen that. Petrol in four-gallon tins and oil in one-gallon tins; billycans and saucepans, a mincing machine, and a camp-oven. Oh! And flour—a 56-lb. bag will do—and half a dozen tins of baking powder. Also two hundred twelve-bore BB cartridges, a hundred high-power '32 Winchester cartridges, and half a dozen bottles of strychnine—and so on.

"How is the track into the Nineteen Mile Rocks, do you know?" Arnold asked languidly.

"I don't think anyone has been down there since last year," replied the storekeeper cheerfully. "Are you thinking of going down for a day or so?"

"Yes. I want to put in time rabbiting and foxing, and do a little fishing in between. It is several years since I was there, but where the track turns off the main road there is a well, isn't there?"

"Yes. That's so."

"Who owns the land there now?" was Dudley's next question.

"Mallory. Just as well to ask his formal permission to rabbit on his property." The storekeeper gazed across his shop as though he dreamed of a life of freedom among the hills and sand-dunes. "If you get any fish you'd find a ready market here," he said. "We can't get fish. The fishermen won't sell their fish locally. They send it all to Perth."

"All right. I'll remember," Dudley answered slowly. "I'll go along now and make camp. I'll be in to-morrow afternoon for the stores and one or two things I expect I'll need. Goodbye!"

Going out, he climbed into his truck, finding the fisherman standing close by eyeing the rabbit-traps and other items of gear not covered by the tarpaulin. Within an hour the whole population of Dongara would know that a strange rabbit-trapper had come to town. This kind of publicity Dudley saw no reason to fear.

He drove seawards, the murmur of the surf coming towards him as a mother's crooning lullaby. At the school, the only real Australian building, he turned to the right and headed north towards Geralton, past the bakery and several old-fashioned cottages, and then the station on the single track that had borne the train carrying Tracy to Perth and back to Geraldton.

And, in his northward journey, the farm lands gradually gave place to raw bush lands which to the west rose in high hummocked coast sand-hills, and to the east in gently rising slopes. Perfumes, sweet and some-times sickly, greeted his nostrils, wafted from the low bush growing it, with here and there tiny open grass-grown glades where countless rabbits raced about or browsed with nervous trembling ears.

Sometimes above the roar of the motor the sound of the waves pound-ing against rocks was audible. On his right he passed a tiny farm where sheep grazed, fat and slow-moving. Where the bush trees were cleared, the grass grew knee-deep. Presently he came to the round coping of a well above which was a windlass, and close by an iron drinking-trough where a black and white butcher bird was drinking.

At Mallory's farm he stopped. Mallory, a young and keen-looking man, whose business was to buy store cattle cheaply in the dry hinter-land and fatten them for the Perth market in his lupin-covered paddocks, readily gave permission to Dudley to trap where he liked, and draw what water he wanted from the well near where the beach-track turned west from the main road.

Reaching the well, Arnold filled two empty petrol-tanks and set off on the last three miles to the coast. The track had been cut through the dense bush that pressed wall-like on each side so closely that branches and twigs slapped the sides of the truck. It rose and fell and twisted over and round the jumble of steep sand-hills, rabbits dashed across it in front of him, and the perfumes of the bush lay heavy in the dells.

Then, climbing a long steep gradient, the engine roaring at low gear, the truck slowly reached the summit of the highest hill ; and quite suddenly, as a picture thrown on a screen, Dudley looked out over the immensity of the Indian Ocean, and down on the fringe of sand-hummocked coast, with its edge of white sand beach and the bluff promontory that thrust shelving, sharp-edged masses of grey and black rock far into the swelling sea.

Stopping the truck, he got out and stood there in front of it, the sunlit vision of wonder space dazzling his eyes, the pure fresh breeze blowing on his heated face and creeping within his rough clothes, touching his body with a million soothing fingers.

He breathed deep, deep, deep. The mist of unreality, the phantasmagoria that had descended on his brain, enveloping him, was torn to shreds and blown away from him by the clean wind as a sail is torn from a ship in a gale. There on the height he regained his mental equilibrium, his right perspective of time, his consciousness of the present; and it was as though a heavy burden had been lifted from his shoulders when he again climbed into the truck and sent it down the hillside, the engine in low gear to assist braking.

Now once again the sand-hills towered above the bush walls, hemming him in, and, following the track, he twisted and turned in its maze till abruptly he came to the track's end on a clear sandy place above the jutting rocks. There, with the vast empty restless ocean before him and the scrub-covered white sand-hills behind, Dudley looked about for a camp site. He saw the marks of buggy wheels and the place where a horse had been tethered. Week-enders, probably. Well, they would not annoy him.

The place he selected was a few hundred yards back along the track. There in a hollow, protected from the wind by a low sand-ridge separating him from the beach, he cut out of the bush a space large enough to erect his ten-by-twelve-foot tent. The task of erecting it and placing within his stretcher-bed and swag—provided by the thoughtful Finlay—and all his gear, other than the traps, occupied him till sunset. He cooked bacon and fried eggs and made strong coffee, and whilst it was still light lay on his bed and slept. It was the first sleep he had had for close on eighty hours.

Contrary to popular melodramatic ideas concerning the state of a murderer's mind, Arnold Dudley slept sixteen hours, never once troubled by nightmarish dreams. True, when he awoke he was puzzled as to his whereabouts, and for a moment thought he was somewhere in the north-east during his pre-Ellen days.

The sun-created silhouettes of bush-tree leaves danced on the white canvas roof of his tent. Clean cool air swept in through the open doorway, fanning his face, vanquishing the last languors of sleep. From somewhere close by a butcher-bird whistled two bars of its favourite song with wonderful clarity and sweetness, whilst omnipresent was the slow droning of blow-flies.

It was with a nerve-shaking rush that remembrance swept through his brain. The sunlight went out, was born again, but it was of a tint as though filtered through a vast sheet of black gauze. No hint of remorse was present, only anger—dull, gnawing anger that sent the blood into his head under pressure. He was glad he had killed Tracy. Realization of the result of his action sent a glow of satisfaction through him—satisfaction slightly chilled by the fact that he could not kill Tracy again.

Why not? Tracy had robbed him of his dearest possession, happiness; robbed him of the body and soul of Ellen. It was a calculated robbery of which no man, not even the thief, could make restitution. If a man, poverty-stricken and starving, stole his watch, the thief would be sent to prison by an indignant magistrate. Yet the value of the watch was small. He could buy a watch every morning before lunch. But a man could steal another man's happiness, another man's wife's virtue, and not even imprisonment threatened him. Financial damages possibly might be wrested from the robber, but the amount would be assessed on the thief's income, making him a debtor, one who owed money, not one who owed happiness and honour, which all the world's money cannot buy.

From the moral standpoint Arnold Dudley honestly believed himself justified in taking Tracy's life—a thousand times more justified than in taking the life of a Turkish soldier in Gallipoli ; one who had done him no harm, a man he did not know. For legalized killing he possessed medals; for the recent unlegalized killing he was in grave danger of being hanged. Where, in the names of good and evil, was to be found logic in man's justice?

"Thou shalt not kill," had said the Voice amidst the thunders and lightnings on Sinai. The command in plain English was expressed by four simple words. There were no riders to that commandment, no exceptions. Dudley had broken that commandment many times during the Dreadful War, he had again broken it three days past; yet, whilst he felt no remorse for killing the man who had robbed him, he often had felt remorse for the killing of men who had robbed him of nothing.

Getting up from his stretcher-bed, he passed outside and, from habit formed many years before, examined the sky to forecast the weather. Lighting a fire, he placed a billycan of water against the flames to boil for tea, washed and shaved, and dressed in his ill-fitting rough dungarees.

Whilst driving to Dongara to obtain the rations he had ordered and purchase fishing gear and a fifty-gallon galvanized tank in which to cart his water supply, Arnold Dudley experienced no emotion other than elation. The loss of Ellen, and all that Ellen represented in his life at Perth, was outweighed by the satisfaction he felt in having upheld the Unwritten Law.

Not that day, nor yet for many more days, did Arnold Dudley again remember that great truth epitomized by the immortal Persian:

"The Moving Finger writes; and, having writ, Moves on: ..."

CHAPTER IV

THE BEACH

ONE morning, about a week after he had established himself on what he was to call the Beach of Atonement, Arnold Dudley was sitting on the Seagulls' Throne. The Throne was a basalt rock, roughly cubical in shape, which crowned a low sand-hill rising at the base of the headland of ugly sea-thrusting rocks. How the cubical rock, weighing at least a ton, came to be where it was, was to him an insoluble mystery; since its base was a hillock of fine sand, covered with stunted coast-shrubs—a hill fifty feet high from its foundation of granite.

He called the cubical rock the Seagulls' Throne because at his first visit the top of it was splashed white by resting gulls. From the Seagulls' Throne it was possible to view the whole length of the beach from the great northern promontory to the southern extremity, where the coast-line curved eastward around hundred-foot cliffs. From promontory to cliffs was possibly a stretch of twenty miles, and where he sat above the short bluff headland was about midway.

Immediately below him lay a comparatively level mass of rock, about two acres in extent, covered by several feet of water at high tide, and at low tide awash by the waves that crashed unceasingly against its crumbling seaward edge. This he called the Pontoon. At low tide there could be seen now and then the top of a rock mass approximately two hundred yards out, whilst farther to the north a flat-topped, oblong-shaped rock he named the Sugar Loaf was visible even at high tide. A little north of these two rocks, where the sea was ever in turmoil, little wavelets cutting back across the tops of the combers, whirling masses of froth thrust this way and that in a wide circular motion, was situated the Boiling Pot.

It boiled the fiercer when the tide swept northward, impelled by a fresh south wind. From Dudley's view-point he could see the back-cutting wavelets, the white froth, and several spars of timber which drifted round; and round, animate things that longed for the freedom of the open beach, but were kept back by the water-devil till such time as the tide changed.

A mile or more at sea, a serried line of deep-sunk reefs broke the larger waves. Out there the sea rolled shoreward in mighty swells—swells that lifted up the horizon-line on their broad backs, high above the general ocean level, high and higher in menacing black lines, forced upward by the reefs, until the peaks curled and rushed forward in foaming lather.

Shoreward from the sunken reefs—Dudley called them the Ramparts—each wave regained a little of its broken strength and came charging in across a welter of chop to climb up and over the Sugar Loaf, take the sunken rock on the south like steeplechasers, and finally hurl themselves against the Pontoon with leaping curtains of white water. And, whilst the main body of each wave was inevitably flung back, tons of water advanced' across the Pontoon with a hissing roar, looking like a charging squadron of white horses in line abreast.

Every wave brought in its quota of dead and living seaweed, carried it over the sunken rocks, swept it across the Pontoon to the narrow shelving strip of sand at the foot of the headland, there to leave it on the sand, and to retreat in the manner of a cat who wants a nearly-dead mouse to run. And the next wave, fearing jealously that the streamers of seaweed would escape, sprang in, grasped its prey, dragged it away from safety and carried it a few yards northward, there throwing the weed up again to await recapture by the succeeding wave.

The streamers of weed were thus teased northward for perhaps a quarter of a mile, when in one of her amazing caprices the sea piled up the weed into a huge hummock, acres in area and twenty feet high.

North and south extended the white glittering sweep of the sand beach, ever pounded by the insatiable surf eternally eating into the sand-bound coast. Above the curling breakers the wind swept shoreward the spray in iridescent veils, and, as if dissatisfied, whipped up the sand on the dunes into a white thin fog.

Never a ship was seen off that coast unless it were wounded or storm-driven. Day after day and year after year the sea was empty of ships ; for sailing ships steered clear of its rock-lined jaws, and steamships, knowing the fallibility of propellers and rudders, passed north and south fifty or a hundred miles away.

Seated on the Seagulls' Throne, Dudley was the only human being in that wild world of roaring water and hissing sand. The small community of gulls, one day numbering seventeen, the next day but nine, the following day again seventeen, deprived of their throne, settled on the Seaweed Mountain, and looked out over the sea with their heads laid rearward over their backs. A solitary shag came winging southward, almost touching the wave-crests, rose several feet to clear the Pontoon, and swept down again when it was past. Sand-martins fluttered over the beach, always watching and waiting for what the waves might leave them.

Nearly all the daylight hours of that first week Dudley had spent seated on the Seagulls' Throne. There was in the eternal restlessness of the sea, the malignant cruelty of the wave-shattering rocks, the wild, wailing wind, an affinity with the exalted mood which at that time governed him. He likened himself to the ever-pounding sea, and Tracy to the ever-pounded rocks. At every magnificent thundering charge of the hugest waves his body tingled with exultation, as though he had Edmund Tracy at his mercy to pound and smash with roaring triumph.

Hour after hour he sat, his face cupped in his hands, watching, fascinated, those rolling hills of water. He seemed never to be weary of watching, never satiated by the thrills experienced, his mind occupied wholly by Tracy, his awful victory over the body of Tracy, his stupendous achievement in sending Tracy's soul to hell.

The relative phases in the evolution of Ellen and Tracy were, in his mind, reversed. It was Tracy who seemed alive, receptive of burning, scorching hatred, and Ellen who was dead and at peace, draped in the white burial sheet of wonderful memory. At the precise moment that he had fired at Edmund Tracy, Ellen's existence had ceased. When Dudley did think of her it was to remember her vivid laughter, which began invariably with a low gurgle and ended in a clear high note; or, again, the trick she had of pinching his ear when especially pleased with him; or how she looked when, at Belmont, she watched Flying Feet pass the judge's box first and win her three hundred pounds; or the recurrent mental vision of her lovely arms when they rose and slipped around his neck:

Tracy was alive, vibrant. He was there beyond the edge of the Pontoon, fighting, struggling in the leaping water, tortured and smashed and pounded by every incoming wave ; he was sunk yards deep in the Boiling Pot, whirled everlastingly round and round, whilst eternally he fought for air and found none.

No man could conceive the exquisite pleasure Dudley felt when he went crab-hunting among, the rocks, armed with stones, when a hit was greeted with a yell of exultation; for Tracy lived within the brittle blue and red and black shells, and Tracy writhed on the spindly hairy legs. Dudley murdered Tracy by proxy and shouted his joy; he murdered him again and again in his mental visions and chuckled gleefully. Because, at the end of his first week on the Beach of Atonement, Arnold Dudley was very near insanity.

It was the coming of Hester Long which saved him.

Seated on the Seagulls' Throne, the laughter-lit shouting of children finally enticed his mind from its inward concentration to the reality of the world of wind and sea and beach. It was some time after midday, and the tide was at its lowest. A miniature lagoon immediately north of the Pontoon furnished safe paddling for two little boys somewhere about seven or eight years old. Their arrival he had not noticed. A woman, evidently their mother—for even at that distance Dudley observed her matronly appearance—stood at one side of the Pontoon, fishing with a hand-line. The way she handled the line, the manner, dangerous even to the most expert, in which she heaved the lead sinker round her head to cast the several baited hooks clear of the rocks, proved that she was no novice at fishing. On the bare sand-patch up back from the beach a buggy stood close, to the single horse, then tethered to a post and feeding from a petrol-box. Near the buggy a second woman, slim and girlish, was coaxing a fire into being.

Arnold Dudley's interest was only momentary. Fleeting resentment at the intrusion on his solitude was followed by utter obliviousness of it. His mind, alive and furious, worked on the body and soul of Tracy, and it was eventually with an unpleasant nervous start that a fresh musical voice broke into that terrible world he alone had created and was developing.

"I am sorry to intrude, but my friend has met with an accident."

Dudley looked up from his lofty perch, oafishly remaining seated, not seeming to realize that the lovely blonde face and slim figure of a young woman of some twenty years of age stood regarding him in the flesh, in reality. He stared at her vacantly, stupidly, and she spoke again, a trace of petulance in her voice.

"My friend has got one of the hooks of her fishing-line buried in her thumb," she said. 'Do you think you could get it out?"

"Er—hook in her thumb?" Dudley replied slowly. "Well, I don't— don't know. You see, I have no hook in my thumb. I was wondering if Ellen was living in a seagull." He frowned, and the young woman's eyes expanded with perplexity, then fear. "Hang it! What am I talking about? I am sorry, but I was thinking of other things. What was it you said? Oh yes! I remember. You said your friend has a fish-hook in her thumb. Am I right?"

"Yes. But don't let it worry you. I can drive her to Dongara, where there is a doctor."

Dudley slid off the rock, to stand immediately at the lady's turned back. "I should be glad to help if I could," he said; "I'll come with you at once."

"Making no reply to that, she moved off down the curving track his feet had made along the steep incline of the sand-hill; followed by the man she had concluded was not quite sane. The other woman was seated on a. tucker-box beside the buggy, one hand and the entangled line on the lap of her white duck dress. When Dudley stood before her he had to make a mental effort to bring himself to reality out of his world of nightmares.

He saw a woman whom at first sight he thought to be about fifty, but a hasty examination of her face reduced that age by fifteen or twenty years. The enhanced age effect was produced by the lines about her forehead, and at the corners of her eyes and her mouth; her real age lay revealed in the steady, limpid grey eyes that regarded him bravely.

"You have a hook in your hand," he said, without questioning intonation.

"Yes. I am afraid it is rather deeply buried," she said in a soft voice which in tone was as beautiful as her eyes were in colour. "Do you think you could get it out? I wish you would try, please."

Holding out the injured hand, she let drop the yards of twisted line, leaving the lead sinker on her lap, and a second hook caught in. her dress. Dudley saw that the other hook was invisible in the ball of her thumb, half-way up its straight length, and he shuddered, because his real nature revolted at the sight of pain and injury in others, and because his imagination was of that vivid order which magnifies things and events out of their true perspective.

"I'll try, if you wish," he said, straightening himself, "but it is going to hurt badly. I am afraid I am very inexperienced. Would you not prefer the doctor?"

"No—if you can take it out," she replied, smiling valiantly. "You see, we are so far from Dongara, and—and I must be home at six o'clock to milk the cows. Besides, the doctor will charge so."

"Very well. Let me cut the hook from the line first," he rejoined, producing a skinning knife from a sheath attached to his belt; then, when the line was clear : " Just wrap the handkerchief round the thumb and try not to think of it, while I run to my camp for one or two things. Why not sit on the ground with the buggy-wheel for a rest?"

Taking a rug off the seat, he folded it and gently assisted her to be seated on the soft sand. There, leaning back against the wheel-spokes, she closed her eyes, her face growing white. Looking up suddenly, he caught the other woman regarding him curiously, as though he were a newly-discovered species of the genus Homo. And in this survey she was supported by one of the children. The other knelt beside his mother crying: "Poor mummie ! poor mummie!"

At his camp Dudley searched for a suitable knife; and, finding none, resolved to use the skinning-knife. It was really a much-used butcher's knife, but the edge was keen, and, finding an oil-stone in a tool-box, he put a still keener edge on it, the while apostrophizing all women in general, and fishing ones in particular. To get a bottle of brandy he was obliged to open a case containing a dozen bottles. He had completely forgotten the spirit, not so far having needed it. Carrying a bottle of the brandy, a wash-dish, and a billycan of water, he walked slowly back to the fishing-party—slowly, because he shrank from the thing he was going to do—an operation he would emphatically have refused to perform, could he have delegated it to someone else.

Midway between camp and buggy he halted, returned to search for an antiseptic of some sort, and found in Finlay's ammunition-box a tin of permanganate of potash. Now fully equipped, with no further excuse for delay, he gained the visitors' temporary camp, where he placed his billycan on the fire and the dish, antiseptic, and brandy on the sand close by.

"How is the thumb-hurting?" he asked with well-assumed cheerfulness.

"It is aching a little," the woman replied, once more smiling bravely.

"Well, I am going to have a nobbler of brandy," he told her, picking up the bottle and producing a corkscrew. "You will have a nobbler of brandy, too. You, please, take the little fellows for a paddle, will you?" he added to the younger woman.

"I—I never—but perhaps a little sip would do me good."

"Of course it will," Dudley assured her, pouring a great many sips into an enamelled pannikin, which he offered her. And, a minute later: "Now, just rest your hand on this step and watch the seagulls sleeping away the afternoon on that hill of seaweed."

Had Dudley's nature been of coarser fibre, he might have imagined, when he possessed himself of the woman's hand, that he had Tracy's throat to cut. As a matter of simple fact Tracy was for the first time banished from his mind. He hesitated for seconds before he gently held the extremity of the hook with his left hand and cut once deeply with the knife in his other hand. He heard the woman's breath drawn in sharply, but there was no tremor, no flinching in her hand, which he sub-consciously saw bore the lines and corns of hard, rough work.

The blood welled up from the cut, ran down on the iron step, and dripped to the white sand. For an instant he thought of giving up, but the woman's pluck and strength of mind shamed him, and he cut again, right down to the buried barb. A second later he had the hook out of the quivering flesh, and, throwing aside the knife, jumped for the billycan and partly filled the basin with the now warm water. Adding a pinch of the potash, he placed the water beside his patient, and himself lowered the hand into it from the step. Her eyes were open, wide and grateful. She tried to smile, but there was a tremble in her voice.

"Have you got it out?" she whispered, to which he said: "Yes. By God! you've got grit. You stand it better than I do. I—I feel a bit sick. I must sit down." Dudley almost collapsed. The bright world about them grew suddenly dark, and as suddenly became light again. Reaching for the bottle, he almost half-filled the pannikin, raised it to his mouth, put it down again, lurched to his feet, almost staggered to the tucker-box, from which he procured a china cup and poured some of the spirit from the pannikin into the cup.

"No, no! I don't want any more," the woman protested. "Drink some yourself. It'll make you better. Never mind me. I—I feel all right."

He drank the spirit neat. Rubbing his eyes with the palms of his hands, he forced himself to walk a few paces from the buggy, to return with the nausea relieved.

"Now let me finish the job," he said quietly. "I am a bigger coward than you. You are a plucky woman, indeed you are! I am going to tear up this cloth for bandages."

"Very well. It won't much matter. It's an old tablecloth, you see."

Not very expertly, to be sure, Dudley bandaged the injured thumb with swathes of the tablecloth until the woman's hand was lost to sight.

"How is that, now?" he asked, standing up and regarding her with admiration. "No, no! Don't get up for a little while. May I make the tea? The billy is boiling."

"If you please," she said, answering his second question first. "Thank you ever so much for getting out that wretched hook. It was silly of me to throw out the line like I did, only there is a deep hole out from the rock, and we did so much want a fish." To the other woman on the beach with the children she called; "Miss Mallory! Come and have lunch."

Standing, Dudley watched the approaching girl, accompanied by the racing children, with suddenly narrowed eyes. The exuberant spirits of the small boys and the joy expressed in the figure of Miss Mallory, who climbed up the low sandy bluff whilst the wind played havoc with her golden hair, inexplicably hurt him.

It did not seem right that there should be happiness on that beach, his beach, where Tracy constantly fought for life and as constantly lost it. Why could not these people go elsewhere, with their fish-hooks, and golden hair, and high-pitched juvenile voices?

"Well—I must be going," he said bitterly, and gathered up his billycan, his wash-tin, and the brandy.

"But you'll stay and have lunch with us, surely?"

For a moment he stared into the steady grey eyes regarding him with surprise. There was something in them which angered him, but what it was he could not then define.

"You must stay and have lunch after what you have done for me."

"No. I must go," was his decision, spoken in a voice that hinted at tiredness, spoke of resentfulness. He left them gazing at him in silent wonder, and from his camp walked and walked over the sand-hills until nightfall.

CHAPTER V

THE ABSENT-MINDED TRAPPER

IT was on a morning early in November that Arnold Dudley, during his breakfast, resolved to idle no longer. He had then been on the Beach of Atonement a little more than a fortnight, but the urge to work was not produced by a surfeit of idleness, but to justify his being there. The people of Dongara, as well as Mallory and the two women who had visited the beach, all knew, as he had intended them to know, that he was a rabbit-trapper. Tongues wag and speculation would rear a dangerous head it he did not prove that he was a rabbit-trapper by gathering and dispatching skins to the Perth market.

Moreover, the mental phase following his sudden departure from Perth was wearing itself out. No human mind can long be dominated by the consuming passion of hatred, the duration of that phase being governed by the strength of the emotion. His hatred of Tracy had been and was a thing so terrible intense as to threaten his reason. Undoubtedly it would have led to madness had not the fierce concentration on his wife's seducer been cut as a thread of cotton by the fishing woman's imperative need. Through the opening thus made extraneous affairs pressed their claims, the proof of his supposed profession or trade being the most urgent. Yet, if his hatred of Tracy was more under command, more subdued by reason, it remained a living flame.

The previous afternoon he had examined the country and decided where he would make his first "set". So thick and close was the bush that it was impossible for trap-setting; but at the edge of the bush, such as that made by the cut track from the main road to the beach, as well as several large natural clearings in the dips between the hills, he found ideal trapping ground.

Rabbit-trapping may not be regarded by the elite as an occupation suitable for a gentleman. It demands, however, qualities that are not always to be found in successful professional men. To be a successful trapper requires not only perseverance and attention to detail, but in addition that formed habit of observation, patience, and untiring energy. The neophyte will set thirty traps and consider the day well spent; the expert will set two hundred, and wish he had set more.

Dudley left camp carrying over each shoulder a dozen traps, and a setting hammer—not unlike a trench-tool of wartime use–slipped through his belt. About a hundred yards along the narrow track leading to the main road, he dropped his load, selected a trap, and with his setting hammer made a bed for it in a freshly used buck-heap. From a hip-pocket he detached from a small block a cut square of newspaper, which he placed over the tongue and that half-side of the plate before covering the whole with dirt. The trap was now set, held to the ground by an iron peg at the end of a short chain.

Here and there were little breaks or clearings in the bush which provided ideal playgrounds for the rodent, and the traps he set in these he marked by making a trail with a stick to the track. Those set beside the track were also marked.

Now to set a number of traps—and Dudley set sixty that morning—requires care and thought. If the places where the traps are set are not marked plainly enough to be found even at night-time, it will be discovered when they are taken up to be reset that several of them are missing; and from the standpoint of economy it would be but a matter of time for the trapper's stock-in-trade to dwindle until he had no more traps than would catch rabbits to the value of a packet of cigarettes.

It is astonishingly easy to overlook marking where a trap has been set. Should the mind of the trapper be exercised by any other subject than the task in hand, he will assuredly omit to mark his set traps. A man in love with a woman will lose many traps; a man in love with his job will not lose one. The number of traps a man loses, or does not lose, thus furnished a clue to the state of his mind.

Arnold Dudley knew all this, and more, quite well. In the old days, whilst he was engaged in making a living by rabbit-trapping, he prided himself on the very few traps he had lost, accounting it a slur on his efficiency if he lost six in six months, Therefore, when he started to set his traps, he resolutely banished from his mind all thoughts of Tracy ; yet in this he found that his hatred governed his mind, not his mind his hatred, and it became essential more than once to force his mind to concentrate on his work.

Not only his will-power but also two separate traps wrenched him back into the world of realities from his world of dreams. He possessed the knack of opening a trap with one hand and flicking the tongue under the catch below the plate with the other hand. A wandering mind failed on one occasion to observe that the tongue was not properly against the catch, and the jaws of the trap snapped against his fingers as a reminder. Half an hour later, whilst covering a trap with soil, his other hand worked too low. It touched the plate and sprung the trap. Both hands were now ripped by serrated, iron jaws. The pain helped him to concentrate on his work; and the work, allied to the fishing woman's demand on him, saved his brain from shipwreck.

Tired to the point of exhaustion by the unpractised toil, Dudley returned to camp about one o'clock, when he washed and treated his injured hands, and ate a lunch of ox-cheek, damper, and tea. He had made himself a rough table in the shade of the bush, the interior of the tent being far too hot during the day ; and, his lunch finished, and a hand-rolled cigarette between his lips, he came suddenly to realize that his camp was in a disgraceful state.

Upon him was falling the mantle of his old outdoor life. Camp cleanliness was with him a fetish. He noted then the litter of paper, of labels from milk and jam tins, a wash-dish half-buried in the sand, a bar of soap flung against a bush-root, empty tins—a great attraction to ants—lying everywhere, shreds of straw from the sheath that he had wrapped the bottle of brandy he had used the day the visitors came. And, seeing the litter, Arnold Dudley felt a qualm of shame, and instinctively knew what any of his old acquaintances would say should any one of them enter his camp.

Even so he made no immediate attempt to remedy his laxity. The temptation to fall again into his stirring day-dreams, wherein he and Tracy were the chief characters, was too great to be resisted then. Seated there beside the littered rough table, oblivious of the hovering flies and the converging—ants, Dudley witnessed with the vivid sight of his mind the death and damnation of Tracy, whilst his physical eyes stared unwinkingly at the wall of bush, here brilliant green, there black with shadow.

A low-flying crow broke the slumbering quietude of the afternoon with its caw, caw, caw-aw and faint swish of wings. Dudley heard nothing. A magpie warbled a few detached notes, and the butcher-bird, perched but five feet above the seated man, produced five distinct bugle-clear notes that composed an utterly sweet melody. Yet Dudley heard nothing. His physical ears were deaf, stone deaf, because the ears of his mind were deafened by the shrieks of Edmund Tracy.

To observe the man then, his strong and now tanned face working successively in triumph, in pure hate, in loathing, was to observe the handiwork of Satan. Hour after hour he sat with contorted face and working fingers, terrible to behold, pitiful to observe, demanding, nay compelling, sympathy.

For in his normal state Arnold Dudley was a most likeable man. He had strange ideas of personal honour, ideas that proved to be the foundation rocks of his success in the business world. His attitude towards his fellow-men and women was reflected faithfully by their devotion to him and his interests. It accounted for the instant co-operation of George Finlay, who risked and was still risking imprisonment for himself as an accessory after the fact, as well as destitution for his wife and children. In fact, Finlay, as he had said, would gladly himself have undertaken the murder of Edmund Tracy. And a man who can inspire that degree of friendship is not to be reckoned mean-spirited, small-minded, sharp-dealing, or snobbish.

Where the birds failed, the sudden piercing scream of a trapped rabbit succeeded in rousing him from his dreams—to face the fact that the day was rapidly dying. From beyond the low sand-hill between him and the beach the roar of the surf was as persistent as the droning of the flies. His camp lay in purple shadow, and above it to the east the rising green slopes were transmuted into gold by the sun then kissing the ocean.

Automatically, Dudley felt the thickness of the paper-wad in his hip-pocket before picking up his setting-hammer to slide into his belt. Into an enamelled pannikin he poured the remainder of the tea made at lunch-time, added sugar, and drank. Then, with a chaff-bag, he began his sundown tour of his "set".

In the second trap he came to his first rabbit, which had run round and round with the trap in a circle, having for its centre the iron pin. Taking it from the trap, he broke its neck with one quick pull ; and, the buck-heap being scattered, carried the trap to another a few yards on.

Working smoothly, with quick expert fingers that had not lost the knack, he went on along the track until in his bag were twelve rabbits. That number always had been reached in the old days before he seated himself to skin, and now it was the assertion of a habit formed long ago which governed his actions. Not yet was his mind free of hate. His hatred of Tracy was certainly weakening. There were recurrent periods, daily becoming more numerous, when Tracy was forgotten; but the sum total of these periods of forgetfulness was but a small proportion of the day.

Seated on the ground beside the little furry heap, Dudley whipped out his skinning-knife and operated on the first rabbit. One cut behind the ears, another cut down the inside of one leg and up the other, a nick under the loose skin at the belly, and the knife was laid aside. One sharp pull at each leg, the rabbit then reversed, its hind-quarters clamped between his boots, a final pull, and the pelt was off. It took him fifteen minutes to skin those twelve rabbits, because his fingers were stiff. When he trapped for a living, the skinning of those twelve rabbits would have taken him but five minutes, and he was never considered a quick skinner.

When he reached the end of his "set" on the summit of the highest sand-hill, he had taken twenty-two rabbits. Then it was almost dark. The gullies below were invisible in the blackness of night, made more intense by the gleaming silver of the upper slopes. Faintly discernible were the sea and the beach, the latter a ribbon of dull white, a ribbon that swelled and shrank everlastingly when each roller added its quota of white foam. Beyond, to the far-flung horizon, the darkness of the heaving waters formed a bar, a base-line supporting the golden edge of the dome of sky. The golden band was the first to catch the eye, and then, whilst vision travelled upward, the cloth of gold changed to purple, and from purple to silver, from silver to cadmium, and on into the indigo-blue of night.

With his chin resting on his crossed arms supported on his bent knees, Arnold Dudley gazed at the glory of the west. As the light of day was fast passing from the earth, so had the sunshine vanished from his life. For the first time solitude spoke to him, solitude which there was omni-present, filling all the universe, hemming him in on all sides as the stone walls of a prison.

Turning his head, he gazed into the southern blackness, his eyes sud-denly immobile, as though he would with his vision leap the hundreds of miles separating him from Perth, the city he knew so well, where he had really lived and known happiness and peace and content, before had fallen the dungeon-gates named degradation and dishonour which had cut him off from the light.

The injustice of his incarceration in the prison of solitude burned and seared his mind to the extent that his flesh shrank as though from actual fire. From the city of sunshine he had been flung forth into the darkness of the world on which he sat. From the community of men he had been thrust into a place where man was not. Taken from the warmth and bliss of Ellen's arms, he had been hurled to the summit of a hill of sand, at the mercy of the elements, garbed in rough clothes, a pariah, an outcast dog, a thing that men would execrate. And for all of that he was not respon-sible. The decree of exile had been signed by another man, one whom he had never harmed, one whom more than once he had helped along the road to success.

Tracy!

Dudley leapt to his feet. Out-thrust were his hands, clenching and unclenching. His head projected forward from his body bent towards, the sea. From him came a moan of anguish, and then a sudden screamed torrent of words.

"Hear me, Tracy! Hear me—damn you! Your body rots, eaten by worms. Your beauty, your magnetism, is but an evil memory. The women you lured and ruined would shudder to see you now. Never again will your thrice-damned soul thrill at a conquest, or your filthy rotting body thrill at a woman's touch. You are there, close by, watching me, Tracy. I know it. Look at me! Alive, able to feel, to breathe, to live. Able, if I wish, to taste good food, good wine, feel the warmth and delight of women, thrill at races and revel in pleasure. Think of it, Tracy, curse you a thousand million times ! Think of it, as you hover there in the night, your soul dead and damned, your body rotting and stinking. You filthy bastard! It was I who parted you from your beloved body. Remember that, Tracy! It was I who cut you off for ever from the pleasures of men. Shriek—go on—scream for life! Your shrieks are divine music in my ears.

"Some day I'll follow you and I'll strangle and smash your soul as I have smashed your body. If you can—ah! but you wouldn't dare. If you can, Tracy, come alive again in another body, and I'll show you what dying really is. I'll burn and sear and cut and rack you, and laugh at you as I laugh at you now, you poor bodiless thing! You'd steal my wife, my Ellen, eh? By God! you've done it. Ellen! Ellen! My Ellen! He's taken my Ellen from me— for ever. Ellen—Ellen—Ellen——!"

The paroxysm wore itself out, leaving him slumped on the ground, his nerves quivering, his body shaken by terrible tearless sobs. What he had done to Tracy was of infinite mercy compared with what Tracy had done and was doing to him. For an hour he crouched, wrestling with the demon of hatred; and when presently he rose and picked up the bag containing the rabbit-skins, he staggered down by the gullies to his camp.

It seemed as though bedecking his hatred of Edmund Tracy in words and phrases acted as a safety-valve, for the articulation of the thoughts that governed his mind preceded a period of mental calmness lasting several weeks. In sharp contrast to his recent mood he ate his supper of damper and tinned meat almost lightheartedly; For two hours he lay and read a year-old weekly paper. It was after ten o'clock when he set off with a hurricane-lamp to go over his trap-line once more.

The value of his trap-marks was now to be appreciated. The bush, buried in blackness of night, took on a different aspect when the rays of the lamp fell on the towering walls. Sense of direction was restricted, and the ground appeared even and without surface irregularity no matter where he looked. When he reached a mark drawn across the track, he followed it to its extremity, where was the trap it indicated. From some he took crouching; large-eyed, frightened rabbits, dazzled by the light, curiosity vying with fear. Others he passed, after swift examination to ascertain that the paper over the jaws was still hidden by the soil.

Towards midnight he returned with nineteen skins, tired out. Boiling the billy, he made coffee, and drank a pint laced with brandy before lying down, not troubling to undress or make up his bunk. Almost at once he slept, falling asleep in the delightful lethargy produced by the unaccustomed brandy. And at daybreak he was up and on his trap-line once more. An additional twenty-one rabbits raised the total of his night's catch to sixty-two. The total would have been sixty-six, had not a cat partly eaten one rabbit and foxes devoured three others.

Dudley was satisfied with the night's work, having averaged a rabbit to each trap. After breakfast he stretched the skins over U-shaped pieces of fencing wire and set them out to dry. His satisfaction was dimmed, however, when he collected the traps in heaps, preparatory to moving them to fresh ground, to discover that he had missed eleven of them. He searched all that morning and found only two of those missing. The remainder of the day he spent searching for missing traps, and found only five. Two he found the following day; two he never did find.

He had been worse than the trapper in love with a woman. He had lost two traps and a whole day's labour.

CHAPTER VI

HESTER LONG

ARNOLD DUDLEY had been trapping for nearly a month when, adding his nightly totals, he found he had almost fifteen hundred skins. That was the month of November, and the first day of December found him vastly changed from the keen business-man of Perth.

Such weeks on the Beach of Atonement had aged him woefully. The coming of many little lines at the corners of his mouth and at the centre of his forehead had transmitted a little of his good looks into a harsh grimness. His hazel eyes, once kindly and laughter-lit, seemed now to have receded into his head, to become almost invisible between the narrowed eyelids, as though their vision turned constantly inward and seldom went outward to examine the things of reality. Yet where his age appeared to be accentuated was in the greying hair above the temples, and the slight body-stoop when he walked. This latter, however, was caused not by his exile, but by constant walking over loose fine sand.

After midday dinner that warm December morning he rolled his habitual cigarette with calloused fingers and observed once again the bale of skins ready for dispatch. Really, it was the wrong time of the year to trap. The fur then was mostly outgoing, and if his return cheque amounted to fourteen pounds it would be as much as he could expect. Even so, that sum would much more than balance his expenditure since he had arrived there. That, however, was not so important. His work would establish him among the people of Dongara as a rabbit-trapper. It had benefited him in yet another way. The work had helped him to recover himself, had kept his mind on the mountain peak, high above the valley of madness.

No longer did paroxysms of hatred of Tracy shake and exhaust him. He had come to realize life as it was, life without man-made comforts, without man-made divergent, without home attractions, without Ellen. At long last he recognized himself for what he was—a man apart, a man dishonoured, a man derided by men and scorned by women, one who had become a law unto himself.

Seated there beside his rough meal-table in the shade cast by the circumambient bush, Dudley decided to take his bale of skins to Dongara on the morrow. He would fish that afternoon, and what fish he caught he would sell or give away. Accordingly he got out his lines, one armed with large hooks and a heavy sinker, another with much smaller hooks and a lighter sinker. These, with spare sinkers, he put into a gunny-sack slung from his shoulder, and, after making another cigarette, set off for the rocks.

Immediately he came to the squat headland beyond the sheltering arm of sand-hill, the north-west breeze, which but just ruffled the tops of the combers, struck him with refreshing coolness. A community of gulls occupied the Seagulls' Throne. The solitary shag stood at the edge of the Seaweed Mountain with wings outstretched to dry.

The sea was calm, the succession of mile-long rollers, sluggishly sweeping shoreward, crashing languidly with low rumbling moans against the rocks. The tide was almost out, and he saw that he could stand at the outer edge of the Pontoon with comparative safety.

It was indeed a wonderful day. Not a cloud sailed in the burnished sky. North and south the beach reflected the sunlight as a crescent-shaped ribbon of white silk, bordered at its outer edge by the green bush-covered hummocks, its inner side turquoise-blue, the sea sending to it line after line of glittering white surf.

Yet that wondrous beauty was lost on Arnold Dudley. His brain was too much benumbed by the tragedy of his life, his mind too self-centred to regard extraneous reality with joy. His heart was not lightened by anticipated sport. Life was too empty of joy to discover joy. Life was no longer interesting, no longer offered anything to look forward to, because after all he had lost, the little that might remain was valueless.

For half an hour he hunted shellfish for bait, gathering large whelks with variously tinted shells. Without qualm, he smashed them with a rock, and put the long curly fish bodies into a tin. Then he proceeded to set the heavy line. Baiting the three large hooks, he unwound the hundred-yard line, to gather it back in neat coils hanging over one hand. His other hand held the line a foot or so above the top hook.

The waves even then surged against the edge of the Pontoon, here dashing spray high in the air, there boiling up above the level of the rock, overflowing it, to rush shoreward in a tiny wavelet. Selecting a point where the sea welled up on the rock, Dudley, dressed in old trousers and boots, splashed his way till he halted within two yards of the sea. Here he whirled the heavy sinker round and round, finally to cast it outward in a high descending curve, almost to the full length of the line. His end of it he secured to an upthrust snag of rock, before paddling ashore for his second, lighter line.

With this baited, he returned to the very edge of the Pontoon, where he lowered the sinker and hooks, and allowed the cord to lie over his stretched forefinger. Wave after wave rolled in upon him, until it met the face of the Pontoon, its own momentum sending it upward till it surmounted the level rock and overflowed it, burying Dudley to his knees in hissing foam. Much of the rock-caught water swept toward the beach, some of it rushing back to cascade over the serrated black lip into the trough made when the body of the wave was sent seaward helter-skelter to challenge and pass through the next incoming mountain.

The Pontoon at that place presented a twenty-foot wall of rock to the caress or fury of the Indian Ocean. Almost as soon as Dudley's sinker rested on bottom, he felt the small fish nibbling at his hooks. He struck when a more emphatic tug was telegraphed up the line to his finger, but missed the fish, and almost immediately after that came a succession of rapid tugs, and the line moved away from the rock whilst he hauled it in and landed a gleaming silver-scaled sea-perch almost two pounds in weight.

Ten minutes later he brought up a crimson backed, pink-bellied rock-fish, a thing of utter splendour of the sea. Followed almost to the edge of the rock a blue-black crayfish, which let go its hold on the tempting bait as soon as it found air. Within an hour he had about ten pounds' weight of fish in his gunny-sack.

The tide now was coming in fast. No longer was the top of the sunken rock immediately opposite to be seen in the troughs of the waves. The green and grey limpet-encrusted Sugar Loaf was sinking ever deeper, and when the waves welled up and over on the Pontoon the water reached his thighs. Dudley decided he had had enough, and was winding in his line when he observed his other white cord cutting through the foam like wire.

Most men would have let the light line go for the sake of catching up the other, which held assuredly a big fish. Most men would have tingled at the prospect of such a catch. Not so Arnold Dudley. As though he little cared if the fish escaped or not, he completed the recovery of the light line, wound it on its piece of board, and placed it among the fish in his gunny-sack before picking up the heavier line.

He found it as taut as a bow-string. Testing it with a pull, he discovered that a mighty fish was hooked. It would have been a far simpler task had he been fishing from a boat, where he could have brought the fish near and gaffed it. Here, with the spouting froth and fume of water a yard from his feet, the knife-like edge of the Pontoon waiting to sever the line; it would be absurd to bring in the fish before it was played out or drowned, when he could draw it close and haul it over the rock edge on the top of a swell. Victory to him, therefore, could result only at the finish of a long battle.

The fight between fish and man developed. Sometimes Dudley had not a yard of line to spare; at others many yards lay coiled over his left forearm. To the north dashed the fish, to be checked ever more strongly till it turned and dashed south. Once it came straight to the Pontoon with amazing speed, rushing to the danger of a shattering collision; yet, sensing the proximity of the granite barrier, it slewed north again, and then out to sea.

Fifteen, twenty, thirty minutes fled. At times Arnold Dudley found the straining line a support against the surging waves, which now reached his thighs, making his position ever more precarious. But now the fish was rapidly tiring. Once he saw its silver-gleaming body, long and thick and beautiful. It came to the surface on the summit of a roller, and Dudley saw it was a glorious king-fish, and estimated it to weigh about sixty pounds.

A human voice behind him cried out with delighted admiration, yet he kept his attention on his line. Any time now he could select a big wave to bring in his catch with a rush and, a hand over hand pull. The wave was coming. A "ninth wave" it must have been, for it was a king of waves. Pulling hard on his line, he saw the fish again, and waited for the roller to reach the place. And whilst the wave raced toward the almost drowned fish, there raced toward it, too, a triangular grey-black fin, cutting the water into two widening wavelets. Dudley pulled hard. The wave lifted the fish high. He saw its gleaming body being sent skyward; saw, too, a dull white streaky body swirl upon it.

With amazing suddenness the weight was taken from his line. The wave was at the Pontoon. It spouted up high, shoulder high, with a white-laced green back, appeared to hang for quite a time above the lip of the rock, then surged toward Dudley, swept him off his feet, enveloped him, hurled him shoreward with a thunderous roar, bumped him on the ser-rated surface of the Pontoon, pounded and pummelled him, finally to lose its strength and leave him gasping and choking at the feet of Hester Long.

When he staggered to his feet, helped by the mother and two little boys, and had wiped the water from his hair, he regarded her grimly, neither fear nor anger nor amusement in his face. Without speaking, he gathered in the line, to regard then half the head of the giant king-fish still on the hook.

"It was a shark which took it, wasn't it?" the woman said, vivid sympa-thy and disappointment in her voice. "I thought I saw its fin and then its white belly. What a shame! Are you hurt?"

"No," he said sharply. "Luck is out to-day. Still, I have the smaller fish."

He allowed her to look in the gunny-sack, whereupon she gave a cry of delight, and into her eyes flashed the real fisherman's joy.

"You have got a nice lot," she cried. "But you must take care. Some of the holes in the rock are dangerous. They would suck you down if you were washed into one of them. But there! you must come and have a cup of tea. I left Miss Mallory boiling the billy. This time you mustn't refuse."

"This time I shall not refuse," he said ; adding: "How is the thumb?"

"Quite well again. For a little while it was most awkward to milk the cows, but Miss Mallory used to ride over night and morning to help."

They splashed towards the narrow strip of beach. Dudley noted that his companion wore a very old pair of elastic-sided riding-boots, and that her unfashionably long skirt was fastened up above her knees. The beach gained, she unpinned the skirt and allowed it to drop to its proper length. Smiling slightly, she said:

"Are you not cold?"

"Not a bit," he told her. "Only vexed at that pirate of a shark." And, when they had scrambled up the low rock barrier and gained the sand-patch back of the head-land, he was quite warm. Even when he seated himself, at Miss Mallory's invitation, between two eager little boys at the side of a spread tablecloth, his clothes were almost dried by the warm sunlit air.

They gave him tea and lettuce sandwiches, buttered scones, and little cakes. The elder woman waited on him with the gentle art bespeaking the habit of waiting on a man well-beloved. Miss Mallory talked seldom, and then only with the two hungry, high-spirited little boys. After a little while Arnold Dudley, with the downright bonhomie of the Australian, said:

"Why not introduce ourselves?"

"Why not?" agreed the matronly woman, smiling. "I am Hester Long—Mrs. Long—of Eagle Farm."

Dudley found himself looking into a pair of steady grey eyes in which was a hint of sadness that could not be banished. He decided she was about his own age, even though at first glance the lines about her mouth and eyes, as well as her weather-beaten complexion, made her appear ten years older. Even in the bloom of youth Hester Long must have been plain. Now her features were almost rugged. Yet till then he had never seen any-thing approaching the spiritual beauty that appeared to radiate from her. Seated on a camp-stool dressed in a white blouse that accentuated the shabbiness of her old fishing-skirt and boots, with an old-time bonnet fastened to her prematurely greying hair with hatpins of the mid-Victorian period, she would have excited laughter, were it not for her wonderful shining eyes. When one looked into them one encountered Maternity. In the glory of the smile that seemed to break over her face as sunlight over a shower-drenched bush-land, the ugly spots of life vanished and were not.

"What is your name?" she asked him simply.

Her eyes and his were joined in level gaze. Dudley's eyes fell before he replied quickly

"Oh! my name is Cain—Hector Cain."

She knew he lied, yet liked him none the less for that. Had he looked into her eyes whilst lying she would instantly have disliked him. She was that sort of woman.

"Now that you and I are introduced, you must let me introduce you to my friend, Miss Mallory. Edith, meet Mr. Cain!"

Now the eyes he looked into were wide and deep-blue. He saw a pretty blonde, probably in her early twenties. Edith Mallory acknowledged the introduction with a cool nod. The accompanying smile was mechanical, for her mind appeared to be occupied with some quite sudden new interest whilst she inspected the new acquaintance.

"Are you a relative of the Mr. Mallory who owns this land?" Dudley inquired politely.

"Yes, I am his sister."

"Ah! Then you might tell him that I have relieved his land of some fifteen hundred rabbits," he said quietly.

"I wish you could relieve my land of a few eagle-hawks," Mrs. Long interjected. "Do you know a good way of catching them?"

"Well, I have caught a good many," he admitted. "Are they worrying you?"

"Not so much now as they have done. They killed nearly fifty of my lambs last August and September."

"Your lambs?"

"Yes—my lambs, now."

Her voice had become infinitely sad. Dudley saw tragedy leap into the limpid grey eyes, and, because having met tragedy he hated to see tragedy, he made a promise which almost immediately he wanted to withdraw.

"Then I will come and catch your eagles. The .Roads Board pays five shillings a head, doesn't it?"

"Yes." Her voice became crisp. "And I will pay also a bonus of half-a-crown."

"Good. Then you may expect me at the farm in a few days."

"You'll come ? Really?"

"I have said so. Not to-morrow, for I have rabbit skins to send to Perth. Nor the next day, which is Saturday. We will agree on Monday."

"I do hope you will be able to catch them."

"How do you catch them, Mr. Cain?" asked Miss Mallory, rolling up the younger boy's knickers. They watched the youngsters dash down to the safe pool which the incoming tide had not reached; whereupon Miss Mallory again regarded Arnold Dudley, this time evidently expecting and waiting for an answer.

"There are many ways," Dudley evaded. "Sometimes they can be poisoned; sometimes it is possible to put salt on their wedge-shaped tails."

She suspected but saw no laughter in his face, and wondered if he ever smiled.

"You won't tell me?" she challenged.

"You would not expect a conjurer to show the way he did his tricks, would you?"

"Well, perhaps not. Are you conjurer enough to catch an eagle with a sieve and a stick and a piece of string?"

"Do not make me betray my stage properties. Give me two days on Mrs. Long's farm, and I'll produce the eagles. Are there many rabbits on your place, Mrs. Long?"

"Yes, especially on the Ridge. You ought to get a lot of skins if you trap there."

"And you wouldn't mind my trapping rabbits whilst I am at war with the eagles?"

"Certainly not."

"Then you may depend upon my arrival in a few days' time. How do I get to your place?"

"Oh! We seem to have known you so long that I took it for granted that you knew," Mrs. Long said, dividing her attention between him and the playing boys. "When you reach the main road you turn north, towards Geraldton. My house is the first you come to on the right. Just look at those imps! It's a mercy I dressed them in their oldest clothes. And look! The tide is coming in so fast. If we are to get any shellfish we must hurry."

For an hour Dudley and the two women hunted for the whelk-like shellfish he had earlier used for bait. Mrs. Long talked continually of the sea, of fishing, of the danger of the rocks and the greater danger of the blow-holes.

"Look at that nasty one there, Mr. Cain," she said, pointing to a circular hole at the shore end of the Pontoon,

He looked as directed. The hole was like a cylinder three yards in diameter sunk into the rock mass. How deep it was he could not then estimate; but, when each roller sent its quota of water swirling across the Pontoon the water in the hole rose and welled up over the rock-lip, thence to fall back and downward for almost five feet. Doubtless the bottom of the hole was connected with the outer sea-wall by a tunnel. Looking up, he found Mrs. Long's eyes resting upon him. She said, very softly:

"Ten miles north there is another rock like this, with several holes similar to that one. It is a fine fishing rock. Two years ago my husband was knocked down by a wave, just like you were this afternoon. He was knocked into a blow-hole, and never came up again."

"Good God!" Arnold was suddenly aghast.

"I was fishing with him and saw him go."

"Terrible!" Dudley was utterly shocked by the look in her eyes. He was shocked further when she said, almost wistfully:

"So you see, like you, I know loss and sorrow."

"Er—like me! How did you find out?"

"I read every word of it on your face," she replied; and, turning, went on hunting for shellfish.

For a moment or two he gazed at her bent back almost blankly. He became conscious that Edith Mallory was regarding him with curious wonder, and, checking an exclamation, joined in the hunt.

Two hours later he harnessed the horse to the old worn buggy, and held the animal's head until the party was seated. Then, reminding him of his promise, Hester Long urged the horse forward, she herself smiling at him with bright eyes, Miss Mallory giving him one more examination, the little boys crying farewells ; and, when the vehicle passed him, he snatched the fish-lines out of his gunny-sack, and tossed the fish remaining in it into the tray back of the buggy.

CHAPTER VII

HESTER LONG'S EAGLES

HAD he not so emphatically promised Hester Long to catch the eagles that menaced her lambs, Arnold Dudley would not have left the beach ; for the windswept immensity of the sea and the stolid, calm, buttressing sand hills were beginning to exert a strange fascination over him. Solitude always had appealed to Arnold Dudley, and when he first had yielded to the appeal he was quite a young man, having run away from a high school to answer the call of the New South Wales bush.

For that his father had never forgiven him. Once he had returned home, after three years occupied as a stockman. His mother, frail and delicate, besought her only boy to seek a living in Sydney and be near her. For ten months he worked in an office, a period of his life spent in fighting down the call of the wild. And when ten months had dragged away the bush had won.

Dudley's mother died the Christmas Day following his second surrender, a day that found him fifteen hundred miles west of Sydney droving cattle. It happened that the boss drover was George Finlay. It also happened that George Finlay was a Western Australian by birth, took part in the gold rush to Coolgardie and several other rushes that followed, and never tired of talking of those halcyon days. He fired Dudley with his pictures of the "West", and a year later they drove two draught horses harnessed to a dray across the continent, blazing a track used afterwards by motor-car explorers who wrote expensive books about their tremendous experiences.

Dudley's love of the bush, of the enormous space and freedom of the bush, had been submerged by his greater love of Ellen who hated it. To retain Ellen he went to Perth, and for a time his love for the bush and his love for Ellen warred against each other. Neither influence gave way, even though Ellen held him to the hateful, cramped, stinking city—held him till city life became a habit, and he had begun to think he had successfully closed the ears of his soul to the siren call of the bush.

The men he had met who had hated the bush with a great hatred! Farmers' sons and farmers' hired hands, men anchored and clamped to a few acres, mentally clogged by the endless drudgery, who had sought the city for an easier life. They had been like the fool who ran to pick up base metal and stepped unheeding over pure gold. They wanted freedom, an easier life, and rushed to the city to become wage-slaves for so many hours a week when they would have found real freedom from man made slavery had they rushed in the opposite direction.

Dudley had known the real freedom of the virgin bush. It attracted him and held him with the allure of a woman. During his life with Ellen the bush was as a memory of a beautiful woman he had loved, even as he loved a flesh and blood woman in his wife.

A flesh and blood woman, however, is but a transient thing, as her love might well be also. She may grow cold, or die. But the bush never dies, never grows cold, never ceases to attract and reward. It is eternal in its allure, no less than in its life. It is able to go on forever calling to its absent lovers in the city, or on the ocean, or in a far country; and often there are moments in the lives of the absent ones when the love-call of the bush pierces the armour of human interests and human demands.

When Ellen had been swept away from him—when the flesh and blood woman had faded out—it was to the bush he had instinctively gone. There on his beach he had met her smiling upon him, laying her protecting gown of green over him, cooling his hate-heated brain with her scents, lulling his racked nerves with her ineffable voice. She was his first love. Let her be his last, was his prayer whilst seated on the Seagulls' Throne. And well might he pray, for as yet he did not realize the depth and breadth of the inspired saying : "It is not good that the man should be alone."

For if Hester Long had been instrumental in bringing to a close the phase of his mentally disrupting hatred of Tracy, she also was to be instrumental in bringing on a phase more prolonged, more terrible—a phase in which the lost Ellen was to fight the bush for the soul of Arnold Dudley.

Yet, whilst the bush triumphed, the man was loth to leave it, even for the few days necessary to relieve Hester Long's farm of the eagle-hawks. Whilst watching the charging rollers laid with a cloth of diamonds by wind and sun, he sighed regret over his promise to Hester Long. He felt then as he used to feel at the moment of parting from Ellen on his business trips, and remarked the strangeness of it.

Two hours later he reached Hester Long's home, a very old white-washed pise dwelling set amidst ripening lupin paddocks that formed the valley between two ridges running east and west. When she came out on the veranda to welcome him, he was not a little surprised at the metamorphosis in her appearance. Dressed in a pale blue overall over serviceable house clothes, wearing shoes instead of the old riding-boots, and without the atrocious bonnet hiding a wealth of brown hair so light as to be almost golden, she looked no more than twenty-eight.

"I am glad you have come," she told him in her sweet voice. "Come in and have a cup of tea, and tell me what you want to do, and if there is anything I can do to help."

Leading him through the house, she took him into a large spotless kitchen, brick-floored, airy, and sunlit. At one side from a ceiling beam hung several sides of bacon. On a white-painted dresser were set polished milking buckets and cream basins. This kitchen was Hester Long's kingdom, and she had taken him there not because he was a rabbit-trapper and presumably on a lower social scale than herself, but because he was her friend. A stranger she would have shown into her drawing-room, not her kingdom, and somehow Arnold Dudley came to realize that, and when he was seated by a small table set before the open window he regarded her with fresh interest.

"You have a nice home, Mrs. Long," he said, because he felt he must say something. "You've a nice farm, too, from what I have seen of it."

"I love my home."

She said it with a slight smile of joy. Holding out the palms of her small yet remarkably calloused hands to him, she added:

"I was a school-teacher in England when I married Fred, who was in the A.I.F. Ours was a hasty war wedding, and everyone said it would be a failure. When I came to Australia with him we had about three hundred pounds between us, and through the Repatriation people we got this farm. We had paid off half our debt when Fred was drowned. The remaining half is almost paid off now, but I have had to work very hard."

"You run the farm yourself?"

"Yes. I milk ten cows twice every day, and make butter which I send to special customers in Perth. I look after four hundred sheep, and manage to fatten fifty store cattle every year for the Perth market. Oh yes, I've worked! I've cleared a hundred acres of land, and built almost three miles of fencing."

"You have?"

Again she showed him her hands.

"Look at the marks of the axe and the crowbar and shovel," she indicated. Then: "Of course the Mallorys have been more than kind. Tom Mallory buys my store cattle for me and has them delivered here, and Edith, ever since poor Fred went and I've had to battle alone, has been teaching the children. They go over to their house every day but Sundays."

For a moment he was silent. He was thinking how plucky a woman could be, how strong in spirit, how wise in mind. Her calloused hands, her lined face, spoke eloquently of the unfeminine labour she had borne, but the light in her eyes revealed—what was it he saw there? And when next she spoke he knew.

"You see, when my husband was taken, the farm. was loaded by, debt, and I had my two boys to think of," she explained. "It meant either going to Perth and taking a situation at anything, or remaining here and carrying on Fred's work. I stopped, as you see. And now I am glad, but there have been times when my sore hands and aching back made me cry. My boys will have an inheritance, after all.

"You're wonderful," he managed to say.

"Perhaps—and perhaps not so wonderful," she told him, giving him tea from a pot enveloped in an old-fashioned bead-worked cosy. "Work helped me over Fred's passing. There is no soul-wound so deep that it cannot be healed by work. Don't you think I am right?"

"Yes," he answered slowly. "Do you know, when I first came here I idled for weeks? It was you who set me to work, and now my heart doesn't ache so much."

"I set you to work?"

"Yes. As I was taking the hook out of your thumb I saw the corns on your hands, and seeing them I felt ashamed."

"Which reminds me that I am very remiss. Thank you for that lovely lot of fish." For a little while she looked steadily at him, and he as steadily at her. Then: "Among several vices, my greatest is curiosity. Why did you give me them?"

"Because you set me to work, and work saved me from madness."

"Then I am glad the hook did get stuck in my thumb. I knew that day you were suffering from great loss or sorrow."

The light of sympathy in her eyes dimmed his own. He knew then that Hester Long had done more for him than save him from insanity. She had saved his faith in his own kind. She was the kind of woman of which there are not sufficient in the world—the woman who does not merely invite confidence, but absolutely tempts a man to confide in her his worries and troubles, knowing that their recital will be received with sympathy and balm laid on his tortured soul.

And, had he not shot Tracy, he would have told her then of Ellen.

It was thought of his blood-guilt which forced him to his feet, saying what had been his business motto:

"Time flies. There is much to be done before night falls. Will you show me which of the two ridges will provide me with trapping ground?"

"Yes. It's that running along my north boundary," she said, leading him through the house to the back veranda. On the veranda he gazed over the expanse of knee-high, fading, lupin-covered paddocks to a low ridge about two hundred feet high, at which she pointed.

"Look! I can see two eagles now."

Dudley had seen them, too. A thousand feet high, they sailed in vast circles with never a flap of a wing, less in size at that height than one of Mrs. Long's many half-grown chickens. Turning to her, he said:

"When you described to me your daily tasks you did not mention the fowls. Who looks after them?"

Why, I do," and seeing him give one of his very rare smiles, she laughed—a golden laugh, a laugh that began with a delightful gurgle, and ended on a high note.

At the sound of it his smile vanished and his face became drawn. She found him staring at her with leaping anguish in his eyes, and, taking a little step towards him, said softly:

"Oh! What have I done?"

"Nothing, really, Mrs. Long. But the sound of your laugh recalled another woman whom it is my task to forget."

His voice, which she had thought very pleasant, was harsh when he said, stepping off the veranda:

"That track along there will lead me to the foot of the ridge?"

"Yes. But wait a minute! Won't you take some eggs and some of my butter? Or will you come back here for meals?"

"Thank you, but I must get on," and he left her almost rudely—left her watching him drive away, with three vertical lines above her nose, and eyes that were saddened.

Ellen's laughter rang in Dudley's ears whilst he drove recklessly along a rough cart-track. The sound of it coming from Hester Long had dragged wide the healing lips of his wound, stirred within him love for his wife which he had imagined was stark and dead. Work! Work was the only palliative for loss and sorrow. Hester Long was right in that.

Parking his truck at the fringe of bush which extended half-way up the ridge, he savagely dragged the rabbit-traps from the truck, and as savagely counted out two lots of twelve each. Assured of a supply of paper squares, and thrusting the handle of his setting-hammer through his belt, he caught up the traps, swung a dozen over each shoulder, and zigzagged up the steep slope to the summit of the ridge. There the bush did not extend. It was open grass country, and a maze of rabbit burrows.

During his recent trip to Dongara he had augmented his stock of traps, so that then he owned exactly a hundred. An hour before sunset he had set them all, marking each with a short stick and dragging a trail from stick to stick. The eagles watched him, and when he descended to his truck they swooped lower. Five of the first-caught rabbits they ate.

That night he went over his trap-line at eight o'clock, at ten, and at midnight. He went over it again at dawn. He then had seventy-one skins. Thirty-seven rabbits were too young to skin, and these he hid beneath a blanket of boughs. The carcasses of the seventy-one he left exposed, divided into fourteen separate lots over a distance of a full mile.

His method of catching eagles he had learned in New South Wales. In Western Australia the method was not nearly so widely known.

About nine o'clock he was breakfasting, when he saw a girl riding a hack up to the homestead, and half an hour later, whilst stretching his skins on the U-shaped pieces of wire, he observed the same horsewoman swinging her mount towards him, and recognized Edith Mallory. Over the crook of her left arm she carried a basket.

It pleased Dudley that morning to be cynical, yet he could not forbear admiration of her easy seat. His admiration was tempered, however, when he observed that she wore breeches and top-hoots, a fashion doubtless prevalent at agricultural shows and in magazine illustrations, but seldom to be found adopted by real bushwomen who ride at stock-work and not for pleasure and effect.

"I've brought you some butter and eggs which you could not stop for yesterday," was her greeting. And then she asked the question Dudley knew she was going to ask: "Have you caught any eagles yet?"

"No," he admitted, with assumed disappointment.

"None!" She stared at him in her disconcerting way. Then: "Did you forget to bring your salt?"

At that he laughed mirthlessly, for at that time he could laugh no other way.

"I have a bag full," he told her. "Anyway, I am not going to give up. I'll try again this afternoon."

"That's right," she said mockingly. "If you've no objection, I'll pay you another visit to-morrow. I hope you get one or two. Mrs. Long and I counted seven a while ago."

"So many!" he exclaimed, mockery also in his voice.

"Then I hope to get at least two."

Watching her canter back to the house, Dudley pondered the fact that this young woman appeared to have the power of raising antagonism in those whom she disliked, and he felt sure she disliked him ; though why, was beyond his comprehension. His experience of women had been limited to one. Miss Mallory's mockery of him, however, was not due to dislike, but was a hastily-donned feminine defence against a growing liking for his strong clean-cut face and lithe body. The man mystified the woman, and few women like to be mystified.

By noon his campaign against the eagles was in full force. The original four in sight settled on the bounteous feast prepared for them. Their nearest neighbours, several miles distant and out of sight, rapidly converged when the first four circled down to the ground. Their coming inward to the centre of the circle; which was the laid-out feast, attracted after them yet other eagles miles farther out still; and when, towards four o'clock, Dudley went again up to the ridge, no fewer than twenty kings and queens of the air fluttered upward lazily from the crumbs, climbed ever more swiftly towards the brazen sky, and drifted back to their seemingly allotted areas.

Ere the sun had set Dudley had gathered his traps into fourteen separate heaps, twelve of seven traps and two of eight traps. Uncovering then the bodies of the unskinned young rabbits, he divided them among his trap heaps. That done, he prepared what are colloquially known as hurdy-gurdies. The rabbits he fastened securely to the ground with long wire pins, and around the carcasses, in a circle with a radius of about a yard, he set the seven or eight rabbit-traps.

That night he went early to bed and rose late the next morning. After breakfast he did several little necessary jobs to the truck, one of which was to erect rails along each side and a few feet from the floor of the vehicle.

Towards eleven o'clock he cut a stout cudgel from a green box-tree and mounted the slope to his traps.

At his appearance nine eagles flew up, joining five others who evidently had just arrived. In the first of his hurdy-gurdies an eagle had got each foot in a trap, and the tip of one Wing in yet another. Dudley killed it with a qualm of regret, a feeling he always experienced when killing eagles, for in beauty, majesty, and power the Australian eagle has few superiors. With a wing-span of from five to seven feet, brown and black plumage, its neck and head feathers of lighter brown, some with feathered legs, clean silver-scaled feet armed with talons of tremendous strength, and a graceful yet wicked-looking beak, to give it the hyphenated name, "eagle-hawk", is to belittle it without excuse. It is no more a hawk in appearance or in flight than the eagle of the Pyrenees.

In the second hurdy-gurdy were caught three eagles. They strove to fly, and glared malevolently at their approaching destroyer: poor, beautiful, devilish birds, the enemies of man because they are the enemies of lambs and sheep, and of new-born weakly calves. One of the saddest sights in the world is to see them caged in Australia's zoological gardens.

One of Dudley's hurdy-gurdies held five eagles. Several held four. Only one was birdless. When he had butchered them all, he found he had secured thirty-one.

After resetting the traps he dragged the eagles down to the truck and concealed all but two beneath a spare tent that he then did not trouble to erect. For he expected Edith Mallory, and presently she arrived.

"I got two," he told her triumphantly, indicating the eagles by the truck.

"My! You are doing well !" she gibed. "How is the salt supply?"

"I have still a little left. I am going to try again presently. There seem to be quite a lot about here, don't there?"

"Yes, several."

Her blue eyes danced, little gleams of mockery and flashes of wonder showing in them alternately. At heart she was not surprised that he had secured two, nor was she surprised that he had secured only two. It was his—to her—boasting of a few days before which rankled in her mind, for Edith Mallory was older than her years. It liked her not to hear a grown man boast as a callow youth.

That evening, between sunset and dark, Arnold Dudley caught eleven more. After dark he trapped for two hours for sufficient "bait" for the next day, and by noon of his third day he secured yet five others, making a grand total of forty-seven. He, himself, was astounded by his catch. Finlay had told him that, using that method in New South Wales, at a time when the rabbits had been numerous for years, he and a partner had caught one hundred and eighty-six eagles in seven days. However, Western Australia was not vermin-ridden as were New South Wales and the neighbouring States, because in the Western State the rabbit is comparatively a new-comer, and it is "bunny" that provides a large proportion of the eagles' food supply.

Keeping watch on the homestead, a splash of brilliant white on an emerald-tinged carpet of brown, he dragged his birds and his traps down to the truck. After he had loaded his gear on the truck, he hung the eagles along the rough rails, so that his turn-out was like a poultryman's lorry on its way to Smithfield with the Christmas turkeys.

At five o'clock he saw the two little boys and Edith Mallory drive up to the homestead in a pony-cart, and when they reached the house he cranked his engine and set off in a mood positively cheerful. They awaited him on the veranda of the house. He saw the women turn excitedly toward each other, and when he stopped the truck outside the little garden paling fence, they were silent and the youngsters vociferous. Standing at last before them, he smiled broadly at Edith Mallory, saying:

"I've run out of salt."

Her eyes were wide, her answering smile provocative. She said:

"I don't know whether to apologize to you or ask you to apologize to me, Mr. Cain."

"Let us consider the apologies as cancelled out, Miss Mallory. And let us both hope that Mrs. Long will not be troubled by eagles for some little time to come," was his pleasant response.

CHAPTER VIII

THE DREAM

THROUGHOUT January and February Arnold Dudley followed the occupation—if occupation it can be called—of beach-combing. It was not that he became tired of work, or that the period of his activity was as a growing and bursting bubble; it was merely because, from the trapper's point of view, those months constitute a natural "close time" in the year. The fur on animals is at its shortest. The old fur has fallen out, and the new has but just started to grow. Consequently the market price of fur and skins is at its lowest, and trapping becomes an absurdity.

He retired late and slept late. The heat of the summer sun made his wind-sheltered camp unbearable after ten o'clock, and sometimes long after the sun had set. The vast sweep of the beach he explored from end to end. He came to know it as a man comes to know his own house; and, as a man comes to regard his house as his particular sanctuary from the world, so Dudley came to look upon the beach. It became his beach, something in which he could experience the pride of possession.

The land-crabs, orange-coloured, which scuttled to their holes high above the tide or ran down to the sea at his approach—crabs that sidled along as though on one edge of their shells, and saw him coming with little black eyes set on the tops of spindly golden cylinders—were the protectors of his beach. The seagulls lorded it from their Throne, and evidenced supreme contempt when he usurped their place and they took refuge on the Seaweed Mountain. The solitary shag, so wise and companionable, met with a violent end.

It was shot by one of three "sportsmen" who spent two days on the beach at Christmas time. They came in a car and camped at the cleared place where Hester Long always tethered her buggy horse, and it was whilst on his way to his own camp one afternoon that he picked up the bird, broken-winged and blood-stained, which the waves had washed up south of the Pontoon. Carrying the bird, he approached the trippers, and with steely politeness inquired if it was their bird.

They admitted having shot it, whilst Dudley idly gazed over, the beach and counted his flock of gulls. All were there, by great good fortune. Knowing the uselessness of argument over the killing of the shag, he dropped it on the running-board of the car and left them without further word, only to come back twenty minutes later with a thick slice of damper. The gulls were then resting on the Seaweed Mountain. The three men watched Dudley climb down on the beach, and with interest saw the gulls feeding from the crumbled bread he tossed almost at his feet. Presently rejoining them, he said:

"I live here alone. Those gulls are my pets. They are no good to eat, and therefore I ask you in all humbleness to spare their lives. I hope you understand."

They thought they did understand. In any case, they appeared to understand the look of cold fury in his eyes, and, not liking it, left the next day.

The absence of the solitary shag, so little a thing of itself, became a poignant regret to the equally solitary man. Dudley had often wondered why that bird elected to live alone, for, unlike him, it could choose its own way of life. For days following the sportsmen's visit he missed something from his beach, just as though a piece of furniture, associated with his life for many years, had been removed against his wish.

He told Hester Long about it when one afternoon she paid the beach another visit with her boys. He told her with petulance in his voice. He was excited at meeting her, and unconsciously told her of his starvation for want of human company.

That was towards the end of February, when he had been on the beach for four months, and during those four months he had spent no more than seven hours in the company of his kind. She was fishing from the Pontoon when he joined her, to plunge at once into the story of the shag's death. Listening to him with sympathy in her eyes and a soft smile on her rugged face, she observed that whilst his clothes were in tatters, whilst his feet were bare and brown and scarred by the rocks, and his hair long, and uncovered from the sun, he was scrupulously shaved and clean. She remarked the peculiarity of that in a man so evidently becoming a victim to his environment.

Hester Long was no woman to stand aside from trouble, or loss, or sorrow. It but aroused her sympathy the more, and there and then she determined, in her own phrase, to have it out with him.

"Come along and boil the billy," she said, after commiserating with him regarding his loss. "This is the first time for ever so long that I and the boys have come to the beach without Miss Mallory. She went to Perth two weeks ago with her brother on holiday."

"Ah! I wondered where she had got to," Dudley said, speaking rapidly.

"Oh! How did you come to miss her?"

"I think it began about Christmas time." Suddenly his eyes were dreamy. He gazed unseeingly out over the glittering ocean. He was talking as he talked when alone. "She got into the way of riding her horse to the brow of the hill just behind the camp, where she tethered it to a bush and watched to see if I were away. If I was away, she would steal down to my camp and wash the utensils and tidy it up. You know, I wish she hadn't done it. I didn't like to tell her that I knew who did that for me, nor do I care about her knowing that I know."

He did not see Hester Long regarding him with wide eyes. She had heard something she had known nothing about. Without being conscious of it he had told her a secret on which but one interpretation could be placed. Whilst she poured the fresh-made tea into the cups there was added to her genuine sympathy for the man a sudden fear for Edith Mallory, who had proved so staunch a friend to her in her hour of need. He went on:

"You see, Mrs. Long, I am not the kind of man in whom any woman should be interested. In strict fairness I should not permit you to speak to me, certainly not allow you to show kindness to me."

"Why not?" Her question was sharply spoken. It shocked him out of his mood, as she intended it to do. Yet, when he looked at her suddenly, he found her face wonderfully soft and radiant, and her voice when next she spoke was not less radiant.

"Why do you live here like this?"

"Because I can live nowhere else."

"How is that? Tell me. Perhaps I can help."

"Help!" He shook his head. "You and Miss Mallory have helped all that it is possible to help. You have helped me to retain personal self-respect. Beyond that you cannot help. You cannot wash out what the Moving Finger has written."

"Perhaps not. But the result of what the Moving Finger has written, where it concerns you, may be eased or lightened by confidence," she argued. "If there is a problem to face, two heads are better able to face it than one, don't you think?"

For a while he sipped his tea. Watching him, Hester Long thought of Edith Mallory and her surreptitious visits to this man's camp to tidy it in his absence. Now, she knew the reason of the change in her friend, those little hardly noticeable things like the smaller pieces in a jig-saw puzzle. She heard him say:

"Could you teach me to forget? If you could, I would become your bond slave for life."

"You must first tell me what you want to forget."

"Very well, I'll tell you." His eyes were suddenly wide and glaring into hers. "I want to forget my wife and the scoundrel who stole her from me. How can I forget when you laugh like Ellen used to ? Tell me how to forget, how I can wrench this torturing agony out of my heart—how I can find peace without destroying myself. Do you know why I haven't destroyed myself? It is because I know, for my mother taught me, that death is but a change."

Again swiftly he moved his gaze from her to the far-flung horizon almost invisible in the sunlight. And when he seemed to have forgotten her she put a hand on his bare, sun-blackened arm, saying:

"Just tell me."

For a full minute after that he did not speak. She removed her hand and idly watched the youngsters playing in the lagoon safe from the rollers everlastingly crashing against the outer rocks. Then abruptly he plunged into the recital of his tragedy. He told her of Ellen, of their courtship, their marriage, and their life together.

"Perhaps she thought I neglected her for golf. I don't know. I had no thought of neglecting her," he said. "A man who was my friend saw his opportunity, though. Someone told me on the telephone that she sent the servants away on Saturday afternoons, when he would visit her at the house I had built for her. I couldn't rest till I had made sure of Ellen one way or the other. I crept into my own house one Saturday afternoon. The servants were absent. I heard her and him talking in her room, the room I looked upon as almost holy because we had made it such. I waited outside in the passage. Seated on a chair I waited for them to come out."

The agony of that time was torturing Arnold Dudley now. She saw his hands clench and unclench, and his body twitch with throbbing nerves.

"What did you do?" she whispered.

His voice was almost a whisper also when he replied:

"I shot him."

The woman's eyes narrowed and quickly opened wide. There was in them amazed horror, and when she did not speak he turned and looked at her. His voice held a hint of a sneer.

"Well, what do you think of that?"

The expression of anguish in his clear hazel eyes had changed to one of mocking defiance. Regarding him, Hester Long sought for a sign of remorse. She found none, and knew that the mood troubling his mind was not remorse. She felt that she had not yet solved the mystery, unless it was that he still loved his wife. Sighing, her eyes fell away from his, and mechanically she filled the teacups.

"Meeting a murderer is not a nice sensation, is it?" he said almost jeeringly.

"No," she admitted slowly.

"I am glad we agree. As you have been nice to me, I will remove myself from your presence. To stay would be fair neither to you nor your children."

He had risen quickly to his feet when she said:

"Stay! Sit down again and finish your tea."

She spoke to him as in years gone by she had often been obliged to speak to a recalcitrant scholar, and he obeyed, partly because he wanted to, partly because the child in him had often obeyed such a voice.

"Well?" he asked grimly.

"As you say, it is not a nice sensation meeting a murderer," she said quietly, adding very slowly and distinctly: "A much more unpleasant sensation is meeting a fool."

"You surprise me." His voice was openly jeering. It hurt her and he saw it, and suddenly his body bent forward and his face became buried in his arms, which rested across his knees. She heard him say, in what was almost a wail: "A fool! Yes, you are right. A fool I am. When I exterminated the vermin I condemned myself to a hell on earth."

"It was inevitable, as you should have known before you committed the deed, that you would live the remainder of your life clouded by remorse."

Once more he was looking at her.

"There you are mistaken," he said quickly. "I do not experience the slightest remorse for having killed him, in so far as killing goes. I could kill him many times over for what he did to me. Where I was a fool was in merely killing him, when I should have cut his vile handsome face to ribbons, and let him live to see the women shudder at him. I could then have sought him out again and again and mocked him, and every woman that I knew would have been taken with me to be introduced to him.

"Remorse! Yes. I feel remorse for having killed him, because killing him was too good. Listen!" He was becoming excited again, and his voice would not have been recognized for the clear, calm voice of the business man of a few months before. Hester Long heard in it the inexorable influence of solitude. "About the time I got all those eagles, my hate of—never mind his name—became dulled, as it were. As though it had grown into a part of me, a habit, I had come to believe that the man's death was full recompense for what he had done. The price he paid was big, not so big as he would have paid had I let him live with a slashed and scarred face, but big enough to satisfy me, as I can't now exact a bigger.

"And then I had the most extraordinary and vivid dream I ever dreamed. I dreamt that with another man I was in an underground passage, like one of those leading from vault to vault in France where they store the wine. Yet somehow this passage was a cul-de-sac, and my companion and I could go no farther. The passage was distinctly visible, even though it was underground. I could see the rough-hewn stones forming the walls.

"We were fugitives—fugitives from what, I do not know. We were standing waiting, and there came to us round a bend sounds of hurrying footsteps and voices. Now, although I didn't know what it was all about, I did know that those sounds meant the end of my life. I knew that the men approaching were going to kill me. It was quite inevitable. There was no possible evasion or escape.

"Two men suddenly confronted us. They were dressed in tunics of light grey which fell to their knees, and their feet and legs were encased in sandals and criss-crossed leathers to their knees. The first man fell back and the other came in front. I stepped forward to meet him. I did that to enable him to kill me first. He said: 'Thus die all traitors,' and, raising a pistol, fired at me.

"I felt no pain. I collapsed in a sitting posture with my back against one of the walls. I knew that the bullet from his pistol had entered my head exactly in the middle of my forehead. I knew I was dead, yet I could see my killer and the opposite wall. I saw a small red flame dart from his pistol and knew that he was shooting my companion. And then what I saw slowly faded into blackness."

Dudley ceased talking and sighed. Hester Long was silent. After a while he spoke again:

"There was perfect sequence in that dream. It was not a jumble of incidents which compose most dreams, and when I awoke I remembered every second of the dream period. But I knew that I had carefully aimed at the two vertical lines above my enemy's eyes, and knew that he died precisely as I died in my dream. And in my dream I had died without the slightest pain.

"You see that I had imagined my enemy to feel agony when I shot him, whereas I now know he suffered none. You think I am a monster. I can see it in your face. If I am, he made me a monster. You don't understand what he took from me. I can't make you understand. When he made me a laughing-stock among men and women who knew me, the injury he did me was little in comparison to his robbing me of my wife. Even the theft of my wife's body was little in comparison with the theft of my wife's love. Don't you see that ? A woman's body can be replaced by another woman's body. If a man wants a woman's body he can purchase one. But he can't purchase a woman's love. My enemy stole from me what all the money in the world can't buy. Not only that, he could not return what he had stolen. No law ever made could compel him to return what he had stolen from me. He could not return it if he wished. He could not make restitution if he possessed and paid over to me all the money in the world."

Hester Long thought she saw the light.

"Let us assume that the man could have returned to you your wife's love. Would you have accepted it?"

"Yes. In spite of her dishonour I would have accepted it. I would have been weak enough to have accepted it because," Dudley stuttered with a sob in his voice, "— because Ellen is the only woman I have ever loved, the only woman I have ever kissed, other than my mother. If he could have given me back my wife's love, I would have accepted it. I would have taken her away to another country and tried my very hardest to forget the nightmare of the past. And, if I did not forget it, my love for Ellen would have relegated it among the least important things."

"Then why not find out from your wife for certain if she does still love you?" Hester Long suggested softly.

"Because, for one thing, there is blood on, my hands." Unconsciously almost Arnold Dudley raised his hands and looked at them.

"That would make reconciliation between you easier," she told him, all Eve in her voice. "You would be on a level, as it were. Your leaving here would be dangerous, probably, but were you able to escape the country it would be worth all the risk."

For a long minute each examined the features of the other. Then:

"You are a strange woman," he told her.

"Perhaps not so strange as you think," she said cheerfully. "I am far from being horrified now by your act of homicide in the circumstances. The man deserved death, although you were most foolish to cause it. If the law made the seduction of married women a death penalty, there would be less misery in the world for both men and women. Have you any children?"

"No." His answer was whispered. His gaze was once more fixed on the ocean. She saw it move inward and rest finally on her two boys, deliriously happy in their lagoon. "No, we have no children. If only we had had one!"

"Then why not seek out your wife?"

"For the very simple reason that Ellen does not now love me," he said with conviction. "I know my wife. She gave herself to my enemy because she no longer loved me, but loved him. Nothing but love would have caused that."

"I wonder!" And when Hester Long said this, there was all the wisdom of the ages in her expression.

CHAPTER IX

IN CHAINS

MEN and women living in the hurly-burly of some great city seldom have time to reflect. A man living as Arnold Dudley was living on the Beach of Atonement has too much time to think. At the end of a day the city man probably remembers half a dozen sentences out of the hundreds of speeches he has heard. From the welter of incessant speech he has retained a few words epitomizing as many ideas. The man living in solitude for long spaces of time remembers every word spoken in the course of a rare conversation. To him the spoken words are imprinted deeply on the tablets of his mind—imprinted words which he reads and re-reads and examines in all their possible, and sometimes impossible, shades of meaning.

Dudley remembered with vivid clearness every word uttered by Hester Long. His own words in that conversation were less distinctly remembered. Seated on the Seagulls' Throne a week after the conversation took place he was pondering her expression, "I wonder!"

What did she wonder at? He had said: "I know my wife. She gave herself to my enemy because she no longer loved me, but loved him." And: "Nothing but love would have caused that." To which she had said, with a strange look in her eyes: "I wonder!"

What was it she wondered at ?

It was an enigma he could not solve. Probably, she knew the answer. She had looked as though she did. Did she believe that it was possible for a married woman in love with her husband to give herself to another man? Being a woman, certainly she possessed authority in the matter. To his male mind it was inconceivable for a man wholly in love with his wife to take another woman. So disloyal an act was an unnatural act.

It was a grey morning, a morning hot and clammy and airless. The sky was the colour of gun-metal, and the sun was like a patch of orange-paper lying in the gutter after a night of carnival. The silence! The silence of the world was as a living omnipresent Thing. It pressed on the sea, flattening it, so that it seemed that the long-spaced rollers found difficulty in rising high enough to wash the Sugar Loaf. There appeared to be no energy in them that morning. They came ashore lethargically as though drugged.

Dudley, too, felt lethargic that morning. He was too brain-weary to continue seeking an answer to Hester Long's riddle. The seagulls, then paddling in the shallower pools on the Pontoon looking for tiny fish, seemed as though they did it from force of habit and not because they were hungry.

Silence and solitude! For three days and nights the silence had been absolute! Even at night the surf had made no perceptible sound. Solitude ! Solitude that passes the understanding of men, with the exception possibly of one in ten million. Dudley's solitude was not that of the romantic white living amidst a host of blacks, nor of the wretch undergoing solitary confinement in a gaol. His solitude was utter, complete. Had he even a dog for a companion his solitude would have been a crowded one.

A dog! Perhaps he could buy a dog from someone in Dongara? A pup! a little pup dog would be better—a pup dog he could play with, go down on his hands and knees and gambol with, as a man would romp with a small child.

A child! Hester Long had said: "Have you any children?" and he had said: "No." And seated on the Seagulls' Throne he, for the first time in his life, wanted to own, to play with, a child. Or was it the first time? The first time, no doubt, that he had actually expressed the wish to himself.

The possibility of Ellen having children had been so remote when he married her that he was almost indifferent, but to Ellen the possibility had been real and vivid. He had been surprised by her knowledge of nativity no less than her fear of having children. She had broached the subject in a manner that tacitly assumed that children in his mind occupied as great a prominence as it did in her own. And she seemed not a little relieved to discover that he was indifferent.

At first he thought she regarded child-birth as a tie that would prevent her accompanying him in his skin-scouting expeditions. The thought pleased him, flattered him. And afterwards, when they settled in Perth and prospered, and lived in a succession of houses each more imposing than the last ; houses in different suburbs, each suburb more fashionable than the last ; and every change bringing into their world a fresh set of acquaintances and new interests —Ellen had still refused to bear children that might hamper her in their social climb. That knowledge, too, had flattered him.

Would Ellen have failed him had there been children? Dudley felt convinced that in that case she would not have given herself to Tracy. Tracy would never have come between Ellen and her babies as he had come between Ellen and her husband. Dudley was sure of that. He knew Ellen's love for the weak, the defenceless.

Hester Long had told him that a much worse sensation than meeting a murderer was meeting a fool. How right that was! Of all God's creatures worthy of damnation none is more worthy than the fool. If he had not been so selfish as to wish never to share Ellen's love with a baby, if he had insisted or even let her see that he wanted a child, her selfishness would have been vanquished, and that day he would not have been sitting on the Seagulls' Throne.

A fool! What a fool sat on that rock, alone in solitude, sitting in a dead dumb world washed by a dead dull sea! What a fool to have pushed God's gift aside in a headlong rush for money and success! And, as with the fabled frog, his foolishness grew and grew. If he hadn't shot Tracy, he still would have the chance of getting back Ellen. He knew that he would have fought to get her back, fought her herself; and, judging by what

Hester Long had said, he might have succeeded. But with Tracy dead, with himself a murderer, the Moving Finger had written that which never could be cancelled. Ellen, even the fallen, dishonoured Ellen, could not be expected to reciprocate the love and the caresses of a murderer. Fool! Fool! Oh, what a fool sat crouched on the Seagulls' Throne!

Quite suddenly Arnold Dudley felt compelling need for movement. Standing up, he looked north, along the wide sweep of beach, till the colour of it merged in that of the sea long before it reached the great promontory. Southward, the sea where it joined the cliffs appeared just of the dull brownish white, almost colourless, of the beetling battlements. North or south? Which way? Direction did not matter. The hours that must be lived! The days, the weeks, the months! Perhaps years lay ahead of his life's march—years of unforgetfulness, sorrow, anguish, repentance.

The lean figure in tattered shirt and dungaree trousers almost lurched southward. Dudley removed his old felt hat, burned and blackened by frequent use as a pot-lifter, and carried it. The air was hot and humid, and perspiration damped his long hair, dark brown at the crown, greying at the temples. His eyes were visible through the slits of narrowed lids, lit as though by a fever, whilst piercing the almost limitless distances. Lean was his face, with accentuated cheek-bones and slightly hooked nose. A strong face, already foretelling the fierce patriarchal mien of old age. But the candle of his life was burning too fast, the leaping flame was consuming the man's vitality at thrice the normal rate.

He kept to the edge of the sand-hills where they skirted the beach, little hills of white sand covered with coarse coast bush. They were as miniature foot-hills to the miniature mountains of sand farther inland. And in the narrow winding miniature valleys he saw the tracks of rabbits, faint and dim of outline, and fox-tracks, four-padded and sharply clear. And down on the narrow strip of clean, dazzling white sand, between the ocean and the sand-hills, chains and spirals and criss-crossed line of one pattern showed the passage of the countless land-crabs. He could see them ahead of him, settled on the beach like pieces of orange-peel on Hampstead Heath after a bank holiday. And when he came to within a hundred yards, the bits of peel quickened and glided down to the limpid waves, or circled about and disappeared in the sand.

They knew not solitude as did he, and the poor lonely dead shag.

Dudley's body was thrust forward whilst he walked on the loose sand, his bare tanned feet sometimes disappearing beneath its fine surface. Dry as dust, yet it was cool ; whereas the air was stifling and still, although the sun was now invisible. In spite of the relaxing heat, or in defiance of it, the man flung himself forward as though he would sweat the salt of memory from his mind as his body sweated its physical salt. He was of iron, tireless. The sea winds, the summer suns, had vanquished all the fat around his muscles which had begun to accumulate during the years of city life.

Here the beach was widely curved, perfect in symmetry, the floor of sand gently sloping till it reached the surging upward rush of water impelled by each crashing wave, where its slope became steep and ugly, so moulded by the hammer of the sea. Now he came to a sharp indentation in the line of beach, as though the sea were a giant, living, hungry thing that had bitten out a chunk of the land. The white dry sand was strewn with flotsam, sawn lengths of timber, casks, boxes, and seaweed. Ahead were low, shelving rocks, similar to his Pontoon, a granite landing place for small boats, had there been a breakwater to protect it from the surf.

Arrived opposite the rocks, Arnold Dudley halted on a pinnacle of sand and looked down on them with weary eyes. The sea was the colour of lead, the sky was the colour of lead; the beach was black with a tinge of white. A mist, so fine, so diaphanous as to appear almost a figment of imagination, shortened the distance to the horizon, and blurred the outlines of the shoreward hills. The green of the little, stunted bushes had changed to greenish grey, on the upper surfaces of the tiny leaves. The undersides of the leaves, where normally would be shadow, were tinged with purple.

Space! He was alone in space. Freedom! He was as free as the sea, as free as the gulls that had accompanied him all the way. Power! He was lord of all he surveyed, the ruler of a world. And yet he was weighed down by chains mental chains that galled and clogged his mind as the sand clogged his feet. And the chains he wore had been wound about him, and locked and interlocked by—Ellen.

Where was the key that would unlock his chains? The key that would free his mind as his body was free? Those questions lay deep in his subconscious mind. They had not crystallized into conscious questions demanding answer, for as yet he was not fully conscious of the third, phase of his life on the Beach of Atonement. His dreams had become more numerous and more vivid, and he had not studied them for their physiological import.

Yet they had become a part of his life in the same way that sea-bites into the wide curve of the beach were a part of the coast. As the sea-bites were an accentuated feature of the beach, so were his dreams an accentuated feature of life. So much so that his dreams had more of the stuff of reality than had his waking actions.

Always were these dreams, which had become of nightly occurrence, of Ellen. If they were varied in scene and movement, their climax was invariably the same. Sometimes in a garden, sometimes there on the beach, at times in his house at Perth, once in a hospital ward, Ellen had drawn near in these dreams. A lovely woman in figure and face—a woman whose eyes were big and violet blue, whose hair was brown as an autumn leaf, a mouth a little large for the oval face, and a small nose that wrinkled at the bridge when she laughed. Lovely and adorable and desirable. A woman, the epic of femininity! Sometimes she smiled at him: mostly her face was tragic in expression, her eyes soft and tender and inexpressibly sad. And always when he was at the point of embracing her she drew away from him as though some evil power impelled her.

Never once did any one of his dreams leave him with any feeling of comfort, or of lightness of heart. They did, however, awaken memory of the happy years of the past—awaken memories that had been forgotten, memories of Ellen as she had looked at a particular instant; and of those memories one recurred with surprising insistence.

When he had held Ellen in his arms, when her face had been so close to his that he could see into the pools of her eyes, he used to search their depths, seeking to see the soul of Ellen, to find revealed that part of his wife which was elusive, her ultimate mystery. And when he searched Ellen's eyes like that he used to see the faintest flash of fear, as though she knew what he was searching for, knew he was on the verge of finding it. The flash of fear was invariably succeeded by an expression of merriment, as though, knowing what he wanted to see, she drew down the blind of laughter to conceal it.

During those moments he loved Ellen with so much passion that he himself was amazed. He knew she loved him with equal fervour. She surrendered her body to him unreservedly, yet never would allow him to glimpse her soul. Was that instinct—blind feminine instinct to guard, even from him, the secret of her soul ? Was it instinct more powerful, more inherent than the instinct of the preservation of life itself?

It was tantalizing to be always on the verge of glimpsing it, yet never to do so. Why was that? Did some women allow the men they loved to look right through the windows of their eyes, keeping up the blinds, letting them view the interior? If they did, why had Ellen never allowed him to do so? Had she kept up the blinds when she lay in Tracy's arms? Had she?

As she had always withdrawn before his ardent, scrutinizing gaze, so she withdrew from him in his sweetly-torturing dreams.

Memories of Ellen filled, loaded, his mind. There were times when his body so ached and throbbed and writhed for the touch of her that he was lashed into frenzied action that sent him rushing madly up the steep bush-covered slopes of the sand-hills in the dead of night, or drove him with unnatural energy to take long tramps along the beach, unwearied by the foot-clogging sand, unconscious of fatigue until his body refused further movement, and there was nothing for it but to fling himself down on his chest, bury his face in his arms, and sob.

And when those mental storms occurred in daylight, driving him along the beach, his bodyguard of friendly gulls accompanied him, calling out sometimes as though with sympathy, sometimes as though in mockery.

Often had death occurred to him. The temptation to destroy himself at times was almost irresistible. Without a shadow of doubt, Arnold Dudley would have killed himself if he could have brought himself to believe that death brought oblivion. Exceedingly few sane minds wholly believe that death is an end and not a change, or a restful interval preceding change. Existence after death has been a belief through so many generations of men that it has become almost instinctive. It is not the clouding of the instinct of self-preservation which is the mark of insanity in suicides so much as the clouding of the instinct of existence beyond death. And Arnold Dudley was not insane.

Death was no escape from the mental torture he was enduring. And if death provided no escape; could there be any escape ? Seated on the sandhill overlooking the shelf of rocks his mind dwelt on the subject of escape. If there was no escape, then the end was, he was beginning to think, insanity. Gazing out on the calm, flattened ocean, it was as though he peered out over the years of life normally remaining with him, each roller a year, and like the rollers, the years, drab and leaden in colour, each year precisely as drab and as leaden as its predecessor.

How to escape? The whole purpose of his life was directed on that problem. Would the gaiety of cities provide a means? Would work, hard, never-ceasing work provide it? Hester Long had said it would, and she was a wise woman. Would drugs open wide the door to freedom? Alcohol! Alcohol was easy to procure when one had money, and he had a good amount.

Into his mind flashed memory of his store of brandy. Brandy would deaden the longing for Ellen: it well might kill that longing. In any case, it would bring temporary oblivion Rising to his feet, he almost ran towards his camp.

CHAPTER X

THE DEVIL IN THE BOTTLE

ARNOLD Dudley's camp-bed lay along one side of the tent. On the opposite side was his ration dump, and from the dump he took the opened case of brandy and set it on the rough table erected a few feet beyond the entrance to the tent. From the case he took out eleven bottles of brandy with seals still intact, and a twelfth bottle about half-full. The liquor he set up in two ranks with as much care and precaution as a child gives to setting up its toy soldiers.

A meal of tinned-fish—fish in tins was easier to procure than fish from the sea to a man in his state of mind—and old and dry damper, with milkless tea to accompany it, had been eaten. Truly it could be said that Dudley ate to live, and did not live to eat. In the dells between the sand-hills lay the first hint of gloom preceding night.

The wind had come. With ever-increasing gusts between ever-shortening spells of calm it blew from the north-west. The sky was an unbroken leaden cloud. The summit of the sand-hill, or ridge separating his camp from the beach, began to smoke, creating a diaphanous veil of wind-blown sand. Already the temperature was dropping, but the heat still clung to the valleys. The wind was sweeping away the scents, sweet and often sickly, of the bush, replacing them with the tang of salt-water and the odour of rotting seaweed.

Above Dudley, perched on the topmost branch of a coast-wattle, crouched a cock butcher-bird, comfortably fed from the man's crumbs, but yet uneasy at the prospect of a stormy night. He warbled five notes forming a complete melody, and his mate, perched in another wattle-tree beyond the truck, which was parked in the cleared space beyond the track, replied with two notes that were not a part of any melody.

It was the cock-bird's custom to render nightly a serenade comprising four distinct melodies, but this night either the comfort of his body or the discomfort of his mind caused boredom. For, after a single rendering of the one melody, he buried his cruel hooked beak in the feathers of his back, and watched the man with one bright unwinking eye until darkness was complete.

Darkness!   It was the blackness of the Ninth Plague.

Dudley sat against the table, revealed by the light of a hurricane-lamp, his profile bold in relief, the light reflected strangely by the wide, staring eye nearest the lamp. On his face was a scowl, and around his jaw were the lines of desperate determination.

Be it thoroughly understood that his mind was made up to do a thing from which he shrank. Alcohol never once had got any grip on him. When he drank at all it was generally wine, and seldom that unless it was at meals. Spirits he rarely touched. The impelling force of an old trapping habit lay behind the purchase of the case of brandy. During those long periods when Finlay and he were rabbit-trapping till the early hours of the morning, or lying out at a water-hole all night shooting kangaroos, a drink of strong coffee laced with spirit ensured vivid warmth in winter-time and mental lethargy in summer, when they threw their weary bodies down to sleep. For the fur game is no mere pastime. Success depends chiefly on opportunity, or the seasons, and when opportunity comes it must be seized to the extent of from sixteen to twenty hours work out of the twenty-four. And for that a man's body must be toned up.

When he took the first sip of neat brandy Dudley shuddered. It was like taking a filthy medicine. Yet it was a medicine that was going to paralyse memory, was going to banish Ellen from his mind for a little while. But how strange, how strong, how vital is memory!

Again he sipped. The spirit sent its delightful warmth coursing through his veins. Another sip, almost a drink this time, and it was as though the Angel of Happiness hovered above him and drew up out of him the miasma that had settled around the cells of his brain. He began to drink.

Around him the roar of the rapidly rising sea and the thin wail of the beating wind were as the orchestra accompanying his damnation. Already his vision was becoming slightly blurred; but his mind was quickened, and the rapid flash of mental pictures for a while became entrancing.

Why had he not thought of the brandy before? How foolish of him to suffer physical torture and mental agony produced by the desire for woman ! The devil of desire was so easily cast out by the devil in the brandy-bottle. To hell with desire ! deeper into hell with woman who stretched man on the rack of longing! and into the bottom-most depth of hell with memories the past !

Good! May hell claim its own! Here's to hell!

A fitting place for all things invented and created for the purpose of torturing man. A nice thing, to be sure, when a man couldn't live a life of ease and freedom, the life of a king, without being annoyed by woman. It was about time man took a tumble, and remembered that woman, as a plaything, was a delight, but as master of a man's mind was altogether out of place.

What a fool he had been! What an utter, arrant fool! To allow himself first to be annoyed because Tracy seduced Ellen, and then again to be annoyed because Ellen was not with him on his beach. His beach! You bet it was his beach. And the next damned sportsman who came to shoot his birds would find out that it was his beach. Let them keep away! He didn't mind Hester Long coming occasionally. There were no flies on Hester, A good mate; Hester Long! None of your shrinking goggled-eyed women about her. Didn't faint or screech when he told her he was a murderer. No fear! Good as told him he did right to carry out the good work. Course he did right in one way ; even so, he was a bit stupid to shoot Tracy. He ought to have collared Tracy and taken him down into one of the cellars, and cut bits off him, little tiny bits, now and then. With proper management, he could have been kept alive for a couple of months.

Poor old Tracy! Wasn't he surprised when a bullet crashed into his brain! Ha, ha, ha! He looked, just before he dropped, as though he was offered the crown of England. It was the stuff to give him all right. No more would he show his teeth in that smile he must have practised before a mirror for weeks, Never again would he stare at a girl, and never again would a girl say : "Isn't he a dear?, I'd love to own a man like that."

"Ha, ha, ha!" Dudley chuckled gleefully. "What a lark to go and find out where Tracy was buried, and dig him up, and shovel him into a barrow, and wheel him down Hay Street and round about Forrest Place, and call on the doting women to come and look at handsome Tracy! Would they say: 'Isn't he a dear?' I could imagine 'em."

The partly-filled bottle was now emptied into his cup, and flung away with a laugh. He laughed again when he lurched to his feet and staggered within his tent, there to curse and laugh alternately, and upset the cases and crash on the bed, laughing again, and again cursing when he reappeared with a mouth-organ.

"Another little drink, and then I'll play a lament to poor worm-eaten Tracy. Poor old Tracy, so full of maggots! Fifteen men jumping on, Tracy's chest. No, that's not it. Anyway, I'll play to Tracy shivering out there in the cold in a nightdress."

Dudley blew discordantly on the mouth-organ. Then shouted with laughter. Came then a short interval of silence, which was broken by a truly wonderful rendering of the Dead March in "Saul". The man, drunk though he was, played the Hymn of the Dead with marvellous skill. He played it right through, twice.

"How's that, Tracy? Good, eh? Come now, don't sulk. There's n o reason to bear me animosity. Come and have a drink, and be sociable. Here, sit down! Dudley kicked an empty case, to the table beside him and uncorked a bottle, his body swaying. Dashing a quantity into his own cup, he groped about the ground beneath the table and retrieved a tin pannikin. This he half-filled and set before the second seat, saying:

"That's right, ole feller. Drink and be merry, although you are dead. How does it feel to be a worm-eaten corpse, Tracy? Now, now! No bad feeling ! You're no worse off than I am, remember. A bit cold? Well, drink up and get warm. How would a song go?"

Once more Dudley drank. He pulled himself to his feet by gripping the table-edge, cleared his throat, and beamed down to where the awful apparition of his imagination was sitting. Then he sang in a cracked voice:

"And the old man said, 'Strike me dead
If Barcoo wins this race, me lad,
We're done---we're up the pole!'"

Then: "How's that? Have another drink. Go on! It'll banish dull care—dull care. My! You make—you make just a lovely corpse, Tracy—'deed you do ! Cold! Cold, are you? I'll get you a blanket. 'Tween frien's, you know."

Half-way to the tent, Arnold Dudley collapsed and lay still, breathing stertorously. The rain came and beat on his upturned face. The wind shrieked and howled about the summits of the invisible sand-hills. The sea, lashed to fury, roared and thundered and swept high up the beach, and from its fury fled the thousands upon thousands of land-crabs.

They scurried up the beach from the ever-rising tide, scuttled up the low sand-bank, and sheltered about the stems of the short scrub bushes. Even there the wind and the stinging fine sand pursued them, and the higher they went the greater became the force of the wind. During the lulls they could be heard everywhere making a "cleek-cleek" sound, sharp and shrill.

The tide, impelled by the north-west wind, set south. The roaring monstrous rollers that raced shoreward with four-foot walls of foam on their gaping crests tore at the Seaweed Mountain, bit into it, pounded and smashed its seaward front, slowly demolished it. South of it the hundreds of tons of weed floating on the surface calmed the breakers as oil cast on the waves. The Mountain was doomed, and from it a grand army of crabs evacuated their quarters and swarmed up and over the ridge, and descended to the little valley that sheltered Arnold Dudley's camp.

The rain became a deluge. Its impact on the stunted bushes was a hissing equal in volume to the hiss of the surf being sucked back into the sea. Hour after hour the deluge fell, and nowhere along that terrible desert coast did the rain make a stream or a puddle. The sand hummocks and hills absorbed it as if composed of sponge.

When day dawned the sky showed great rents in the flying cloud masses, rents aflame with brilliant stars. The eastern summits were silhouetted against a background of dark grey, which magically turned to dove-grey, thence to pearl-grey, and successively, with marvellous rapidity, to yellow, orange, crimson. The wind died out as though from very exhaustion, and veered to the south, a mere zephyr. The racing hills of water, white-capped and splendid, were tinted turquoise blue. When they rose as leaping horses at the outer reef, they lifted the horizon line high, paused as though surveying the land, their enemy, curled over and outward, and with undiminished speed charged on the rock-bound shore.

It was the clear flute-like song of the butcher-bird which awakened Arnold Dudley. He thought it strange that a butcher-bird should be at sea with him in such a storm. He marvelled that the ship did not turn right over, marvelled at and groaned from the sensation of the deck of a ship at sea. An arctic cold gripped his legs and his arms, and encircled his chest as a steel band. Someone was beating his head with an iron bar, the blows of which were oddly rhythmical, and in between the blows he became conscious of the silence surrounding him, and of the roar of the sea thousands of miles distant.

To open his eyes to admit the light was an agony. Once he tried, and decided to do so never again. Fire burned in his mouth, a foul, stinking fire. What a sea was running! How the vessel that bore him was sent high, high towards the sky, and then down, down into a veritable sea-pit. Another sound came to him, a peculiar sound. "Cleek-cleek-cleek-cleek!" It was like a chorus. Something cold and hard touched his chin, something loathsome ran across his face.

That forced open his eyes and jerked him upright in a sitting posture. First, he was astonished to find himself surrounded by the walls of the bush; secondly, his astonishment was succeeded by chilling fear. For the ground was orange-tinted. Everywhere he looked, across the track, close up to where he sat, under the ramparts of bush-trees and shrubs, the ground was a sheet of orange. And upthrust from the sheet were a million tiny cylinders, each supporting an eye—black, malignant, cold and evil.

Dudley leapt to his feet with a scream. He was answered by a hundred thousand crabs, which chorused: "Cleek-cleek-cleek!" incessantly. His sudden jump to his feet, to stare about him with horrified eyes, was as the dropping of a stone in an orange-coloured lake. Over the orange surface, in an ever-widening circle, passed a ripple, whilst the countless bodies swayed from him to escape, as though the fear in his mind darted into the minds of those nearest him, to pass thence from crab to crab to the outer edge of the mass.

Five minutes later Arnold Dudley still stood staring about, a little less wildly, a little more sanely. There was not a crab to be seen.

The man brushed his eyes with a forearm, looked round again, and laughed in a cracked voice. In the ensuing silence he could distinctly hear the crabs' "cleek-cleek cleek" on their way beneath the low bush back to the beach.

The sun, topping the eastern ridge, shone through a vaporous haze. He felt no warmth from it. He was as cold as the dead, his teeth a-chatter, his hands and arms blue. The surrounding sea-green hills took on the aspect of gigantic waves that moved and closed in upon him threateningly.

Yet, though his eyes played him tricks—he had come almost to believe that the crabs were evidence of a waking nightmare—his brain was sober enough. His body cried out for warmth, and his brain set about contriving means of producing heat. The bush was then a vast shower-sprinkler. Every piece of dead stick was soaked through and through, and only by first starting a tiny blaze with paper and a smashed-up pinecase did he manage to get a fire going.

Later, crouching over the mounting flame, he surveyed the bottle-littered table, noted the half-filled tin pannikin, and the case set close beside it. He knew why that case was there; remembered the invitation he had given his enemy. He remembered, too, that the invitation had been accepted, and that a foul, rotting, eyeless, faceless thing had been his guest. How his head ached! How his stomach turned over and over upon itself! How like to the most terribly imagined hell was life!

Perhaps a wee nip would steady the heaving ground. Lurching to the table, he picked up Tracy's pannikin, and, lifting it to his lips, vomited instead of drank. Flinging the pannikin from him, he almost collapsed over the fire, but dropped close to it, and was fervently thankful to feel its scorching heat on his face, his arms, and his chest, feeling it penetrate his soaked clothes, from which uprose a cloud of steam into the still air.

And, whilst lying there, his mind went back over the incidents of his orgy, of which he remembered every one. He remembered his wild laughter, the feeling of exultation that preceded his invitation to Tracy to join him in a drink. He knew now that the invitation had been accepted by a Tracy of his imagination, and realized that he was unafraid of his self-created phantom because he had always been unafraid of Tracy. Similarly, he had experienced no remorse at sight of the phantom, since he never had experienced remorse at having killed the fellow.

Thinking of Tracy automatically brought thoughts of Ellen. As clearly as though he was then in his own house in Perth, he saw her sitting up in bed drinking the early cup of tea. Her blue eyes were sleepy still. Her hair was dishevelled, for her boudoir-cap had fallen from her head. The pinkness of her throat and breast was as the pinkness of a rose, colour wonderful and alluring, and when she caught him looking she wrapped about her still closer a rose-pink bed-wrap.

Dudley closed his eyes at the sweet agony of it. When he opened them again he saw the bottles on the table, the tin pannikin where he had thrown it, the mouth-organ half-buried in the water-darkened sand, the litter of paper, empty tins, pieces of board, and straw sheaths. His tent, wet and heavy, sagged in the middle. Within was wild confusion. His bed was on its side, the blankets in a heap near the door, cases and tins of meat and fish were scattered and jumbled.

His body was tingling from the new-found heat. His nerves were on edge. When he got to his feet it was with difficulty that he restrained his surging anger, unreasoning, insane, against the inanimate objects he possessed. The mental storm passed, and was succeeded by a fit of weeping, which he made no effort to control. Whilst he filled a billy-can he wept.

He continued to weep whilst he waited for the water to boil, tears running down his face, his body shaking, and through his mind ran words ceaselessly reiterated:

"I wish I were dead! I wish I were dead! I wish I were dead!"

He was still wishing that, and still weeping, a man on the verge of mental collapse, when he made himself strong coffee. Pouring himself out a cupful, he added a generous measure of sugar and a most generous measure of brandy. And when it was cool enough he sipped, and with his sip-ping his weeping ceased, and once more his mind was exhilarated, and from the Slough of Despond he rushed to the mountain summit. Half an hour later he was laughing.

About noon he suddenly groped for and found the mouth-organ. Wanting music, he blew on it, to discover that several of the holes were clogged with sand. With half closed, blurred eyes he gazed at it stupidly, knowing it was out of action, nevertheless. With a mumbled curse he tossed it inside the tent and slumped down beside the table once more. The pannikin he raised to his lips clattered against his teeth. And whilst he drank he looked over it, to see Edith Mallory regarding him with horror-filled eyes.

CHAPTER XI

EDITH MALLORY'S CONFESSION

THE day was gloriously fine. The night of rain and wind had cleansed the coast country of its almost stagnant bush scents and replaced the heavy sultry heat with a bracing clearness. The world was washed and bright and new. Even Hester Long's cattle appeared to shine, their colours fresh and vivid against the ruddy brown of autumn paddocks.

Hester was inconvenienced by the rain, which had come, for her, too early. It delayed her "burn", which that year would add no less than fifty cleared acres to her farm. Throughout the summer she had wielded an axe for several hours of each day, chopping and felling the thick low scrub eastward of her house-work that had been subsidiary to the ordinary tasks of milking, feeding the pigs and the fowls, overlooking her cattle, and sometimes yarding her sheep to operate on some with a pair of shears in her battle with the blow-fly.

Work! Incessant work from dawn till dusk, work that taxed her small feminine body to the utmost, that made her sigh with weariness, but that filled her days with the gladness of achievement.

Hester Long was that kind of woman in whom the maternal instinct is a deathless passion. Her love for her husband was a consequence of his suffering from the effects of gas. He lay in the bed next her brother's in a hospital in the south of England. Long had come out of the Australian bush that the Empire might be preserved, and especially that Australia might be reserved as a play-ground for politicians. The War left him shattered in health. And the strength that he had laid down, his wife took up.

The farm had been made not by Long but by his wife.

A semi-invalid, Long was unfit for rough work. He tended the pigs, fed the fowls, and overlooked the cattle and sheep. Hester did the cooking and, when not burdened with children, repaired the old fences, erected new, and cut down scrub. Hers was the mind that ran the farm immediately she had grasped the essentials of that peculiar kind of farming. Hers was the spirit that raised a hedge of security around her man and her boys. And when her man was taken, her life became devoted to making the hedge thicker and stronger around her children.

It is refreshing to turn from our professional politicians, everlastingly chanting praises of the British Empire on which they batten as parasites, to the Hester Longs, the quiet workers who in the past have made the British Empire and to-day are remoulding it.

By noon on the day after the storm the sun had dried the scrub, so that to cut it or move under it was not to invite a shower-bath. The midday meal over and the utensils cleaned and put away; Hester Long donned an old tweed skirt and a pair of man's thick boots, and then, calling her children from their own allotted little playground, she and they walked out to the scene of her summer labours.

She had cut down the fifty acres on a gentle rise of ground. Everything within that area had fallen to her axe, from the whip-stick mallee-like bush to the several large box-trees lining a tiny creek. Over most of the area the cut branches had been laid out evenly, and around the stumps dry limbs and sticks had been packed, so that when the fire went through it the stumps would be completely burned out.

A little of this work yet remained to be done, and, helped by the children, who had become adepts at packing a stump, Hester Long proceeded to do it.

It was the "doing" of all that work which had helped her to live down the grief caused by her husband's death ; for when her husband was drowned she lost also a lover. It was the idleness of Arnold Dudley's life on the beach which had kept his loss so vitally alive. Three months almost of idleness spent in utter solitude had emphasized his loss of Ellen so fiercely that the serpent of desire, kept quiescent during his life with her, now writhed convulsively and was strangling his soul. Had Ellen died, the loss of her sex companionship would have been made up for by intensified application to business. Her loss being unrelieved by business or even social demands on him, but accentuated by forced banishment from the world of men, even climatic conditions putting a stop to his trapping work, Dudley was left with no occupation but to think and live wholly in the past.

To one placed as he was, a man's greatest and most deadly enemy is himself.

Whilst the two boys worked on the clearing they directed each other, criticized each other, but manfully stuck to their task. There had been no sulking when called to labour from their play. At six and eight respectively they fully realized, even at that early age, the necessity for work. They knew that their efforts not only pleased their mother, but also in some mysterious way would benefit themselves. Hester Long sang whilst she worked, dragging a branch here to cover a bare place, another there away from a heap, so that the branches lay evenly over the whole of the ground, for clear spaces would balk the fire.

Towards four o'clock, when Hester Long was thinking of returning to the house to put on the dinner before beginning the evening attendance on her live stock, she was halted in her singing by the sound of horse-hoofs thudding on yielding turf. The boys simultaneously shouted the fact that Miss Mallory was coming, and a moment later Edith Mallory pulled her mount up almost viciously, slipped from the saddle, tied the reins to a dead bough, and suddenly faced Hester Long with wide, horror-filled eyes, her face white and drawn. A picture of woman sorely distressed, she almost tottered towards Hester Long, who stepped quietly forward to meet and catch her in her arms. The small boys were silent at this some- what dramatic interruption of their labours. Their mother, seeing that the young woman was hysterical from some severe shock, said to them:

"Miss Mallory has hurt herself. Not much, though."

"How would it be if you both ran home and brought a billy-can and something to eat? Harold, you could get the billy-can, and the cups, and some milk in a clean bottle, and a tin of tea and sugar; and you, Jim, could fetch a loaf of bread, a jar of butter, and a big knife and spoon. Put everything in that apple-basket with the wicker-handle. And when you come back we'll have afternoon tea here beside the creek."

The lads departed with enthusiasm, and when they had scampered off Hester Long led Edith Mallory to the trunk of one of the cut box-trees and gently urged her to be seated.

"What has happened, dear?" she said coaxingly.

"I-I-I! Oh-oh-oh!" and Edith Mallory laughed and cried alternately. Hester Long shook her.

"Stop it!" she ordered sharply. And, again: "Stop it, I tell you!"

After a while she managed to calm the girl, and then, holding her hands in one of hers, her other arm around the shaking shoulders: "What is it, Edith? Just tell your old pal."

"I—I went down to Hector Cain's," she said, almost whispering. "I—oh! don't you understand?"

Hester Long smiled, and her smile held wonderful sympathy.

"Yes, I know," was all she said then.

"He found out, then, about my going to his camp, and told you ? I can't explain about that now—it seems so silly of me—and yet—and yet, I just hated to think of the way he was living, so down, so, so abandoned. You know, Hester, how he lives, don't you?"

"Yes, I know," the elder woman repeated. "But tell me what has sent you here like this. Tell me everything. Is he dead?"

Edith Mallory's eyes were tragic when she searched Hester Long's lined face.

"No—no, not dead. Much worse than being dead. We—Tom and I— got back from Perth last night. I was glad to get back. Perth didn't seem to be the same. After lunch I rode down the beach track and tethered Moky just this side of the big hill. I always had done that, and as I have always done I walked up to the summit and examined Hector's camp with my binoculars to make sure he was away. Funny of me, isn't it? Why don't you laugh?"

Edith Mallory's lips trembled. Hysteria again threatened. Said Hester Long with conviction:

"I shall swear if you don't tell me at once what happened."

"I wish you would swear, Hester. Well, I couldn't see him about the camp, nor did I see any smoke from his fire, so I went down. And there he was, sitting beside his rough table littered with bottles of whisky or brandy. He saw me at the instant I saw him. His face was dirty and unshaven and flaming. His eyes—oh, his eyes, when he saw me! They grew big, like cat's eyes, and in them was sudden green fire. He was drunk, mad drunk. He held to the table with his hands and glared at me. Suddenly he rose to his feet and shouted :

"Ellen, by God ! Ellen at last!"

"And then he sprang at me. His face was awful. And his eyes, Hester— his eyes ! He frightened me so that I couldn't move. I could do nothing but stare at him, do nothing till the instant he almost reached me, when I found myself suddenly running. I ran towards the beach with him close behind me, and he was shouting all the while:

"Ellen, I've got you! Why run, Ellen? Never again shall you leave me, Ellen!"

"The sand clogged my feet, Hester. It was just like having a nightmare, you know, when one is chased by a terrible monster and one's feet are made of lead. I screamed as I ran. I heard him fall with a crash behind me. I took to the bush, I remember, and next I was standing on Big Hill, hardly able to get my breath. Then I saw him, down on the rocks, running back and forth along the edge of the Pontoon, waving his arms towards the sea. The waves knocked him down again and again, and sometimes I could hear him shouting:

"Ellen, come back! Ellen, come back!"

"Well?" urged Hester Long, after a short silence. She felt her work-scarred hands seized in those of the girl; she saw a tear-drenched face, marred by anguish, thrust close to hers ; heard Edith's voice suddenly hardened:

"Who—who is Ellen? Do you know?"

For a moment their eyes held.

"Yes," Hester Long nodded. "Ellen is his wife."

"His—his wife!"

The proudly-held head suddenly bent forward, and with fierceness in her movement Hester Long drew the shaking figure within her arms, patted a firm shoulder with one hand and smoothed the golden hair with the other. And thus they remained till the boys came back with the loaded basket.

"Now, Harold, you light a tiny fire over there beside the creek, and Jim can fill the billy with water," Hester Long directed. "Get busy, now, and make us some tea. Miss Mallory is better, but she wants to tell me about her holiday in Perth. To-morrow she is going to tell you some wonderful stories about Perth."

"All right, mum!" responded Harold, the elder boy, cheerful-ly-frank-faced, steady-eyed, sturdy. "Come on, Jim: fill that billy, quick. I'll get some sticks."

"You think that Mr. Cain did not recognize you ?" inquired Hester Long quietly of Edith Mallory, now a little more composed.

"No. No—he took me for—for his wife. "He was drunk?"

"Yes. Not ordinarily drunk. Mad—just mad with drink. Did he tell you about his wife?"

"Yes."

When Edith looked at Hester Long it was to find the elder woman's face turned towards the sea, her eyes wide and blank, and not registering the scene upon her mind.

"Tell me what he told you," she urged, the hint of tears in her voice.

"Edith!" Hester Long turned quickly. "Edith, you have got to call upon all your strength and kill your love for Hector Cain. In spite of your fright of this afternoon, I can see that you love him now no less. You must realize the fact that Hector Cain can never, never be anything to you."

"Why?"

The girl's eyes were wide and brilliant. Hester Long saw in their violet depths the living flame of youth awakened—youth courageous, con-fident, defiant of failure. And Hester Long came thereby to know that no bars of convention would restrain the flood of passion till then pent up by the gates of hope. She knew in that moment that Edith, Mallory was from that mould of women who forsake all, sacrifice all, for love. Hester Long felt a slight glow of satisfaction that she had been armed by Hector Cain himself with a weapon that would protect Edith Mallory against her own heart.

"The world is a beautiful place, dear," she said softly, "but some of the men and women who live in it tend to foul its beauty. At first one is shocked by the evil in human beings, but as one grows older one is able to shut away the nasty things and regard only the beauty. I'll tell you about Hector Cain and Ellen his wife only because you love Hector. They say a woman can never keep a secret. I can keep a secret. So can you. Keep the one I am going to tell you."

She related the manner in which Arnold Dudley had first become acquainted with his wife's infidelity; described how he had stolen into his own house, how he had heard voices in his wife's room, and how he had sat outside the door in the passage. Incredulity was followed by amazement, then horror, in the changing expressions in Edith Mallory's eyes. The girl's gaze was fixed entranced on the narrator's old, seamed, maternal face. She heard how Arnold Dudley had waited; how the door of his wife's room had opened to reveal his wife embraced by the seducer ; and how he had shot the man dead.

"So you see, Edith dear," said Hester Long in conclusion, "that there can be no question of your winning Hector Cain through death of his wife, or divorce from her. He is a murderer, a man-killer, a man condemned by man—and God."

"He may have killed the beast, but he is not a murderer," came the counter-statement fiercely. "He was within his rights to kill. I would have killed, had I been a man situated as he. Hector did a manly thing. Had—had—had it all happened two hundred years ago, he—he would have been honoured for wiping away the stain from his name. He should have killed her, too, the hussy, the slut, the—the wanton."

"Hush, dear," Hester Long said soothingly. "She may have been what you called her. Hector may have done the right thing. But this is nineteen-twenty-nine, not seventeen-twenty-nine. If ever the police get him he will be hanged as a murderer; or, at the very least, he may escape with his life to live the remainder of it in a prison. You see, he can't plead self-defence; he can't plead overwhelming provocation, as he might have done had he stepped into the room and found them together. He did the very worst thing for himself by waiting in the passage."

For a moment neither spoke. When Edith Mallory did, her voice was low, calm, almost without intonation.

"It's terrible—terrible," she said slowly. "It is even more terrible because it seems that he still loves her. Oh! I know he does. His love was in his voice when he took me for his wife. And I—it's terrible for me, too, because I love him. I think I loved him when I spoke to him sitting on the rock on top of the sand-hill the day you got the hook in your hand. I didn't know it then. Actually I disliked him when he boasted, as I thought, about getting the eagles; but I knew it so well that day he brought them to your house hung round the truck. I shall—It doesn't matter to me if he has killed a hundred men. I love him. Hester!" she gripped her companion's arms suddenly. "Hester, you know what love is, don't you? Would you love your boys the less if they turned out bad, wicked men? You know you wouldn't. You know you would love them even more, and try to make them good."

"Yes, maybe, Edith. Nevertheless, you cannot become anything to Hector Cain. Apart from the impossibility of your winning him, a murderer, he does not love you, because he loves his wife as deeply as ever he did. You see, don't you, how hopeless it all is? You must see it, realize it. You must let your love of him be swamped by the waters of common-sense."

"You speak as though that would be easy."

"It will not be easy, God knows, Edith dear. But it can be done. And the greatest aid in the doing is work. Work enabled me to keep living in happiness and content when I thought there was nothing in life when my man was taken."

Mention of the death of her husband revived in her companion's mind memory of Arnold Dudley's being knocked down by the waves on the Pontoon.

"Oh, Hester, suppose Hector is hurt out there on the rocks! Suppose he is drowning, or is drowned," Edith said tearfully, hysteria threatening again. Hester Long, observing the sign, said:

"It will save a lot of trouble if he does get drowned. He will be all right, though."

"But he mayn't! Anyway, there is still a lot of spirits left. I saw several full bottles on his table."

"Wow, look here, Edith! It's no good getting yourself into a pet. We must keep calm and think. It is too late to do anything to-day. As it is, you will now have to stay and milk my cows and cook the dinner. To-morrow, if you come over early, I'll go down to the beach and have a heart-to-heart talk with Hector Cain. He has got to stop drinking, and he has got to start working. I am forgetting what he has done. I only remember what he is, a nice man rapidly going to perdition, and I am woman enough to stop him if I can,"

"Then—then you don't shrink from him? You don't loathe him because he is a—a murderer?" Edith said very softly.

"Shrink from him?" countered the wonderful Hester. "He was a fool to take the law into his own hands, and I told him so. I don't shrink from a fool; I try to make him wiser. I don't care what the law would say about it all, but I am going to save Hector Cain from himself."

CHAPTER XII

DUDLEY GOES HOME

HESTER Long rose very early the following morning, despite the fact that it was very late when finally she slept after hours of thinking of the separate tragedies of Arnold Dudley and Edith Mallory.

Edith she had come to regard affectionately as a younger sister. In the first years of her Australian life, when her husband was alive and the motherless Edith came home but seldom from school, she watched the girl grow into a beautiful woman with the fervent interest she always felt when face to face with the beautiful. Continually searching for beauty, she continually discovered it. She was amazed that late afternoon at the beauty of the soul of her irresponsible, outwardly cynical brother, when it left its war-shattered habitat. She never ceased to be amazed at the beauty of her husband's love, and at the greater beauty of the unfolding flower of her babies' lives.

She came to know that Edith Mallory's beauty was not skin deep at the tragic period of her life, following the death of her husband. Then a capable young woman of twenty-one, Edith had been a rock on which was set the light of Eternal Hope. For a time Tom Mallory, a bachelor, and his two hired hands, fended for themselves; for Edith left them to live with and help with all her young strength the older woman weakened and broken by grief.

It would have been Hester Long's delightful ambition to have helped her friend win the man she had come so unfortunately to love, had not circumstances made so happy a consummation impossible. This being so, her efforts would have to be directed to helping Edith Mallory to live down her new-found love, even as Edith had helped her so wonderfully to live down her loss of husband-lover. Time would show her the way to deal with that problem The other problem, the problem of Arnold Dudley, was impatient of Time for its solution. Quite apart from the man's confession that he had killed another man, Hester Long was assured that he was a man frightfully wronged. He was an outcast, first because of that wrong, and a long way second because he had exacted a terrible vengeance for it.

To Hester the consummation of that vengeance had been a very natural climax. A stern puritan by nature, she regarded the violent death of the seducer as no more than a just punishment, simple justice avenging the spoliation of another man's wife.

A woman of vivid but balanced imagination, Hester Long visualized Tracy fairly accurately. She made of him a man ordinarily good-looking, abnormally magnetic, and utterly without scruple. Ellen she visualized even more clearly. She saw her as daintily-lovely, gay and passionate and weak. At one angle was the man with the magnetic personality ; at the second angle the gay, weak, and passionate young woman ; and at the third angle the confident, proud husband of the woman, possibly absorbed in his business, which had outrivalled the love of youth. And there again was the eternal triangle.

Because she herself was a woman, Hester Long understood her sex. She knew that it was possible, quite possible, for a woman to be in love with one man, and yet capable of allowing herself to be swept by passion into another man's arms. She understood how such a paradox in feminine character could be arrived at. At least she thought she did. The passionate side of a woman's love for her husband may wane, leaving the maternal side still strong and ardent. It remains then for another man with suffi-ciently attractive sex-magnetism to reawaken for himself the woman's pas-sionate sex-love, a conquest easily made of a woman weak in will-power.

It was whilst she was sipping a cup of tea before the dawn of another day that she asked herself why it was the man she knew as Hector Cain aroused her sympathy so keenly. Ever ready at self-analysis, she probed first her heart, and found that although she liked Arnold Dudley she did not love him. To her own question why she liked him, she found the answer to be because in his character she found beauty.

Memory of her first meeting with him remained fresh. There was beauty in the way he shrank but steeled himself to cut the hook out of her thumb. There was beauty, too, in the incident of his slipping the fish into the back of her buggy; and surely there was beauty in the sadness he felt and revealed over the shooting of the shag, regarded by most as winged vermin?

She had found nothing coarse in Arnold Dudley's make-up. A strong man mentally as well as physically, she knew him to be tender-hearted and loyal. The man who still loved his wife in spite of the wife's failure, the man who would replace his wife on the pedestal after she had deliberately cast herself from it, proved emphatically his loyalty. That was it. Loyalty was the trait in Dudley's character which chiefly attracted Hester Long.

Her reverie was interrupted by the melodious notes of a butcher-bird roosting in the topmost branch of the fig-tree, outside the kitchen. Clear, in perfect harmony, the bird sent forth one of the four identical tunes rendered by another of his species who had come to overlord Dudley's camp. Knowing it would be the prelude to the most exquisitely beautiful fantasia in the world, she quickly went to the kitchen-door and stepped outside.

Beyond was the east. The morning mist lay black along the ground, hiding the trunks of the near apple-trees, blanketing the paddocks back of them, shrouding the stately box-trees left standing to provide shade for the stock. Higher, through the branches and withering leaves of the apple-trees, the mist was almost white against the background of the softly-pink dawn.

The world was hushed. It was as though a vast, silent, electrically-expectant concourse of people awaited the performance of a super-orchestra. The woman was the sole audience, a few birds the musicians. She awaited the rendering of what she called "The Melody of Heaven", a melody that no composer could write for instruments to reproduce, a melody not to be heard in any other part of the world.

The bird in the fig-tree repeated his five notes and paused. He was invisible, yet Hester knew that his black and white head would be held slightly on one side, listening. Out from the mist came the lower and softer notes of the Australian magpie. Far away a hen butcher-bird piped two notes. Hester's bird sent out his four melodies in challenge, and the challenge was instantly taken up by butcher-birds and magpies stationed in near trees, and trees far away in the bush. So still was the air that birds a mile away could be heard.

Now without cease Hester's bird sang his melodies over and over again, other birds warbled the same bars, magpies piped and throbbed, so that from the very sky there fell on the woman's straining ears the music of God. God's music it was, a glorious pæan of praise, earthly only in its likeness to the swelling chant of men and women within a vast cathedral accompanied by a mighty organ and heard from a distance on a quiet, magic summer evening in England.

And people crowd in cities, and are satisfied with life. Poor people, to be satisfied with counterfeit!

The topmost level of the mist became pink, shell pink; the sky above it was pale orange, to deepen whilst the seconds fled. If only Time would stop for a minute, just one brief minute, to allow each divine shade of colour to sink in one's mind and be a possession for ever! Lower sank the shafts of pink into the mist, as though forced downward by the bars of purple laid by the brush of the Almighty. Upward to the zenith fled the golden light of coming day, extinguishing the brilliant stars.

Colour and song allied! The softer chirpings of small birds intermingled now with the louder tones of the larger songsters in the grand finale. The fantasia was almost over. The colours of the dawn seemed suddenly to vanish. As suddenly the birds stopped their anthem. It was day. The mist was white now from top to ground. The dew-drenched spiders' webs among the fig-tree branches and the dewy grass beneath appeared as blown glass. Hester's butcher-bird dropped to earth to uphold his name.

And people live in cities and slumber when the dawn of day arrives. Poor people! Sleep on, sleep on!

Hester was smiling, a radiant yet wistful smile, when she realized that her "Melody of Heaven" was finished. It had been a fitting prelude to the day she intended setting aside to rescue Arnold Dudley from his Slough of Despond.

Re-entering the kitchen, she added fuel to the stove, and took her milking buckets to the cow-bails. Out then into the paddocks to drive in the cows, regardless of the wet grass which soaked her feet in the first dozen yards. As usual the cows were at the far side, and twenty minutes were spent in rounding them and getting them to the stockade enclosing the wall-less shed thatched with small scrub.

She was milking the last cow when Edith Mallory arrived on her horse, and, seeing Hester at work, she removed the saddle and took the animal into the cow paddock before removing the bridle. Hester met her outside the stockade with a cheerful smile, which brought to Edith's flushed face a wistful expression.

"Are you going down to see Hector this morning, as you said?" she asked almost eagerly.

"I am going to give Mister Cain a piece of my mind, Edith. Do not let us forget that he is not yet an intimate friend, permitting us to call him by his Christian name."

"I call him Hector because I think of him only as Hector."

The girl took up one of the buckets of frothy milk, a hint of defiance in her eyes. With two other buckets Hester and she walked to the house. Hester Long did not speak again until they were in the kitchen, when suddenly she turned to Edith, and, laying hands on her shoulders, said softly:

"You have a battle to fight, dear. Let me help you win it. I am older than you, and I am covered with the scars of life. Please don't call him Hector, or think of him as Hector. To us he is Mr. Cain."

Tears sprang into the blue eyes, and Hester turned to the boiling kettle on the stove and made fresh tea. Without glancing at Edith she knew the girl had seated herself beside the small table at the window, and was crying. It was best to let her cry then. Hester Long left her there, went to the boys' bedroom, aroused them chidingly and cheerfully, told them what clothes to put on, and to be quiet and well-behaved, because their goddess, Miss Mallory, was in the kitchen waiting to breakfast with them. And they must be good boys, because mother. had to go away for the day to visit poor Mr. Cain, who was sick.

An hour or so later she was driving in her worn buggy on her way to the Beach of Atonement. The air of early morning was laden with bush scents, which one met in waves, sometimes sweetly fresh, sometimes raising strange elusive hauntings of memory, sometimes heavy and sickly. The quiet old horse she drove ambled along the main road to Dongara which skirted the coast sand-hills along the eastern slopes, the pace and the scene unregistered on Hester Long's mind.

She was thinking how she would carry out the task ahead. Much, of course, would depend on circumstances. She trusted that circumstances would not prove too much for her, such as her having to deal with a man wholly mad with drink. She had no liking for the prospect of being pursued as Edith Mallory was pursued, for if it did come to a struggle she would be at a hopeless disadvantage.

Almost automatically her hands reined the horse to the right at the junction of the narrow beach track with the main road. Familiar with the way, the horse ambled along the level stretches, slowly pulled up the stiff gradients, and as slowly, proppingly, descended. It was with no consciousness of time that Hester Long found herself at the summit of Big Hill, where the immensity of the ocean lay below and before her, and the beach with all its many peculiarties lay stretched for inspection.

Pulling her horse to a stop, she gazed steadily at Arnold Dudley's camp, marked in the mass of green-bush by the white roof of the tent. There was no smoke denoting a fire and the presence of man, nor could she espy Arnold Dudley anywhere along the beach. Had he in his madness fallen from the rocks, or been swept into one of the terrible blow-holes of the Pontoon? Had his tortured soul found peace? Or was he down there at the camp, seated before the liquor-laden table, not drunk enough to be helpless, but in that stage of drunkenness when a man is a ravening beast?

Hester Long proved her dauntless courage when she urged her horse down the steep hill towards the camp.

She began to wish she had not come. She realized that she was perhaps foolishly placing herself in a position of grave danger. She also knew that her errand might well turn out to be one of mercy. Instead of a madman she might find a human being physically injured, in urgent need of help.

Horse and buggy finally reached the foot of Big Hill, and then, with nerve-shocking suddenness, Arnold Dudley leapt out of the bush wall into the seat beside her.

Hester Long fought back the scream that was on her lips. Dudley's appearance had affected her as one is affected by the sound of a voice immediately behind when one has imagined oneself to be alone. The first shock was succeeded instantly by another.

The man's torn dungarees, his ripped foul shirt, his face, unwashed and covered with inch-long stubble, his truly ferocious eyes, would have been shocking to anyone, even if iron bars had held him prisoner. Her worst fears were realized. His insane laughter, rolling and echoing between the hills, sent a horrible chill through her body, and her physical frailty cried out against the iron grip of the hands that fell on her shoulders and wrenched her round to face him squarely.

"You're a funny old thing, Ellen, aren't you?" he cried gleefully. "You go and throw yourself in the sea one minute, and the next you come riding along through the bush as fresh and innocent as a babe. Ha, ha, ha! Still, I knew you would come back. I knew you would hear my call and come back." Then, with complete seriousness: "You see, Ellen, I have been sending out wireless waves calling you here; and all my friends, the crabs and the gulls and Tommy the shark, have been calling you, too."

"Very nice, I'm sure," agreed Hester, with sarcasm that astonished her.

"Of course, it is," he said with a roar of laughter. "Go on, drive the chariot to my castle in Spain. The Lord of the Beach comes here with his wife. Say, Ellen—you haven't kissed me yet."

His eyes, orbs of green fire, glared down into hers. His breath gave off the fumes of hell. His iron hands were upon her, clutching her arm, pressing her waist towards him. She wanted to scream, but found that to scream was beyond her power. Woman's hideous fear of imminent outrage was upon her.

"Elusive, eh?" he leered. "You always were elusive to me, Ellen, my sweet. Always wanting to run away, and always liking to be caught. There is no running away this time. You are going to let me see right down deep into your eyes. By Moses, you are! Your soul isn't that pure that Arnold Dudley can't look at it. No! Not after showing it to poor old maggot-eaten Tracy. Come on, now—a kiss—with your eyes open!"

Hester saw his eyes close to hers. She felt his mouth on hers, hot, devouring. In that instant she saw Ellen, dainty, lovely, fastidious, gentle—and the way of her salvation was revealed even whilst his mouth covered hers and almost suffocated her. When he threw up his head and laughed with the triumph of a devil, she cried out passionately:

"You damned skunk! You blasted filthy dirty dog!   You . . . !" From her mouth poured as a river in flood a torrent of oaths and foul language which would have silenced an enraged bargee. "How dare you mistake me for your slut of a wife? Do you think every woman you meet is the harlot you're married to? Let go my arm, damn you! If you don't, I'll tear your throat out with my teeth."

The weapon of vile abuse which for this one time in her life she used, knowing that it was the only weapon likely to save her, seared the gentle soul of brave Hester Long. Most of the foul words had no meaning for her whatever. She was not conscious of ever having heard them, and their use and repetition stunned her no less than they stunned Arnold Dudley.

His hands fell away from her. His body moved to the extremity of the seat. Into his eyes came an expression of shocked, horrified wonder. The impossibility of Ellen uttering so terrible a string of obscenities—the impossibility divined by Hester in her desperate need—penetrated his drink-inflamed mind, shocked and shattered his brandy-created illusion, swamped and extinguished the furnace of his desires. The weapon of horrible words Hester Long had unsheathed served her better than she could have hoped; for Dudley had known intimately but one woman, who was his ideal still, an ideal utterly incapable of using vile language. Why, this was worse than coming upon his Ellen drunk!

"Sorry!" he mumbled.

Hester saw her victory. She clinched it by saying viciously:

"Get out! Do you hear? Get out, and walk behind. I am going to your camp. Don't you speak to me."

Arnold Dudley got out—and stood swaying at the side of the track, his body more at the mercy of the drink now that the madness of his mind was subdued. Hester drove on slowly, and, without looking back, knew he was following. Elation at her conquest of him surged through her, warming her body as old wine. She had him whipped, and was prepared if necessary to continue the whipping until he regained his normal senses.

Arrived at the camp, she managed to turn the horse and buggy in the narrow way, when she descended and regarded the scene of litter and desolation with a sinking heart. Hands on hips, head thrown back, she examined the tattered, tottering figure of Dudley, and said in almost a snarl:

"You'll want some clothes, Cain. And some boots. You can't work on my farm without boots, and I am not going to have my friends see you in those rags. Get yourself clothes and boots, quick. I'm in a hurry."

"I—I—you don't wansh worry about me. I'm or'ish, orl-right," he muttered.

"All right!" Hester echoed with withering scorn. "You look it! Get those clothes and boots. Go on, don't argue."

He tried to meet her gaze, failed, and lurched into the tent obediently. Hester walked to the table, and inspected the now disordered array of bottles. One was partly filled. Two were full. The rest were empty. The partly-filled bottle and one of the full ones she smashed with Dudley's setting-hammer. The single full bottle remaining she placed in the cavity beneath the buggy seat.

When Arnold Dudley staggered into the sunlight he held in his arms several serviceable garments and his working boots. He was ordered with biting curtness to place the articles in the back of the buggy.

"Now you can get in with me," Hester commanded. And when, after several attempts, he did manage to climb up beside her, she said: "Keep as far away from me as possible. You stink."

The horse dragged the buggy up Big Hill and down the farther side. Arnold Dudley nodded. Presently he sank back with closed eyes. He slept, and on his face was an expression of utter weariness. Regarding him, Hester Long smiled gently, wistfully. She wanted to cry at the sight of him. She was trembling from reaction. Yet she was supremely happy whilst she drove him "home".

CHAPTER XIII

A LADY WITH A LAMP

DUDLEY awoke in strange surroundings. It was unfamiliar noise that awakened him—sharp metallic sounds, irregular in, sequence and in tone. The noise demanded an explanation, yet he felt too lethargic to seek it. A sharp stabbing pain back of his eyes forced him to close them, and when he turned over on his side he found that whatever he was lying on gave way with luxurious softness.

Possibly he slept. When again he opened his eyes the pain in his head was more subdued. This time the noise above him shrieked for a name, and, knowing he would get no peace until he had labelled it, he sat up and swung his legs over to the floor, to look half-wildly about him.

Then it was to discover that he had slept on a flock mattress laid over a wire spring mattress supported at each end by empty kerosene cases. He was in a small corrugated-iron room which contained, besides his bed, an old washstand on which was a glass carafe and a tumbler, a butter-churn, a clothes-mangle, and a heap of bags. Beyond the window the sunlight was reflected redly by the dense-leaved branches of a pepper-tree, and the tint told Arnold Dudley that the sun was setting, and he realized that the sounds that had awakened him were caused by the diminishing heat of the sun allowing the sheets of iron on the roof to contract.

As to the place wherein he found himself he was completely at sea. That was a mystery to be solved later. The glass water-bottle and tumbler on the washstand caught his attention, and the only matter of importance then was to quench his terrific thirst. Standing on his legs he found that, although his mind was clear, he was still physically drunk. His walk to the washstand was as that of a man long confined to bed. But the water ! It gushed down his throat, sweet and cold, swept away the brimstone and carbolic, and weakened his legs still further. He almost fell on his way back to the bed, on which he rolled with a groan.

Then memory, starting from a blank and fading out in sleep, brought partial enlightenment. He remembered quite clearly being in a buggy drawn by an old brown horse. The vehicle was at a standstill. He was listening, almost paralysed with astonishment, to some awful language hurled at him from the mouth of Hester Long. Even in the old wild days he had seldom heard such words from the lips of a man. The words uttered by the woman he had come to admire for her brave yet gentle qualities and sympathetic understanding were so terrible that it was worse than finding a baby's corpse in a bed of lilies.

How he came to be sitting with her in the buggy, why she was using that dreadful language, and why she spoke afterwards so sharply as she did, he could not remember or fathom. He did remember hearing her tell him to get some clothes and boots. He remembered obeying her, and, whilst doing so, hearing her smash the brandy bottles. That act, he decided, in summing up matters from the bed, was unwarranted and inexplicable. It was his brandy, his property. Anyway, he remembered being told to get into the buggy with her; remembered, too, being informed that he smelt—no, stank. That was the word. And the word stung, because Dudley had always been fastidious as to his person. And then he went to sleep, and now he was in this strange room or store.

It was all very perplexing. Perhaps this was a dream, and the buggy incident as well. Doubtless he would awaken on his beach with the everlasting rumble of the surf filling the world. And then something gave a sharp tug at his hair, so sharp a tug that the pain of it sent him upright. He saw standing at the head of his bed a little boy about five years of age, golden-haired, rosy-cheeked, with mischievous eyes. The child regarded him steadily for a moment before clambering on the bed beside him, and, jumping on his back, pulling his hair again.

It was by no means a playful tug. Dudley ducked his head and threw himself sideways, whereupon the child hid himself beyond the bed. The man, who seldom swore, uttered an oath and gazed wildly about for the extra-ordinary child.

The sunlight had vanished and already gloom was settling within the room. Dudley felt tired and sick. Again he lay down. A few seconds later his hair was violently tugged once more.

The second assault was too much for him. He cried out, leaping from the bed. On it stood the boy laughing silently, a cold malevolent light in his blue eyes.

"What do you mean by it?" Dudley almost snarled. "Go away and leave me alone. I'm sick. Go away. D'you hear?"

The imp apparently heard. Jumping off the bed, he ran to the but-ter-churn and disappeared. Dudley blinked his eyes. The disappearance was amazing, since the churn was but half the size of the child, yet it had distinctly gone into it. The man stood and stared at the butter-churn, then yelled when he felt something on his back and knew before it happened that his hair would be painfully pulled.

"You little devil!" he screamed. "Go away—go awa ! Leave me alone—leave me alone, I tell you !" He stood in the centre of the room swaying on his feet; tears of mortification and anger in his eyes and voice. He heard the door open, and, spinning round, saw Hester Long enter hurriedly, and to her he burst out:

"Why am I here to be tormented by a brat? Why don't you look after your children, Mrs. Long? Take the little swine away before I—before I kill it."

"Ah!" said Hester Long softly. "Anyway, I am glad you have awoke, Mr. Cain. Now lie down again, and I'll fetch you a nice cup of strong tea. The little boy won't worry you again, or at least not after you have had your tea. Would you like a nice thin slice of fresh bread, with some of my own made butter?"

"No, thank you." Dudley almost collapsed on the bed. "I would appreciate the tea, though. Ugh!"

He saw squatted on one of his knees a hideously loath-some toad with a child's face. He heard Hester Long sigh a fraction of a second before he picked up a pillow, whirled it about his head, and brought it down on the reptile.

Hester fled to the kitchen, where her two boys were at work over their evening lessons. As quickly as she could she uncorked Dudley's bottle of brandy and poured a liberal portion into an enamelled pint pannikin. Filling it to the brim with milk and tea, she added sugar, and, not waiting to cut bread, picked up a canister of sweet biscuits and hurried back to her guest.

She found him standing on the washstand, his eyes distended, his lips drawn back from his teeth in a look of absolute horror.

"Get down, Mr. Cain," she said firmly. "I'll keep those things away while you drink your tea and eat a biscuit or two."

"Do you see them? Those scarlet centipedes? Look out! they'll be all over you," he said hoarsely.

"Come down at once! Do you hear?"

The clear ringing command had its effect. Dudley got off the washstand and edged in eccentric curves towards her, his gaze riveted to the floor. When he, with effort, hook up, she was before him holding out the brimming pannikin of not too hot tea and brandy. The smell of the spirit reached Dudley's nostrils, and he clutched the pannikin with both bands and drank as a man will who is dying of thirst. The biscuits he refused. The hot tea and brandy rushed through his veins as an ignited river of petroleum, flooding his body with exquisite warmth and pacifying his shrieking nerves. The empty pannikin he landed back to the waiting anxious Hester, and when again he looked on the floor he could see no awful Things in the dusk.

"They are gone," he said with relief that was almost ecstasy.

Hester responded cheerfully. "They have a funny name. Do you know what my brother used to call them?"

"No. I've never seen them before."

"I am most pleased to hear that. My brother used to call them 'dingbats'."

Dudley stared at her. Then he laughed mirthlessly.

"Thank you! I am glad I know," adding seriously : "They horrified me. And the child—was he a dingbat, too?"

"Of course he was. Are you feeling better now?"

"Much. Mrs. Long, you're a good Samaritan. Did you bring me here? Is this your place?"

"Yes, to both your questions," she said. "To-morrow, or the next day, I want to burn off fifty acres of scrub, and I badly want help. You want to get as much sleep as possible if you are to help, and you will, won't you?"

"I certainly will," he agreed heartily. "I think I shall sleep now. I felt awful."

She smiled at him and straightened the bed-clothes, turning down the sheets invitingly; and when she was almost at the door she turned to say good night.

"Would you mind telling me why you swore so fearfully at me down at my camp?" he asked her.

"Swore at you!" Hester Long echoed. "Really, Mr. Cain, I think you are too bad. I am not in the habit of swearing."

Dudley felt ashamed, as he was meant to.

"I am sorry I made a mistake," he said contritely. "It must all have been a horrid dream. I don't know. I think I have been a little mad. To-morrow I'll try and apologize."

"To-morrow you'll be a new man," he was assured, before Hester left him in the dusk of evening.

"Half an hour later, when Hester Long crept into the store-hut, she found him sleeping peacefully. In a saucer she held was a night-light, and this she set down on the washstand, and beside it she placed a glass of milk in which was a very moderate portion of brandy. For Hester knew that the best remedy for brandy-created devils and insects was brandy, and she knew moreover that Dudley would be almost sure to wake before morning, to see once again things of unnatural aspect and colour.

For a moment before leaving him she stood looking down on him with an expression that doubtless had been often on her face when she gazed on her sleeping children before going to her own bed. His face was weather-beaten and dirty and hairy. Yet she could see so plainly the nobility of the man, the cleanness of his mind—and the marks stamped on its index by the mental turmoil he had lived through. Even in that minute Hester Long was glad, more than glad, that she had brought him out of the hell on the beach into her own quiet haven of peace and purity.

Leaving the door open, she stepped across the yard, through the little garden gate, and entered the kitchen to find Edith Mallory reading a fairy-tale to two entranced little boys. Looking up quickly when Hester entered, Edith saw on the work-scarred, lovely face that which made her glad, too, and it was with a song in her voice that she completed the reading.

"Now, we are all going to bed," Hester announced. "Mr. Cain has gone to sleep so as to be strong and able to help with the burn. And you two little men are going to help, too, aren't you?"

"Can we light the fires, mummie?" eagerly asked six years.

"You'll let us, mum, won't you?" pleaded eight years. "You shall each of you have a box of matches. And must have a wet bag, too, in case the fire gets into the lupin paddocks. Now, come along into the Land of Nod."

Miss Mallory was kissed with affection and abandon, and returned the kisses with equal fervour. She seemed very happy just then. Her eyes were a-sparkle in the lamp-light. Yet when mother and children had left the kitchen her beautiful face became sad, and into her blue eyes entered an expression of pain.

When prayers were said, and the little boys were safely in their respective beds, Hester Long gave each a final hug before going to her own room. She had decided to do something that to her bordered on sacrilege. The urge came to her whilst she stood looking down on the sleeping Dudley, and now when she drew from beneath her bed a brass-bound double-locked oaken chest she hesitated, her mind occupied by thoughts of Arnold Dudley and her husband. Her candle lit up the scene—a small white-washed room containing a narrow single bed, a chest of drawers, a washstand, and a chair : no pictures on the walls and only one ornament, a crucifix made of sea-shells, hanging above the head of the bed. That moment was ever to remain a vivid memory, because, when her mind was occupied by the one man she loved and the other man she could have loved, a sentence of living words came to her with the force of a command:

"Now as I serve you, you go out and serve."

How deep must be the subconscious mind that will throw up into consciousness a phrase that has been read and thought about and forgotten perhaps many years before ! No longer did Hester Long hesitate. Grave doubt had been vanquished by decision. Kneeling swiftly, she set the candlestick on the floor, and, unlocking the chest, raised and pushed back the shut lid. With the candle now in her left hand, she took out of the chest, slowly and reverently, object after object wrapped in tissue-paper, and when each object had been looked at it was set on the floor beside her. There were broken toys, a baby's rattle with a tinkling bell, a baby's dummy with an ivory ring, and little garments pressed and folded and scented. Next came the cabinet-size photographs, one of her husband taken in his military uniform, and one each of her children at twelve months of age. She unwrapped and for an instant looked at a masonic apron within a morocco-leather case, a pair of pipes in another case, a man's glove, a white glove—her bridegroom's glove.

At last she came to what she sought, an oblong electroplated box, and this she placed on the bed whilst she gently put back the articles lying beside her. The chest, her "treasure chest," was relocked and pushed beneath the bed.

For an hour she sat with Edith Mallory in the kitchen, talking of the coming burn, the cows, and the sheep, and the market reports, and the illness of old Mrs. Black in Dongara, whose husband had been one of the first to settle there. Neither spoke of Arnold Dudley, and each knew that the other wanted to talk about him.

After supper they took a hurricane-lamp and went out to the stable to feed Edith's hack and Hester's buggy horse, and then they made a round of the chicken-runs to see that doors were shut and fastened against the marauding fox. By ten o'clock they were in bed.

Several hours later, Hester awoke, and, lighting her candle, looked at the clock and discovered the time to be ten minutes after two. She wondered if her guest was sleeping, and, wondering, realized that she would not herself sleep again until she had found out. Very quietly she arose and slipped into an old dressing-gown, and, picking up the candle, stole along the passage to the kitchen, where she left her light, out through the door, which was never locked, and across to the store-hut. Through the open door of the hut she saw Arnold Dudley seated on his bed, gazing steadily at the night-light.

The glass containing the brandy and milk was empty. Hester was sure that it had been emptied some time before, because whilst she watched Dudley now and then brushed an imaginary insect off his clothes. He was a stage further on the road to normality. For he knew that the things he saw did not exist, whereas before he had believed them to be real.

Hester stole back to the kitchen. When she emerged the second time she carried the candle in one hand and in the other another glass of milk with a yet smaller portion of brandy in it, and in it besides three powdered aspirin tablets. Dudley looked round sharply when she entered, for an instant frowning, and then, when she asked why he could not sleep, laughed shortly, and explained that something running across his face had awakened him, and banished sleep.

"What is the time?" he asked.

"About half-past two," she replied. "Thinking you might be awake, I thought a glass of warm milk would do you good."

"You should not have troubled. Why do you bother with me?"

"Why!" Hester echoed. "Didn't you bother about the hook in my thumb? Besides—"

"Well?" he prompted.

"Oh! just because. Now drink this milk. I have put a few aspirins in it. That'll make you sleep, I'm sure."

When Dudley stood up—the state of his mind made him forget to do so earlier—she saw there were tears in his eyes. His hands shook when he accepted the glass, and whilst he drank the glass clattered against his teeth.

"Funny what a beast a man can make himself, isn't it?" he said.

"Not so much a beast as a fool, Mr. Cain. To-morrow you'll decide never to be a fool again. We'll have a long talk sometime. You'll find that

I understand men, or you will say I do if you will but follow my advice. Now lie down again and try to sleep. Good night!"

"Good night!" he answered, and wondered if there were any more Hester Longs in the world.

He slept late that morning, but when he did awake, about nine, the pains in his head were gone, and when he stood up he discovered that the ground no longer heaved and swayed beneath him. Memory caused him to feel a shame never before experienced. He wondered what he looked like, and, seeing a small mirror on the wall behind the washstand, he went to it and gazed long and miserably at himself.

"Arnold, you're a dog," he whispered. "She was right when she said: 'You are a fool'. Fool! Yes, you're a fool."

His gaze fell to the water ewer standing in the basin. Beside it lay a cake of soap, and near that a small electroplated box. Picking it up, he pressed a button, where-upon the lid fled up to reveal an ivory-handled safety razor, flanked by small ivory boxes containing spare blades. There was engraved matter on the inside of the lid, and he read:

"To the Dearest Man in the World,

From Hester, his wife,

23rd January, 1921."

He knew then what lay behind the loan of Hester Long's gift to her dead husband. He knew, too, that he could never accept that loan. Suddenly he realized that he could not possibly look into Hester Long's eyes as he then appeared.

She saw him, a minute later, running down the farm track to the main road. Edith stood with her. Dudley ran as though in a race to his camp. When he returned it was midday. He was shaven and washed and dressed in clean clothes. He drove in his truck and told them he had come to work.

CHAPTER XIV

"BRAVO, HESTER LONG!"

THE burn actually took place on March 20th. For two days the wind had come from the north-east, come from the vast sun-baked interior of the continent, hot and dry.

At ten o'clock that morning, Hester Long left the house with a billycan of tea and fresh buttered scones in a basket, and set off to one of her far paddocks which was being re-fenced by Arnold Dudley. He was sinking holes and erecting posts that he had cut out of the bush and brought to the "job" on his truck the day before. The unaccustomed work made him perspire and caused the muscles of his arms and back to ache atrociously. The cutting of the posts had made him perspire much more than the erection was doing, and because of it he already felt a different man.

A perspiring body is the most healthy, which is the reason why Australian bush people are the most healthy in the world. People in towns who lounge in offices, shops, trams, and theatres seldom perspire, which is why they are white of face, dull-eyed, and limp. A bushman will tell you that he feels "dopy" in the morning until, by using an axe or other implement of labour, he sweats the "dopy" feeling out of him. Then he is his own man.

After Dudley had swung an axe—which he could use—for nine hours, his body had exuded not only the result of an orgy of brandy drinking, but also impurities that had collected during months of idleness. At the end of the day's work he had taken a towel to the little creek east of the house and had lain down in the shallow stream for half an hour. Although his hands were blistered, and his arms and back ached, he felt like an athlete of twenty, and ate supper in company with Hester Long, Edith, and the children with avidity.

Whilst Hester crossed the paddock to where he was putting up the posts with evident skill, she smiled. She felt glad to be taking the morning lunch to him, glad to match him working, because she knew that the labour would benefit him in mind as well as body ; for, if one works willingly, one has to centre one's thoughts on the work. And, if a person's thoughts are on work, thoughts of anything else cannot intrude. That secret she had learned through her own bitter experience. It is Work, not Time, which is the healer of wounded hearts.

Dudley had put up forty-one posts when Hester Long reached him. She saw at once that he was no novice in fencing, the posts being accurately set apart in absolute alignment, and all exactly five feet three inches out of the ground. Then, in dark-blue duck trousers, cotton singlet, and an old straw hat on his head, the man was not to be recognized as the drink-maddened ruffian who had leapt into her buggy three days before.

"'This is not the first fence you have put up, Mr. Cain," she said brightly.

"Well, no, it is not. But it will be the first one I've erected for many years," he told her in a manner that was quiet and yet different from what she had known it to be. "I am not so young as I was, nor am I as hard as I was. What have you there—some tea?"

"Yes; and some buttered scones. Let us go over into the shade, shall we? You see, I've brought two cups."

"Bravo ! And where are the boys?"

"They are at school on the veranda," she told him, seating herself on the grass beneath a wattle and spreading out a miniature table-cloth. "They are having a half-holiday this afternoon, because I think the time has come to burn off that fifty acres."

"Good ! You'll fire it, which end?"

"If the wind does not increase, I think we'll fire the lower end, don't you?"

"Yes. The fire will go through it the quicker, and I see you ploughed a fire-break along the top end yesterday."

Arnold looked at her curiously. "Do you know, you are a first-rate ploughman? Those furrows are as straight as a die."

"Not so bad for a school-teacher," she laughed.

"Harder work, though."

"Indeed it is not. There is no harder work in the world than teaching school," was her instant reply. "I can go out all day and plough—yes, even swing an axe all day—and at night I can sing and romp with the children. After one of my days teaching school, I wanted to go to bed at six o'clock."

"Still, ploughing all day must be monotonous," he persisted.

"Not at all. I was never satisfied that the furrow I had just ploughed was straight enough. There is no monotony in any task if it is done with one's heart as well as with one's hands."

"You are right there." For a moment he sipped his tea. Then "The paddock on the south side of the fifty acres is tinder dry. We shall have to have a few buckets of water and plenty of bags handy."

"The water and the bags and the wielders will be there," Hester Long said with suddenly twinkling eyes "There will be the Mallorys, the Jessops, the Smythes, and the Browns. They'll all come, because I have told them to. You see, Mr. Cain, they have always come every year to my burn. They look upon it as a picnic, something like we Pommies look upon a harvest-home in England. For twelve months and longer, after my husband was taken, they came and ploughed, and dug and cut and built for me. They're just a wonderful lot of people."

"We Australians are a wonderful people," he said with mock gravity.

"You are no more wonderful than the Canadian people, or the English people, or the Scotch people," he was informed seriously.

"I am justly rebuked."

"You are!" Hester Long said laughing, and the timbre of her laughter brought back to the man memory of his wife. How strange, he thought, that two women, so different in looks and temperament, should laugh alike "You are rebuked because when you said you Australians were a wonderful people you thought only of those British people born in Australia. To me it seems to make no difference where the British people are born."

"When I said: 'We Australians are a wonderful people', I was but quoting our politicians before an election."

"You were not; you were teasing me!" Hester said with ill-assumed severity. "For that you can smoke or go back to work I am leaving you. I've piles of scones to bake, and cakes and sandwiches to make. Come in to lunch at twelve sharp, please. Edith has to go round the neighbours directly after, to tell them we will be burning off this afternoon."

"All right. You'll want me this afternoon, too?"

"Of course."

"Then I must continue man-handling those posts at once."

Looking up from his work now and then, he watched a little figure in its blue print dress swing along back to the house, and to the crowbar murmured: "Yes, the Australians are a wonderful people, because the Hester Longs came to Australia over twelve thousand miles of sea. Who was the fool who said the British Empire was decadent? He was a darned sight bigger fool than I was, and that is saying something."

Immediately lunch was over, Edith Mallory saddled her hack and rode off on her round of the neighbours, the nearest of whom, apart from her brother, lived four miles south. For Hester Long's children the burn was more thrilling than any Guy Fawkes bonfire. They changed their school clothes for the oldest they possessed, and naturally their oldest clothes were several sizes too small. When they appeared before Arnold Dudley they looked like scarecrows, the only substantial article of their apparel being their boots, which were exceptionally stout and heavy.

Dudley spent an hour making buckets from four-gallon kerosene tins, and a second hour taking them, filled with water, to various strategic points. By that time the first of the visitors arrived in a very ancient Ford car. They were the Browns. Mr. Brown was small and wiry and sixty; Mrs. Brown, fifty, fat and fair. Joe Brown drove the car: Joe was thirty and, like his father, thrifty. He owned the car, and, although able to own ten new ones, his first love was evidently going to be his last.

About three, the Jessops and the Smythes arrived together. The Smythes came in their new single-seater, Mr. Smythe being very fat, ever bubbling with laughter, and his wife painfully thin and appearing prim and severe, which she certainly was not. They had no children, but their lack of them was made up for by the super-abundance of Mr. and Mrs. Jessop. Mr. Jessop drove two spirited horses in a buckboard with a single seat, built high above the long floor. Two of the daughters sat with him, girls of perhaps fourteen. Mrs. Jessop sat on the floor nursing a new baby, and around her in such numbers that the poor woman was almost submerged in a mountain of humanity was the rest of the family. In that district there were other people who could have come, but they were the "grandees"—a class of person unfortunately rapidly increasing in Australia—and they were not Hester Long's "neighbours", which was their loss. Had the Jessops, the Smythes, the Browns, and the Mallorys congregated in the market-place of any British town, most certainly they would have been arrested as people without visible means of support. The clothes they wore were amazingly dilapidated, and one can imagine the incredulous disgust on the face of any tramp had Joe Brown's pants been offered him.

Hester Long received them all with a kiss or a hand-shake, and above all a gladsome, welcoming smile. The women kissed her as though they meant it, and the men grinned shyly and wiped their hands on their tattered trousers before taking hers and squeezing it with genuine admiration. The Browns and the Smythes were people of affluence, the Jessops were as poor as mice, Tom and Edith Mallory could individually have bought up the other, whilst Hester Long was at last set on her own financial feet. Wealth and the snobbery of wealth were there non-existent. The clothes they wore had been selected to suit the particular labour they were embarking on that afternoon. Joe, of the ancient Ford, cracked a joke with Mrs. Smythe of the new single-seater, even Mrs. Jessop, her voice raised to overcome the chorus of juvenile voices around her, handed her baby to Miss Mallory, precisely as one girl will loan her doll to a special friend to nurse for a few minutes.

Hester brought out to them a kerosene-tin full of tea, and a great tray piled with buttered scones and little cakes. She set tea and cakes on the veranda, Mr. Brown filled the cups and pannikins, and Mrs. Smythe handed them round, whilst Mrs. Brown dispensed the scones and cakes. The children shrieked, the women laughed, and the men discussed the weather outlook.

About half-past three the party set out for the burn. Arrived at the windward side, they stood in sudden silence whilst Hester Long's children, their high spirits temporarily subdued by the importance of the act, lighted the first two fires, which they had carefully prepared two days before. Now, with the two fires well alight, Hester Long cried: "Go!" and the men each seized a burning brand and, running along the edge of thick-lying dry branches and leaves, set up a chain of fires.

Into the brazen sky rose a cloud of bluish-white smoke. The fire hissed and crackled, spread, grew, leapt into its stride. The women and children watched, fascinated: the men separated and rapidly took up positions along the south side, where the dried lupins would invite the fire. The column of smoke quickly became a rising mountain with a crimson fiery base—a mountain of smoke seen at Dongara, where speculation became rife as to whose burn it denoted.

Somewhere, invisible in the smoke, a man shouted. Dudley and Mallory, with chaff-bags heavy with water, raced to the point and madly beat out the fire among the lupins caused by a flying spark. Onward swept the main fire, eating up. Acre by acre, the tones of dead rubbish which had met the axe of Hester Long.

From within the smoke farther away along the south side a youthful voice cried : "Hi-aye!" and Dudley rushed in that direction to join forces with one of the Jessop lads in beating out another fire. And so it went on. Eyes smarted and burned, arms ached from flailing the wet bags, and the heat-parched throats to lime-kiln dryness. The sun, shining sometimes through the high, whirling smoke, resembled a sovereign and gilded the world beneath. Towards four o'clock, the fire had reached the farther side of the burn. A little before five, the wind dropped to a calm. The smoke rose to the sky in a straight column, and people at Dongara who looked that way saw how it mushroomed two thousand feet above the earth in a flat-topped, motionless black cloud.

All danger of the fire spreading outside its prescribed bounds had disappeared. The stumps and logs from the larger branches still burned redly in the smoke sent up from the heated ground in a million tiny spirals from the hot ashes of leaves and twigs and sticks.

The sun, now almost at its setting, whitened the pillar of smoke and tinted the cloud resting on it bright yellow. Hester came along to invite everyone home for tea, and in twos, threes and fours the visitors reached the neat white house, where the men and boys washed at the well and hurriedly assisted Hester Long to bring out to the cool veranda dishes of cold meat, dishes piled with cooked eggs, heaped with tinned salmon, plates of bread and butter-bread that was famed around Dongara and butter famous in many magnificent homes in Perth—plates of cakes and apples, the repast being set out on a snowy white table-cloth on the veranda floor.

"You've had a good burn, Mrs. Long," announced the enormous Mr. Smythe with little twinkling grey eyes. "The rubbish was well laid and the wind just right. What are you going to put in it?"

"I don't think I shall have much time to put anything in, Mr. Smythe," Hester replied doubtfully. "If the stumps burn out well, I could just scarify it and broad-cast clover."

Mr. Smythe fell to examining the rising column of smoke, his beaming face as that of Friar Tuck smelling a cooking haunch of venison. Mr. Brown gazed at him with peculiar hopefulness. Jessop waited also.

"Seems a pity letting that fifty acres lie fallow this winter," presently remarked the fat man to no one in particular. "What about it, Bert?"

"Anything you says goes," encouraged Mr. Brown, looking at Joe. Joe's mouth stretched in a grin, and he nodded.

"All right, then," Mr. Smythe again observed to no especial person. "To-morrow you and me, Bert, will fetch over our tractors and ploughs, and get going. The next day Bill Jessop and Joe can bring over their teams and seeders ; and, Mrs. Long," and Mr. Smythe paused, apparently to allow his smile to widen to the limit—"in three days' time we'll have your fifty acres ploughed and sowed."

"I-I, oh! it is too kind of you, really it is," Hester told them with shining misty eyes, her seamed face suddenly radiating an inward glory that made it lovely. "You've all been so helpful ever since I came here. It is like imposing on your generosity."

"Of course it's not!" cried the thin and dismal-looking Mrs. Smythe. "They'll come bright and early, won't they, Mrs. Jessop?"

"They certainly will," agreed the burdened Mrs. Jessop, as though at the last minute the men would wish they hadn't promised, which was absurd.

"Don't I get a part in this play?" asked Tom Mallory.

"You bet! Your job will be to keep the tea up to us," Joe Brown pointed out.

"All right," laughed Mallory; "but you, Jessop, needn't bring your team eight miles. Let Brown bring your seeder behind his plough, and I'll have a team of my own here for you to work."

And so it was arranged.

The sun having gone down into the sea beyond the towering sand-hills, the men sat and smoked whilst the women cleared and washed up, and the children raced around the house and orchard.

Dudley and Mallory, sitting a little apart, discussed rabbits and other vermin in the district and idly watched the smoke cloud hanging above them change in colour from white to yellow, yellow go gold, and gold to purple. The column became violet-blue when night settled at its base, where it was alive with lightning flickered from the countless fires over the burn. The cries of the romping children were intermingled with the warbling of the sleepy magpies and the occasional throaty melody of a butcher-bird.

"First time you've been to Dongara?" inquired Mallory.

'Well, no. I was here for a week before the War," Dudley replied.

'Ah! Then it will be the first time you met Mrs. Long?"

"Yes. Our acquaintance dates from some five months ago. She is a wonderful woman."

"Indeed she is. A battler, if ever there was one. Her husband was crippled by the War, you know, and Mrs Long came here straight from England, and, she tells me, straight from teaching at school. To bog in at once and do a man's work better than the average man does it.

"Long got the Repatriation Department to buy this farm. The Department paid a boom period price for it, and from the beginning the land was over-capitalized. How they managed to pay the interest, let alone the capital, I don't know—or rather I do know. You know what a Government Department is—it demands its pound of flesh. The Repatriation Department had no mercy on Hester; when her husband died it wanted to seize the farm from her, so that it could be sold at a profit to the Department. Smythe and me paid out Shylock, and to-day Hester owns her own farm.

"Yes, a wonderful woman, our Hester," Mallory went on softly. "The pity of it is there are not more of her sort in the world. They are the people we want in Australia instead of those Southern Europeans who, directly they come to understand our values, loaf far worse than the Australians when the boss's back is turned. I know. I've employed 'em, more shame to me, but never again!

"Ah well ! Come on. They're going back to finish the burn."

Rising, they followed after the men and boys and joined with them in the final operation. With long-handled shovels and crowbars the still burning logs were rolled against one another and against the stumps by the crow-bar wielders. The shovellers knocked charcoal away from the logs to help the eating fire. The countless separated fires burned up with renewed life, and to these the boys dragged the remaining branches and sticks too green for the general fire to have consumed.

The women presently came and watched. The scene was like some imaginative artist's idea of hell. Lit by the flames of a hundred fires, the men and boys worked as so many devils with their crowbars and shovels, their faces crimsoned by the heat and colour of the conflagration. Then became apparent the wisdom of wearing the oldest clothes and the stoutest boots. Sparks dropped on the workers' old hats and tattered garments, burning fresh holes. Thick-soled boots trod underfoot red-hot ashes.

At nine o'clock most of the work was done. The Jessops were the first to leave in their buckboard. One hour later the Smythes drove off, and shortly afterwards Joe's Ford roared like twenty aeroplanes, and the Browns departed. Tom Mallory remained with Arnold Dudley until midnight, when they decided that there was nothing more to be done.

Utterly weary, but happier than he had been since; coming to Dongara, Arnold Dudley went to bed, and was at once asleep. At dawn he arose, refreshed and reinvigorated, and hurried out to look over the burn. The work had been well done from the very start. Not a branch or stick remained. Not a stump protruded above ground. Even the roots were mostly burnt out. A carpet of grey ash and black charcoal lay spread over fifty acres which a few months before had been covered with dense, tangled, sweet-smelling but useless bush.

Fifty acres! Fifty acres added to the British Empire; wealth to the amount probably of five hundred pounds added to the wealth of the British Empire. Fifty acres of ash and charcoal, soon to be fifty acres of luscious clover, a monument raised by a lone, dauntless woman to the greatness of her race—a monument that bore the words: "To my children."

And when Arnold Dudley heard footsteps behind him, and, turning, found Hester Long coming to see her work, his hat was removed automatically from his head in homage.

"Bravo, Hester Long!" he said with sincerity.

CHAPTER XV

BEAUTY SURFACE DEEP

ONE afternoon, in the first week of April, Arnold Dudley returned to the Beach of Atonement. Reaching his camp, he drove his truck off the track into its bush-cleared parking space, and before alighting surveyed the litter-strewn neglect of what was his home.

The tent sagged sadly. The bush-built table was messed with empty brandy bottles, pannikins, and remnants of food. Over the naturally clean sand lay enough paper to provide a "scent" for twenty paper-chases. Billy-cans, a fry-pan, jam and milk and fish and meat tins lay everywhere—an eyesore amidst a scene of sylvan beauty.

Dudley's face reddened. As a pig in its sty he had wallowed there until Hester Long had come to his rescue. The camp would have disgraced an aboriginal: as a white man's habitation it would have disgusted the lowest vagabond.

When he jumped to the ground he halted, urged equally by two opposed longings: one to set to at once and tidy the camp, and the other to hurry along to the Seagull's Throne and gaze upon his beach. For he was like unto the man who hugs to himself his chains. The heavy, sickly bush scents, the tang of the sea air, the soft thundering of the ceaseless surf, were as voices welcoming him home. If it was a home wherein he had suffered the agonies of the damned, it was no less a home for that.

For the vision of the vast deserted beach was as the vision of a city man's house: the northern stretch of white sand being one room; the Pontoon, with the adjacent Seaweed Mountain, the Sugar Loaf, the Boiling Pot a second room; whilst a third lay to the south as far as the beetling cliffs. Rocks, sand-hummocks, lagoons and pools, tiny bays within the greater bay of the beach, and the flotsam and jetsam of the tide, were all separate entities, pieces of furniture within his house.

There, too, dwelt the spirit of Ellen, the elfin, elusive, desirable, lovely Ellen, whom he had loved and married and possessed. And out among the rocks that other spirit, that wailing lost soul of the man who had fouled and dragged down into the muck—the lovely Ellen. In the wind and surf he heard, standing twixt bush and camp, the fretful sighs of his lost Ellen and the remorseful, restless, pain-racked cries of the vile Tracy.

Arnold Dudley knew which longing would master him, even before he admitted decision. The camp could wait. When he returned from the beach he would set to and clean it; but first he must visit his beach, his home, and examine with loving care each article of its furnishing.

From the truck he took a large biscuit-tin, which he carried along with him. It contained bread-crusts. When he rounded the southern spur of the coast sand-dune and came to the open sandy space, he saw that the gulls were resting on their throne; and there he stood and called them, and, hearing as well as seeing him, the birds fluttered upward, and then swooped down to hover with harsh welcoming cries above his head. The man laughed and shouted at them whilst he jumped down on the beach and almost ran to the Pontoon, then well above the low tide. And into the pools on the great rock he tossed the crusts and watched with a thrill of pride his birds feed, the while carefully counting them, and finding them all to be there.

Now with the empty tin he regained the sandy space, where he left it, to climb unencumbered to the hillock of sand and seat himself on the Seagull's Throne.

The Beach! It lay spread far away north and south, white and delicate and slender as a new moon, cradling in its gigantic curve the rushing lines of white surf sweeping across a floor of turquoise blue, which towards the horizon deepened to living steel. As of yore the squadrons of white horses charged far out over the Ramparts, lifting high the horizon line in contemptuously leaping the sunken barrier, thence to regain formation and strength to rush on the Sugar Loaf and the outer wall of the Pontoon, there to be flung back in disorder.

Ah! And there, too, was the old enemy. Dudley could see the sinister triangular fin of his shark cutting the water, rising and falling with the chop between the Pontoon and the Sugar Loaf, sending out behind it radiating ripples. Everything was as it had been, and strangely enough at that moment he felt the loss or absence of the poor lone shag, and fell to wishing that another would come and occupy his beach.

The wind blew softly from the south, whispering of icebergs and ice-fields and freezing snows which it had passed over. The world was a-glitter with light and colour. Vivid green behind him, white at his feet, and brilliant blue before him. The sun, now in the north, was reflected at a million points, its radiance sent back by the rolling sea beyond the Ramparts and the chop beyond the Pontoon, sent back by gleaming brown and green and red seaweed, and black and grey water-washed rocks.

Nothing in that great open world lay visibly decayed. Nothing therein was impure, nor did there exist ugliness in any shape or form. Arnold Dudley saw and studied and understood. He had come to his beach as a man returns to his house in the early summer after the spring-cleaning. That the beach was the same beach, yet a beach more brilliant, more beautiful, without blemish, he was dimly conscious was due to the change in him brought about by Hester Long. She had spring-cleaned his mind: she had swept down the winter cobwebs from before his eyes and permitted the light and the beauty to enter into him.

His mind dwelt on the marvel of Hester Long. He recalled her picture when she stood looking up at him sitting behind the steering-wheel, the engine running. Her work-lined, plain-featured face appeared wonderfully lovely, and whilst he gazed thereon the thought had occurred that if a woman's eyes are beautiful and her hair is beautiful, the face catches beauty as a night-closed flower opens in beauty at the touch of the sun.

Just then there was an appealing look in the limpid grey eyes as though she were his mother, and he departing for the metropolis where temptations awaited inexperienced youth. He thought, too, that then he had seen behind her grey eyes that which he had vainly sought in the dark-blue eyes of Ellen, a vision of the innermost, the real woman. And what he saw, or fancied he saw, startled him. He knew, whilst he sat on the Seagulls' Throne, that in Hester Long there was no guile, no deceit, nothing whatever to hide. There was no mental cupboard containing little skeletons for Hester eternally, and instinctively to guard. Time had written nothing on her heart but what was wholesome, sympathetic, and beautiful.

To her Dudley's heart warmed. She was Woman, the Woman, the ideal of every man since Adam. A woman true as tempered steel, firm as a lighthouse rock, pure as water at the spring, courageous, gentle, and—feminine! A woman to whom a sin-stained man could take his troubles, confide his transgressions, sure of understanding and of sympathetic advice; rather than one who could arouse admiration and the passion to possess. Her sweet voice echoed in his ears:

"Don't forget that you have promised to come and take dinner with the children and me every Sunday," she said. "Let your body be exercised with work and your mind with thoughts of the future, and seldom of the past. Good-bye for the present, Mr. Cain. And good luck!"

He had come away loaded with gifts of apples, of eggs and butter, a batch of bread, and a mysterious gift wrapped in brown paper. He had left her with hope in his heart once more, that he would find content and happiness once again, and determination that there should be no back-sliding into that Slough of Despond out of which she had dragged him.

Ellen! He knew that his wife was alive, yet that day Ellen appeared to have drawn farther away from him. The impression that she was dead and had died true to him persisted. In all but reality she was dead to him, and he mourned her as such, and sometimes asked himself with his honest bluntness if he hated her for her betrayal of him. And always the small voice of his conscience said: "No ! He still loved her no whit less than he had ever done, and in his heart he knew that if she stood confronting him he would hold out to her his and cry aloud his joy at the touch of her.

Had Arnold Dudley not been a one-woman man—it is surprising how large a number of men are, in spite of the feminine cynics—it is quite probable that he would have turned to Hester Long; but the actions and the spoken thought of Ellen were too deeply imprinted on his mind and his heart ever to be marred or dimmed by a fresh experience. It was because he was a one-woman man that he had suffered so deeply her loss and was still to suffer it. The past was revealed, the future hidden from him; though it was less hidden from Hester Long, who had opened the book of his mind and had read therein.

For an hour he sat there high above the beach, reveling in its beauty, in his possession of it, sometimes thinking of Ellen and often of Hester Long. With an audible sigh he rose, descended the hillock of sand, and, retrieving the empty biscuit-tin, returned to his camp, where for several moments he paused, undecided where to start. Then with sudden fierce energy he seized a shovel and dug a pit, and, collecting the empty tins, the bottles, and the paper, he dumped the litter into it and covered it out of sight. He proceeded to build a fire and boil water, making tea with some of it, and with the remainder washing down the table. Afterwards he brought out of the tent his blankets and hung them over bushes to air; then he fell to work within the tent, tidying it, and setting the mass of jumbled rations in their proper places and order.

About three o'clock he donned his old tattered dungarees and boots, the latter now hard and dry and cracked by salt-water; and again went along to the beach with fishing lines, a song on his lips, and a gladness in his clear hazel eyes. Hatless, the wind played with his wavy dark brown hair, and its freshness touched his sun-burned face as though with cool, caressing fingers.

The tide was coming in fast. Beyond the Ramparts the sea looked as calm as the proverbial mill-pond. Beyond the Pontoon the water was chopped by meeting waves, but even there the sea was comparatively calm. That day the serried ranks of water-hills did not fly high above the Pontoon edge with their usual brilliant abandon. They seemed hampered by lethargy or the desire to conserve their strength for a future onslaught, for when they met the wall of rock they rose sullenly and welled over upon it in a sweeping rush of white water.

Dudley gained a position about a yard from the edge and cast the lighter of his lines. The heavy sea line he retained in his bag. He brought up a scarlet-backed, pink-bellied rock-fish, then a three pound bream, and later an emerald-green rock-fish round about a pound in weight.

It was whilst rebaiting his hooks that the shark came slowly cruising by. The purposefully moving, sinister, triangular fin fascinated him, and he watched it with the hooks held in his two hands. From the north came the sea-brute, along a water valley, skirting the Boiling Pot, and cut the chop with its fin beyond the watching man. Now and then he caught a glimpse of its blue-grey back, and saw shivering in the surface water the dull white of its belly. It passed him, and still he watched it. He saw it circle and return, this time closer to the rock on which he stood with the welling waves sending their overflow sometimes almost as high as his waist.

Whilst the beast drew opposite, Arnold Dudley noted how the symmetrical body was lifted and lowered by the incoming sea-hills, observed with admiration the mastery the beast had over its native element. Whether it saw him or smelt him he was undecided, but suddenly the moving fin slowed to a stop and disappeared.

He thought the shark had gone deep after an unwary fish, and waited for the fin to reappear some distance further on. At one instant the level of the near sea was as high as his waist, the next it had sunk ten feet below his rocky platform. The fin did not appear at the expected spot, and at last he prepared to cast his line again.

In the very act of drawing back his arm for the throw Dudley saw the shark directly opposite him, and not six yards from the Pontoon. It lay motionless, only the tip of its fin being visible. When the swell carried it upward it cut the horizon line, and when the water sank, Dudley gazed down on the motionless fish staring at him with horrible, malignant, agate eyes, even though they were softened by a few inches of translucent water.

With the sea level with his waist, Dudley experienced a qualm of fear. He pictured the shark making a dash forward and seizing him the precise second it lifted above the rock. But reason pointed out his safety, and for a while he stood and watched.

With marvellous ease the brute kept itself motionless, counteracting in some subtle way the attempts of the sea-currents to move its mass. Second after second, minute after minute, it lay watching the man, invisible, hatefully contemplative, terrible in its placidity.

Dudley shivered. The beauty of his beach, after all, was only surface deep. Beneath the shimmering wonder of the sea lay ugliness, bestial and horrible. It was as though smiling, lovely nature kept hidden away her monstrosities conceived in storm and passion, or as a prosperous city magnate standing in his hall welcomes illustrious guests, knowing that in the back rooms of his house men and women he has ruined are waiting to receive alms of him.

A poignant loathing swept over Dudley, held by those unwinking agate eyes. In a bouquet of roses he had discovered an adder, and with quick decision he retreated, determined to cast out this reptile fouling sweet-scented beauty.

Winding the line on its short piece of board whilst he stumbled to the shore, he walked rapidly to his camp. There he unpacked a leg of mutton given him by Hester Long, and in this he made deep gashes with his skinning knife, and along the gashes inserted the white crystals of strychnine.

Now running, he raced back to the Pontoon and stumbled over its uneven surface to its seaward edge. The shark, he saw, was north of the Boiling Pot, and, waiting, he saw it disappear in the distance beyond.

For five long anxious minutes he waited—waited to witness its return, revealed by the triangular fin, yet he did not see its return. Suddenly he was shocked to behold it watching again in its former position. As a cat with a mouse, it had feigned retreat, intending to spring back unobserved within reach of its prey.

Dudley tossed it the poisoned leg of mutton.

The meat fell with a splash where the shark had been. Even whilst it was in the air, the fish had sunk. Dudley saw the meat disappear, saw it rise again to the surface, saw it carried upward by an incoming wave, up and up almost to the level of his head. He saw a streak of white, two inward-curving crescent rows of white teeth, then a blue-grey back, long and graceful, and the wide tail-fin.

When the water fell the bait had gone.

"It's you for the tummy-ache now, you beast!" Dudley shouted.

For a while he stayed there, watching the sea. But no more did the giant fish appear. He stayed for an hour, until the sun kissed the horizon and laid across the darkening sea a narrow carpet of crimson. And then far, away to the north, he observed a small flock of gulls, his gulls, hovering, hovering low over the water.

With a feeling akin to exultation Arnold Dudley reached the narrow strip of sand lying along the rear of the Pontoon, seeming to divide it from the bluff headland, and there in a pool he gutted and scaled his fish. Again in his camp, he added wood to the embers of the fire, boiled the billy, and, after changing into dry clothes, fried the fish.

He ate his supper whilst the stars appeared one by one, and his butcher-bird rendered his repertoire of melodies ; and, when he had finished and washed the utensils and put away the bread and the butter, he rolled a cigarette with thoughtful care and smoked it with the relish of a man who smokes but little.

The recent exultation was replaced by a feeling of satisfaction, for that day he had removed two ugly blemishes from his beach—the indescribable litter of his camp, and the dreadful monster of the sea. With the darkness the wind fell to an utter calm. The birds slept, but the unsleeping sea rolled against the eternal rocks with subterranean thunderings, and on the steeply-shelving sand-beach with reverberating, sharply-defined crashes. The orchestra of the deep soothed Dudley to dreaminess, and he fell to wondering how much older the world would be when the sea-music ceased. And, thinking thus, he suddenly thought of Hester Long and her mysterious gift.

Procuring his hurricane-lamp, he lit it, and from the truck took the flat brown paper parcel tied carefully with string. He took it to the table, and from his belt pulled out his skinning-knife. Yet he did not cut the string. For a while he stood, looking down on the parcel, the knife held under the cord. His mouth softened in a smile, and slowly he, laid aside the knife.

He untied the knots with his fingers, asking himself who he was, to cut with a knife knots that the fingers of Hester Long had made? And when he had accomplished the task and spread out the covering, he discovered a book with light-blue covers. It was of foolscap size, and when he lifted a cover he saw that it was a new day-book. The pages were crisp and white, and at the top of each was a line of writing.

Bending low, he read the writing, done in a neat round-hand, and found that each page was headed with a date beginning with 6th of April. Between cover and fly-leaf was a half-sheet of cheap notepaper, on which was written:

A steam-engine has, of necessity, a safety-valve. Write your thoughts daily in this book. You will find keeping a diary a safety-valve, something through which you can pour off all those little things you feel unable to tell anyone.

HESTER LONG.

For a long time Arnold Dudley sat beside the table, thinking. Before he went to bed he got out pen and ink and wrote a few words on the flyleaf of the book.

CHAPTER XVI

DUDLEY'S STEP FORWARD

THE Sunday following Dudley broke his promise to Hester Long. The decision that he could not keep it was made on the Saturday night, when he went over his trap-line with a hurricane-lamp. The line lay parallel with the beach, and at its farther end he climbed to the summit of the dividing sand-ridge and sat and gazed out over the sea, bathed in the light of the moon.

The vivid daylight colours were reduced to a couple of silvery shades. Under the moon the heaving sea appeared the colour of new silver. On either side stretched a vast sheet of old silver, tarnished by the ages. The beach itself showed as a moonbeam sent downward beyond a veil of falling rain, whilst the sand-ridges took to themselves the shapes of strange blotched beasts deep in slumber.

Seated there alone in limitless space Arnold Dudley came to feel his solitude. In that immensity he was as much a castaway as the lone sailor on a frail raft in the middle of a shipless ocean; but, whereas the sailor is cast away through misfortune, Dudley was cast away by his own act. For the first time full realization of that situation was evidenced to him.

He had killed a man. Deliberately he had waited to kill. Apart from the ethics of the deed, its justice or otherwise, he had not the right to kill. The law of the country expressly forbade killing. In effect, the law laid it down that, no matter what the wrong, the wronged must not kill. It applied even to those cases where the law was helpless to right the wrong done. Civilization demands that there shall be no killing; the demand is based on self-preservation, which itself is blind instinct. A man who kills is hanged, but a man who robs another man of his woman and his honour is let off with a cash fine. In one way the fine assesses the woman's value. A price is set on her chastity, and the price varies according to her social station. A poor woman's chastity may well be assessed at ten pounds, and a rich woman's chastity at ten thousand. To assess chastity in money is indeed not to honour woman.

Dudley came to see the dishonouring of Ellen in a new light. It mattered little if his wife's honour was valued or not valued. It mattered still less if the seducer was com-pelled to pay for his destruction of it with ten pounds or ten thousand pounds, or with his life. If it were possible to compel him to pay ten thousand millions, or his life ten times over, the woman would not regain her chastity.

Had civilization decreed that the dishonoured husband be permitted himself to hang his wife's seducer, there would be remarkably few domestic tragedies; for, unlike the murderer, who ninety times out of a hundred is mentally unbalanced, the seducer of a married woman is sane enough to weigh the consequences. But civilization decreed that a seducer must not be killed, decreed that the fallen wife should be ticketed in pounds, shillings, and pence.

Dudley saw that, being a unit of civilization, he had outraged it by his killing of Tracy. And outraged civilization would avenge itself by killing him if and when it received the chance. It would ally itself with the dead Tracy against him. The shooting of Tracy was not merely a violence done to Tracy, it was a violence done to civilization.

Cain slew Abel and was branded by God. Dudley had killed Tracy and was branded by man. He sat there above the silver sea, lonely and in solitude, because he was so branded, because he feared death at the hands of man ; and because, if he died at the hands of man for the killing of Tracy, Tracy's blood atonement for the wrong done would be wiped out, and the wrong would remain unpunished to the debit of civilization.

That was the basic reason why Arnold Dudley was there. A normal man, he wanted to live, but sincerely hoped that when death did come he would be able to meet it with fortitude. Life becoming as it then was, death would be welcomed if that death was not the result of his killing of Tracy.

Dudley's heart, as Pharaoh's of old, remained hardened.

Yet he came to take one step forward towards clearing his destiny. Fully recognizing what he was in the eyes of man, without questioning what he had become in the eyes of God, he saw that to fulfil his promise to Hester Long would be to place her in danger of legal trouble. She knew he was a murderer. The law demanded of her to become an informer, an accuser. That she was an ally, a defender, was, of course, natural to a woman like Hester Long. She insisted on continuing as his ally at least, and because of that Dudley saw that he must protect her against the greatness of her heart.

Not again could he go to her house. To do so would but continue to expose her to the vengeance of the law. It would be an act unworthy of an honourable, a decent man. It would be repaying her gifts of gold with base metal.

Solitude weighed heavily on him that night. The killing of Tracy had made him accursed, a man forced to shun his fellows, unable to accept the hand of human friendship, because acceptance would endanger the owner of that hand.

It was as though the soul of Tracy laughed at him in mocking triumph. It was as though Tracy and he had been playing a game of poker. Tracy had won the Jack-pot when it was Jack high. He, Dudley, had scooped the pool when it was Ace high ; and now that the game was Jacks-on-the-Down Tracy had won again—won all that Dudley had won, and a little more besides. Yet the game between Arnold Dudley and Edmund Tracy was not finished. It was to proceed even up to the point when Dudley would toss his all in the pool between them.

The sea midway between him and the horizon became strangely darkened, and it was this quite ordinary phenomenon that roused him from reverie. Glancing up, he saw creeping over the moon a small but dense cloud. Its eastern side was thick and reflected the moonlight dazzlingly white. The cloud was flanked by others, and they were the advance guard of an unbroken mass sweeping in from the west.

The shadow on the glittering silver sheet raced towards him, uncontrollable as the tide. Second by second the silver sea was blotted out, second by second it shrank shoreward, now a broad ribbon, now a narrow ribbon, now but a wisp of silver straw. The gleaming beach faded magically. To Dudley it seemed as though the beach and he were being hurled through space into the shadow. It fell over him as a garment of dark purple velvet, and, standing up, he turned to see the shadow eating up the sand-dunes and tiny valleys, and finally the towering sand-hills beyond.

Was it indeed rushing towards envelopment by the shadow of destiny? What lay behind that night and the to-morrow? Darkness! Eternal Darkness, wherein happiness and life are no more!

Far out at sea he saw a patch of twinkling jewels. As though an Aladdin's genie had created them from nothing, the jewels increased in number. They lay thickly, spreading every second north and south and east. The edge of them rolled towards him as the unrolling of a magic carpet. The sea-swept rocks were littered by countless diamonds. The sea-foam was laced with them.

Out of the darkness sprang the beach in all its snowy purity. The purple velvet cloak was torn from him, and once more he stood in the radiant light. The darkness had been but a veil. Was he to pass through that other veil of darkness to gain the light of Eternity?

Fantasy! It was only cloud shadows on the sea. Shadows only, preceding a greater shadow that spelled rain. Picking up his lamp and his bag of rabbit-skins, Dudley made his way to the end of the trap-line. Two hours had elapsed since he had last gone over it. Some of the traps held wide-eyed, terrified animals. These he did not reset. The others he sprang in passing by, merely pressing down the plate with his boot.

The rain came before he reached camp. It rained as it can rain along that coast, and long before he arrived at his canvas home he was drenched to the skin. The fire was drowned out. The clock on the empty case at the head of his stretcher-bed notified him that it was twenty minutes past two.

The butcher-bird awakened him at dawn. It sang merely a few bars, in a tone that expressed no joy. The rain still beat on the tent roof, little and big drops being clearly distinguishable by sound. It fell in sharply accentuated rattles driven before a rising wind, and from the beach came the voice of the surf, raised in an angry snarl.

Arnold Dudley was thankful for the rain. Hester Long would not now expect him. He was thankful, too, that he had sprung the traps, for by doing so he was not compelled to go out over the line to take out a few unfortunate rabbits. He had worked hard that week, averaging probably eighteen hours in every twenty-four, and the coming of the rain gave him an excuse to lie abed. Good old rain! I t would make Hester Long's new-ly-cleared fifty acres leap into green life.

When again he awoke it was eleven o'clock. He rolled and smoked a cigarette before dressing. The rain still fell, but the wind was half a gale. From beneath his bunk he drew out a box of pine chips, stored there for such a day as this, and with them soaked in kerosene he made a roaring, leaping fire that defied the rain and beat off the chill of wind.

It is a peculiarity of solitude, acting on the brain of a man, that he becomes given to impulse far more than is the case under normal con-ditions. Unless he holds to strict self-discipline he will inevitably slide downhill to a mental morass in which personal cleanliness and care for what he eats become almost non-existent. Every little task concerned with the welfare of the body becomes too utterly boring to perform. He sinks finally to the level of the ape.

Whilst Arnold Dudley still performed the ablutions and shaving as fastidiously as when living in civilization; he had unconsciously arrived at the stage when cooking food was a task to be got through as easily or lazily as possible. To open a tin of herrings or corned beef was easier than catching and cooking fish. Baking-powder bread was a necessity, as also was boiling the billy for tea.

The supply of potatoes and onions he had bought in Dongara months before had been thrown away, rotting. He had lived principally on canned food, damper, and tea. Apart from the labour of cooking a rabbit, Dudley never ate one. Only a few Australian rabbit-trappers can bring themselves to eat rabbit. Whilst lying in his bunk that rainy Sunday morning, however, he felt the impulse to cook himself a proper breakfast.

The inconvenience of doing this with the rain pouring on sizzling bacon and eggs was not so great as being compelled to eat it sitting on his bunk inside the tent. Therefore that afternoon he dumped his canned food and many accessories on a flooring of sticks outside the tent and covered the heap with bags. The space thus gained enabled him to rebuild the table within the tent. Several other small jobs were attended to, and by the time darkness fell he was better able to meet the approaching conditions of winter, and sat down to his dinner of a slice of boiled bacon, flanked by potatoes and hot tinned peas, with a dish of stewed apples and a cup of black coffee to follow.

An hour later he sat at the table with Hester Long's gift lying open at the page apportioned to that day's date. Impulsive again, he had decided to take her advice and write down the things in his heart clamouring to be told to sympathetic ears. For a little while he read and re-read the words he had written on the fly-leaf, and for a little while gazed through his cigarette smoke at the lamp with eyes that saw it not.

Presently he took up a pen, dipped it in the ink, and wrote two words, when he paused before writing a third. That third word he never did write. For half an hour he wrote rapidly, when the page was filled with his somewhat neat handwriting, and than he rolled a cigarette and, after lighting it, read what he had written.

DEAR HESTER—

You seem to be totally unaware of the kind of woman you really are, and it seems far from being right that you should stoop to reach a man with blood upon his hands. There is a saying that "They that touch pitch will be defiled", and of all women I have known you must not be defiled by contact with me. You and I are what we are. You had the courage and the intelligence to make adversity serve you and not be governed by it as I was governed when the test came. You were as clear cold water untouchable by the fires of human emotion; I was as inflammable spirit to an electric spark.

I know the reason why you made me promise to dine with you and your boys every Sunday. You thought that that single connecting link with human friendship would save me from utter damnation. You exacted the promise not merely because you delighted to entertain, but because you could not fail to stoop and lift a poor wretch as that other was tended by the Good Samaritan.

I cannot keep the promise, and I am not a little perturbed at that, and regret keenly having given it. Your estimation of me will fall, and yet I broke my promise because you are what you are, Hester Long.

To have kept it, to have continued the friendship you have given me, would have been for me to repay good with evil. I killed Tracy because he robbed me of my most valuable possession—the love of my wife. I feel no remorse whatever. I know he deserved to lose his life. I know that he did not love Ellen as a decent man loves a woman. I know he seduced her to gratify his passions and his vanity. I know why he seduced married women—so that the natural consequences of his alliance might be shifted to the woman's husband. He was not man enough to face the same consequences for a single woman.

That is why I killed him. If he had been honestly in love with Ellen, and she with him, had he been honestly desirous of marrying Ellen divorced from me, I would have given her the opportunity to be free of me. If he had come and manfully told me that he loved her, wanted her as a wife, and up to that time had acted honourably, I would not have shot him.

The world would say, and says, that I am a murderer. In my heart I know I am not a murderer, any more than is a lawful hangman. You believe I am not a murderer. So does Miss Mallory. But no other would. It is more than possible that the long arm of the law will find me even here, and when it does find me I must be no friend of yours ; I must be the friend of none, least of all of you, whom I esteem almost reverently.

The rain beats down on my tent. There is no other sound but the surf. I can almost hear my heart beating.

To-morrow will be as yesterday, and next week as this week——

Arnold Dudley sighed and closed the book, and fell to thinking of that awful afternoon when he had heard voices within his wife's room. He saw again the slowly-opening door. Again he saw the comical expression on Tracy's face before he collapsed, as though he were utterly surprised at being killed by an enraged husband. At that point Dudley pulled himself up. He was beginning to realize that it was necessary to govern his thinking. Time itself was softening the blaze of his hate, and deliberately to undo the work of Time would be a foolish thing.

Yet what else was there to do but think? He had no books, not even an old newspaper. He had not wanted to see anything in print about his crime. Now, for the first time since his banishment, he felt the need of papers and books. He did not know it, but this was a healthy sign. His mind was satiated with itself, it was seeking something other than itself to feed upon. Undoubtedly he was rapidly becoming normal—that is, mentally normal.

It was not eight o'clock. To sleep then after his late rising was impossible, and, impulsive for the third time he brought forth his mouth-organ and played, seated at the table, his elbow resting on it.

Finlay had said often, not entirely in jest, that if he could play a mouth-organ as Arnold Dudley played it, he would go through life playing at hotel bars and keeping perpetually drunk on the free drinks showered upon him. In common with most bushmen, Dudley had taught himself to while away the hours in lonely camps.

He played hymns first: "Now the day is ended", and "Knocking ! knocking! who is there ?" But presently he broke into waltz music rendered in very slow time and with infinitely delicate variations.

It was whilst playing "Drifting down a silver river" that a king moth as large as a man's hand flew into the tent and spiralled round the lamp before alighting between Dudley's elbows. Quite suddenly he stopped to look at it with admiration of its marvellous markings.

And distinctly he heard somewhere outside a horse champ at its bit.

From the moth his gaze tried to pierce the canvas walls of his tent and the impenetrable darkness without. So sure was he of what he had heard that he passed out into the rain and called:

"Who's there?"

No reply came to his question. Blanketed, beaten down by the moisture in the air, the surf rumbled and moaned. The hiss of raindrops on drenched scrub leaves and the soft patter of raindrops on sand were the only other sounds.

"Is there anyone there?" he called again, this time doubtfully.

Deciding that his ears had tricked him, he turned to re-enter the tent, and paused as though turned to stone when he heard the soft creak-creak of leather. Into his mind flashed two words, words brilliantly lit by imagination:

"Mounted police!"

So the long arm of the law had reached him! The police were surrounding him, believing him desperate, knowing him to be armed. Well, he would not fight, certainly he would not attempt to shoot. The men were but doing their duty. There would be a trial. He would be the focus of public attention for a little while. Then would come early one morning a man with shackles to lead him out to death. What of it? He was tired. And no longer was life desirable.

He waited for the rush. It did not come. Only the sound of the rain and of the surf fell on his straining ears. He brought out the light and stepped on the track, peering between the walls of bush. No horse was to be seen. But there, a few yards from the tent, he did find a horse's track in the soft yielding sand—the tracks of one horse only. They told him that a horseman had come to that point, halted a while, and had gone back up the track.

For a long time after that he sat in his tent and waited.

CHAPTER XVII

TEMPTATION

AT the first hint of dawn the next morning Dudley's butcher-bird put unusual energy into its singing. It appeared incredible that so great a volume of sound should emanate from so small a body, but little larger than an English thrush. For a full five minutes the melodies were rendered one after the other without an instant's pause. The music awoke Dudley; and, before he arose and dressed and passed outside to the light the fire, he knew that there was not a cloud in the sky.

It was a day like one of those rare March days in England which almost persuade one that it is mid-June. The moisture still on the leaves of the scrub accentuated their greenness. The absence of wind permitted the scrub scents to be wafted low on the ground by the unnoticeable air eddies and currents made by the warmth of the rising sun. Dudley yawned, stretched luxuriously, and smoked his before-breakfast cigarette with thorough enjoyment.

Until the second that recollection came of the night-visitor.

During his breakfast, thoughts of the visit worried him. He was worried because the visit was not followed by immediate action. That it was a police visit he felt certain, and because the horseman had retreated he concluded that the retreat had been for the purpose of securing rein-forcements. That made him smile wryly. There was not a little humour in one man going back for help to arrest a man quite willing to be arrested. However, the visitor could not have been expected to know that.

For Dudley had reached the point of mental resignation which ordained no effort to escape the law when once the law had discovered him. In his inmost heart he believed thoroughly in the ancient maxim that "murder will out". Also he was intelligent enough to know that once the law got on his footprints it would be but a matter of time before it caught up with him. Nevertheless, he must make sure whence came that night-rider, for he was a man who hated doubt, as was shown at the beginning of this history.

Breakfast over, he slipped a handful of cartridges into a pocket, and, taking his double-barrelled breech-loader, set off on a tracking expedition. In no sense was the gun taken to resist arrest. He took it by force of a habit, formed years before, of going out equipped to destroy vermin as opportunity served.

In spite of the rain that had fallen since the tracks were made, they were quite distinct on the moist white sand of the dunes. Only in the deeper dells where the ground was of black soil had the rain washed out the traces completely. They kept to the twisting switchback roadway, right up over Big Hill and beyond throughout the three miles, until the gate was reached in the fence skirting the main coast road.

Once through the gate, he expected to see them turn south towards Dongara. Yet the muddy sand-outlined points of horse's hoofs indicated clearly that the rider had come from, and had returned to, the north. When he saw that, the riddle was explained.

His non-appearance at Hester Long's farm had sent one of two women out into a wet and pitch-dark night to ascertain if he had been unable to come through physical disability, or had merely-forgotten. And, because he knew very little about women, he docketed the incident in his mind as feminine inquisitiveness.

By that time the sun had dried the bush trees and shrubs, and he decided to walk straight over sand-hill and bluff to the south-west till he reached the coast, there to walk northward along the beach until he came to the Pontoon. That decision, at least, was not an impulse.

He had long wanted to scout the surrounding country, to ascertain if there were dogs or foxes about, and, if so, their likely number.

He knew, of course, that to walk through that dense low bush would not be so easy as walking a city pave-ment, even during peak hours. He was obliged to push his way through the scrub, at times to make a detour round a particularly dense belt, and from the moment he left the road his direction led him upward along the steep slopes of a gigantic hill of sand.

A passing crow, observing him as a possible food-producer, circled and alighted far above him to watch with cunning white-lidded eyes. In all probability it was one of half a dozen who long before had found it worth while to keep this particular human under observation. For this human left rabbit carcasses about. He left scraps at his camp, too, but the butcher-birds saw to it that the precincts of the camp were well pro-tected against crows.

Rabbits there were a-plenty, and Dudley noted how the coming of the rain and the approach of winter made them excessively wild. High in the sky, so high indeed that the eyes failed to follow it continuously, circled an eagle. Possibly it was three thousand feet overhead, yet it watched Dudley, too, and would see if Dudley dropped a match. He wondered why it was that eagles never flew over the beach.

It took him an hour to gain the summit of the enormous sand-hill, and there the scrub was no higher than a man's knee. He sat down then to observe and enjoy the view. To north and south stretched the coast-hills, looking to him like a carpet in three colours—one of those old-fash-ioned cottage carpets laboriously made of innumerable strips of cloth. The green-black patches denoted the dells and gullies, the light-green splashes the hill-slopes, the greyish-white the summits of those hills so wind-blown that no scrub could take root.

Westward lay the blue ribbon of sea, its nearest edge frayed by sand-ridges, its farther edge bounded by the sharp unbroken line of the horizon. Away to the east, beyond the long valley down which came the Geraldton road, other valleys jutted into it, and one could surmise that they were originally sea inlets and the arms of high sea headlands, and that the coast sand-hills were of comparatively recent origin.

Far to the south a cluster of white buildings marked the homestead of the Smythes. Nearer, to the north-east, Dudley could see the white house and paddocks belonging to Hester Long; and that occupied by the Mallorys farther north still. Beyond those farms stretched the uncleared bush, as far as the eye could see, bush-land awaiting the settler when it was freed from the relentless grip of the land monopolists.

Almost in Dudley's chosen line of direction he espied, at the foot of the hill on which he then was, a large natural clearing, whose existence till then he had never suspected. Towards this clearing he made his way, and when he got down to its level he came across a very old cattle-pad, which he followed until he reached the edge of the clear space, covering ten or eleven acres.

It was of deep rich soil, and was one of Nature's surprises. Despite the obvious depth and richness of the soil, despite the fact that knee-high grass grew over it, there was not one single tree or bush. A veritable rabbits' paradise, there could be seen quite equally spaced the bare surface of some twenty enormous rabbit burrows. Hundreds of rabbits squatted on the burrows dozens played at the edges of the burrows where the grass was eaten down ; and yet dozens more raced along the lanes through the thick grass. And all those rabbits were utterly oblivious to the fact that a fox was busily digging up one of the burrows.

Whilst it dug, Dudley could see the red-brown arched back behind which was flying a constant shower of moist earth. Now and then the digging temporarily ceased, when the fox sat down for a rest, which brought its head up from the hole to gaze around with lolling jaws and eyes that held no fear.

At heart Arnold Dudley was a naturalist, as indeed is every successful trapper. He knew what purpose lay behind that furious digging. When rabbits were first liberated in Australia, they were governed by habits or instincts adapted to the conditions of their countries of origin. The does hid their young in shallow holes well away from the burrows. With the coming of the fox to Australia, he, like the rabbit, increased enormously. He thrived on the young rabbits, at first so very easily obtained.

Animals, we are informed, are unable to reason. It is a thesis difficult for a bushman to believe. The rabbit, coming to understand that its method of leaving its young in shallow holes during the day would determine its extinction, now rears its young in the depths of deep burrows, in some cases yards below the surface. The fox, also supposedly without reason, does not follow a rabbit-run down to the youngsters' nest. Either by scent or hearing, probably the latter, the fox digs straight down from the surface to the nest.

Every time the fox in the clearing went on digging down to its little luxury, Arnold Dudley moved a few more yards round the clearing towards it, being careful to keep hidden behind a scrub tree. The buck rabbits saw him and thumped their warnings. The fox became uneasy and his spells of digging were shortened. From two-minute breathing spaces he advanced to five minutes, thence to ten.

At sixty yards Dudley fired his choke-barrel, and a quarter of an hour later had the fox skinned from nose to tail-tip. The time expended was well repaid. For the head and tail the Government would pay a bonus of two pounds, and the skin at that time of the year was worth at least ten shillings.

The shooting of the fox, the poisoning of the shark, the visit of the sportsmen and those of Hester Long, were as landmarks to Dudley during his sojourn on the Beach of Atonement. They were the rare breaks in his otherwise monotonous existence. As milestones passed in a fast motor-car are noticeable against long strips of uninteresting country between, those incidents stood out milestones in Dudley's uneventful life.

They were events to look back upon, to keep fresh in memory like ports of call during a long ocean voyage. Of necessity, in a written history they occur in close succession ; therefore it must be emphasized that during Dudley's solitude the periods of drudgery and the periods of self-contemplation were enormously protracted as compared with the few fleeting occasions of exceptional interest.

Whereas the walk from his camp to the road had taken barely an hour, almost three hours were occupied pushing through the bush from the road to the beach some two miles south of the Pontoon. Cresting the last sand-ridge, the blue of the sea and the white of surf and sand that brilliant day brought to his mind the gaudy pictures of home or foreign resorts used in advertising sea trips. In all that panorama of land and sea there were remarkably few colours, but those colours were astoundingly brilliant.

Tired, he seated himself on the ridge, rolled himself a cigarette, and fell to wondering which of the women had braved the darkness of a wet night to ascertain if he were all right. And, whilst thus thinking, half an hour later he heard the same sound which had come out of the night. A horse champed its bit. It made him leap to his feet and swing round, and then he saw down in the gully behind the beach a black, spirited gelding on which sat Edith Mallory.

The distance between them was a possible sixty feet, and for quite sixty seconds the two regarded each other with unconscious interest. She saw a lithe athletic man, dressed in dungaree trousers, and blue cotton shirt opened wide at the neck and the sleeves rolled to his elbows a man whose hair glinted as old copper in the sun, and possessing, set in a ruddy handsome face, a pair of keen, narrow-lidded, hazel eyes, He saw seated on a young horse the spirit of feminine youth, a vision of feminine loveliness entrancing enough to dazzle a St. Anthony.

She, too, was hatless. Her unsheared hair glinted as new copper wire, wire so fine that there seemed to be millions of strands. A pair of wide blue eyes set in a rose-complexioned face gazed up at him with an expression wholly baffling. And when she dismounted with effortless grace he came to appreciate for the first time her beauty of face and form. It was then he spoke.

"Good morning, Miss Mallory!" he called out affably. "Come along up and say how-do-you-do to my Beach."

Waiting, he watched her tie the horse's reins to a bush before climbing up the sand-slope to his side. He saw that she then did not look at him, nor did so until she had gazed first north and then south over the wide stretch of sand and rolling surf.

"Mrs. Long is anxious to know why you didn't go there to dinner yesterday," she said, with evident serious-ness. "You promised to go every Sunday."

"Promises, like laws, are made to be broken."

"Not by nice people." He found himself regarded in her old provocative way, through eyes that examined him with curious interest.

"I am not a nice person," he pointed out.

"Don't let us equivocate," she said, stressing slightly the pronoun. She waited as though still desirous of an explanation. For a second their eyes met, his full of bitter sarcasm, hers undeniably stern, with the sternness of youth.

"Let us sit down and talk," Dudley proposed, and when he was seated with her face turned to the sea he went on.

"You know, don't you, that I killed a man?"

Her lips moved, and very, faintly came the affirmative.

"You know what they call a man who kills—a murderer," Dudley said quietly. "That neither you nor Mrs. Long has, so far, informed the police of my whereabouts makes you both my accomplices or accessories after the fact, or something equally obnoxious to the law. Both of you have been kind to me, exceedingly kind. It would, indeed, be a poor way of returning your kindness were I to risk the law finding me in your presence and discovering that you know me for what I am."

Pausing, he waited for her comment. None came, so he went on:

"You see; by accepting Mrs. Long's hospitality in these circumstances, I am taking advantage of her goodness. Also you must see that my association with her children is not, and could not be, good for them. They must not grow up influenced in the slightest degree by contact with such as I am. I am sorry I made her a promise, but her wonderful kindness to me made me forget for the time that I am a criminal. Will you please explain what I have said to her?"

"No."

"Why not?" Dudley stared at her in surprise.

"Just because!"

"Why not tell me?"

He was looking at the clear-cut profile and saw the white lids flutter before her eyes. And quite suddenly the face was turned on him and in her eyes were tears. They surprised him more than her refusal to convey to Hester Long the reason of his failure to keep his word.

"Don't you understand that Hester is one of the sweetest women alive?" she cried. "Haven't you yet found out that she is the most understanding woman in the world? Do you think that if she thought for a moment that your presence would harm her children, for whom she had fought and is fighting so hard a battle to protect from poverty and harm, she would have asked you to spend every Sunday with them?"

The fervency of her utterance surprised him yet further. Her effort to keep calm during what, to him, was a matter-of-fact discussion puzzled him. He remained silent, a silence that invited her to proceed.

"Have you ever read the New Testament?" she asked.

"I read it right through once."

"Do you remember if Christ turned away from a sinner —a murderer even?"

"No."

"Then why should Hester Long? Why should I? You say you are a murderer, meaning that you are some-thing foul. As though you wanted to rob the man you killed of something, whereas he had robbed you of something he could never give back, even had he wished: I—I'm afraid I can't reason very well, Mr. Cain; but it does seem to us that you had right and justice on your side.

"Then, again, once Hester had cause to feel as you felt when you found out things. She doesn't know I know, and never you breathe a word! There was a woman who tried to get her husband. She lives in Dongara. She tried her hardest in a most brazen way, and Hester had to fight to keep her husband. Not openly, you know. Hester Long's too fine a woman for that. If I had been Hester Long I would—would have killed her."

Dudley shook his head.

"No, you wouldn't," he argued in an effort to change her mood, which he could not understand. "You are too sensible for that. Quite aside from the immorality of my act, the act was that of a fool. Mrs. Long was right there. I should have let them alone. Time would inevitably have avenged me much better than a bullet. What we have to consider is that the act was committed, that the law of the country says that such an act is murder, and clearly states that the penalty is death. It also lays it down that to knowingly harbour a murderer is an offence to be punished. Mrs. Long, I know, willingly risks punishment. We agree that she does so because of her wonderful sympathy; but that makes it all the more urgent for me not to permit her to run the risk.

"You see, Miss Mallory, don't you? I am doomed to live an outcast life. To accept friendship is to risk involving my friends in my troubles. You two are just wonderful in keeping my secret. Your thoughts of me and for me are worthy of a better object."

"But you can't go on living like this?" she expostulated, her face vivid with sudden colour.

"I must, for I can't go on living otherwise. I must lie on the bed I've made."

"The bed is not of your making," she said fiercely.

After that outburst she fell silent, and they both stared out over the sea. Presently he sighed, knowing not why. When he again looked at her he saw tears slowly falling down her cheeks.

"Why, Miss Mallory, you're not crying, surely? Have I said any-thing to hurt you?"

"Everything you say hurts me. Everything about you hurts me. I hate to see you here on this lonely beach. I hate to think of you being here. There is no justice in it. I—I— Oh! won't you go away? Can't you go to some other country where you could mix with people and be happy?"

"Happy! I shall never again be happy."

"But would you go? I could—I could lend you money to go with, and you could pay me back some day. I—I wouldn't want any interest, of course, excepting just a letter now and then. I'd like to know where you were, and if you were happy."

Arnold Dudley was too fine a man to laugh or sneer at her suggestion. He saw that, after all, she was almost a child, quite inexperienced in the world—a child who evidently liked him, and wanted impulsively to help. He said gravely:

"You are very kind, and I appreciate the spirit in which the offer is made. To go back to a city, even in a far country, would not help me to be happier. Every time I saw happiness it would embitter me further. I would rather stay here on what has become my beach. Yet, if you wish it, I will go away, far away, and find another beach. Although why you should wish it I don't know."

"I can't tell you."

Suddenly she stood up. Her eyes were dry and clear and shining. They made him think of Ellen's eyes when she first had loved him, and often after they were married. And then he knew. She was too unsophisticated to hide it from him. He never knew how it was that he came to hold her hands in his, and stand looking down into her upturned face. Even his voice sounded in his ears as that of another man.

"Don't tell me," he advised her gently. And then, with well-assumed harshness, he said sharply: "I'm a married man. I am a murderer. My wife is still alive." Their hands fell away. He saw the hurt in her face and said stiffly: "Good-bye Miss Mallory!"

Rudely he turned his back on her. He heard her moving away, and twice he heard her sob. When three long minutes had passed he turned, to see her riding slowly over the crest of a northern sand-ridge. She never looked back, and when she had gone Arnold Dudley flung himself down and hid his face in his arms.

For when he had heard her sob a small thin voice had whispered: "She loves you, Arnold. Take her—take her—take her!"

CHAPTER XVIII

BATTLING WITH SATAN

FOR the next ten days Arnold Dudley worked at high pressure, forced on by a mental feverishness that had had its re-birth in the meeting with Edith Mallory on the southern sand-hill.

The first long battle with the devil of sex had ended when Hester Long rescued him from a drunken debauch —had ended in the utter rout of the devil. Hester Long's influence had been an all-powerful ally, and so long as that influence continued the outcast had enjoyed a period of mental quietude. A man living in a great city, or even a small town is armoured by various interests, amusements, books, ambitions. A man living alone, cut off from his fellow men, utterly without the armour of the city man, is wholly defenceless. Not only that, but the unnatural life he leads is a breach in his defences, a breach inviting attack by his hereditary instincts, and this crafty sex devil strikes when the defender least expects the attack or has temporarily forgotten the enemy.

When Edith Mallory, herself going through a hell of unrequited love, unconsciously betrayed herself to the man she adored, she gave the devil of sex his chance to strike. The blow was shrewdly given. The effect was first to tempt Arnold Dudley to take advantage of his new-won knowledge that Edith loved him. That temptation he successfully resisted—a success highly creditable to one in his position—but the effect passed on, and inflamed his old longing for the reciprocal love of Ellen.

The revelation of Edith Mallory came to be an obstacle lying in the straight path of his desires—an obstacle that had temporarily balked, but one that he had rounded easily, thence to continue along the straight path.

For to the one man was the one woman. Dudley's love for his wife was supreme. In the years before he met Ellen he had flirted with several women more or less seriously. He thought then that each flirtation was the manifestation of love. He knew that that was not so when he came to love Ellen. After three years of married life his love for Ellen was far more profound than before their marriage. The intimacy of married life proved the real foundation of sexual love. In Ellen he found the twin of himself, the second half of every human being. The realization of that, the tranquil satisfaction it gave him, had possibly made him a little inclined to take Ellen's love for granted, but not a whit the less appreciative of it.

Edmund Tracy had disrupted that sublime state. Yet so powerful a hold had it got over Dudley's very existence that, had it not been for his disastrous crime, he would gladly have taken Ellen back, and honestly tried to banish from his mind the incident of Tracy so that he and Ellen might re-enter their former blissful estate.

In his solitude that former blissful estate remained the one goal of life worth striving for. It was not so much woman that his body craved for, as Ellen for whom his spirit craved. His solitude taught him that Ellen's body was a magnet to the metal filings of his body in a far less degree than the magnet of Ellen's soul to the meal of his. The possession of Ellen satisfied the longings of body and soul alike, which was the intention of God when he created Eve.

Had Ellen died, Dudley never again would have taken a wife. City interests would have armoured him against the sex devil, relieved him of the terrible warfare of sex instincts, enabled him to go on living his life steadfastly alone, keeping before him the ideal of his past life with Ellen.

The ideal was yet his, in spite of the devil's subtle assaults. The assaults at first only caused more poignant desire for the ideal state of marriage which had been his. Succeeding assaults showered upon him in his defencelessness wore his nerves to a thin edge, and drove his mind to the very verge of insanity.

The temptation to take what Edith Mallory offered him when she gazed straight at him with shining eyes affected him little, in comparison with the dreams that disturbed his short snatches of slumber. They were not dreams quickly forgotten, if remembered at all. They were dreams vivid, in perfect sequence of action and time.

In them he was chained to his bed with Ellen standing beside it, her hair dishevelled, her face distorted by mental anguish, in her eyes that shining light that every man has seen in the eyes of a woman who loves him. Trying to rise, he knew he was unable, and coming to know that he watched, Ellen slowly retreated from him as though drawn back and away by the spirit of Tracy.

Or they would be standing each on a rock with a chasm between them. Ellen would smile at him wistfully, the mystery of woman in her violet eyes, the lure of her sex visible about her adorable mouth. He would look at the chasm and see it could not be crossed, and then wildly seek a way round to her whilst slowly she drew away into the mist.

It was always thus. Always did Ellen invite him, always did she call to him. And always was he unable to respond, always was she drawn away from him.

From those dreams he awoke trembling. In a while the trembling subsided and a physical ache grew and grew into sharp pain below his heart. Whilst his body and his mind cried for rest he forced himself to rise and stride with faltering steps down to the beach or over the endless sand-ridges till dawn came, when he returned to his work and kept at it till nightfall and long after.

His mind flogged his tortured muscles into continuous action. Work was the antidote. Hester Long had said so repeatedly. Work, therefore, he did as seldom man has ever worked. His trap-lines radiated from his camp as the spokes of a wheel. In ten days he trapped over a thousand rabbits. Between visits to the traps he employed himself digging out the rabbits from their burrows, moving tons of sand. Or laboriously he tracked a fox for miles, and if he ran it to earth fell to like a maniac searching for gold in an ash-heap, digging that fox out of its hole.

Hester Long's advice that work was the healer of all spiritual wounds, was the weapon with which to defeat any kind of devil, was sound in so far as the receiver of the advice lived among his kind. Her advice failed to meet the needs of this man, living in unnatural solitude and haunted by such a love as he held for his wife.

There came a day when Dudley's body refused further to obey the commands of his mind, when even his brain refused to function. For seventy-two hours he had not slept. He had not dared to sleep. Those sweet, alluring dreams were too terrible to face. Night and day he had trapped and dug, drinking much tea, eating little food. It was a supreme effort to flee the torturer named Desire. And it failed. The torturer dogged his weary, shuffling feet, nudged his elbow constantly, and incessantly whispered in his ears:

"Ellen! The lovely Ellen! You've lost Ellen! Fool! Fool that you were to shoot Tracy! Tracy alive—and Ellen you might have re-won!"

On her way to the beach to ascertain why he had failed to keep his promise to take Sunday dinner with her and her boys, Hester Long came upon him sprawled across the winding track midway between his camp and the main road. He lay in a sharp bend, and her old horse stepped a yard from his rough-clothed body to gaze on it unconcernedly.

With the colour suddenly drained from her plain face, her clear grey eyes quickly clouded with dread, she bade the two children stay in the buggy whilst she jumped out and ran forward to the outcast. He lay on his face, which was pressed into the fine moist sand, one arm lay beneath him, the other stretched out beyond his head.

Hester Long, when she flung herself to her knees beside lane, had all she could do to repress a scream. She thought him dead, and, thinking this, came to know that she almost loved him. Her actions to herself appeared abnormally slow. Thoughts of Edith Mallory, and her hopeless love for this man, raced through her brain even when she touched Dudley's neck and found it warm. The relief that surged through her at discovering that he was not dead almost deprived her of power to regain her feet. Her face was aflame with glory the instant she stood over him, her head thrown back, her hands pressed to her breasts.

An instant of reaction only. Swiftly she bent down and turned him over. Sand, white and moist, lay scattered in his long brown hair. It adhered to the corners of his closed eyes and about his mouth. Death had spared him, for the sand had been too moist to trickle down into the cavity his face had made, which would have meant suffocation.

Hester Long moved his arms, and decided they were not broken. She could see no sign of injury. The drawn lines over his face made her want to cry out. She saw, with a catch in her breathing, how scrupulously shaved he was, and even whilst she looked on him the lines were banished by a tender smile, and from his lips came:

"Ellen, oh Ellen, stay with me!"

As suddenly as the smile came it passed. Again he spoke, but this time in his voice was anguish:

"Ellen ! Ellen ! Come back—come back!"

The watching woman's hands flew to her lips. Dudley struggled in his sleep, and sat up with the name of his wife voiced in loud tones. Looking into his opened eyes, she saw first comprehension, then perplexity, flash into them. The distended pupils frightened her. Then he smiled again, saying:

"Funny That's funny! The first time Hester Long ever took Ellen's place."

Then he sighed, sank back on the track, and, closing his eyes, slept again.

For a moment or so the puzzled woman stood irresolute. She could not understand precisely what was wrong. In any case, whatever might be wrong, Arnold Dudley could not be left there lying on damp ground with but a few hours of daylight remaining.

Taking him by the shoulders and partly lifting him, she dragged him along to the buggy step, whilst the youngsters demanded to know what was the matter with poor Mr. Cain.

"I don't know," Hester Long panted. "We must try to pull him into the buggy and drive him to his camp. Jim, get out and hold Brownie's head. Don't let him move, That's right ! Now Harold, old man, let us think."

A moment later she reached into the buggy and drew out the horse's neck-rope, and, fastening one end of it round Dudley under his arms, expertly tied a non-slipping knot. The other end she passed up to young Harold and told him to pull.

In spite of a degree of emaciation, Arnold Dudley was no light weight. In any case, a man's live body is the most awkward of all objects to lift. Hester Long exhibited amazing strength and tenacity. Her strength surprised even herself, whilst her brain cried out that the task must be accomplished. Little eight-year-old Harold manfully assisted, and at long last Dudley lay along the floor of the vehicle in a crumpled heap.

The youngster at the horse's head climbed up, and slowly the old horse drew the buggy uphill and down dale till Dudley's tent was reached.

Getting him down from the buggy was less arduous then getting him into it. Hester Long, unable to carry him, dragged him by the shoulders into the tent, pulled the blankets off the stretcher-bed, and heaved and panted in her final efforts to lift him on it.

Exhausted, she sank down on a wood case and looked at him for a minute or two whilst recruiting her strength; her children regarding first their mother and then the inert man who seemed to them always to be ill.

"Light the fire, Harold, and then fill a billy with water," she instructed, and, whilst both boys were thus busied, she removed Dudley's boots and covered him with blankets. Afterwards she searched his ration dump for meat extract, but, finding none, made a billy of strong coffee. When it was sufficiently cooled she took into the tent a pint pannikin, and set to work to arouse the sleep-drugged man.

Once again Dudley opened his eyes, red and hot, and blinked even at the soft canvas-filtered light. A frown of perplexity drew his brows together.

"Why, Mrs. Long! Why are you here?"

"We found you lying on the track, Mr. Cain," she replied with sudden briskness. "You must have fallen. Are you hurt?"

"Hurt! I don't think so. Yet my eyes are as heavy as lead. God! I'm tired."

"Well, just drink this. Please—please do," she urged.

"All right. If you wish… But I want to sleep. All right." With his eyes closed, Dudley drank all the coffee. Hester Long held him up with an arm about his neck, and when he had finished it, he murmured:

"Those traps! I must go over those traps again. I—I—"

Hester sighed. A poignant thankfulness made her supremely happy. If Dudley were merely tired, all was well. He appeared to be unhurt. Yet for all that his condition was a mystery, and the cause of it a greater mystery still. There was nothing further she could do, and it was needless to stay the few remaining hours of daylight. In the morning she would return.

Perplexed and worried, she turned the vehicle in the space cut out of the bush for the camp, and, explaining that Mr. Cain had been working too hard, she urged old Brownie up the steep slope of Big Hill and down its farther side to the gate and the main road. She came to persuade herself that her explanation of Dudley's condition to the children was the correct one, and, if that were so, if Dudley had worked himself to collapse, then the power of his wife over his mind must indeed be both subtle and marvellous.

They were half-way from the gate to the farm when she was obliged to pull to the near side of the road to allow an overtaking truck to pass. In its passing she saw a man of about fifty, with greying hair and ruddy-complexioned face, driving alone a truck that evidently was not new. A hundred yards ahead of her the man also drove to the near side of the road and pulled up. He got out, to walk slowly back to meet them, and when she pulled Brownie to a stop she found herself regarded by a pair of shrewd grey eyes half hidden by narrowed lids, which years of fierce sunshine seemed to have fixed perpetually.

"Good afternoon, marm!" he said. "Can you tell me whereabouts I turn off to reach the Nineteen Mile Beach?"

"Yes," was the instant reply. "It is back about a mile and a half from here. Are you going fishing?"

"Yes'm. As a matter of fact I am looking for a man. He is probably trapping. The storekeeper at Dongara told me that last September a stranger trapper came to Dongara and gave out he was going to trap along the coast at the Nineteen Mile Beach."

Hester Long's veiled eyes searched the man's face. In physique he was robust and well set up. It flashed into her mind that he might well be a detective, and at the thought, a mental picture of Dudley as she had left him was thrown on the screen of her mind, and her maternal instinct then and there prompted her to protect the outcast at all costs to herself. The assumed hardness she invariably adopted when doing business fell upon her in that instant, and thereupon she proceeded to embark on the telling of a chain of lies in a manner worthy of Ananias as prompted by his wife Sapphira.

"What is his name," she asked briskly.

There flashed into the truckman's eyes an expression of uneasy perplexity. There was distinct hesitation before he replied:

"I don't know what he calls himself."

That hesitation, followed by an obvious falsehood, decided Hester Long that the man was a detective. Her old suspicion that Hector Cain was not the outcast's real name was confirmed, but she decided that she would not take the risk of naming him. Incidentally she had forgotten the names uttered by him in his drunken. ravings.

"There was a trapper camped at the Nineteen Mile Beach," she said. "He came and worked for me for two weeks, as he didn't do any good there, or said he didn't. His name was Lowery, and he went up to Walk-away when he left me."

"What sort of a man was he, marm, to look at?"

"Tall and very thin," Hester Long said instantly, pre-pared for such a question.

"Clean-shaven, dark brown hair, hazel eyes?"

"I don't recollect his eyes or his hair," laughed Mrs. Long. "Clean-shaven, yes."

"Well-spoken chap?" pressed the stranger.

"Hum! Hardly that," came the lie. "A Londoner, I think he was—and not much of a hand at rabbit-trapping."

The other frowned, and gazed pensively at old Brownie. Hester Long saw that her disparagement of Dudley's trapping abilities had won for her the credit which her former lies had failed to do. Then:

"You seem anxious to find Mr. Lowery?"

"Yes. I am anxious. I've been looking for him since Christmas. I started at Geraldton and worked up to Meekatharra, and then down to Sandstone and Burracoppin, and round about Merredin and Bruce Rock. I'd like to get a sight of this man calling himself Lowery. What's his Christian name, do you know?"

"Yes. Hector."

"Umph ! When did he leave you?"

"About three weeks ago."

"How far is it to the beach when you get off the road at the Nineteen Mile?"

"Oh! About four miles," Hester replied with some dismay. "But you would never get there with a truck, I'm sure."

Keen grey eyes regarded her steadily. As steadily she returned the look. He looked away precisely one second before the mounting colour in her cheeks would have betrayed her.

"Well, I'll get along to Walkaway. Thank you!"

With relief she watched him stride to the truck. He appeared to be a long time starting the engine, and it seemed to her, too, that he drove very slowly northward towards Geraldton.

CHAPTER XIX

AT THE PRECIPICE EDGE

AT noon the next day, Hester Long, driving in her ancient, weather-worn buggy, reined in old Brownie at the summit of Big Hill. A boisterous south-westerly wind swept up the seaward slopes and gave velocity to the particles of white sand blown in her face.

The sea was a mass of white horses far beyond the Ramparts. From her elevation she saw them marked by an irregular line of heaving, tossing foam. The water about the Sugar Loaf leapt twenty feet in the air as often as it met the foaming surf; it boiled into snow over the sunken reef directly south of it, and crashed against the Pontoon, to be shot skyward in a long solid wall of water topped by a diaphanous veil.

The noise of it all came up to her in an incessant roar. Two miles to the north and two miles to the south the usually plainly-marked beach was indiscernible in the mist of spray and sand. The sand-ridges smoked as a thousand railway engines racing in all directions—smoked so that beyond three miles north and south all that was to be seen was a dun-covered fog. Above the maelstrom of wind-lashed water and sand, ominous-looking clouds rushed in never-ending succession across the watery sun.

It was cold. For Australia it was bitterly cold.

Tiny specks of white fluttered or were settled on the brown velvet knob of the Seaweed Mountain. Hester saw there the uneasy gulls. Her gaze moved slowly south to the hummock of sand immediately behind the Pontoon, there to remain whilst her eyes carefully examined the Seagulls' Throne.

Seated thereon, motionless, was Arnold Dudley; and at sight of him there amid his wild solitude Hester Long was sad.

Life! The cruelty of life! So especially cruel to men and women who have fallen. How little removed is man from the beast! A wounded wolf is killed and eaten by its kind. Let a man deviate an inch from the path of moral rectitude, and men fall on him and rend him. Let a woman fall, and women are ready and eager to keep her down.

Men had sent Arnold Dudley to sit on the Seagulls' Throne and watch the raging sea for the term of his natural life. They reckoned not the injury that man had done him, because the injured party was beyond the law. Dudley, still alive, was not beyond reach of the law, and men would satiate their lust of vengeance on him if ever he returned from exile. Buffeted by the wind, stung by spray and sand, his flesh blue with the cold, at the mercy of the elements: alone, tainted, marked, living out thus the few remaining days of his life, chained there on the beach as her eagles had been chained to the ground by rabbit-traps, and, also as the eagles, waiting for death itself to give release; the punishment seemed out of proportion to the crime.

The cold blast of wind was too much for her horse to face for any lengthy space of time, and without urging old Brownie started on the downward slope to the jumble of lesser hills nearer the coast. He was pulled up before the shelter of the beach sand-hill was left, and there taken out of the shafts and tethered to the wheel.

When she reached the open space where usually she camped with her boys and Edith Mallory, the wind tugged at her luxuriant hair beneath the comfortable velvet tam-o'-shanter, whipped the blood into her face, and brightened her eyes. Her slim, agile little body seemed as though in danger of being blown away, whilst slowly she climbed the hill of sand to come eventually to the side of Arnold Dudley who, seated on the Throne, stared vacantly across the welter of furious water.

The roar of the angry sea filled the world. Ribbed with white, it heaved and sank, its body almost black. Twenty-five times every minute a wall of deep green and snowy white leapt into existence along the entire seaward edge of the Pontoon, blotting out the horizon line already made almost invisible in the fog of spray swept from the summits of the combers beyond the Ramparts. Columns were spouted upward from south of the Sugar Loaf, which itself seemed the kernel of an everchanging mountain of suds.

Dudley, crouched on the Throne level with Hester Long's head, was watching the turmoil with complete absorption. He was totally unaware of the woman's presence until she reached up and tugged at his coat, and when he moved his head slowly to look down on her his eyes were vacant for many seconds.

"Come down, Mr. Cain! I want to talk to you," she called out, obliged to shout to make him hear her above the sound of furious waters.

Unsmilingly, showing neither pleasure nor annoyance at seeing her, Dudley heaved himself off the rock and stood beside her, looking down into her upturned, flushed face. The effort to talk there in the full blast of the wind was too great to be sustained, and, motioning him to follow her, she led down to the sand-patch and thence to her buggy in the shelter of the coast sand-dune. From the buggy she took the horse-hair stuffed seat and, laying it on the ground near one wheel, seated herself thereon, and invited him to sit with her.

"You are not looking well, Mr. Cain. What have you been doing with yourself?"

Looking into her eyes, he saw them bright with concern, and noted that her face was beautified by a smile, gentle and wistful, of understanding. It occurred to him in a detached way that Hester Long became in appearance a strangely different woman when she smiled. Her usual plain self was transfigured by a radiating light that made her far more beautiful than a beautiful woman in repose. The thought caused him to forget that she had asked him a question, and, since he did not speak, only stared at her, she repeated the question, and saw that he had to make a strong effort to bring his mind to even the simple task of answering it.

"I am all right, Mrs. Long," he said, mumbling.

His face was deeply bronzed, but his cheeks were sunken, and his mouth more prominent than it had been ; and his eyes, she saw, were sunken into his head beneath the brows drawn together by much mental concentration. His features told a tale of incessant hardship, but his eyes revealed the ravages of the fire that was consuming him. Quite impulsively she caught his forearm in her horny grip.

"Boy! you've been thinking too much," she said.

"Maybe," was his reply.

"What have you been doing since you came back here?"

"Working when awake; dreaming when asleep." Hunching his knees, he rested his elbows on them, and his face in his cupped hands.

"Tell me your dreams," she urged softly.

"They are always of Ellen." Arnold Dudley, in a dull monotone, described his haunting dreams. "Always has she wanted me, and always have I been unable to reach her. Is it not enough that every wakeful second I know I shall not again reach Ellen, but my sleep must torture me also? Work! God! how I've worked! Work is no use. It cannot help me, cannot give me peace and rest.

"For years I have loved Ellen. For years she and I have been always together. She grew on to my life like a rose-sprig grafted on an apple-sucker. She lived on my strength, and I lived on her sweetness. And then Tracy came. The rose-sprig was torn away from the apple-sucker, and now the frosts have seared the wound. I am like a man used for years to consume tobacco, and suddenly deprived of it. Just like such a man am I. Think of a man whose nerves are red raw because he is deprived of his cigarettes, and telling him that work is as great a sedative as tobacco. Take a drug-fiend and seal him up in the King's Chamber of the Pyramid of Cheops, and you may liken him to me."

"Fresh scenes may help," Hester Long suggested softly. "The novelty of this beach has worn away and there is little left to interest you. Why not go away? Why not travel up to Darwin and thence to Central Queensland? And, when you have been there a little while, you could get a passport and go out of Australia, to America, or to England. You cannot stay here. You can't go on like this."

"There is nothing else but to go on," he told her dully.

"Indeed there is," she said eagerly. "Let your beard and moustache grow. You'll be safely disguised in a week. If you haven't much money, I—I could lend you all you wanted."

For several seconds the man sat motionless. Her suggestion appeared to occupy that time to sink into his mind; but, when it had done so, he suddenly raised his head, straightened his legs, and turned to her sharply.

"Miss Mallory offered to lend me money to go away," he said. "Is she making the offer again through you?"

"No. I know nothing of what Edith has offered or suggested. I did not know she had spoken to you since you came back."

"Tell me," he demanded, "have you ever received the impression that I bore any affection for Edith Mallory?"

She saw that his eyes were clear and alert, and in his voice she detected entreaty to be told the truth.

"No," she said firmly. "Why do you ask?"

"You are a woman who can guard secrets, so I will tell you why I ask. I have never consciously done anything to arouse in Edith Mallory affection for me. Of her I have not made a confidant as I have of you. Your friend I have always looked on as a young girl just blossoming into womanhood. She is young, beautiful, and innocent. I never thought of her as a man will sometimes think of a woman. When not in her presence I don't think I have thought of her at all. Yet she loves me. She, too, said I could not go on living here. She, too, offered to lend me money, as much as I wanted, to go and seek happiness in another country. Do you also love me?"

The blood rushed into Hester Long's face. The beating of her heart became irregular and accentuated. The abrupt, stupendous question appeared to drain away her strength in sudden egress. She became weak, and into her reeling mind came the desire, the impulse, to fall forward into Arnold Dudley's arms. Yet in that fatal moment reason came back to her. Even as the light of day brightened into a flaming radiance of new-won knowledge, she saw plainly the path she must tread. Laughing softly, tremulously, she answered him:

"No, I don't love you, Mr. Cain. What a foolish question to ask!"

"It was not foolish at all," he said swiftly. "Listen! I came to this beach to hide, to live in solitude. I met two women who, from the first, treated me as a human being and not as a mad dog. Through no conscious fault of mine one of them falls in love with me. Her innocence protected her, Mrs. Long. She had no inkling of the furnace which is devouring me. Before me she laid down her beauty. Think of that! Before me! Then think of what I have been and what I am. I was tempted. I was like the man in the Pyramid suddenly released and offered unlimited quantity of the drug he was deprived of. With harsh words I sent her away. Why? Because I am an honourable man? Because I am a noble man? Not at all. I sent her away still pure because I saw that the drug she offered me in her innocence was only a substitute for the real thing, which for me can only be given by my wife."

Hester Long was mentally stunned by this revelation, following so closely that other relating to herself. Dudley went on speaking, with increasing excitement in his voice.

"Edith Mallory was kind to me, and I have done nothing but give her pain. You have been kinder still. You have gladly risked your purity of mind just to help one who cannot be helped. I would be an ingrate dog not to recognize it, not to appreciate your kindness which, being a part of you, you are unable not to render. If you had said you also loved me, my cup of bitterness would have overflowed, and I would have walked off the Pontoon.

"I want you to understand that the furnace now burning me up is not the furnace of lust. It is of something far deeper-seated than that, something which goes deeper than my body, something which is rooted in my very spark of life. I have come to see that my love for Ellen is not such as the matter-of-fact emotion so glibly described by novelists. When I began to love Ellen I surrendered to her my soul's independence. No longer was I a separate entity. I became a part of her, she a part of me. And now that we have become eternally separated, my soul is as a blind man's body, rushing here, creeping there, in a fruitless search for the light. And it will never see the light."

Bent forward once again with his face supported by his hands, Hester Long watched a man in the throes of mental torture. She came to understand in a dim kind of way that which he was trying to tell her. She understood more plainly what a great love was, and was unable to swamp a sudden feeling of shame that she should so far forget her husband as to love this man. That she had loved her dead husband she was certain. That she loved Arnold Dudley now she was equally certain. Was that love? In loving two men was she loving either? The man she now loved, loved but one woman and was being eaten up by that love. If this man's love for his wife was a sublime love, what degree of love was it she had had for her husband, and what was that which she now was being thrilled by? Was her capacity to love so small that her love was counterfeit?

She did not know, and could not know, that the devil which added fuel to the furnace eating up Dudley was the devil of Solitude. If she had discerned that, she would have insisted on his leaving the beach and travelling, travelling anywhere. She was not to see, never having lived in solitude, that in solitude a man makes an all-powerful enemy—himself. Without natural association with his fellows his mind, instead of receiving impressions from without, is overwhelmed by the impressions, sub-consciously gathered and stored away, which it has received from the hereditary instincts of the body.

Dudley's desire for Ellen was becoming exaggerated because his mind was receiving no impressions from without himself. Prompted by the instincts of his body, Ellen had become abnormally necessary to him. To him, then, the future was void of any importance to his life.

He possessed neither hope nor ambition. His mind derived nourishment only from the past, and like a healthy body fed by an unbalanced food diet his mind was being slowly poisoned to the living death we call madness.

Whilst she did not understand the process, Hester Long could visualize the abyss towards which Dudley was rushing. If he was to avoid that abyss he must no longer continue to live alone there, or indeed anywhere else alone. Yet she wanted time to think before coming to the point of being able to put before him a proposition that was likely to be acceptable to him.

"Tell me about your meeting with Edith," she said.

He related that meeting to Hester Long just as it had occurred. In so far as the speeches were concerned there was nothing in them to suggest that Edith Mallory loved the outcast. Arnold Dudley described the sequence of incidents as a parent might describe his child's faults to a teacher, or his child's symptoms to a doctor. Already knowing of her friend's passion for Dudley, the fact of that was not so important as the fact that Edith had visited him, urged him to go away, offered him a loan to enable him to do so. And Edith Mallory had said not a word to her about it.

Seated there beside this piece of human flotsam cast up on the beach of her life, Hester Long vainly sought a solution to a problem that was of more vital concern to her friend than to herself. Edith Mallory came first. At all costs to herself her life must not be wrecked as assuredly it would be if Dudley were tempted again. It was not fair to him. Hester Long decided there and then that Edith must be shown the precipice on which she stood. She must herself open before the girl the book of life and read to her some of its pages as yet unread.

If it were so important to Dudley that he should give up his hermit life, it was a thousand times more important to Edith that he should do so. And for the first time since she had been there with him she remembered the stranger in the motor-truck.

"Listen, Mr. Cain," she resumed in her low voice.

"Yesterday a man was asking about you. He looked like a detective. His questions were like those a detective would ask. It seems that he has been searching for you for months, and he seems to have got scent of you at Dongara. You see, you cannot stay here. I put him off. I told him you had gone north weeks ago. But he'll come back again to Dongara, and the next time he will be sure to come here. You must not be here when he comes. You can see that, can't you?"

Dudley was staring across the gully at the further sand-hill, and failed to answer.

"You are not listening, Mr. Cain," she accused.

"Indeed, I am," Dudley replied. "While you were telling me of this detective I decided that I don't care a curse if he finds me or not."

"But think!" Hester cried, aghast. "Think what they'll do to you if they find you."

"They will see to it that I find rest and peace," he rejoined grimly . "No. I've reached the stage when I no longer care what happens. I stay here."

"Very well. Then, if you won't go for your own sake, go for the sake of Edith Mallory."

"I am sorry for Miss Mallory. But she need never come here again while I'm here. I am six miles from her. What difference would it make if I were six hundred?"

"A great deal. If you were all that distance away she would no longer be able to yield to the temptation of seeing you."

"I cannot agree," Dudley said stubbornly. "She knows I am a married man. I have told her I love my wife. She knows I can never love her. She knows, too; that it is folly to even hope that I should."

"You would not deliberately injure her, would you?" Hester was press-ing an argument with the fervour of a politician.

"No. I would certainly not injure her."
"Then remember that she is young, beautiful, and passionate. Whilst you remain here she will come to see you again and again. In the end, Mr. Cain, you will irrevocably injure my very dear friend."

"I tell you I shall not."
"Are you then a St. Anthony?"
Suddenly she saw him looking at her, almost glaring at her. When he spoke he nearly shouted.

"No—I am not. But why, because she should be a little fool, should I leave my beach? Tell her not to come again, unless with you or her brother. Tell her to leave me alone. Why can't I be left alone? Because I have made a hell for myself, why should she want to come into it? Make her leave me alone. You leave me alone, too! Let me be, damn you! Let me be."

"Mr. Cain!"

Dudley sprang to his feet, the mental storm disfiguring his face. Raising his arms above his head, he beat his forehead with his clenched fist, and shouted to be let alone. Hester rose, too, frightened at his outburst, torn by pity and love for him. And then, as suddenly as he had leapt to his feet, he turned to her and threw himself down before her, bowing his head, and crying alternately for forgiveness and patience.

"I didn't mean that, Hester," he moaned, and her Christian name on his lips sent the blood to her face and her hands to her lips. "Oh, I didn't mean that. I didn't think. I don't know what I am saying half the time. I'll go away. I'll leave my beach, because—just because you want me to."

"I don't want you to go," Hester Long said firmly. "But I think you ought to go for your own sake, as well as for the sake of Edith Mallory. You can see that now, can't you?"

"Yes. Yes, I'll go. I'll go now, directly you have gone. But no! I must first say good-bye to my beach. I must feed my birds for the last time. You go now, Hester. I'll put in your horse."

Swiftly he arose, and with practised skill backed old Brownie into the shafts and harnessed him to the vehicle. He led the horse along to the cleared sand-patch, and, turning it there, led it back to the waiting woman, whose eyes now were bright with unshed tears.

Restoring the seat, he handed her in and placed the reins in her hands, then stood and gazed idly, vacantly at the horse.

"You will call in at my farm before you go right away, won't you?" she asked softly.

"Yes. I shall want some crusts for the gulls," he said.

"They always look for the crusts. Good-bye, Mrs. Long, good-bye!"

Her hands were seized by his and tightly gripped. His face, as she saw it then, was terrible. The corners of his mouth twitched, the corners of his eyebrows twitched, as though afflicted by St. Vitus's dance. His eyes! His eyes were green flames in whose depths his soul writhed in torment.

"Good-bye! And don't forget to call," she reminded him, with stupendous courage.

And then he let her hands go, and vanished. And when she looked back round the edge of the buggy hood, she saw him running up the sand-hill towards the Seagulls' Throne. He was standing on the Throne when she reached the summit of Big Hill, standing as motionless as the rock itself.

Whilst Brownie dragged the buggy home, Hester Long wept.

CHAPTER XX

FINLAY COMES TO THE BEACH

AFTER a week spent fruitlessly in the locality of Walkaway, George Finlay returned to Dongara. For seven months he had toured the country and the pastoral districts of Western Australia in search of his old friend and recent employer. He had undertaken the search in the first place at the urgent entreaty of Ellen Dudley, and in the second place because his friendship with Dudley had been created and cemented by their sojourn in the lonely places of Australia.

Put two men in a spot of the world where they seldom see a fellow-human, and in less than a month the probability will be that they will hate the sight of each other. If not that, their companionship will result in esteem, if not affection. The middle line of indifference is impossible.

Ellen came one afternoon to George Finlay's wife bearing the lines of tragedy on her chalk-white face, and an indescribable haunting regret in her beautiful eyes. Mrs. Finlay, a gaunt Irishwoman from County Clare, had met Ellen with a countenance as hard as quartz, but had succumbed with Irish quickness when she saw what lay in the depths of Ellen's eyes.

Arriving home from the warehouse, George found no dinner ready for him, and the two women locked in the front-room. Hugely indignant, he demanded to know why he was expected to live on air, and why his wife should entertain women visitors at an hour when she should be preparing for him necessary sustenance. He demanded this through the key-hole, and on being requested to "shut his face" had made himself tea and boiled four eggs. Afterwards, as an indication of annoyance, he had stormed the Swan Hotel, where he remained till nine o'clock, the hour when the working-man's clubs are closed by law. Not being a plutocrat or a politician, he was then compelled to return home, determined to assert his manhood even to the extent of wrecking the furniture.

To his vast surprise he found his lady and Ellen Dudley drinking tea in the kitchen, where on the table a strangely benevolent spouse had set in readiness for him two bottles of beer and a glass. Being a mere man, George Finlay fell head-first into the feminine trap, and, instead of describing to Ellen the various kinds of idiot she had been, he smiled on her and wished the world good luck—with one full bottle and one half-full bottle at his elbow, and one glass of beer in his weather-roughened hands.

Of the ensuing conversation he retained but the essential points. There were three, all told. The first was that Ellen had become fascinated by Edmund Tracy's personality. The quite ordinary friendship had gradually become more intimate in proportion to the growth of Tracy's ascendency over her. Ellen's fall occurred one evening when she and Tracy were motoring through the Darling Range—an evening planned weeks ahead by the astute philanderer.

The result of that motor trip was to put Tracy in the position of a blackmailer and Ellen in the position of the blackmailed. Tracy pursued her during those week-ends he could escape from his business at Geraldton, threatening, if she did not submit to him, to expose her to her husband. And Ellen, knowing she could not fall lower than she had fallen already, was compelled to meet his demands.

The second point was that Ellen did not love Tracy and never had loved him; that she had always loved Arnold Dudley and loved him still. It was a point entirely beyond Finlay's comprehension, but a point nevertheless.

The third and final point was of tremendous importance to George Finlay. Ellen Dudley wanted him to seek out her husband. She was by no means penniless, owing to Dudley's generosity and her own prudence. She was willing and anxious to fit out Finlay with a new car or truck with which to carry on the search, besides financing him and his family. When successful, Finlay was to "pump" Dudley to ascertain if it were possible for Ellen to receive forgiveness. If so, Finlay was to return immediately to Perth and take Ellen to him, when she would be able herself to fight to regain his love, and to start life afresh with him somewhere remote from the chances of discovery.

The reason why this third point was of paramount importance to George Finlay was that the search for Arnold Dudley would mean a short return to the glorious freedom he had so foolishly sacrificed when he allowed himself to become married to Nora Chancey.

Steering a good second-hand truck, he left Perth three days later and drove straight to Geraldton, where he expected to take up the chase that would not last long—worse luck! Yet it had lasted month after month. The first month was great. He scoured the district around Mullewa, and proceeded then as far east as Magnet and Youanmee. The second month he drifted south along the great No. 1 Rabbit-proof Fence, and earnestly talked with the boundary riders. The third and the fifth month saw him eastward to Kalgoorlie, southward to Ravensthorpe, thence all through the "cocky" district in the triangle formed by the towns of Southern Cross, Bruce Rock, and Wyalcatchem.

By that time he was becoming tired of his freedom. Nora's cooking was remembered with increasing vividness, and Nora's company, after all, was essentially preferable to his own.

About the time of Hester Long's burn he returned to Perth, admitting failure, having covered twenty-seven thousand miles without having discovered a meagre clue. He then felt certain that Arnold Dudley had left the State, probably left Australia. He found Ellen thinner and wan with hopeless waiting, but he found his wife grimmer and more determined. It was she who suggested the possibility of Dudley never having gone as far north as Geraldton. The country between Perth and Geraldton Finlay had not touched ; and three days later, after the truck had been over-hauled, he set off again, spurred by Ellen's poignant grief and his wife's unconquerable hope.

And at Dongara he had talked with the storekeeper and obtained a description of a trapper which tallied with that of his friend. His meeting with Hester Long had balked him, but after examining the Walkaway district he determined to hark back to Dongara. Once again at the store, he learned that there was a track into the beach nine miles out, and also a track at the Nineteen Mile peg. Outside the store again, he was about to climb into the driving-seat when the storekeeper came out with Tom Mallory, who had entered a few seconds before.

"This is Mr. Mallory," the storekeeper said with evident respect.

"You are looking for a man named Cain?" Mallory asked.

Knowing that Dudley would almost certainly have changed his name, Finlay instantly recognized Dudley's choice of the name, Cain, To choose that name would be just like his friend.

"Yes," he agreed. "Bloke about thirty-five. Roman beak, brown hair, and green eyes which don't blink much."

"That'll be him. He's trapping at the Nineteen Mile Beach."

"Thanks for the information," the delighted Finlay said ; and then, added remembrance of Hester Long coming to him : "He worked for a while for a little woman who drives an old buggy. Got a farm near there."

"Yes. Mrs. Long, that will be."

Again thanking Mallory, George Finlay left Dongara, wondering vainly why Mrs. Long had lied and put him off. That little mystery most likely would be cleared up when he talked with Dudley; and, so blithe was he at the prospect of being near the end of the wearying search, that he whistled and sang when he passed the Dongara railway-station, and was still whistling when he reached the beach track at the Nineteen Mile peg.

Immediately he turned off the main road he saw the wheel- and hoof-marks of Hester Long's horse and buggy, and the tune of his whistle changed to one long significant note. Arrived at the summit of Big Hill, he involuntarily stopped the truck to take in deep breaths of the clean west wind, and examine the beauty of the beach with appreciative eyes.

"Ah! Now if that ain't Arnold's camp down there; I'll go hopping from here to hell," he observed aloud, the old bush habit of talking to himself still strong in spite of the years of city life. "And me gallivantin' around W.A. for six months. Now then, friend and boss, to give you a shock!"

With the truck in low gear and brakes hard on, he dropped down Big Hill slowly to the smaller hills, and drove along the narrow, green-walled, twisting corridor until finally he drew up at Dudley's camp. As soon as he saw Dudley's truck, which had been his own, Finlay knew his search was over.

For a while he surveyed the camp, with evident approval written on his brick-red face. It was spotlessly clean, not an empty tin or a piece of paper was there to be seen. Getting out of the truck, he peered into the tent, and, finding it empty, entered, to see some of his own blankets on the stretcher-bed, which also had been his. On the rough table he espied a foolscap-sized book with blue covers, and, lifting the top cover, read a few words only, written on the fly-leaf, before he closed it, sharply realizing that he was prying into personal affairs not his own.

After seven months' hunting for a man, Finlay might reasonably have walked from the camp to find the absent owner. Not so the experienced bushman. Having found the "home" of Arnold Dudley, it would be but a matter of hours at the longest before the owner came "home". He examined the ashes in the fireplace, estimated correctly that Dudley had been gone from camp an hour or less, threw more wood on the red coals, and hung the billycan over the leaping flame. He was eating fried bacon and chipped potatoes inside the tent when Dudley burst in upon him.

"Good day-ee, Arnold, old lad!" Finlay greeted with the real bushman's calmness. "How's things?"

He was smiling broadly, with not so much as a flicker of an eyelid to betray the shock he suffered at Dudley's appearance. That appearance he instantly attributed to remorse, and at once decided that Dudley must be brought to see that the killing of Tracy was of less importance than the killing of a cattle-maiming aboriginal.

"Why! George Finlay! What are you doing here?" gasped Dudley, no less shocked to find Finlay there than Finlay was at his appearance.

"Come along to do some fishing," replied Finlay blandly. "Recognized me old truck and added two to two. Knoo you would be home sometime afore dark, and wired in getting a feed ready. Bacon and spuds waiting for you. Well, how are you bucking?"

"Gad ! I'm glad to see you," Arnold exclaimed, and then sank down on the stretcher, there to sit and stare at his friend with trembling lips and tears in his eyes.

The sight of him, a wreck of his former self, gave Finlay a sensation akin to that he felt when his baby almost died. Hastily he arose, and, going out, brought in the warmed bacon and potatoes and tea, and set the food out beside his own on the table.

"How's the fishing here?"

"I—I—oh! good, I think," Dudley stuttered. "I—I can't get over it. Just fancy you happening along like this ! I can hardly believe you are sitting there. When did you leave Perth?"

"Come and eat some tucker," growled Finlay, his face averted. "You talk worse'n Nora. See you bin getting a few rabbits. Skins went up an average of fourpence a pound last week's sales. Gonner be a keen demand this year. Stocks in London pretty low. Minx and sable still fashionable."

"Have you seen——."

"Wonderful wot can be done with Australian rabbit fur," Finlay cut in. "Come on, the grub's getting cold. Friend of Nora's called the other day wearing rabbit-skins wot she swore was Arctic fox. Haw, haw, haw! You could sell 'em anything, these days."

"Ellen——."

" 'Ad a nargument with a squatter's manager last Christmas Day," Finlay went on, blithely, cutting off a thick slice of damper for Arnold. "I told him that Brer Rabbit was the greatest blessing that ever happened to Australia. See it? Not him. Rabbit skins and carcasses brought nine million pounds odd into Australia last year. That nine millions was earned and spent by Australians in Australia. The measly wool-clip is worth fifty or sixty millions every year, and most of that money is spent by the damned capitalists in every country in the world bar Australia. Come on, do eat up! I want to go fishing. Yes, sir ! The blasted sheep provide silver cheques for absentee squatters, but the good old rabbit provides employment to thousands of Australians in Australia. If I 'ad me way, I'd protect the rabbit for three years, and declare all sheep as vermin with a quid on their scalps."

"But tell me, George——"

"Aw, shut up and eat! You interrupt me worse'n Nora," Finlay complained. " 'Ere's me and you got a good living out of rabbits ; there's thousands of other men getting a good living out of trapping ; there's the auctioneers and their staffs, and the thousands of blokes and girls in the felt hat factories, all living on bunny. And there's laws passed and millions of the people's money spent to exterminate the rabbit, so's a few squatters can live in luxury in Europe."

"I'm eating now," Dudley said at last. ."Can't you see that I'm about all in? Tell me of Ellen, do you. hear?"

When George Finlay finally looked at his friend he saw Dudley's eyes blazing with unnatural light, and an expression on the drawn face which indicated that further equivocation was impossible. He saw, too, that his deliberate effort to calm Dudley by extraneous discussion had been a failure.

"Ellen's all right, as far as I know," he said slowly, at the same time lighting his pipe.

"When did you leave Perth?" came the quick question.

"Last week. Got sick of work, so thought to do some fishing for a change. Storekeeper at Dongara told me about this place."

"When last did you see my wife?"

Dudley had forgotten his food. He sat sideways on the empty petrol-case, his hands clasped tightly, an infinitely pathetic look in his wide eyes.

"Nine or ten days ago," Finlay said, nonchalantly blowing tobacco smoke towards his host.

"Well, tell me! Damn it! tell me of her," commanded the now desperate Dudley. "Is she all right? What is she doing? Where is she living? Is—is she living with another man, George?"

"Wot's that?" inquired Finlay, removing the pipe from his mouth and glaring. "Ellen living with another man! Not much. Wot do you take her for? Think, because she came a thud over that Tracy swine, that she be living with Tom, Dick, or Harry?"

"Well, no. I didn't really think it," replied Dudley, almost apologetically. Finlay was quick to note the subdued manner, an attitude so strange in the Arnold Dudley with whom he had "droved" cattle and trapped. It mystified him no less than Dudley's appearance, and equally as much as the falsehoods told him by "that Long woman".

"You're crook, Arnold, old lad," he said contemplatively. "You've been worrying over Tracy. I think I told you afore that you wouldn't make a real murderer's shadow. Neither you wouldn't. Forget it! You done Australia a great deal of good when you corpsed him, for he was far worse a snake than me and you first thought. Nora got it out of Ellen, got the whole dirty devil's history of the affair. Listen!"

Finlay related that history in language vivid with expletives and adorned by his own emphatic opinions.

"You see now wot happened," he said, in conclusion. "'E mesmerized Ellen, that's wot 'e did. Ellen ain't that unbending kind of tart like Nora. She's weak and clinging and pretty. You began to think more of golf and cash than of canoodling with her, and her the sort of woman 'oo must be made love to or bust. Along comes Tracy once again and sees 'ow things are, and proceeds to bait his fishing-line while the fish are biting good. If only you 'ad just told me, and allowed me to slit his throat kind of slowly, everything would have turned out all right in the end."

"Is Ellen still in Perth?" The question was spoken softly, and on Dudley's face was a look as that of a man suddenly set free by the Inquisition's torturers.

"Ya-as. Still living at Belmont. Lives alone with two servants. 'Ow do you like your bacon and spuds stone cold? Fat lot of good cooking a feed, ain't it?"

"Eat, man? I can't eat. Ellen! I want to know about Ellen. Is she well?"

"She's goodo. Sort of worried a bit. Nora goes along sometimes and bucks 'er up, and takes 'er to the theatre or the pictures. I don't mind Nora going, anyway. Them nights I get three bottles of beer as a bribe to stay at home and see that the baby does his 'ome lessons."

Dudley was silent then for a full minute. He sat motionless, just staring at Finlay with eyes that saw him not, for the pictures flashing through the outcast's brain were those of memory and imagination. Finlay, too, remained silent, a great pity in his heart for both his friend and his friend's wife, well hidden by his robust and jovial exterior. Then:

"George, tell me, do you think Ellen still thinks about me?"

"I expect so."

"But do you think so?" Dudley insisted.

"Wa-al, yes, I do. You see, Ellen never did love Tracy. She says she didn't, anyway. And Nora says she didn't, and Nora is always cussedly right in everything. How she came to carry on with Tracy, not loving him, beats me. But why worry about that part of it? Ever since the day when it became infra dig. for a man to thrash his wife twice a week, men have worried about the tantrums of women."

"I am glad you think she still loves me," Dudley whispered. "It will help me to carry my chains. If I hadn't been such a fool as to murder Tracy, I could have gone to her and told her—told her I still loved her—in spite of everything."

A long silence ensued, suddenly broken by Dudley.

"What are the police doing about me?" he asked. "I am expecting to see them any day."

"You'll be disappointed," replied Finlay easily. "When I left your car at Guildford I put 'em in a quandary. You were gone without trace. While the police were fishing for you in the river, looking for you on the railway; waiting for you at the ports, and broadcasting your picture and details of clobber everywhere, your real track got as cold as this feed you're not eating. Even I, who had watched you bumping along the Dongara road, overshot the mark and went thousands of miles astray till Nora, who knows everything without learning it, put me right. The police had no Nora to put them right. They have given you up long ago as probably drowned in the Swan and carried out to sea. Some fresher mysteries are interesting them at present. A lot came out about Tracy, and it is agreed he deserved what he got."

Finlay stayed a week on the Beach of Atonement. Then he remembered he had forgotten to send Nora some necessary money and departed, ostensibly to repair the omission, promising to return for a longer stay at the end of a week.

CHAPTER XXI

HESTER'S DEFEAT

GREAT events generally have small beginnings. On the other hand, the fates of ordinary people are affected more or less by great events. An established institution in Australia is the Arbitration Court, to which all industrial disputes are taken, and which also reviews existing awards when those awards are due for renewal. The Judges in this Court are appointed by the political party in power. At this precise time, had not the party in power directed the Arbitration Judge in making an award between the United Road Contractors' Association and the Blue Metallers' Union, the ending of this history undoubtedly would have been different.

It happened that the fresh award was wholly against the Blue Metallers' Union. The opinion of the members of that Union was that the acceptance of the award meant a lower standard of living; and, since the standard of living had been materially reduced during and after the War, the Blue Metallers' Union declared a strike.

There followed much recrimination. The number of blood-sucking capitalists and blood-letting Communists discovered in Australia became truly appalling. We are not concerned, however, with capital and labour, which at such times become figuratively two street urchins ya-hooing each other from opposite sides of the road. What does concern us is that one of the results of the Blue Metallers' strike was a sympathetic strike of the workers on the Midland Railway of Western Australia.

The day George Finlay left Arnold Dudley, promising to return within one week, witnessed this railway workers' strike in full swing. The cessation of rail traffic along the north-west coast was not in itself an all-important factor in the fulfilment of Finlay's promise, but became so when the ball-race in the off-side wheel of the truck heated and cracked, ten miles south of Mingenew.

Now it is impossible to drive a car or truck with a faulty front-wheel ball-race. Finlay walked back to Mingenew and interviewed the proprietors of two garages. Neither establishment could supply him with the ball-race to fit his truck-wheel. And until the strike was over it would be impossible to obtain a ball-race from Perth.

Finlay swore. The situation and the man were such as to produce bad language. Unfortunately, a constable overheard the bushman's remarks on the industrial situation, and arrested him. Unwisely, Finlay resisted arrest and was awarded fourteen days' detention in the local gaol.

So that the indirect outcome of a political party's direction to an Arbitration Court Judge was the gaoling of George Finlay for two weeks. The effect of that judgment was to be passed on from Finlay to Arnold Dudley and the three women who loved him.

Towards evening on the day Finlay received sentence of fourteen days from an irascible magistrate, Hester Long emerged from her kitchen door carrying a pail of water, a butcher's knife and steel, and a small-calibre revolver. It was Friday, and invariably on that day she killed a sheep.

There was but one task to be done on her farm which a man could do and she could not. A bushman or a butcher can kill a sheep in one second by cutting the throat and breaking the neck of the animal in almost the one action. Hester Long recoiled from that method, quick and humane though it is.

Adjoining the gallows were the sheep-yards, in a small section of which waited a "killer". The sheep she dragged from the yard in a manner denoting practice, and, throwing it on the wooden floor beneath the gallows, she tied its back legs and one fore-leg together, and then shot it through the brain. Whereupon, the animal being dead, she cut its throat to bleed the carcass. Cutting the animal's throat when alive and then breaking its neck was the operation she could never bring herself to perform.

The skin was lying over a rail in the skin-house, and Hester Long was washing down the carcass hanging from the gallows when her boys arrived from "school" at Tom Mallory's house in their small pony-cart; and with them, mounted on a spirited grey mare, was their teacher. Edith Mallory had come to spend the evening, having been urged thereto by Hester, who had written her a note. For over a week the elder woman had not seen her friend, and was beginning to wonder why Edith absented herself so unusually long. She waved to Edith, prior to slipping a calico bag up round the carcass and tying its mouth.

Her boys, remarkably self-reliant for their years, unharnessed the piebald pony and led it to the water-trough preparatory to stabling it, whilst Edith slipped from her hack and as efficiently watered and fed it. The horses attended to, the youngsters raced into the house after their mother, and when Edith entered the kitchen she found Hester Long taking from the oven a joint of roast pork.

"Where have you been this last week, Edith?" Hester inquired, with a bright smile. "You have deserted me, for sure. Sit down there beside the fire, and I'll have the dinner ready in no time. Now, boys, into the wash-house quickly. I've made your favourite apple-pudding."

With joyful shouts the children rushed out to perform their evening ablutions.

"I've been so busy," Edith excused herself, laughing half-heartedly. "What with Tom worried to death by not being able to market some fats on account of the wretched strike, and having to visit poor Mrs. Brown, who doesn't seem to get any better from her illness, I've laid my hands full."

"Yes, to be sure," Hester agreed, yet thinking of the time Edith had spared to visit Arnold Dudley. "I don't think," she went on, "that Dr. Cars quite understands the case. Mr. Brown should get a specialist from Perth to see her."

"He was saying that he would next week if his wife did not improve. Shall I light the lamps? The days are getting short."

Five minutes later they sat down to dinner. Through the large window the sky was rapidly becoming invisible against the lamplight within. A wakeful magpie away in one of the paddocks warbled a few notes of even-song, answered sleepily by the butcher-bird roosting in state in the big fig-tree beyond the door.

Watching her boys eat with keen appetites, joining in the juvenile con-versation, she furtively studied the face of their teacher and her warm friend, and was made uneasy by what she saw. Edith talked a little too loudly, a little too fast. She laughed often, and at nothing. A hint of mental excitability tempered her usual calmness, and it was seldom that her frank blue eyes met those of Hester Long.

In honour of the visitor the boys were excused the task of helping their mother to wash up the dinner-things. The table cleared, the red-shaded lamp placed exactly on its centre, Edith Mallory read to them from Grimm's Fairy Tales, the absorbed youngsters kneeling on their chairs, one on each side of her, their faces cupped in their hands, their eyes watch-ing the girl's lips, their ears never missing a word.

The grandfather clock in the corner, which Hester had brought with other furniture from England, ticked away the peaceful seconds. The wood fire in the wide cooking-range hummed softly, and, to avoid disturbing the reader and listeners, Hester moved and worked quietly as possible. The work done, she seated herself in the easy-chair beside the fire and prepared to enjoy an hour's rest, the first she had taken that day.

What a volcano is human life! By most of us life is spent in long monotonous periods broken by eruptions of grief, or success, or supreme happiness. Sitting there watching the small quartered logs she herself had cut burning in the range grate, Hester Long looked back on her volcano. It had erupted when her father died, again when she was married, for the third time when her husband was drowned. Now it was in the throes of another eruption. For two years the volcano had been quiescent. For two years her life had been a period of work, of sublime hope, of passionate yet subdued devotion to her children.

And them came the man calling himself Hector Cain, just the kind of man placed in the kind of circumstance who would arouse in her her real womanly instinct to love and protect. Alas! If only the issue had been clear cut! Yet what a tangle Fate was making of it, with two women in love with that one man, and that man desperately in love with a dishonoured wife! From a period of quiet she had come to an eruption of a hopeless love, sincere and deep sympathy for the friend she had come to look upon as a sister, and constant gnawing anxiety for the physical and mental welfare of a murderer.

The thought never entered her mind that Edith Mallory was in effect her rival. A feeling of commiseration and desire to serve her friend overwhelmed even her own fully recognized hopeless love. Had Dudley not so emphatically stated that he loved his wife, Hester Long would most certainly have done her utmost to have brought them together.

At half-past eight she sent the boys to bed and, after giving them five minutes, went to their room to conduct their prayers and tuck them into their neat little cots. And somehow that evening, when she kissed them goodnight, she felt fervently thankful and happy that she had two such children to work and plan for.

Going back to the kitchen, she found Edith preparing coffee, and again experienced that happy thankfulness that she had found such friendship just when friendship was so utterly needed. Hester had never ceased during the last two-year period of quietude to admire the beauty of the girl's face no less than her open, transparent, beautiful nature. Whilst she herself was capable of anger, of harshness, capable of lying when she thought it necessary, Edith Mallory was wholly incapable of lying, subterfuge or deceit.

"Did you find the morning's cream in the safe, dear she asked cheerfully, despite Edith's evident moodiness.

"I haven't looked yet." There was a hint of defiance in the low sweet voice.

"I'll get it," the elder woman decided, and said no more until the coffee was poured into the china cups and the cream added. Then: "Have you seen Mr. Cain lately ?"

Edith and Hester gazed at each other with sudden and significant directness.

"I saw him yesterday."

"Ah!"

"Why do you say 'Ah!' as though you knew it and just wanted to be told?"

"I didn't ask you wholly for that reason," Hester Long replied gently. "I understood he was leaving the district, and, as he promised to call and say good-bye before he went, I have been wondering if he broke that promise also."

"Leaving the district? Did he say he was going to?" Hester nodded, noting with pity the girl's quickly-paled face and the nervous clenching of the hands.

"Yes. I persuaded him to go away. He said he would."

"When—when was that?"

"Last Monday."

Edith looked at her friend, her loved friend, with a hint of hostility in her large wide eyes.

"Why should you make him promise to go, Hester?"

"Because you failed."

A silence followed pregnant with emotion. The two women regarded each other steadily, each knowing that for days past each had realized the inevitability of this crossing of swords, knowing now that the swords of their wills were at last crossed.

"He told you I asked him to go?"

"Yes. In that you did a brave thing, Edith."

"No, I didn't!" Edith burst out with sudden vehemence. "Far from being brave, I am a coward. I asked him to go away and hunt happiness just because to me it was unbearable to think of him there alone. I am always thinking of him, day and night. I picture him slaving at his trapping in a fruitless effort to forget. I see him seated on the Seagulls' Throne, gazing out over the sea, or playing his mouth-organ with his poor eyes leadened by misery ; and, while I think of him like that, my heart hurts me and my poor mind reels. It was to ease my agony that I entreated him to go, for the pain would be less if I knew he was happy.

"There is nothing brave in selfishness, Hester. I didn't think of the risks he would run, were he to go travelling about of recognition. He knew it, which was why he refused me. Why did he not refuse you?"

"Because I showed him that by remaining there you would meet your moral ruin."

"You showed him—what?"

"I showed him the precipice at your feet, dear. He guessed you loved him. A less honourable man would have taken advantage of that. You remember the legend of the temptation of St. Anthony, don't you? When St. Anthony was tempted he was an old man. Hector Cain is neither an old man nor a human iceberg. Just now he is a raging fire, a fire of desire and love for and of his wife."

"Hester!" The name was wrenched from between parted lips. Edith's face was scarlet.

"Listen, dear!" said Hester; and calmly and dispassionately she turned over before the gaze of an inexperienced innocent girl certain torn dirty pages of the Book of Life.

"I—I don't love him like that," Edith cried wildly.

"How do you—know?" demanded the inexorable Hester. "You would find that you did—you would find that you, as any other woman passionately in love, would be as inflammable spirit to the flame of his lips when once he kissed you. You can't keep away from him ; you know you can't. You used to watch for him to go away, and then steal down and tidy his camp, because everything in it was dear to you as it belonged to him. You went to his camp one dark night in the pouring rain just to satisfy yourself that he was safe. You went to the beach one day and offered him money to go away. Then you let him know, in your voice, the love you have for him, and let him see in your eyes that same love. You knew he was a married man, you knew what the law names him, you knew that he could never marry you, even if he wanted. You know now, Edith, the narrow escape you had that day, for which you have to thank Mr. Cain's wife; for it was her memory and his love of her which turned the scales in your favour."

Hester Long slid from her chair and knelt before the now frigid girl. She took her hands in hers and pressed them to her flat bosom, and from her glorious eyes tears fell fast.

"Edith, darling!" she cried softly. "Can't you see how impossible it all is? He can never love you, and your love can never find expression in marriage with him. See—try to see the path you are deliberately following. Our woman's strength is our weakness. I know—I know. I knew it when my husband kissed me on my bridal night, for my strength was shattered by the touch of his lips, and I knew even as I surrendered that I was but a feather, unable to resist the wind of desire blowing a tornado through me. Our real strength, sweetheart, is in acknowledging our weakness.

"I don't want him to go, yet I persuaded him to promise," Hester went on chokingly. "I was thinking only of you. When he goes far away, and no more are you able to see him, time and work together will ease and cure the pain in your heart. Such pain doesn't last, if the twin doctors are given a chance. Oh, my dear, my dear! If it were possible, I would gladly give ten years of my life to make it so."

"He won't go now, Hester. I met him coming from Dongara, when he seemed much more cheerful."

Through her tears Hester Long saw triumph in the other's eyes. She saw, too, the indescribable flame of youth in Edith's face, the courage of youth, and the obstinacy of youth. She realized that Edith Mallory was suddenly glad that not only was Dudley not to run the risk of recognition, but also that the torture of unrequited love was to remain. With dismay she understood that Edith either did not even then understand her danger, or, understanding it, ignored it with the defiance and the calm disregard of youth. Shaken, knowing defeat, Hester Long rose from her knees and regained her chair.

"Why will he not go?" she asked dully.

"Because I asked him not to. I told him that he would he recognized if he did go. He said he would rather stay, intended to stay another week, anyway. A man has visited him, and promises to return and stay with him when he has done some business. So you see, Hester, that with Hector having a companion with him, I can't burn myself at the fire as you seem to think."

After that, for a while, neither spoke. Hester wondered if this friend of Dudley's was he who had inquired for him of her on the main road. Doubtless it was. The dark cloud of misgiving was swept away from her mind. She realized that Edith spoke the truth when she said that the arrival of Dudley's friend would be a guard between her and the fire of passion.

She determined that when the friend did come back she would see if she could not persuade him to induce Dudley to leave the beach; for, until the fire was removed, it would still be a danger, in spite of any safeguard.

Quite suddenly their late positions were reversed. Edith rose and fell on her knees before Hester Long, hugged Hester's knees, buried her face in Hester's lap, and broke into a storm of weeping. And, as the voice of a gull above the pitch of the tempest, Edith Mallory wailed between her sobs:

"Oh, Hester! I love him so. What matters if I am burned? What matters anything, anything at all? I wish I were dead, and no longer could feel this pain and misery, and—and want. My body screams for the touch of him. I want his kisses—I want his love. Oh ! I cannot go on, Hester—I cannot—I cannot! God! let me die, please let me die, let me—let me die!"

CHAPTER XXII

MADNESS OR REPENTANCE?

IT was Sunday, and that day was the eighth of Finlay's detention in the Mingenew gaol. Weather permitting, Hester Long had decided to spend the afternoon on the beach with her boys, and, possibly, with Arnold Dudley; but Jim, the younger, had contracted a cold and, therefore, she had to stay at home.

What day of the week it was, and what day of the month, Arnold Dudley would have failed to name, even if it were of importance to him, which it was not. One of the first effects of solitude is forgetfulness of time periods. Alexander Selkirk, when relating his experiences to Daniel Defoe, emphasized that point, and Robinson Crusoe meticulously cut notches on a stick as an aid. The only safe way is to keep a diary. Putting a pencil mark daily through the dates on a calendar is safe enough, provided not a day is missed ; for, should a day be missed, it will be found that memory is a tricky jade, and at once a doubt will arise as to whether yesterday was marked off or not.

Dudley did not keep his diary regularly. There were periods of several days when not a word was written, and periods when several day pages were filled at one sitting. Every time he wrote, what he did write was prefixed by "Dear Hester". Under Hester Long's written date, 10th April, he wrote on 11th May:

Your detective came and revealed himself as my very good friend, and one-time partner. I shall not put his name in writing, as I must take care not to betray my friends. Let him be known as George. He has told me all about Ellen, the way she was tricked and ruined by Tracy. It was this way.

[Here he gave a succinct account of Edmund Tracy's crime against Mrs. Dudley.] My poor Ellen was damned by the vilest scoundrel of the century, and I am glad, tremendously glad, that I shot him. All day I have whistled and sung and laughed, just because I am so happy at having removed such a beast. This morning I actually baked biscuits to throw to my gulls because I had no crusts, and they knew I was happy, for they laughed, too, and three of them settled on me—one on each shoulder and one on my hat.

And then, too, George saw Ellen only a few days ago. She was pale and dejected and sad. She thinks of me, and George says he is almost certain she still loves me in spite of everything.

How happy am I to-night! Just realize it, dear Hester, dear beautiful pal! Tracy robbed me of my wife's body, but he was unable to rob me of Ellen's love. It doesn't matter that he didn't want her love. What matters is that he never got it. I feel more of a whole man than I have done since I found Tracy out. One part of me, the most important part of me, feels complete once more. Why! I have not had those terrible dreams of Ellen drawing away from me since George arrived here. My sleep has been extraordinarily restful, and because of that the evil whisperings, deep in my mind, have ceased. And now I hear, as though a real voice repeated it : "Ellen still loves me! Ellen still loves me!"

George has been gone a few days now. I don't know how many, but no more than three. He will be coming back here in three or four days from now, and we might go away to the far north. I shall hate leaving my Beach. Nevertheless, to leave will be wise. Your friend is very lovely, and I am just a man. You will understand, Hester, won't you?

George Finlay had been gone ten days, yet such was the extraordinary effect of his visit to Dudley that his mind measured that time as, three days. From a state of utter depression Dudley had swung into a condition of high-pitched elation. Both conditions were emphasized by the fact of his solitude, for he was still without the city man's armour of outside interests, and if the former condition of depression was dangerous, the latter was almost equally so. For there was bound to be reaction.

The Sunday Hester Long had intended taking her boys to the beach turned out to be the third brilliant cloudless day, warm and still. The gentle wind came from off the land and quieted the restless sea. It seemed as if the ocean were tired by the ceaseless tossing, and smilingly relaxed into the restful lethargy. The northern sun caressed the coast waves, so free from white surf, and dried the rocks no awash, and warmed the sand of the beach so that the thousands of orange-coloured land-crabs came out and basked in its radiance and went about their mysterious affairs less alert for the coming of the strange inquisitive man.

Whilst Dudley walked northward from the Pontoon along the low sand-cliffs bordering the beach, the scents of the bush in the sheltered dells inland were wafted about him, warm and sweet and cloying. The foot-high thick-growing scrubs covering the sand-dunes close by the sea gave forth no scents. The little green bushes were hard and brittle, and the leaves of them were hard and polished by the wind-blown sand, and reflected the sunlight in millions of tiny points.

For a little way the gulls followed him, but, finding he had no crust to offer them, they flew southward in two and threes and gathered on the Seagulls' Throne, where they seemed to sleep. Above the sky was empty. Not a trace was to be seen of the eagles, who patrolled the sky but a few miles inland. They shunned the coast because it was covered so densely by bush; and, being shy and wary birds, they preferred the comparatively bushless headlands and hilltops whereon no enemy could evade their look-out.

Dudley carried a .32 calibre Winchester repeating rifle. The object of his expedition that day was to obtain a kangaroo, since he had been without fresh meat for many days and had suddenly found himself meat-hungry. Meat-hunger! It is a fierce, ravening appetite, demanding that which has appeased it daily for years. Place a dainty society lady, on a desert, or uninhabited island, feed her on biscuits and tinned food for a month, and then offer her two pounds of raw steak. She will not wait for the meat to be cooked, or cook it herself—even if she knows how. She will bite and tear at the bloody flesh as though she were nearly dead with starvation. So thin—so thin, indeed—is the veneer of civilization.

Meat-hunger having assailed Arnold Dudley, he set out to appease it. To him, a rabbit-trapper and skinner, rabbit was out of the question. Fish was no substitute. To travel to the butcher at Dongara for meat when there were kangaroos in the district was equally unthinkable to a man like Dudley.

He was making for a narrow valley running back from the beach for several miles among the sand-mountains. Its junction with the beach was marked by two towering hills of sand, so wind-blown that they bore not a single bush. Months before he had discovered the valley, and, having followed it inland for a little way, had seen several 'roos and the fresh spoors of many.

The two hills of sand reminded him strangely of the huge mullock-dumps of the mines at Broken Hill before a German scientist discovered that the mullock held gold and silver and some commercially valuable acids. They towered above the neighbouring beach-dunes, conically shaped, and about a hundred yards apart. The space between them also was a stretch of pure white sand, which added its sun-reflected brilliance to that of the hills to dazzle the eyes of man.

At Arnold Dudley's first visit what had interested him most about those hills and the sandy connecting-link was that on all that expanse of sand there was not a single track of animal or bird. Now, however, when he arrived there he paused, the trapper in him thrilling at sight of the apparently aimless lines of tracks criss-crossing and twisting around the sand-mountains. They were the tracks made by foxes.

At the sight of them his eyes lit. Kangaroo-hunting was for the nonce forgotten, for a greater thrill than bagging a 'roo after a long stalk is the sight of lovely fox fur waiting to be taken from a carcass early in the morning. Dudley hurried in from the beach to pause at the first set of tracks clearly imprinted on sand that had lain undisturbed by wind for three days and nights. As a setter-dog following a scent, he followed the interlacing lines of tracks for almost an hour, by which time he decided that at least three grown and seven half-grown foxes had made them.

A further hour he spent in endeavouring to ascertain the attraction for the foxes at that place. There were no rabbit-tracks to indicate that they came there hoping to catch an unwary rabbit far from a burrow. Here and there the sand bore evidence that a fox had sat on its haunches to scratch itself against the tormenting rabbit-ticks. He saw where a fox had begun to dig, and near the shallow hole were smaller holes dug by two young foxes, either from native instinct or in imitation of their senior. It was only after careful survey that Dudley gave up the puzzle, to which he could conceive that one possible answer.

The attraction of that place might have been its salt.

It is possible for man and meat-eating animals to live without meat ; wholly impossible to exist without salt : remembering which fact, Dudley remembered, too, that he had plenty of salt in his camp, but not the red meat for which he craved. The foxes could wait. They would visit the place next week and the weeks following that, until the day came when the lack of water among the dunes, added to the sultry summer heat, would send them inland. And when he did lay poisoned baits, the baits would be salted fillets of fish.

Passing eastward along the floor of the miniature winding valley, Dudley had proceeded but a quarter-mile when he came to grass-ground and dense bush-covered hills. Precisely in the centre of the valley ran a fifteen-inch-wide "pad", evidently made by cattle; and, whilst now there were no tracks of cattle on it, Dudley discovered rabbit-tracks, fox-tracks, kangaroo-tracks, and the tracks of goats: these last probably the descendants of those goats brought to that part of the continent by the early settlers.

Of the several tracks, those that now interested him were made by kangaroos. He saw the regularly-spaced twin marks made by the 'roos' hind feet, and sometimes the clear outline of a 'roo's paw appearing as though a little child had pressed the soft soil with its hand. Only once did he espy the tapering fifteen-inch impression of the animal's tail.

Ahead of him the valley took a sharp northerly turn to avoid the steep slope of a great sand-mountain, and when he drew near the turn Dudley edged to the left-hand side to gain cover. At the angle he moved with caution, and, edging round the turn, suddenly halted at sight of four kangaroos sitting up in the middle of the valley, alert and alarmed by even his quiet coming.

Of the four, one was a monstrous fellow with a white chest and red back. Sitting on its shanks, balanced back against its thick yet tapering tail, it measured slightly over five feet in height. Two others, evidently does, were six inches shorter. One of them was red-backed, the other bluish-grey-backed, with white front. The fourth almost a baby. It stood near the blue animal.

Faces turned towards him, ears taut and motionless, Dudley thought they saw him and waited for him to move before racing for the shelter of the bush. As a statue he, too, waited. Three hundred yards separated hunted and hunter, a distance too great for reliable shooting. From the waiting game the man emerged victorious, for after a while the blue 'roo went down on her fore paws and began feeding. Shortly after, the other doe began to feed; but the "old man" remained suspicious for a full further five minutes.

Dudley allowed them ten minutes of quiet feeding before he walked straight towards them, no longer bothering about cover. He had shortened the distance by fifty yards when one of the does suddenly sat up. The man as suddenly halted, to stand immobile. To move an arm then, even as much as an inch, would have alarmed them. Followed by the "old man", the other doe and the baby also sat up to regard him with soft curious eyes, unafraid still.

One could almost imagine the "old man" grunting annoyance at his suspicious wife when he went to ground, gracefully turned, and moved away several yards on all fours, for all the world as though he were some gigantic, ungainly spider.

The blue doe, however, remained sitting with unabated curiosity, her young one keeping very close, ready to dive into the protecting pouch, large though the infant was. At long last she went to ground, but only for a second or two, when up she came again, cunningly expectant. But Dudley was too wily a hunter to have moved so soon. He expected that little trap set for him, and when again the four 'roos were feeding he gave them five minutes before he moved, and then he walked rapidly, arms stiffly at his sides, prepared at the instant to stop. When he did stop he was within a hundred and twenty yards of them.

Unable to remove his gaze from the kangaroos, he trod on a dry stick that snapped no louder than a man can snap his fingers. At once the "old man" and the two does sat bolt upright, whilst the young fellow jumped for, and into, its mother's pouch.

Even then, with Dudley so near and quite revealed to them, they did not flee. He almost feared to wink his eyelids at this point, when movement would have spelled failure. And in that position he and the 'roos remained for minute after minute, until at last Dudley could have cried out with the cramp slowly eating him up. And when he found that he could endure it no longer and decided to take a standing snap-shot, the "old man" 'roo went to ground with a contemptuous grunt, and—instead of following his example—the two does edged close to each other and began to play. Face to face, sitting well back securely against their supporting tails, they gave open-pawed clawing blows, and defended themselves in precisely the manner of boxers. Their occupation gave Dudley his chance. Both fighters were intent on watching each other, and slowly Dudley sank to his knees in the long grass, and slowly he fell forward on his chest pushing the rifle in front, till finally he was lying full length on the ground, his rifle sights bearing on the hip of the blue 'roo.

It was whilst waiting for movement to cease—for the combatants, if not changing position, at least swayed in their efforts to avoid each other's blows—that Dudley remembered the young fellow, whose head and shoulders showed above the rim of the pouch. From the blue he shifted his rifle-sights to the red.

What it was that alarmed them was unapparent, for they were not alarmed by Dudley's going to ground. Possibly the youngster's interest in the fight or bout had waned, and it had seen the slight movement of the rifle. In any case, the bout suddenly stopped. The blue 'roo sprang into the air about nine or ten inches, and at the instant her hind feet again felt the earth she brought her tail down with a thump on the ground. It sounded like a carpet struck by a stick. The old fellow sat up with amazing swiftness. Three beautifully-coloured, noble-looking beasts faced the hunter.

Aiming at the red doe's chest, Dudley fired.

He expected her to collapse. The impact of the bullet readied him a split second after the sharp report. The struck 'roo rocked on her haunches. The blue doe never moved. The "old man", made uneasy at long last, turned away, and with short unhurried jumps made off to a more peaceful spot.

Dudley stood up. The blue doe turned in a flash, and, taking double-length jumps, overtook the "old man" as an express train passing a signal-box. Once the "old man" looked back. He saw Dudley running toward the stricken 'roo, when he heaved himself along the valley , after the doe at extraordinary speed, covering thirteen feet at a jump.

The wounded kangaroo remained, shocked by the bullet, yet still sitting up. She waited, poor brave thing, to give battle, seeming to know that escape was impossible then for her. Dudley stood four yards from her and fired again at her chest. The bullet sent her backward, but with extraordinary vitality she sat up once more facing the man, regal, beautiful. For three seconds she sat thus, whilst Dudley ejected the empty shell and pumped another cartridge into the barrel of his rifle.

He was about to fire a third shot, sick at the sight of her, racked by the pity and the cruelty of it, when the doe's head very slowly fell forward, and at first slowly, then with sudden finality, she lay down on the green grass and died.

In all his hunting life Dudley had never seen a kangaroo he had shot die so hard. At the last there was neither hate nor fear in the soft, deer-like, black eyes, only an expression of great reproach ; and, whilst he stood gazing down on the soft-furred graceful body, memory, vivid blazing memory, revealed in the 'roo's place the body of Edmund Tracy.

Late that night he wrote in his diary:

... There have been many times when I have recognized clearly the danger of insanity. Too many poor devils, lonely and at grips perhaps with some grisly skeleton, have I come across during my wandering in the bush, harmless yet quite mad, not to see the danger in my life of solitude.

Standing in the green valley gazing down upon the kangaroo, I saw its carcass vanish and in its place the body of Tracy. He lay precisely as he did when I shot him dead, clothed in a light-grey lounge suit, black shoes on his feet, hat and stick clenched in his left hand. Upon his face was the identical expression of comical surprise. I might have put this strange occurrence down to a trick of vision, or some unexplainable mental phenomenon, had it not been for the fact, stranger still, that at sight of the man who blasted my wife and destroyed my happiness I felt no hatred, only a very poignant regret that I had killed him. I know now, Hester, that it was a fit of madness. It will come again and last longer, and again and yet again, till it will last all my life.

CHAPTER XXIII

THE FALL OF ST. ANTHONY

THE sea beyond the Sugar Loaf and the adjoining southern sunken rocks was like a sheet of widely ribbed blue glass. The low swells now did not crash in foaming white against the Sugar Loaf and the Pontoon, but meeting these obstructions they rose and rolled back without breaking, as if exhausted by their ocean-wide journey.

Never, since his arrival on that beach, had Arnold Dudley seen the sea so calm and languid. From a cloudless sky the sun, noticeably northward when at zenith, was heated almost to midsummer fierceness. It sucked up the countless scents from the coast bush and the inland pastures, and the east wind wafted the fragrance west-ward to the glittering beach and far out over the still waters, far beyond the horizon, bearing news of land to people in ships.

For that time of the year—towards the middle of May—the weather was abnormally free of rain-clouds and wind. Over the great pastoral areas eastward sheep and cattle staggered about in search of the ground feed that in the absence of rain had withered and died. Beyond the coast areas the autumn was as dry and as hot as in any of the drought years that are the affliction of Australia. The squatters despaired, the farmers waited anxiously for rain to permit them to plough and seed, whilst already city business languished and the standing army of unemployed gained many recruits,

Dudley, however, was entirely unconscious of these conditions. So far from being interested in the problem of drought facing the pastoralists, or the problem of the Midland Railway sympathetic strike, or the political-ly-controlled Arbitration Court, he had lost all concern for dates, seasons, or public events ; although the weather conditions and the industrial upheaval combined to affect his destiny.

Seated on the Seagulls' Throne, he surveyed the sea and the beach below him. That day the beach revealed yet another of its infinitely varying moods. To the lonely man it appeared vaster in extent, and in proportion he seemed immeasurably smaller. The sky, void of content other than the sun, was sunken towards the earth and the sea, giving the impression that presently it would fall on the world and crush him.

The horizon, an ink-stroke on a sheet of cadmium-coloured paper, hid, or seemed to hide, cat-like monsters of wind and tempest waiting, waiting to spring on the midget on the rock, sweep him off, and dash him down into the very bowels of the planet. The sun was monstrous in size, and he imaged it as the unfaceable eye of an ogre watching him with scientific interest before lifting him up and dissecting him.

And on all the world Dudley sat alone, and into the brain of Dudley came the thought to hide, and into the heart of him a great fear, a fear of the world on which he sat. It was so terrifically big, and he so hopelessly little. Points ten miles distant in reality appeared to be within one mile. The sand-mountains, two miles back from the beach, hovered in the heat haze and towered above him in close proximity; whilst the horizon-line was so close that had he but taken a short walk he would have come to the awful gulf down which the sun sank daily.

In him was aroused the primitive instinct of man for a shelter, a cave, a house, a place to live, a refuge where he could be safe from danger for some little while. He was leading the life of an eagle who even sleeps a-wing, whereas man's natural habitat is the earth. He had been wrenched away from the living habits of man implanted in him by countless gener-ations of ancestors, who had dwelt first in caves and then in houses. Now he was as a snail without its shell, blistered or frozen by the elements, at the mercy of every enemy, naked, unprotected, lost.

It came to him, sitting there above the beach with the glittering sea for a footstool and the sand-mountains for a back-rest, that after all he was a poor puny thing, of less account in the scheme of cosmos than any one of the foxes that had left their tracks on the twin sand-hills. He was a man banished to the desert from a lovely city of men because of the brand that was upon him. In the desert he must wander until he perished. Never again could he return to the city, never more could he mix with his fellows, be one of them, delight in their delights, thrill and sorrow, hope and fight for success as did they.

There, marked on the sea-chart by the low hill-lines of water, was the number of the years he had to face, or the number of months, or of days, left to him to live. They stretched, those marks, to infinity, wherein lay the change called death. And after the change, the weighing is the balance, the judgment—as inevitable, as fixed, the spaces into which he gazed!

The Judgment Seat—the Sitter thereon—the accuser—the witnesses—his defence—the verdict!

"I accuse this man of having destroyed my life on earth," Tracy would state.

"I witnessed this man destroy Edmund Tracy," Ellen falteringly would add; earthly relationship not counting in that Court.

"I killed the man because he robbed me of my wife," would be his ready defence.

"Vengeance is MINE!" would come as thunder from the Sitter on the Judgment Seat. "Can one injury be wiped out by inflicting another? Of all sinners against me a Fool can I suffer least of all. Pass, Fool, to thy damnation!"

Almost could Arnold Dudley hear the Voice coming from the brazen sky, whilst there, on the rock, his soul was as naked as his body seemed to be.

Regret! That moment which revealed Arnold Dudley to Arnold Dudley was poignant with regret. Perhaps one or two further moments of self-examination would have produced Repentance, a softening of his adamantine heart. We know how Jacob wrestled with the Angel.

An Angel was pleading with Dudley—when the Devil intervened, insinuating into the ambit of Dudley's consciousness the soft, sweet voice of Edith Mallory.

"You don't appear to notice me, Mr. Cain," she said softly; and, turning his head, he saw hers on a level with his granite seat, her face made radiant by a wistful smile. There was something so childishly frank about that smile that the crust of self-centredness which had been thickening during the months was split open, and for the first time during his sojourn on the beach he felt sympathy for someone other than himself.

"Certainly I was unaware of your presence, Miss Mallory," he told her, swiftly removing his old felt hat. She saw the ghost of an answering smile on his face, now lean and hawk-like, and even whilst her heart leapt she likened him to an eagle on its eyrie, gazing into the distances with all-seeing eyes, yet an eagle that never more would spread its wings and fly.

"I have been standing here for at least two minutes," was her reproof. "Please help me up. I want to sit up there with you and see what you have been seeing."

The strained hard look returned, and she thought the smile had fled from her suggestion to sit with him, whereas it had vanished before memory of what he had been seeing. Kneeling, he held down his hands to her, and she, putting one foot into a narrow crevice, helped him to pull her up beside him. Then, their bodies touching, so small was the flat summit, she said with forced gaiety:

"I went to Dongara this morning and noticed, when passing the beach-gate, that there were no motor-tracks. I knew then that your friend hadn't come back. Then in the store at Dongara I was looking over some new novels just arrived, and found among them a reprint of 'A Master of Fate', by Guy Willow. Have you read it?"

"No. I don't remember having read it."

"I'm glad of that, for I have brought it with me for you to read."

"Is it worth reading? Have you read it?"

"Yes; I read a cheap edition of it three or four years ago," she replied.

Dudley glanced sharply at her, and she encountered his too brilliant eyes with unfaltering steadiness.

"What is there about the book which causes you to recommend it to me?" he asked.

"I would rather not tell you. I would rather you read it; but I will tell you if you wish."

"I do wish," Dudley said simply.

"Well, the hero killed a man because this man ruined his sweetheart—the hero's sweetheart, I mean. Afterwards he escaped out of the country, went to some place in South America, and there he fell in love with a beautiful Spanish girl. On the eve of their wedding he found that he could not marry her unless she knew about his killing the other man. He did tell her, and it made no difference with her. And afterwards, for several years, he was saddened by his vengeance, but she clung to him, and led him always away from his thoughts until at last she conquered the past and made real happiness out of the present and far into the future."

"And you think reading this book will help me?"

"It might point out a road for you to follow."

"It might," he conceded. "I will read it. I appreciate the thought behind the gift." Dudley was silent for a moment or so. Then: "You, say the book is called 'A Master of Fate'. According to the tale it appears that the hero wasn't sufficiently master of his fate to see the stupidity of becoming a murderer."

"Ah! But in that you are wrong," she countered. "The hero became master of his fate only through the love and sympathy and help of his beautiful wife."

"At what part of the characters' lives does the book end?"

"When they had been married about five years."

"Yes, it would be, to end happily. The author knew where to stop. He would not have dared to carry on the tale till the hero had reached very old age, or even further —beyond death. Have you read Omar Khayyam?"

"No."

"He was a very wise old poet who put very big truths into quite short verses. One of the truths he versified was:

"'The Moving Finger writes; and, having writ,
Moves on: nor all thy Piety nor Wit

Shall lure it back to cancel half a Line,
Nor all thy Tears wash out a Word of it.'

"We may be masters of our fate by planning ahead, but we cannot put the clock back or obliterate one act, one thought."

Dudley was looking at her shapely face in profile, and remembering what Hester Long had said about St. Anthony. Dressed in navy-blue, with a light-grey hat fitting low over her head, Edith Mallory made a delightful picture. Without turning her head she said:

"Agreed that the act has been committed, should we not try to live it down and make the best of life nevertheless?"

"There are some acts that can never be lived down," he told her quietly. "Murder is one of them. Atonement has to be made, not only to man, but to God also. I am not a religious man, but I still believe what my mother taught me as a child. I believe in God. I believe in a future existence. And, most important of all, I believe in the just punishment of our sins.

"Even if I did not believe in the first two articles of faith I must, being a man of ordinary intelligence, believe in the third. If I do not believe in God I must believe in Nature. And, after all, God and Nature are one. I am realizing this more fully these last few days. I have come to recognize that my banishment to this place is a just punishment for having committed murder. A far juster punishment than hanging. The agony of death by hanging lasts but a few seconds ; my agony in life is worse than death, and has lasted for many months. The sentence was passed upon me the instant I pulled the trigger. Assuming that in the circumstances my fellow-men acquitted me of murder, I should still have to face the judgment of God."

"And why should God's judgment be less merciful than man's?" she questioned swiftly.

"Because God's judgment is invariably just; and, if man did acquit me, man's judgment would not be just, for man's sympathy would overcloud his reason."

"I cannot see it from your viewpoint, indeed I can't," she said earnestly. "I think the trouble is that you are living so much alone that the whole matter of right and wrong is distorted in your mind. If you would but go far away and mix with other people, you would come to look upon the act in its true perspective, as merely an act of folly. Being merely a foolish act, though quite justified, you would soon almost forget it and find happiness again."

Slowly Dudley shook his head.

"I shall not find happiness again, never," he said. "Even were I to deceive the people I finally settled among, even if I loved and married again and deceived the woman, it would always be impossible to deceive myself."

"Not if the woman truly loved you. She would make you forget. A writer or poet once said: 'A man remembers nothing when he is in the arms of a woman who loves him'."

"Maybe there is truth in that," agreed Dudley, wondering if the girl fully understood what she had quoted. "But such moments of forgetfulness are fleeting, and Time is without end. We come back, you see, to the relentless Moving Finger."

Edith sighed. Dudley knew why. He knew she realized that reason was on his side, as indeed it was. At that meeting he was thinking more lucidly than he had done for months, and the cause thereof appeared to be this girl's determination to show him a way out of the morass in which he had sunk. She demanded reason of him, and found it.

"Your friend has not come back," she said abruptly.

"Not yet. He said he would be away a week. He went to Perth to fix some business which would assure his wife a small fixed income for a year, so I understood. When he does come, we shall probably go north on a prospecting expedition."

"How long do you think he has been gone?" she asked, her brows knit with perplexity.

"Three or four days. Why?"

"You are losing count of time, Mr. Cain. Your friend has been gone twelve days."

"Twelve days!" he gasped.

"Twelve days," Edith Mallory repeated. "It was twelve days ago when he passed through Dongara. I learned that from the storekeeper this morning. You see now how this sort of life is treating you, don't you?"

"Twelve days!" Dudley repeated. "Impossible!"

"Twelve days it is."

The man stared out on the sea. The girl watched him keenly, agonized by her love of him, and hurt by every line on his face which told of suffering. The longing, the desire to throw her arms around him and cradle his head in them there, to stroke his hair and soothe his wounds and make him forget the horrible past, caused a feeling of faintness.

As for Dudley, he had for the moment forgotten her. To him was the future made vivid. The signs were plain, writ in letters of fire before his eyes. The body of a kangaroo became the body of Tracy. Nine days and nine nights had slipped away unaccounted for, unaccountable. How had he passed those days and nights? Think! Remember! He must try to remember. He put his hands over his eyes to shut out the memory-clogging light, and sat thus for a full minute trying to remember. To remember meant merely that that lost period of time was but forgetfulness ; not to remember it, not to recall an important incident or two, meant but one thing, the thing he had suspected—the madness born of solitude.

At last his hands fell. Edith Mallory saw the terror in his eyes, the terror that made the corners of his mouth to quiver. The elements at long last had made impression on him. Space itself had worn away the shell covering his soul. Wind was ever increasingly whistling through the cracks. Temperature, cold and hot, sent shafts of fire and ice against the thinning, weakening body-armour. And now behind him, tracking him as a relentless aboriginal tracker, drawing closer and ever closer to him, was the Thing called Madness.

The writing on Dudley's pain-racked face made Edith Mallory catch her breath. There was nothing now in the world that mattered but the saving of Arnold Dudley. She believed—woman-like, she had finally come to believe what she wanted to believe—that she could save him from himself, could make him forget the past by the power of her love—believed that her love was powerful enough to create love in him to compensate it.

"Hector! Hector! Listen to me," she cried, gripping him by the arm. "You can see now where this terrible life is leading you. Let me help— please let me help!" Dudley was looking into her tear-drenched face almost stupidly. "You must go away—indeed, you must go away. You want taking care of, you want sympathy and love. Let me go with you, Hector! Let me take the place of that other woman. We could go away to some place where neither of us is known, and start life afresh, perhaps presently in some other country."

He made no effort to speak, showed no sign that he understood her meaning. In her earnestness she shook his arm held in her two hands and twisted her body towards him, so that she came to be kneeling and sitting on the heels of her riding boots.

"Don't think, Hector! Please don't think of what you know, what I know, is coming if you stay here," she pleaded with trembling voice. "Just realize that I am here now and want to be with you always, to take care of you and love you and make you well and happy. Lean against me, Hector! Let me be your support till you have forgotten and are yourself once more. Take me away with you in your truck now, this day, this hour. See, here in my handbag is money. I drew it from the bank at Dongara this morning. There is a thousand pounds, and presently, if we want more, I can send for it. You need worry about nothing, think of nothing, care for nothing. You needn't love me, or try to love me, or think of me if you would rather not. I don't matter in the least. It is you, you, you that matters. Let me give all I have, all I can. I shall demand nothing of you in return, nothing but to be permitted to be near you, to watch over you and for you."

She paused only to regain her breath. The words came in a torrent, low-toned, vibrant with passion, with entreaty, with the desire to serve. In those moments she was indescribably lovely. Her eyes were pools reminding Dudley inexplicably of the Psalmist's description of green pastures beside running water. Her mouth, a-quiver with emotion, fascinated him with its infinite invitation and allure. Her voice soothed the chaos of his mind into a semblance of orderliness. And that devil-voice within him cried aloud:

"Why not? Why not?"

Why not? Why not fling the past further behind? Why not take from this lovely girl all that she entreated him to take? She offered him escape from the Thing called Madness living there on the beach of desolation and ever creeping nearer to him. She offered him temporary forgetfulness of Tracy and of Ellen. What use, to what purpose was it to go on there dreaming of an Ellen who would eternally evade him just because he had shot her seducer? Why not race away from the past with this alluring, desirable woman, rush out of the present into the future, accepting joyfully the God-given gift, even if the gift faded and vanished in a few years? He heard a voice. Was it his own?

"You would some day regret it."

"Regret! Hector! Oh, Hector! Never would I regret serving you, working for you, planning for your happiness."

Again that voice. Again the doubt that it was his own.

"Are you sure—sure?"

She saw the light of desire flash into his blazing hazel eyes, was lifted up by the surge of triumph, and cried loudly:

"I am sure. Please believe I am sure."

He was smiling, a smile such as she had never dreamed to see. She knew she had won her fight, and the knowledge almost made her heart stop with its exquisite portents. His face seemed to become larger, so large that presently all that she could see was the hunger in his eyes. She felt his lips upon hers, and the fire they sent rushing through her veins burnt out her sight of him. The world stopped. She lived in a stupendous silence, broken at last by a well-known voice that held a sob in it, seeming to come from a far distance:

"Edith! I have come to take you home."

Onward rushed the world. The gentle roar of the waves, the faint murmur of the wind about the Seagulls' Throne, came again into her consciousness, as into her flame-lit mind entered the calm, pure light of day.

Standing near the rock was Hester Long. Edith saw in the grey limpid eyes a great sympathy and under-standing. Dudley, looking down into the same grey eyes, saw neither sympathy nor understanding, but reproach. And what he saw there sent him to his feet on the Throne, and the idea, the thought, which came to dominate his mind, was that he had betrayed his wife, had been disloyal to her, and also to the ideal she was to him.

He forgot Hester Long. He forgot Edith Mallory. He knew only that he had been untrue to Ellen. In that supreme moment it was the woman who had dishonoured him, and not the woman who had laid her all at his feet, who dominated his mind and his soul.

He jumped the rock, tore madly down the sand-hill, and rushed across the gully and over the next and the next, whilst Hester Long helped the wildly-sobbing Edith down from the Throne, then gathered her in her work-hardened arms and hugged her to her flat bosom.

CHAPTER XXIV

THE FOX HUNTER

THE sun was touching the horizon, a disc of concentrated fire which crimsoned the sky above it and the sea on which for an instant it rested, joining sea and sky as one vertical sheet of flame.

A further twenty-four hours had passed, and still the sea remained as blue glass at midday and rose-pink to emerald-green at sunset. Still the wind blew fitfully and softly from the East. That day had been almost hot, even for Australia, and the coming night promised to be warm and kind.

When the sun sank into the sea, causing passing wonder that it made not the sea boil and steam, Arnold Dudley turned eastward from the beach between the twin hills of pure white sand. With satisfaction having no basis other than the instinct of the trapper, Dudley noted that the hills, as well as the narrow stretch of sand between them, carried far more fox-tracks than they had done at his earlier visit. That, however, did not indicate an increase in the number of foxes visiting that place. The absence of wind allowed Time to multiply the original number of tracks by the number of nights since the last wind or the last rain had obliterated those made before.

On account of its numbers, as well as its destruction of lambs, the fox is considered and dealt with in Australia as vermin. A price is placed on his scalp ranging from two pounds in Western Australia down to half-a-crown in many pastoral districts over the Eastern States. The pelts, of which many thousands are sold to foreign buyers every season, range from three and sixpence to sixteen and seventeen shillings apiece. Therefore the fox is closely studied by all fur-getters.

Dudley had learned a great deal about the fox from George Finlay, and had found out a great deal more for himself. His knowledge, however, had been gained in New South Wales. In Western Australia the fox is a comparatively recent immigrant, like the rabbit. The rabbit came westward one bumper year. It came in droves, and after it came the dingo, and in lesser numbers, the fox.

That evening in mid-May Dudley carried a "drag" and a quantity of baits, as well as a canvas water-bag, a small billy, and sufficient cooked food for two meals. He made his camp by lighting a small fire a quarter of a mile inland along the green-floored, bush-bordered valley where he had shot the kangaroo, and then hastily breaking off a quantity of bush-boughs for a bed. Leaving the food and water-bag, he snatched up the "drag" and the baits, and hastened back to the twin sand-hills.

By then it was the magic period of the twenty-four hours called half-light, neither full daylight nor twilight. During the few minutes of Dudley's absence the green of the sea had changed to deep-blue north and south of the wide ribbon of pearl-grey at the farther end of which the sun had vanished. The white surf, the white sandy beach, the drab white sand-dunes, had softened to pale cream. The bush on the westward slopes of the dunes reflected the sheen of yellow-green satin; the bush on the eastern slopes pale purple; whilst that deep in the shadow of dell and valley was blackening rapidly.

It was a world painted wholly in three colours—green, white, and blue, vivid and brilliant, but colours having each a thousand differing and ever-changing shades.

Dudley waited, regardless of the beauty surrounding him. He waited because two white-eyelidded crows—sleek, glossy, funereal black, and sinister—were watching him intently, whilst pretending to be searching for the worm caught by the late bird. Of all living things that fly the crow surely is the most intelligent. Seeing the observers, Dudley laughed and spoke aloud, as was now an established habit.

"And there were two crows, an old fellow and a young fellow. And the old fellow said: 'My son, beware of the man who stoops to pick up a stone, for assuredly he will throw the stone at you.' And the young fellow said: 'All right, father, I will remember and act on your advice. When I see a man stoop to pick up a stone, I'll make myself scarce. But, father, what am I to do if the man puts his hand in his pocket?'

"Ha, ha, ha! you wily devils," Dudley cried to them. "It's a hard road for the dog and sandy for the pup. You'd like me to lay the baits now, wouldn't you, so that you could come along and gobble them up? Wait, friends, wait! To-morrow morning I'll do better for you than that. All I have now is some little cubes of fish seasoned with strychnine. They would make you mighty sick, though I believe you know enough to fly to a tree and hang upside down till you disgorge them again. That's a trick worth knowing. The devil must have taught it you."

Crows are late as well as early birds. This especial pair pretended to hunt industriously for the late worm until it was almost dark, when disgustedly they flew away to roost in the branches of a wattle farther up the valley. Safe now from their interference, Arnold Dudley stood up and took the end of a short line attached to a ten-pound gummy shark—known in English waters as a species of dogfish—and proceeded to drag a trail. The shark had been caught five days previously, and was in that state of decay when its oils were oozing from it. Upon every particle of sand it passed over the "drag" left its pungent oily fish-smell.

Dudley dragged the shark around the base of both hills and zigzagged over the sand-patch between them. The passage of the fish made a broad shallow line on the white sand, and at intervals of fifty paces he placed on the trail thus made two half-inch cubes of rock-fish flesh to one side of which adhered powdered strychnine crystals. Where the twin baits were laid he marked the sand with the heel of his boot.

A casual observer at this point might ask: "Why two baits together? Why not one, or more than two?" The fur-gatherer is not a casual observer. If he were, he would soon have to take to a pick-axe for a living. He knows that were he to drop a single bait at intervals the fox might well pick it up and carry it between his teeth for a considerable distance before swallowing or burying it. When, however, the animal, running along an alluring trail, comes upon two baits, he will be obliged to swallow one, even should he desire to pick up the other and carry it away, possibly to bury it. It is needless to say the second bait is not carried very far, seldom over the next stretch of fifty paces. To lay a number of baits at one spot also is foolish, because too large a quantity of strychnine will most likely make the animal vomit what it has taken, and it will get far away before succumbing to the effect of the small residue left in its stomach. And to poison a furred animal without a chance of getting the fur is considered by trappers nothing short of a crime.

Dudley laid twenty pairs of baits before returning to his temporary camp with the drag, which, being no longer needed, he buried in the soft fine soil of the valley.

Night was now come, soft, warm, comforting—comforting because the vast spaces of the beach were blotted out and the sense of defenceless-ness, ever growing upon him, for the time being was banished.

The flames of his fire hissed and leapt upward, licking the small black-ened billycan filled with water for tea. He washed his hands by pouring water on them from the canvas water-bag; although his hands were clean, for never once had they come in contact with fish-cubes or strychnine. The pungent odour of man on the baits would warn any fox not raven-ously hungry, besides which to touch strychnine needlessly is the act of a careless fool, who, by avoiding such acts, might live to a wise old age.

The huge sand-mountain on the one side and the lower jumble of hills on the other were then mere inky-black walls unrelieved by a single feature. Their summits, firmly curved, were outlined against the indigo-blue of the sky, clear and ablaze with stars, there never so clear and brilliant as they are above England when frost grips her. To the south-west, low and setting, was the constellation of six stars set in the shape of an irregular cross, no brighter and no more distinguished than their neighbours. The Southern Cross has been unduly honoured by romantic imagination.

The night appeared to shut off many daylight sounds to accentuate the few that were of importance. It was a night full yet empty of sound—a paradox easily understood by a bushman. The silence of the windless night could almost be felt, as though silence itself were a living entity; as was the fox which "quok-quoked" far up the valley, as the tail-thumping 'roo, suspicious of the figure outlined by the fire, as the many tiny frogs whose "queek-queek" was kept up marvellously in perfect time, and as the waves crashing with a low rumbling sound on the sand-beach.

Whilst Dudley stood and waited for the billy to boil he was but subconsciously aware of the night sounds. Night had contracted the uttermost walls of space to the radius of his firelight. He felt easier in mind and better clothed of body when thus within the narrow limits of a camp-fire world ; and standing there, as often in winter he had stood with his back to Ellen's drawing-room fire, Arnold Dudley carried on aloud a complete conversation between Edith Mallory and himself. For the Thing called Madness was very close behind him, "sooled" on by the Demon of Solitude.

Some men, in the stage of capture Dudley then was, will argue or converse with a hat placed on a stump or a fence-post. Political and economic questions will be thrashed out from two distinct angles or points of view. Perhaps the theme of the one-man conversation is the pros and cons of Protection. The hat may be for Free Trade and the hatless for Tariffs. Argument will be keen and lucid ; whereas the man's thoughts when he enjoyed the doubtful advantages of sanity would be neither keen nor lucid. The mind of a man reduced to arguing with his hat is quite pleasurably excited. He is conscious of new-found mental superiority, never experienced before Solitude found him ; and, as with the taking of a drug, indulgence occurs with ever-increasing frequency.

Dudley knew this, realized that his dual soliloquy was a sign and a warning, yet nevertheless he was unable to resist the desire, and did not wish to. He there told Edith Mallory how fortunate Hester Long's coming upon them on the Seagulls' Throne was; and proceeded then to inform himself how Edith Mallory was in despair of him, and how she would have proved her love and devotion to him. He told her that nothing she could do or plan would for long banish from his mind the loss of Ellen and the killing of Tracy. And he told himself, mentally in Edith's place, that he was wrong, that love and passion and devotion would win him from the black past and carry him along into a brilliantly happy future. And he pleaded more eloquently than ever any woman could have done.

The conversation closed. The elevation of his mind waned. He remembered the billycan and found it boiled almost dry, and with wry laughter refilled it from the water-bag to boil again.

He supped standing, gazing down into the fire. He ate cold boiled fish and hard, cracked, old baking-powder bread. He was unconscious of what he ate. Of a truth he ate to live and lived not to eat.

For an hour he sat on the heels of his boots in regular bushman's style, and gazed into the glowing coals of the fire, wherein he saw strange faces, animals' heads, and fantastic scenes, now silently smoking cigarette after cigarette. For most of that spell of day-dreaming his face was hardened by an expression of hopeless desolation, but now and then he smiled gently, and once he laughed long and loud. At the sound of it, echoing between the hillsides, two sentinel kangaroos, one just beyond the fire hidden by the darkness, and the other further up the valley, sprang into the air, raising their tails to bring them down with a resounding thump of warning at the instant their hind-legs met the earth.

The frogs never ceased their litany of praise. The fox that had "quok-quo-ked" was answered presently by another fox over the sand-dunes with a "worle-worle", and later the queer sound between a hiss and the screech of an owl informed Dudley that two or more foxes were contending over the body of a rabbit somewhere east of him.

In that he recognized Nature, blood-raw and ivory-toothed. The foxes were fighting over a morsel of food which one, possessing initiative as well as luck, had snared. Greater even than sex instinct was the instinct to kill, the instinct to eat to survive coming second. And of all animals man is the most predatory, the most horribly ruthless, the most indifferent to suffering. That truth had come to Dudley more than once in driving his luxury car to his luxury home at Belmont. He passed by groups of work-less men, shabby and down-at-heel, and in passing by he never could bring himself to look any one of them straight in the eyes. He felt as if he had stolen his luxury from their necessity. Always was he hurt by the cynical reference to the workless as the "work-won'ts" by fellow club-members—sleek and glossy and well-fed: men who regarded an army of unemployed as a gift of God where—with to break strikes and lower the wages of their producers. As with dogs and foxes, one of the things undreamt—of was to share a bone.

The prosperous period or peak of Dudley's career appeared to him at that time to be wholly foreign to the course of his life, in the same way as a vivid dream of affluence can be to a poor man. His sojourn on the Beach of Atonement seemed to follow naturally from the point when he had left the bush and his skin-buying operations to go to Perth. In retrospect his former bush life was much nearer to his present existence than had been the years spent in the city. Ellen of the bush was more vivid in memory than Ellen of the city. Memory of her in Perth was rapidly blurring in ratio to the increasing vividness of his memory of her before they went to Perth. That, too, was another sign of the approach of the Thing called Madness. The effect solitude was having on Dudley was very similar to the effect increasing age produces on ordinary sane people. As the aged become increasingly reminiscent of their activities decades before, when in the bloom of youth, so, too, does the dweller in solitude. The immediate past is quickly clouded; the fog gathering about the far-distant past is swept aside and that long-vanished past is re-lived again and again.

Eventually Arnold Dudley spread out his heap of bush-boughs in the form of a mattress near beside the fire, and, removing only his hat, laid himself down on them and almost instantly was asleep. The lullaby of the surf drifted up the valley and was lost in the maze of the countless gullies. The kangaroos forgot their suspicions and fed themselves to the full, when they, too, laid down on their sides and slept, leaving one of their number sitting up to watch—a strong proof of animal intelligence, this. With the passing of time the silence seemed to increase, until towards dawn it was complete, save for the ceaseless moan of the surf.

Long before Venus—then the morning star—showed palely above the summit of the eastern sand-mountain, Dudley was up, boiling water for breakfast tea. Breakfast was eaten, and he was smoking a cigarette waiting for day half an hour before it became light enough for him to follow his fox-trail. The crows arrived almost as soon as he.

Carrying a tin and a twig, Dudley started back over the now clear-ly-defined trail. Coming to his last mark, he found the two fish baits undisturbed, and these he scooped into the tin with the twig. The second and the third pairs of baits he found and likewise secured. The fourth pair was missing, and there he hastily made a fresh mark with his heel. The tenth and the eleventh pairs were missing. One each from the ninth and the eighteenth pairs remained, and those places where baits were missing he marked.

There were three pairs and two single baits gone. Along parts of the trail the four-padded, diamond-shaped tracks of several foxes were plainly imprinted. By now it was broad daylight, and Dudley, arrived at the beginning of his trail, looked about him. There, on the seaward slope of the southern sand-hill, lay the red-brown body of a fox. Another lay stretched in death on the sand-patch between the hills. Almost at a run, Dudley raced up the southern sand-hill and brought down the fox to where lay the second. Both were dogs in their second year, with fur at top grade.

The carcasses he took up the valley to the fringe of the more robust bush, where he laid them in shade from the rising sun, and covered with broken bushes to protect them from the crows. The crows! They were gone. Dudley raced back to the twin hills of sand and climbed the northern one, slightly the higher. Almost at once he espied four black dots dancing about a larger brownish dot two hundred yards along the beach. He reached the third carcass in time to save the skin from being torn by sharp beaks. The eyes of the dead fox, however, had been taken.

With less haste now, he skirted the base of the sand-hills carrying with him the third fox, an old vixen whose teeth were discoloured and worn short by age. A second-grade fur, for it was thin and uneven. A fourth fox he found by luck in a clump of low bush east of the northern hill, and when the four were well hidden he climbed the higher of the two hills and from that vantage-point looked for the crows.

So far he had beaten them. Their number had miraculously increased to seven. They flew singly, here over the beach, there along the valley, and there over the sand hills, and down into the dells, their needle-sharp eyes piercing the bush and travelling along the pads made by kangaroos or goats, and the rabbit-runs. Hopeless for Dudley to search all that dense bush for a fox or foxes, which, after all, might not lie poisoned there. Should dead foxes lie hidden there, the crows would find them quickly enough. Dudley made and lit a cigarette and watched his enemies, the crows, do his work of searching.

Presently he saw one wheel, bank high, wheel again, and alight on a dead limb of a coast wattle. It cawed raucously, and another flew to join it. Both birds began to caw, lowering their heads as though bowing whilst they did so. The remaining five came back from their self-allotted sections of country, so that very shortly all seven birds were gathered in near view of some centre of interest.

Dudley smiled grimly, stood up, made mental note of the position of the dead wattle, and walked to it, pushing his way through the close-growing scrub. And within four yards of the wattle he found the fifth fox, so obligingly indicated to hint by the crows. It was a dog fox, two years old, fur super class, long, even, clean, nut-brown with grey specks, glossy, and lovely.

Half an hour later he had five pelts, each rolled into a ball and hung from his belt. The crows had as their well-earned breakfast the carcasses.

Walking back to his tent, Dudley felt no elation what-ever. Hanging from his belt were fur and scalps to the value of at least thirteen pounds. He was wholly unconscious of the colourful sea, the beach, the sand-hills. He was living over again the moment when he first met Ellen in a station-owner's garden.

CHAPTER XXV

STORM

GEORGE FINLAY was released from gaol on the 14th of May. He found the strike of the Midland Railway still in full swing; and, since the ball-race for his truck had not arrived from Perth, he wired Ellen Dudley to leave for Mingenew in a hired car as quickly as possible. Three hours later Ellen wired him that she was about to depart.

That afternoon found Arnold Dudley tramping north-ward from the southern extremity of the beach, where he had been prospecting for fox-tracks. He had been away from camp since early that morning, and, although he had walked some twenty miles over loose sand, he was unconscious of fatigue. When half a mile from camp his seagulls came to meet him, flying about his head and screaming a welcome, and he acknowledged their comradeship by tossing his hat high in the air, and shouted when the birds converged on it with daring wing feats. Whilst he walked on they accompanied him, till he began to climb the hill behind the Pontoon, when they preceded him to the Seagulls' Throne, on which they settled. When he reached it they rose, hovering, and when he climbed to its flat top they dropped down to the sand base. Love had conquered their shyness.

For mid-May the weather was superb. For days the wind had come from the centre of Australia, warm and gentle. Day by day, although the sun was swinging farther to the north, it yet became hotter, so that on this day the atmosphere was humid and the great rock on which Dudley seated himself was uncomfortably warm. Still no cloud whitened the sky, and over all that vast expanse of water not a wave broke into foam. During many days the calm had continued, and to a person whose sojourn on the beach was shorter than Dudley's the first indication of the coming of the greatest storm the people of Dongara had ever experienced would have been unnoticed. Dudley saw it immediately he sat on the Seagulls' Throne, for from that elevated position he looked down on the sea. The tide was low, one of the lowest tides he remembered. Not a drop of water rolled over the Pontoon. The Sugar Loaf was revealed in the wave troughs to its foundation, an immense mass of granite, whilst the sunken reef south of it was occasionally disclosed, studded thickly with shellfish as large as oysters. Sky, sea, and beach were exactly as they had been the day before and for days before that. There was no sign of the coming storm in the sky or the sea. It was the beach crabs that predicted the coming change.

The first crab to attract Dudley's attention arrived at the summit of the sand-hill on which rested the great boulder he called the Seagulls' Throne. Watching it idly, he saw it move straight to the clustered gulls, who made way for it ; and it struck Dudley as curious that he had never seen a gull kill a land-crab for food, although its shell is exceedingly brittle and it is incapable of self-defence against a bird the size of the gull.

Excepting to move away at its approach, the gulls ignored the many-legged, grotesque beach-urchin moving on with its flat body on edge and its two black eyes tipping the high cylindrical towers. The crab, without haste yet with uncanny fixed purpose of direction, deviated not a hair's breadth, and passed the Seagulls' Throne to move down the landward side of the sand-hill, where it disappeared among the low coast-bush. Shortly afterwards Dudley saw two more travelling together and in the same direction. From his eminence the Seaweed Mountain appeared in shape and colour a flat wet rock lying at the edge of the beach. From this seeming rock he saw tiny points of orange become detached and move slowly across the narrow sand-beach till they disappeared in the coast-scrub. The moving points of orange were countless. The Seaweed Mountain must have been the home of many thousands of these peculiar crabs, and they were then evacuating their fortress for the greater security of the scrub-studded sand-dunes.

So unusual an occurrence aroused his interest, and, climbing down from the Throne he made his way to the beach, there to walk along it till he arrived behind the Seaweed Mountain, which then cut him off completely from the sea.

Its brown mass, interlaced with black-studded streamers, and spotted by scarlet sponge not yet dead from exposure to the drab atmosphere, was pointed by countless beach-crabs, reminding Dudley of a community of ants whose nest has been disturbed. They swarmed over the seaweed and appeared and disappeared from and into crevices and holes. An army of orange-uniformed soldiers moved from it up the beach, passing him on both sides, "cleek-clecking" acknowledgment of his presence, but strangely unafraid of him.

The migration fascinated him. The naturalist in him marvelled, and for a while he was absorbed by the problem of their collective purposeful movement. He wondered what the impulse was behind that migration, what had come to them from space ordering their evacuation. Dudley remembered then that one of the surest signs of heavy rain in the hinterland of the continent was shown by ants removing their eggs from ground nests and carrying them up into trees.

Of a certainty these crabs were not afraid of rain. They had no need to be. Wind, however, did disturb them. Wind-driven sand appeared to frighten and hurt them; and, after more thought than he had given to anything for some considerable time, Dudley decided that they were hurrying for shelter at the approach of a storm long before a single indication of its coming was observable to man.

For dinner that evening he ate kangaroo steak fried with sliced potatoes, accompanied by the inevitable tea. Through the open tent-door came the occasional "cleek-cleek" of a crab; and, when finally he went out for the wash-up water, he was greeted by a chorus of "cleek-cleeking" from dozens of the amphibians, mostly concealed by the surrounding bush.

It still wanting half an hour to sunset, Dudley returned to the beach, carrying damper crusts and small pieces of kangaroo meat for his gulls. They were waiting for him, circling his camp into which they never would come, and they flew around him whilst he walked down to the Pontoon, where he tossed their evening meal into the rock-pools, for they preferred to pick up the bread and meat from water.

The lonely man's attention to these seventeen gulls was pathetic. It revealed a human soul starved and hungry for affection. The most depraved of men, hated and loathed by his fellows, will receive adoration from a dog, friendship from a bird, or even toleration from a reptile. A man must love something; he must receive solace from the affection of something living, and if he lives in solitude he will take infinite pains to secure from other sources the need of affection denied him by his kind.

Remarkable is the number of sudden and serious quarrels caused by the ill-treatment of a man's pet. There are instances when the quarrel has culminated in murder, for the instinct to protect is as great as the instinct to love. Dudley would have fought off any danger to his gulls, forfeiting his life if necessary. The shooting of the solitary shag meant as much to him in his state of loneliness as the death of a child to a man living in normal circumstances.

His gulls fed and duly chided for their greediness, Arnold Dudley mounted to the Seagulls' Throne, there to make and light a cigarette. The sun was very low, big and crimson. The wind was a little stronger. It covered the sea with cat's-paws and laid a carpet of rubies before the sun.

Over the Pontoon welled the waves of the incoming tide, and to the south-west and west the horizon-line was being lifted and dropped by the rollers sweeping over the distant Ramparts. The sea was rising. On its surface it bore no different aspect, yet even to Dudley's untrained eyes it was evident that the incoming waves were bigger than they had been at noon. They were what are known as ground swell. Raised by the growing weather disturbance far in the Indian Ocean, these long, distinct hills of water outran the storm in speed to become its pilots.

Into its bed of fire sank the sun, and when it had sunk from sight it revealed low on the horizon a ribbon of clouds with the substance of mist, clouds of gauze with centres of scarlet and edges of pink-dream clouds, unearthly, Martian clouds. And whilst Dudley watched he saw their colour turn to orange and yellow, to cream and white, and then appear slowly to disintegrate and vanish.

The Sugar Loaf was being washed by the rising swell. Low, thunderous vibrations came from the seaward base of the Pontoon at the instant tons of water rose up its concave face and welled shoreward in a white-fronted swathe of green water, three to four feet thick. The tide set southward and the Boiling Pot was free of flotsam. The incoming breakers gradually drew nearer and nearer to the Seaweed Mountain, as teasing monsters confident of power to destroy when they willed.

Dudley sat on the Seagulls' Throne when darkness fell and hid the water, but was unable to conceal the softly gleaming stretch of sand-beach and the lines of incoming surf. With the fading of daylight the easterly wind, warm and bush-scented, freshened. It rustled the dwarf bushes and disturbed the fine dry sand with a hissing sound so low that it was as the bursting of soap-bubbles.

When he walked behind the low sand-ridge backing the beach, to his camp, the bushes on both sides of the rough track were full of the "cleek-cleeks" of the crabs. They were still fleeing the Seaweed Mountain and assembling in their thousands in the shelters between the dunes. Their strange voices appeared to Dudley to hold indignation at his presence among them. He still could hear them all around his tent whilst he recorded his observations of them in his diary, and he heard them later when he lay down to sleep.

At dawn he awoke from a dream that left him stiff with horror, and sent him out to light the fire and boil the billy for tea, as a man who has passed through a frightful experience. Undoubtedly dreams are made up of memories stored by the subconscious mind. Often we can trace the substance of a dream to a recent thought or happening. When the thoughts entered Dudley's mind which produced the nightmare that was to lead him to freedom from his chains, he did not know. So far from trying to recall those thoughts to account for the dream, he believed that it was a vision sent him by God to soften his heart.

He dreamed that he was dead and walking along a white sandy road towards two low, thick pillars of marble. When he drew nearer to those pillars he saw on the summit of one seven seagulls, and on the summit of the other ten seagulls. They were his gulls. He recognized each of them with joy and called to them, and as one they left the marble pillars and flew to him and attacked him. Their bills he saw, with a feeling of terrible loathing, were fouled by flesh and were hooked as beaks of eagles. Screaming vile oaths, they pecked at his face and his ears and his hair, and when he wildly waved his arms to beat them off one pecked out his right eye and held it in its beak, so that with his other eye he could see his lost optic regarding him with malevolent hatred.

Another gull pecked out his left eye, and even when suffering untold terror and pain he considered it strange that he could still see, could see the two gulls each holding one of his eyes in its bill. And both eyes shone with an awful hatred blazing from their green depths.

Limb by limb the gulls tore him to pieces, and his disembodied soul hovered about them whilst it screamed for the return of its covering. It was then that he heard the voice of Edmund Tracy, whom he could not see, but who he knew was near. Tracy was crying, pleading for life, imploring the gulls to give him Dudley's body, so that he might live his allotted span, and work out his redemption on earth. The gulls cried their familiar welcome, and there upon the ground built up the body of Tracy with the limbs of Arnold Dudley. And on Tracy's face was a wonderful joy, whilst the gulls flew down the sandy road, beckoning him to follow them whence Dudley had come.

The pillars of marble turned to living flame, and beyond them the road led to and vanished at the foot of a perpendicular grid of red-hot bars which ran up to the vault of the livid sky. And from the grid along the road came four figures carrying a stretcher with black leather handles which once had carried Dudley from a train to a hospital in England. Waiting there, he knew with sudden awful terror that those four men were coming to lift him on the stretcher, and carry him back to the fire beyond the grid. And when they drew near, and he shrieked and tried to flee, he saw that each of their faces was the face of Ellen. The four Ellens came, and, laying the stretcher beside him, bent over him, smiling with shocking evilness, and stretched down their beautiful white hands.

That was the moment of his awakening. The next found him outside his tent, trembling, his temples damp with ice-cold sweat. The patches of orange laid on white helped him to regain his nerve, for the patches of orange swayed over the white sand, and the hundreds of crabs of which they were composed greeted him with their chorus of "cleek-cleek".

The effect of the dream was still upon him when, having breakfasted hastily, he went along to the beach. The day had brought but little change to sky and sea. The sun rose into a clear, brilliant sky, as had become usual, and the surface of the sea was but faintly marked by the soft easterly wind. The tide, however, was high, and racing into the beach. Widely spaced and evenly formed were great hills of water whose summits were as whales' backs until they reached the Sugar Loaf and the sunken reef, or came to within fifty yards of the Seaweed Mountain, when the rollers reared and broke, thence to charge on the obstructions with the slow weight of terrific power.

Obsessed by his dream, Dudley walked to the edge of the low headland abutting on the Pontoon, leaving the gulls feeding along the beach, since the tide was too high to afford any placid pools. Whilst he sat with his feet dangling over the water-combed edge of the headland, he felt an instinctive warning of coming danger, and thought of the migrating crabs, and wondered if their finer instincts or intelligence had received the same warning. Consideration of this hypothesis was rudely stopped by sudden conviction that his more than habitually depressed state of mind was due to the dream.

It haunted him. Tracy's cries for life rang yet in the ears of his mind. Vision of the faces of the four Ellens was still vivid to the eyes of his mind, whilst the horror of that doom awaiting him still made his hands tremble and the corners of his mouth quiver.

Idly watching each roller leap and rush forward over the Pontoon, now many feet submerged; idly noting how each incoming wave rushed, fronted by a wall of water, to the base of the headland, careering over the comparatively still grey-green water, then sweeping backward to join the greater volume sliding southward with the speed of a racehorse, he tried to solve the enigma of his dream.

The hours sped and time brought him no solution. He could make nothing of the stretcher, nor of the four Ellens. That his dead body should be taken from him and given to Tracy to enable Tracy to live again and die a natural death after having had full time to repent his evil ways, was but justice. As a man in a dark room searching for the switch to turn on the electric light, Dudley had been groping toward real understanding of his act of killing. That part of the dream which directly concerned Tracy and himself became the switch that turned on the light. By it he saw clearly that when he shot Tracy he not only deprived him of his life, hut also deprived his soul of the hope of Redemption, in which he, Arnold Dudley, had always so thoroughly believed. He not only had hurled Tracy out of a world of pleasure, but moreover had hurled the man's soul into Eternity, blackened by his lustful amours. Not only had Tracy lost his life; he had lost also the right of regaining Paradise by repentance and amendment which he might have exercised had he lived.

That was the thought which became dominant in Dudley's mind during the rest of his life. It absorbed him so intensely that morning that he failed to observe the knife-edged bank of clouds rising from the sea towards the north-west. This bank, dense and bluff-faced, with flat blue-black underside and its top side a glory of snowy white, rose to the zenith with astonishing swiftness, travelling south-east. He did not observe that whilst the general mass of clouds raced towards the south-east they also drifted eastward. They were as the outside edge of a wheel which spins slowly from right to left whilst the wheel itself moves steadily in one direction.

During the approach of the cloud-mass to the sun the wind veered with infinite slowness to the north, at the same time increasing in velocity. By noon the sun was hidden. The summits of the sand-hills were faintly smoking, the sand-smoke sweeping over the beach to the sea, now grey-green and whipped by tiny wavelets that rushed away to meet the growing swells. The sound of them breaking along the beach and crashing over the now invisible rocks had risen to a low continuous roar, accompanied by the whine of the wind steadily ascending in tone. It came steadily, not in gusts, and in its rising pressure there was mysterious significance.

As the wind increased, so seemed to increase the weight pressing on Arnold Dudley's mind. Regret became an agony. He saw the fullness of his folly, the atrocity of his act, that day. Never since that fateful telephone call had he been so sane. In correct perspective he saw Tracy's act, Ellen's act, and his own act. After all, civilized man was right when he demanded that there should be no murder without death or life-imprisonment to the murderer, no matter what the provocation. Man was merely upholding a law of God.

There was now no recall, no going back. What the Moving Finger had written could never be washed out. Not only had he destroyed Tracy, he had destroyed also himself, for there on the beach lived but a ghost of Arnold Dudley. He was enduring a living death, and why? Because he loved Ellen and had lost her? No. Because he hated Tracy? No. Because a man had pricked the bubble of his vanity? Yes.

The afternoon waned. There had entered into the voice of the surf the roar of fury, and into the scream of the wind the anger of hell. No blaze of crimson glory laid the sun to rest that evening. The sand stung Dudley's face and neck, and swirled around the Seagulls' Throne high above his head. The whole beach beyond a quarter of a mile was hidden by the sand-smoke from the dunes, and the spaces between the ridges were obliterated by the white fog.

The tide remained stationary. The pressure of the coming cyclonic disturbance held it at its abnormally high level. For a mile from the beach the sea was covered by endless lines of sweeping surf. Every roller crashed and spouted against the Seaweed Mountain, and from it tore its quota of weed, which drifted past the headland over the Pontoon in a dark mass acting on the chop as oil on greater waves.

Not a crab was in sight. They huddled together in compact masses in the shelter of the scrub, and singly ran with apparent aimlessness as far inland as Big Hill. Dudley saw the clouds lower and come racing out of the sea. He watched the day weaken and die in a world of tossing, swirling water and flying, hissing sand. And not until midnight did he stumble into his tent and throw himself on his bed, oblivious of bodily wants of food and drink and warmth, realizing only that he had damned himself merely because his vanity had received a wound.

CHAPTER XXVI

HESTER LONG'S ORDEAL

THUNDER awoke Hester Long, and if there was one thing that daunted this brave woman it was an electric storm. The electrically-charged atmosphere seemed to play on her nerves as a musician's fingers on catgut. Nevertheless, a lightning display had a powerful fascination for her ; and, being awakened by a heavy roll of not-far-distant thunder, she lit the lamp at her bedside and noted the time to be five minutes past four.

Slipping out of bed and throwing on a wrap, she went to the window and, drawing aside the blind, peered outside. Her room faced south, and the window was almost fully open. Quite invisible in the black darkness was the fig-tree near which opened the kitchen door. The stillness was profound.

When she had gone to bed the wind was blowing half a gale from the north. Invariably, when a weather disturbance was due, the wind veered from the east to the north, thence to swing westward whilst the disturbance heightened, and southward when it had passed. These weather disturbances were almost always accurately foretold by the meteorologists in Perth from data wirelessed by ships at sea, and the result of the charted information was broadcast twice daily from the Government Broadcasting Station. The Mallorys, therefore, possessing a wireless installation, were well posted as to the approach. of these disturbances, and Hester

Long, through Miss Mallory, had been advised of the coming of what was to be a notable storm.

The dropping of the wind sometime whilst she was asleep was not unusual, but an electrical storm at that season of the year was most unusual. It predicted an unusually severe disturbance, and, whilst looking out through the open window, she thought of Arnold Dudley in his flimsy calico tent.

The tree was illuminated for fully two seconds by lightning blue as turquoise. The thunder, following instantly, shook the house, and in the ensuing silence she heard two sounds, the roaring of the surf on the beach four miles away, and her younger son crying for her in the next bedroom. Even when she dropped the blind the lightning came again, flickering and terrifying, and her answer to the lad's call was lost in a burst of thunder. With madly pounding heart, the lamp carried unsteadily in her trembling hand, she passed out of her bedroom and entered that of her two small boys.

Their round childish eyes winked into her light. Harold, the elder by two years, was still lying down, manfully hiding his fear, but James was sitting up, frankly terrified.

"Mummie! the thunder frightens me," he wailed.

"But there is nothing to be afraid of, darling," Hester told him cheerfully.

"That's what I said," Harold put in with scorn.

"Oh, mummie, it's getting worser!"

"There is no such word as 'worser'. We'll see that we cannot find it in the dictionary in the morning. And it will soon be light. Now I'm going to get into your bed, Harold, and Jim can come in, too; and while we wait for day to come I'll tell you a story about two little boys named David and Jonathan."

Yet that night Hester Long's story was not successful. The storm broke on the coast about an hour before dawn. The blinded window, aided by the lamp, baffled the vivid lightning, but nothing could deaden the appalling crashes of the thunder. The very bed on which the woman sat with her two lads huddled against her shook from the concussions, as though it and the house were set beside the mouth of an enormous naval gun. The thunder rumbled from a far distance, it crackled with many rapid reports immediately above them, and once one single ear-splitting crack set the children frantically hugging her, drew the blood from her face, and caused her heart to miss a beat.

Minute after long minute, after longer minute, the thunder roared and crackled and crashed without cease. The house shook and Hester thought it would collapse. To speak was almost impossible, and all the comfort she could give her children was to tighten her arms around them and alternately brush their hair with her face. Above her concern for them and for herself was her wild anxiety for the welfare of Arnold Dudley, there alone in the bush at the utter mercy of the elements. A fox in its hole, a rabbit deep in its burrow, would be infinitely more secure.

Supposing the lightning struck him? Vividly Hester Long saw him lying twisted and charred beneath the smoking ash of his tent, and she wanted to cry out at the picture drawn by her own imagination. Dead! supposing that the new day found him dead ? At least he would have found peace, at the least his agony would be finished; for surely there would be no further punishment after death? And after death Hector Cain would meet her husband, and they would be friends, for they were so much alike in temperament and in spirit; else why had she loved both?

Presently the intervals between the thunder-claps lengthened, and then she heard another sound, the hissing fall of tremendous rain. No tent without a protecting fly pitched over it would keep out such a downpour. Dudley's tent she knew was unprotected. In a short time he would he drenched, and everything belonging to him would be drenched also.

The dawn, when it came, brought yet another terror to succeed the thunder and lightning. Above the fall of the rain on the tin house roof, above the roar of the surf so far away yet seeming so close, she heard another sound, low-toned, humming as a top revolving faster and faster. That sound, strange to her, made her uneasy and fearful.

How she managed to put genuine cheerfulness into her voice when she spoke to the children was beyond her accounting. The increasing humming sound forced her out of the bed to the window, when lifting the blind she peered without.

It was almost light. The leaves of the fig-tree hung downward from the weight of the falling rain. It fell straight down, a swishing, roaring, tremendous downpour. Beyond the tree, through the leaves and branches, she could see no farther than twenty yards. The milking-shed and yards, the paddocks beyond, and the virgin bush beyond them, were obliterated from human vision by the falling sheets of water.

And above the roar of the rain that other sound, sinister, mysterious terrifying. It reminded Hester Long of the throbbing hum of German raiding aeroplanes. No other sound did it resemble.

"In God's name, what is it?" she whispered.

"Mummie, come back to bed," James cried, half-fretfully, half-fearfully.

Turning from the window, she regarded her two boys sitting upon the one bed, their eyes wide, as shown by the lamp.

"Just a minute, sweetheart! I must fasten the window." She spoke almost automatically, listening—listening to that throbbing hum growing in pitch, wild, menacing. If only she knew what it was! It seemed to be something monstrous, tearing across the world to destroy them. What should she do? The underground cellar! The cellar where the butter cream was kept during summer was fourteen feet underground. It would offer security against that frightful thing that was coming.

If only her husband were alive! If only Hector Cain were there, or even Tom Mallory or Joe Brown! Never during all the days of her lonely solitary fight had she felt the need of a man as at that moment. The sound, that devil's tune, was now as one played by a thousand insane violinists.

Time! Had she time to get her boys out from the house to the underground cellar some ten or twelve yards from the kitchen door? There might be time. She flew to the bed. The children, used to discipline and obedience, acted as well-trained soldiers.

She gave them no time for questioning. They made no effort to ask, seeing that on her pale face which frightened them more than the roar of the rain and the humming horror. Sweeping up the bed-clothes, she led them out of the room, past her own bedroom, where she did not stop to secure a gown to cover her night attire, and thence to the kitchen. A lad at each side of her, the three reached the door. She fumbled at the latch, the bed-clothes hindering her fingers. The latch was released, and the door flew inward under pressure of the south wind being sucked northward to meet the storm.

With the opening of the door the devil's tune roared into gigantic crescendo. The rain slanted in upon them, blinded their eyes, stung their faces and naked feet. How it rained! And that awful sound!

Hester Long waited no longer than that momentary pause. The clothes she held in her arms hampered her ; yet the urge, the need for haste, was no more compelling than the necessity for warmth in the stone-cold cellar.

"Run!" she screamed.

Out in the full force of the rain the children sped, she at their sides shepherding them as a dog shepherding lambs. Leaving the kitchen door was like taking a plunge into the sea. She clung to her blankets. Several garments were dropped by little James, who, wanting to cry, was unable to obtain sufficient breath.

Gone now was the throb in the dreadful sound. One omnipresent note encompassed them, low-pitched and vibrant. It seemed hours and days before they reached the brush-covered shed protecting the steps leading down to the cellar, a journey of a hundred miles through a surging torrent of water.

Arrived within the shed at the head of the wooden steps, she threw her bundle of clothes down to the door of the cellar, and, lifting James in her arms, scrambled down them, slipping at the third step from the bottom and falling in a heap on the bed-clothes. Gripped by panic, yet thoughtful only of her boys, she flung inward the cellar door, and, dragging the lads inside, slammed it shut.

Each second that they stood in the darkness seemed an eternity. She wondered later why at that moment she methodically counted the auger-holes in the door which gave the cellar ventilation and some light. There were nineteen two-inch holes in the form of a diamond, and the fact was impressed on her mind that it was the first time she had noted the number of holes, although she herself had bored them.

The children clung to her. Both now were crying and whimpering alternately. Dropping to the semi-saturated bed-clothes, she drew them down beside her, and the same instant that their bodies pressed against hers Hester Long's panic subsided and the stunned lethargy of her brain was replaced by a delicious calmness.

"Let's pull the clothes round us, sweethearts," she said with amazing cheerfulness. "The storm will soon be over now, and we'll go up and get breakfast. Cuddle in and get———."

Her voice was drowned by supreme cacophony. A monstrous roar, a ripping tearing of corrugated iron, a bump, bump, bump down the wooden steps without. Something struck the door and sent it flying inward on its hinges. They were flooded with daylight. Within their vision was the rain streaming on the now glistening wooden steps, and a mass of broken squared timber that had supported the roof of the shed. As a fire roaring up an open flue the mighty wind sped across the uncovered descent to the cellar, and within the roar other sounds, smashing of crumpling sheets of roof-iron, and wind-driven kerosene buckets. And, some thirty seconds after the door flew inward, there came to them an earth-quaking crash that wrenched cries of fear from the children and a gasp of terror from herself.

It seemed that that tremendous crash marked the apex or crisis of the storm, for shortly afterwards the wind slackened its terrific even pressure, and came in ever more accentuated gusts and comparative lulls.

"It has almost gone now," she whispered ; and Harold on her right sighed as a man of forty, and James on her left clung to her fiercely and shook with sobs. "Hush, hush, darling ! It is all right. See, the rain is stopping, and soon the sun will come out. Just let us stay a little longer, and then we'll go up and get breakfast."

"The noise, mummie! What was that noise?" the younger cried, eyes staring, chubby face tear-drenched and uplifted to hers. She bent her head and kissed the wet eyelids.

"It was only the wind," she said, forcing a laugh.

"Yes, mummie," Harold chimed in. "But that other noise-the big noise?"

"Oh! that was the pig-sty roof blown away, I expect. But let us see what clothes you have, and then you can dress. By that time the rain will have stopped, I am sure."

James could not find his jacket and Harold had lost his shirt and braces; but, as Hester Long had prophesied, by the time they had put on the garments they did have, the rain had almost stopped. The wind, however, blew tempest-strong, and with the squalls of a tempest, and down upon them rushed cold currents of air.

Hester Long stood up, and wrapped about her small but strong body one of the white woolly blankets. Followed by her children she reached the steps, and the water on them, as well as the water lying at their base, struck chilly against her naked feet. Helping the younger to ascend the slippery, littered steps with her, she finally reached the ground-level—and there stood aghast, confronted by the ruins of her home strewn on the ground like a collapsed house of cards. The red pisé-built walls, two feet thick, lay broken and jumbled beneath battered twisted sheets of roof-iron ; wooden veranda posts were snapped off ; brick chimneys lay partly buried in the little plot of kitchen garden, whilst here and there, visible and protruding, were parts of a bedstead, a table, a broken picture-frame, and, oddly enough, a book, laid open as by a human hand, resting on an upturned, uninjured kitchen chair.

The children were stricken dumb. With the wind whisking the hem of the blanket about her, oblivious of the biting coldness of it, Hester Long surveyed the destruction of the home she had worked and struggled so hard to maintain. With infinite slowness the corners of her mouth drooped, with infinite slowness tears welled into her limpid grey eyes and, unheeded, trickled down her lined cheeks. The house wherein she had known great joy, great sorrow, and deep loneliness, the house that had been her protection and the protection of her fatherless boys, was now but a mullock-heap.

But in that moment Hester Long felt no anger against God, or against Fate. Whereas a man would have wrung his hands and cursed, Hester Long stood holding in each of her hands the hand of a small boy, and wept. The balance, she recognized, was in her favour. The house, with each article of furnishing which she had loved for its associations, was no more; but her boys were alive and uninjured, and she was alive and uninjured, and able to go on fighting for them. God, as it were, had given her a pound and had taken away but a shilling.

It was then that the voice, deep and vibrant, and oh ! so welcome, of Tom Mallory fell on her ears ; and, turning, she saw him mounted on a great grey gelding, splashing through the water running in rivulets everywhere.

"Gad, Mrs. Long! This is a smash, to be sure. I feared the house wouldn't stand that cyclone, for it was built in the year One. But how did you manage to escape?"

"We—we hid in the cream-cellar. I heard the wind coming. I didn't know it was the wind, but the sound frightened me. And now look—look at our home, Tom! What are we going to do now? It's gone. It's all gone. Everything."

Keen-faced and lithe of figure, Tom Mallory slid off his horse and tied the bridle-reins to the one remaining upright of the cellar shed. He then came and stood before Hester Long, and in his eyes was a gleam she did not then see. His voice was very gentle when he said :

"Nothing is ever so bad that it cannot be mended. Here is Edith coming with two horses and a dray, because a light horse could never drag a buggy or buckboard through the mud. You must come home with us as soon - as we can get you there, and to-morrow we'll all start in and salvage your undamaged possessions and then rush up a new house."

Hester Long saw her friend Edith driving two powerful draught-horses along the flooded track towards them. The girl was standing upright on the dray and urging the animals with whip and voice, like a charioteer in a Roman arena. From her Hester looked up into the sympathetic face of Tom Mallory, and, smiling wistfully through her tears, she said:

"Everything is never utterly lost until one loses one's friends."

Two hours later she was dressed in Edith Mallory's clothes, which with a little alteration fitted her passably well. The Mallorys' farm had suffered comparatively little damage, but to what extent the storm had damaged their neighbours they were unable to learn for several days, since all telephone wires were down. The Broadcasting Station at Perth was equally without information for the same reason.

Whilst Edith Mallory fussed about her and the children, Hester noticed how strained was her face and the frightened hungry look in her blue eyes. It was whilst they lunched in the Mallorys' light and airy dining-room, with the sun now and then peeping through the cloud-wrack and brightening the drenched landscape outside the french-windows, that she said softly :

"You are worrying about Mr. Cain, Edith?"

"Oh! I can't help it," the other burst out, gripping one of Hester's arms. "I am frantic with fear now that we have you here safely. His camp must have been in the line of the storm centre, for I saw how the trees between it and your house are torn up. I want to know, Hester—I must know! You must release me from my promise—you must let me go to him."

He should be all right, dear. Remember that his camp is well protected by the coast sand-hill; better protected by far than was my house."

Whilst she honestly believed this, Hester Long herself, too, was suffering an agony of anxiety; yet still she endeavoured to persuade her friend from going to the beach that day, or any other day: The promise she had exacted from Edith Mallory, that the girl would not again go to the beach alone, Hester Long knew would be kept. It was Edith Mallory's pleadings to be allowed to know the worst that won Hester Long's consent to leave the children in the care of the maid and accompany her friend on horseback to the Beach of Atonement.

"I only want to see him, Hester dear, to be sure he is unhurt," urged Edith somewhat wildly. "If we can see him moving about from Big Hill, it will be sufficient."

"Very well; we'll go. But your brother will think us mad."

CHAPTER XXVII

DEATH—AND LIFE

ONCE again Arnold Dudley sat on the Seagulls' Throne. It was noon, yet he had eaten nothing, for the magnetism of that terrific storm had drawn him, early that morning, irresistibly to the beach, and had held him there spellbound by its magnificent aftermath.

From the rocky summit he watched the coming of the wind with the lightning ripping and sizzling about him and the deluge flattening the sea. And out of the rain-fog had sprung the wind, bringing in its mouth a ten-foot wall of water and pressing down the sea behind as though by its enormous weight. With a hideous shriek it came, giving him just time to sprawl flat on the Throne and cling with lacerated fingers to its sharp edge.

Between eyelids lowered to mere slits he saw the sea rush up to the low sand rampart backing the clear beach on his right and left; saw the water kept to its level by the force of the wind, whilst the summits of the beach sand-hills were blown away in smoke, and in the smoke the small tenacious bushes that had held the sand together. Deeply into the hills of sand bit the wind, tearing across them gutters that magically widened and deepened into gullies. Across the permanent gullies it screamed to the slightly higher hills beyond. With an ear-shattering blast it swept up and over the sand-mountains in the background, blotting them from sight with sand and debris. A hundred-mile-an-hour wind had pounced on the beach, and in ten seconds had shifted countless tons of sand, wiping out sand-hills that had stood for years, and creating new hills of pure sand where before had been level beach.

How long this devastating pressure lasted Dudley could not estimate. It banished all physical feeling, save that his face smarted as though bathed in boiling water ; for the sand on the steeply-rising slope below him had played on him as a flaying sand-blast.

The scene of chaos chained his mind as the wind his body. Watching the rain lift, his vision leapt to the far horizon. The sea, the usually calm and lovely sea, was white and hideous with passion. It showed a million rows of serrated teeth—long, low wavelets of foam—leaping landward at amazing speed. The entire ocean was boiling as a stupendous cauldron.

Almost as suddenly as the wind had reached the beach it passed over, leaving a dead calm that lasted possibly ten seconds. The sea sank to its normal level, with the effect of the backwash of a monstrous wave. As though the entire beach had shaken itself free from the gripping wind, it sent outward into the face of the next gust an enormous counter-wave. As though hell's fires had been lit beneath, the ocean rose in hummocks and mountains, seemed to pause, and then to rush madly shoreward impelled by the wind, now blowing from the south-west.

Whereas on ordinary days the Ramparts had been marked by the rising and falling horizon-line, their position now was lost in a smother of high-flung spray, which wiped out the horizon altogether. Shoreward from them raced waves of a monstrous, an incredible hugeness. The crests of them appeared to be on a level with the awed Dudley, and he was a hundred feet above the Pontoon. The pitch, or distance between crest and crest, appeared to be fully half a mile. They were mountain ranges racing against the beach, threatening to overwhelm the land and to surge up the slopes of the sand-mountains two miles eastward. Their height, where they met the submerged Sugar Loaf and the Pontoon, was enormous, bearing on their upflung crests low walls of water that were swept into spray by the following wind, to pause for a fraction of time, curl over landward as some vast, green, white-laced, wonderful sea-shell, and rush on the bluff headland or the open sandy beach on either side.

As for the Seaweed Mountain, it was gone. In its place twenty-foot waves curled over the beach, thence to dash up the steep slope of sand and slap the wall of the first sand-ridge. In foaming masses each wave surged over the Pontoon and struck the limestone headland with a reverberating roar, shooting up spouts of water from its face, water to be whipped into fine spray and carried to and past the watching man.

Black and evil were the troughs between the waves; white and terrifyingly beautiful their crests. Their power was fearful to watch, their aspect paralysing. Arnold Dudley felt much as the man probably felt who was bound to a post surrounded by chained lions, who every now and then were given a further foot of chain.

At noon the racing cloud-wrack broke up, affording glimpses of sun. The wind pressure was relaxed, coming now in fierce squalls with comparatively calm intervals between; yet, whilst the wind slowly eased, the seas seemed to rise to greater heights. The smoke from the sand-ridges thinned. Saturated by the rain, it was marvellous that they smoked at all. Towards one o'clock the conditions had moderated to those of an ordinary gale.

Another day was passing. The vision of frantic water was losing its grip, and the mind of the man was becoming increasingly aware of the discomforts of his body and the hideous monotony of his existence. It was as though the cyclone had frozen his brain, which the peeping sun was slowly melting, releasing first the impressions of an awful world and then thoughts of his frightful exile.

Another day was passing. How many more were to pass before freedom came, before the shackles of his supreme stupidity fell from him ? He sat upon the Seagulls' Throne and buried his smarting face in his crossed arms supported by his bent knees. The old feeling of nakedness came over his spirit, and his body visibly shrank towards the rock.

How long had he really been there on that rock? A few hours? Or hundreds of years? It seemed to him that he had been there before Time was, and sudden terror, more exquisite than terror of the wind, made him raise his head and open his eyes to the light of day-then spring to his feet and gaze with wild bloodshot eyes over the vast welter of maddened water.

And, as suddenly as he had broken into violent movement, his body stiffened when he saw, for the first time off that forbidding coast, a ship.

It was about a mile from the beach. At first sight Dudley knew there was something amiss. It was without power, incapable of self-movement. It wallowed even in rising to the highest crests, and each time it sank into the long troughs Dudley had no hope of seeing it again.

A ship! There! On that coast! Disabled!

Again it rose into sight, and he saw and noted its colours. A black funnel with one narrow white band, two squat masts, white-painted upper-works, and a black-painted hull with a red bottom. Every time it heaved upward into his line of sight tons of water cascaded from its fore and aft well-decks. Squat, tubby, a tramp. An ocean tramp of perhaps two thousand tons.

Dudley pressed his hands to his eyes, and when again he looked the ship was not there. So after all it was another trick of the devil. But no! There it was again, nearer, driven nearer by the wind straight towards him.

"Mad! Mad! I'm going mad!" he shouted suddenly. Then, in what was almost a whimper: "It can't be. I tell you it cannot be. No ship could get there. No ship could get across the Ramparts and float. And yet—and yet it is there. I see it. I can almost see—yes, I can see men. They're lowering a boat. Dear God! as though a boat could live, could ever come ashore."

For a little while he watched. Then: "Yes, that must be the reason. A huge wave must have carried her clean over the Ramparts. What's wrong with her? Hey, you, captain! What's wrong? A broken propeller? Slipped your propeller? No? Ah yes, yes! I hear. Smashed your rudder. Poor, poor ship with a smashed rudder!"

Dudley's firm mouth seemed to disintegrate and become a slobbering gap. From his eyes fled the ever-keen, fierce gaze which, added to his faintly outlined Roman nose, gave his face that slight resemblance to an eagle's. The sight of the helpless ship, the thought of the sure inevitable doom of its people, seemed to snap the last thread that had held his sanity. His face was pitiable, his attitude abject. His fingers hovered tremblingly about his mouth. His hazel eyes were clouded, yet still fixed on the shoreward-driven tramp.

The Thing that men call Madness had laid one claw on him. It had stalked him, tracked him with the pertinacity of a tiger-cat following a kangaroo. Now it had caught him up.

Arnold Dudley leapt from the Seagulls' Throne. Lo! it stood twice its original height, its secret bared. It was not a casual boulder after all. The Throne was the top portion of a pillar forming the core of the hill of sand, and the storm had blown tons of its sand covering away from it, leaving fifteen feet of it exposed. Dudley dropped on his feet, but the distance he fell upset his balance, and he pitched forward on his face and rolled clown to the narrow ledge of rock edging the headland.

On his feet once more, unhurt and unshaken, he stepped right to the edge of the low headland and shouted at the ship, now half a mile nearer and drifting directly to the Pontoon. Below him the monstrous waves roared against the face of the headland, shaking the rock beneath him a second before the sheet of spouting foam sprang upward, blotting out the ocean and the ship and drenching him. His eyes cleared of their cloudiness, and, raising his fists above his head, Arnold Dudley screamed:

"Fools! Fools! Your boats are no use to you. You've got to die! You've got to die! You're better off than I am. I've got to live—live for ever and ever and ever!" His voice sank to a whisper. "What do you want to come here for? You're not going to have my gulls. D'you hear? They're my gulls. I've fed them and looked after them. They're my gulls, I tell you! My gulls!" Again his voice rose to a scream. "Don't you hear what I'm telling you? They're my seagulls. What's that? Ellen! Ellen coming ashore! You are sending Ellen ashore for me? Liar! Captain, you're a liar! Ellen is a broken vase. What's the use of a broken vase to me? Tracy broke the vase. A vase full of cracks and lines, chipped and in pieces. Ha, ha, my bonny heroes! Fifteen men on a dead man's chest! Die, damn you! Why can't you drown like men instead of hitting my brain with wireless hammers? Yes, that's what you are doing. But I can stand it—you bet I can——."

"Mr. Cain, what are you saying?"

The words were shouted at him above the wind and the roaring sea, and, turning his head, he looked down into the horrified face of Edith Mallory. And, seeing her, the fire seemed to be quenched within him and his face fell into lines of pitiful weakness. It was as though he stood on the verge of tears because of what he saw in her wild eyes and strained, ghastly face. His eyes left hers quickly, shiftily, and again his hands flew up to his quivering mouth, which his trembling fingers seemed as though trying to still. Then suddenly he saw Hester Long on his other side.

"Have you seen a broken vase?" he stuttered. "The captain said he had left one here for me and Ellen to pick up.

"Think of a broken ship, Mr. Cain," Hester Long said sternly, believing that she had to deal with hysteria. "Can't we do something to help those poor people out there?"

She saw him gape at her with vacant eyes, whilst a second passed, two seconds, three. Straight into his eyes she stared, her heart almost stopped by the look of him, realization dawning of his madness.

Hester Long never knew precisely what it was Arnold Dudley saw in her face which for the time restored his reason. With wonder she saw the vacant look give way to intelligence, watched the lines of his face straighten and harden into the semblance of those she knew. He rubbed his eyes with his open hands as though the light were too strong, and when again he looked at her she saw in them bewilderment and surprise.

"Why, Mrs. Long, I did not see you come," he said slowly. "What brings you here on a day like this?"

"We saw the ship from Big Hill," she told him, pointing to it.

"The ship! Miss Mallory, too! The ship—what ship?"

He saw the tramp, now less than half a mile from them, and his body stiffened and his brain froze with the sudden horror of it beating on his clear mind. The last period of sanity had come to him, and because it was the last his mind was crystal clear. He saw all that he had seen before, and remembered. He realized that there was no hope for either ship or crew, for nothing that he or the two women with him could do would avert its fate. Cut off from civilization and without the most elementary life-saving appliances, the three onlookers were powerless. There was nothing they could do but stand and watch the end, and perhaps pray, or try to pray, for the welfare of departing souls.

"Can't we do something?" Hester Long cried.

Dudley slowly turned and looked at her, shaking his head.

"What can we do? See! they are lowering a boat."

Hester Long's plain face was white with pity and horror. She stood, small, frail, yet dominant, her hands rigid against her sides. Edith Mallory held Dudley's right arm in her two hands, her breath coming in sobbing gasps. The man between the two women watched the fated tragedy, drenched repeatedly by the leaping walls of water shooting up the face of the headland, oblivious of the hissing, roaring, pounding sea at their feet, or of the gulls that arrived in twos and threes to settle on their Throne, high above the watchers' heads.

The launching of the boats was a pitifully forlorn hope. The wind was driving the steamer northward as well as eastward to the beach, driving it directly towards the Pontoon. From the Pontoon southward for four miles the beach was open and sandy. The forlorn hope lay in reaching the open stretch of beach, for against the Pontoon no boat constructed by man could live. And even if men managed to get a ship's boat to the open beach the chance of escaping from the undertow was small.

The watching three saw one boat launched and clear of the ship, evidence of superb seamanship. Not for many long seconds was it possible to see the small boat in the trough. Then into view it sprang, tossed high by a mighty foam-capped wave. Six or eight men, tugging frantically at their oars, managed to keep the boat's stern to the crest that rose behind and above them. The boat was a match, the crest a match-box on edge. It curled over and down on the boat, hiding it in white foam, and Dudley and his two companions saw neither boat nor men again.

"Gone—they're gone!" he cried.

Hester Long closed her eyes. Her lips moved, but if she spoke the wind blew away the words. The girl's face was as white as chalk, her features as immobile. Even her eyelids never flickered whilst she gazed at the hapless ship.

Now broadside to them, each wave that carried her up out of the water-pits showed the watchers the decks tilted their way, and they could see broken deck-rails and twisted and splintered wood and iron. Over came the ship, so that almost they could look down her solitary squat funnel.

Tons of water swept up her topmost, almost horizontal, side to pour over on the slanted decks. And then, when the wave passed under her, the ship gallantly righted herself, thence to heel seaward and reveal a third of her red-painted bottom before again she slid down into a water-pit. And each time she appeared she was fifty yards nearer the Pontoon.

The end came when but a quarter-mile separated ship from shore. Sliding down a water-pit, her bottom came with smashing impact on submerged rocks. The hollow, metallic crash of it reached the watchers, a sound utterly horrible. The rocks must have torn her bottom clean out. Coming into sight on the following wave, they saw that her funnel had gone, lying as a black stick across the bridge to the fore well-deck. Her masts, too, were down. She was a ship no longer, for her hull was below water and it seemed as though only her ripped and torn decks were afloat. They were submerged by the wave-crest, blackening here and there the white foam. That was the end, for nothing was seen on the crest of the following wave.

"It is all over," whispered Dudley unheard.

Edith Mallory was clinging to him, her hair swept loose, head thrown back, great tears sliding down her face. Her eyes were wide and strangely vivid, and from her mouth came one phrase screamed over and over again.

"I'll never forget it—I'll never forget it—I'll never forget it!" Dread of unfailing remembrance, of unfading vision, was upon her haunted face, and frantically she shook Dudley's arm, perhaps because he continued to stare at the sea, unconscious of her presence.

And now the sea began to exhibit its spoils, bringing in wreckage to sweep it over the Pontoon at their feet. A barrel riding high was the first to come. Then a plank, followed by an upturned boat miraculously saved from destruction against the Pontoon. A packing-case and the top part of a swivel-chair came next, and afterwards a hundred and one wooden things or their fragments.

The flotsam came careering across the Pontoon, escorted by countless streamers and bunches of green, black, and brown seaweed. The tide, forced by the north and north-west wind, had carried the wave-disintegrated Seaweed Mountain southward along the coast, and now that the

wind had veered to the south-west the tide set northward and was bringing back the seaweed to build it again into a mountain at its former site
immediately the waves subsided. Already its position was marked by acres
of floating weed, among which the curling surf was unable to penetrate.

A four-knot tide raced across the Pontoon, now sub-merged by twelve
or fourteen feet of water when a wave roared against the headland, now
covered by a bare three feet when the wave rushed out to meet the next.
The flotsam was beaten and battered by the incoming walls of white water,
pulled round and past the headland, and there divided by the currents.
The heavier items were drawn seaward again into the Boiling Pot, north
of the Sugar Loaf, a spewing, racing cauldron ; but the lighter and great
majority of the items of flotsam were carried on to be embedded among
the floating mass of seaweed, presently to be buried within the mountain.
It was a whim of the sea, one of countless whims of the eternal sea, feminine in its softer moods, masculine in its placidity and its rage.

Of his companions Arnold Dudley was but dimly conscious. He was
alive when twenty or more brave men had died. He, an outcast, bloody
and damned, lived when decent men, some certainly with women and
children dependent on them, had perished. The irony of it bit deep, and
its breath scorched his soul. Regret! Regret! Tracy had come out best. He
had won over Ellen in life and over him in death. And in the end, when
death claimed him, Tracy would win again; for he was a martyr and his
slayer a murderer, abhorred by God and man.

"Look! Oh look!"

The command was hurled at him by Hester Long, who was pointing
her outstretched hand at the sea south of the Pontoon. Edith Mallory saw
what she pointed out before Arnold Dudley emerged from his reverie,
shaken out of it by two suddenly frantic women. Not a hundred yards
from where he stood, but a few yards within the shooting water-wall at
the edge of the Pontoon, the tide was sweeping towards them a hatch-grating, and on it lay, face upward, a man. The grating was either small or
broken. About it and through it twined a length of heavy rope. The rope
lay coiled about the man's arms, as though he had used it in haste to secure
himself to the hatch.

A rushing ledge of water swooped on the hatch-grating, buried it in white suds, swept it forward on its lip, left it to sink down into the trough whilst it sprang to the headland, was dashed backward, and ran out in a lesser ledge to fall once more on the hatch-grating, pass over it, and leap to meet the next incoming wave. Buffeted and flung forward and then back again, the castaway was brought to the very feet of the watchers.

Now in the grip of the north-bound tide, grating and man swept past them. They saw a calm bearded face, in which the eyes were closed, and a great muscular body covered by a ship's officer's uniform.

"He's alive—he's alive still!" cried the older woman, her voice vibrant, her small body tense and dangerously near the cliff-edge. "See! His eyes are closed. If he were dead they would be open."

Dudley understood that. He knew, knew absolutely, that the man was alive, although unconscious. How it had been possible for him to live through all that hellish water was of no concern to Dudley then. What wholly occupied his mind was which way would the tide take the grating? Shoreward to the floating seaweed, or far out into the rushing, leaping smother marking the Boiling Pot? And as certainly as he knew that the man was alive, so certainly he knew that the Boiling Pot would be his destination.

If, however, a swimmer could push it farther shoreward before it reached the point where the tide separated all flotsam, it would be a comparatively easy task to bring man and grating right to the beach before it was claimed by the seaweed mass. For immediately north of the headland was created by wind and tide a back-water, gentle in movement and sheltered by the formation of the Pontoon.

To Dudley then was given the hope of redemption. The hope was as a light flaring through his mind, expelling the depression that had held down his spirit as beneath a weight of many tons. It washed him clean of blood, that amazing hope, it flung off the baffled Thing men call Madness, and when he turned and faced the two women they were startled by the radiance emanating from his face, so changed, so beautiful.

"He'll go to the Boiling Pot for sure," he cried, and, stooping, whipped off his elastic-sided bushman's boots. "You see—it's my chance. If I get him out, I atone for Tracy's life which I took. If I lose my life in the effort I make atonement also. Don't I?"

He stood now with his coat off, his back to the sea, the wind blowing his over-long brown hair low over his broad forehead, and when he said: "Don't I?" Hester Long saw that he was looking straight at her, clearly, steadily, sanely. A woman screamed.

"No, no, no! You shan't—you shan't! You haven't a chance. Hector! Dear Hector! You cannot! you must not! you'll be drowned ! you can do nothing. Oh, my God! you shan't go—you shan't !"

Edith Mallory clung to his arms, hung on them. Her wild, staring eyes were terrible in their intensity, reflecting the horror of her thoughts. Yet never did he look down on the anguished, upturned, lovely face, but gazed steadily over it into the eyes of Hester Long.

And Hester Long knew that the choice lay with her, knew that Arnold Dudley awaited her response. Time stopped. Death, death, death lay waiting for him in the sea. It was impossible for him to accomplish the salvation of the castaway. She heard, within, a sound of many voices calling, shrieking. The voices took sides and, benumbed her brain with their clamour. "Death awaits him in the sea. You cannot let him go. You know how much you love him. Loving him, how can you send him into that terrible water?—Let him go, Hester! What is your love against his atonement? Let him go now, before again the madness springs upon him."

The agony of indecision tore at her nerves and stabbed her heart. Standing there waiting, his lips still parted after having said: "Don't I?" radiant with the vision of redemption in his eyes, splendid in his virile manhood, Hester Long shrank backward and raised her hands in supplication. From her lips at last came the fateful word, distinctly, firmly spoken, but low, as fraught with the awe of a decision made for eternity:

"Yes!"

The woman of her wanted to rush to him and help her friend to restrain his mad impulse. The soul of her sang triumph at her sending him forth to grasp this one and only opportunity held out to him of winning salvation. The roar of the sea became a monstrous sound in her cars. Her heart! Would her heart stop? Why could she not move ? How was it she could not roach him and cling to him as Edith Mallory was doing, and give vent by shrieks to the horror eating away her vitals? Her eyes appeared to fail her, for her vision became blurred; yet she could see him smiling at her, such a smile as she never had seen on his face, and above the roaring in her ears she heard him say:

"Thank you, Hester! Dear old pal! You understand."

Gently, yet quickly and firmly, he forced the girl's hands from his arms, pushed her away to give himself a start, then raced along the headland to its north-west point. Edith Mallory stumblingly raced after him imploring him to stop, but if he heard he never once looked back.

Hester Long saw him standing at the cliff-edge. A wall of water leapt up in front of him, and when it sank he jumped feet foremost into the smother. She saw her friend on her knees looking downward. She wanted to go to look down also, but found her legs held as by immovable weights. She knew he was drowning even at that awful moment. But no! There he was, being swept away from the headland, swimming with thrashing strokes after the grating a bare dozen yards away. Her heart leapt with exultation at the thought that victory would be his, in that he would push the castaway on his raft into the currents racing towards the seaweed.

Almost had Arnold Dudley reached the grating when he went down, sucked deep by the water-devil. One year, two, three, five years dragged slowly away, and still he did not come up. Time! There was time no longer. Pain! No longer was there pain. Hester Long felt neither pain nor sense of time. As a statue she stood, whilst the man she loved died unseen.

And presently she felt a strange gladness. Life became a thing of warmth once more. Flooding her as brilliant sunshine, knowledge was vouchsafed her of Arnold Dudley radiant, triumphant, gloriously redeemed.

Without curiosity she saw the man she had met on the main road and thought to be a detective standing beside Edith Mallory. She saw her friend's pitiful face for an instant lifted to his whilst she pointed to the place where Dudley had vanished. She saw beside this man a slender girlish figure dressed in navy blue, and wondered idly who she could be— idly, because in her ears rang the voice of Hector Cain, saying :

"Thank you, Hester! Dear old pal! You understand."

CHAPTER XXVIII

A WOMAN OF EMPIRE

THE three months following the wreck of the S.S. Eipeluera on the coast north of Dongara, with the loss of twenty-three lives, was a period of tremendous activity for Hester Long. Leaving the Mallorys' house every morning in her dilapidated buggy drawn by old Brownie, she returned by the same slow but sure conveyance in the evening of the day spent on her farm.

The railway strike hindered the erection of her new home by a month, but when finally the men returned to work, without having won those union wage standards for the Blue Metallers' Union, the material was quickly delivered at Dongara and the work started.

Mr. and Mrs. Jessop being also badly hit financially by the cyclone, the fat and prosperous Mr. Smythe obtained the requisite assistance to make good the damage. Mrs. Brown having recovered her health, she sent her husband and her golden-hearted Joe to join with Tom Mallory in putting Hester Long on her feet once more. Under the supervision of a house-builder from Dongara the three men built Hester Long's new house in a little less than eight weeks.

It became her duty to keep the volunteer workers supplied with tea and food, a duty cheerfully and lovingly performed as the only possible expression of her gratitude; for those big-hearted Western Australians not only refused to accept wages, but also were most extraordinarily remiss in being unable to tell her what the building material cost and from whom it was bought. When the labour of love was finished, Hester Long possessed a six-roomed up-to-date bungalow-house.

There followed in due course a house-warming, to which Hester Long invited all her friends, who were all her neighbours. The party was timed to start at five o'clock in the evening. To it came the Jessops with their innumerable children packed tightly on a buckboard ; Mr. and Mrs. Smythe in their ultra-modern single-seater; Mr. and Mrs. Brown in Joe's antique Ford car ; and Tom and Edith Mallory, who rode over on hacks.

Two surprises were given at that party. It was in full swing when Joe Brown arrived with a stranger driving a strange truck, on which was a case, many lengths of strong iron piping; and much wire. Hester wanted to go out and bring them in to supper, but Mrs. Brown and the other women cornered her in the new sitting-room, leaving the children and the men to slink out to join Joe and his companion.

Hester Long did not see the wireless masts erected and the aerial swung from them, but she was astonished to see Joe and his father carry into the sitting-room an expensive wireless set, which they put on a table near the big-paned wide window. Through that window crawled the stranger, trailing copper wire behind him.

They made her sit on a chair before the set. Whilst the stranger did things with a pair of wire-cutters, Tom Mallory fitted over her beautiful hair a pair of ear-phones. Expertly and silently the stranger worked, now with head-phones to his ears, and suddenly Hester Long heard the broadcasting announcer in Perth telling her that egg were from two and nine to three shillings per dozen. And, whilst listening, she caught sight of a small metal plate fitted to the front of the set and read on it :

To HESTER LONG, who saved the sole survivor from the wreck of the S.S. Eipeluera, 16th May, 1929. From Hester Long's Friends.

For a little while her head was bowed, and then she stood up, took off the gleaming head-phones, and turned to her guests with moist shining eyes. Her lips were trembling. "My friends—my wonderful friends—" she said before she broke down. They smiled on her, patted and fussed about her, but it was Edith Mallory who hugged her and cried softly with her. And after a little while it was Edith Mallory who whispered:

"Tell them now, Hester."

More composed, but her eyes still bright with tears, Hester Long began to speak clearly and firmly. Without faltering, she said:

"You all remember the man who attempted to save the captain of the ship, and lost his life in the attempt. You met him here the afternoon of my last burn. His name, as you know, was Hector Cain.

"Edith and I first met him on the beach, and eventually got to know him rather well. There was some tragedy he was trying to live down, and he was bravely doing it when he sacrificed his life.

"He came here when he heard that my sheep were being attacked by eagles. I promised to pay him a bonus of half a crown for every one he caught. He caught forty-seven, yet he would not take from me my promised bonus. Afterwards he worked for me for a few weeks and put up a line of fence for which I stipulated to pay twenty-two pounds a mile. This money also he refused to accept, saying that he owed me far more for friendship than the amount I owed him for work. Altogether he should have received from me seventy-five pounds twelve shillings and sixpence.

"Mr. Cain at one time rendered Edith a great service, and she proposes to make the amount I have just named up to a hundred and fifty pounds. With this money, Edith and I want to create a lasting memorial, making the money a trust fund. It is not very much, and the annual interest would probably only amount to eight or nine pounds. Now that you are all here, we would like you to decide the form the memorial should take."

For a little while there was silence, excepting for Mrs. Jessop's low crooning lullaby to her current baby. Joe Brown scratched his head unashamedly. Mr. Smythe pinched his fat upper lip. Mr. Brown suggested devoting the money to the purchase of clothing for the poorer children of Dongara, from which Mrs. Brown disagreed. Jessop's eldest boy suggested the upkeep of a local cricket team, and was severely frowned down. Tom Mallory proposed the scheme that eventually was adopted.

"Why not devote the annual interest to the expense of sending the best scholar at Dongara school every year to Perth for a certain number of days? The cost could be easily assessed. Perhaps at times the current interest could be increased by some such means as a bazaar. For instance, if three boys and three girls in charge of the schoolmaster and his wife could be sent every year to Perth for three days, the trip would be of enormous educational benefit to the children if they were shown the historic places of Perth and Fremantle.

"You know this is the Centenary Year of Western Australia. Considering the wonderful growth of the State since Captain Stirling landed on the bank of the Swan River from the—the Parmelia, I think it was—to the present time, to my mind the rising generation should be guided to recognize the responsibilities of citizenship and become possessed of a keen pride in their State, their Country, their Empire."

"A good idea, Tom ! What do you think of that, Mrs. Long?" asked Mr. Smythe.

"I think it is splendid," declared Hester Long. "Don't you, Edith?"

"I do, indeed," Edith cried, her face alight with an inward glory. "Yes, it is a good idea, Tom. And let it be called 'The Hector Cain Educational Trip'."

And thereafter the house-warming proceeded to its destined hilarious end.

.   .   .   .   .

It was a few days later that Hester Long drove behind old Brownie to the Beach of Atonement, and pulled up for a little while in the clearing beside the track where Arnold Dudley had erected his tent and parked his motor-truck.

Nothing now remained of his occupation other than a few empty tins and a piece or two of discoloured paper. The little cleared spaces cut out of the thick-growing bush were memorials provided by Dudley himself. At one time Hester Long had thought of keeping those spaces always clear from the mass of space-hungry bush, but the idea of spending the money she owed him in perpetuating his memory had occurred and seemed better worth while. Already bush shoots were appearing from the old stumps and roots, and a year hence the clearings would be no more.

Sighing softly, Hester urged on old Brownie and came at last to the open sandy place back of the Pontoon and directly against the hill of sand crowned by the Seagulls' Throne. The birds were resting thereon, and at her coming rose and flew out along the beach for a little way, and then back again to the buggy suspicious of her, yet undoubtedly remembering the crusts thrown to them by that other benevolent human being.

After hitching old Brownie to the post, Hester Long took from the seat of the buggy a large biscuit-tin and clambered down the low sand rampart to the rocky floor of the Pontoon, there to toss handfuls of crusts into the rock-pools left by the previous high tide, and standing watching the birds flutter and swoop upon them.

Their number was eleven. Only eleven! She wondered what had become of the other six, and if those six would come back with the summer. Her plain, lined face was wistful, and from her lips fell the words:

"Your gulls, Hector! I am feeding your gulls."

Afterwards she returned to the buggy for a book, and, knowing that now she could not possibly climb up to the Seagulls' Throne, she walked out along the edge of the low bluff headland and seated herself at its point, there to look on the beach that had been his.

The sun was warm and comforting. The sea was smiling, vivid blue, diamond-sprinkled. It caressed the squat Sugar Loaf and lazily welled up over the far edge of the Pontoon to send in to her line after line of milk-white foam. The Seaweed Mountain rested at the foot of the gleaming beach, a hummock of black and brown, mighty in aspect, yet an easy victim to the sea's fury.

His beach ! He called it the Beach of Atonement. There over those rocks he had died, and, dying, had sal-vaged his wrecked soul. Sad yet glad was Hester Long whilst she sat there, the pages of the Book of her Mind revealing pictures of him during those last tempestuous months— pictures of his stirring battles with the demons of solitude, and that last great moment when he had shot at her the brief, fateful question :

"Don't I ?"

And then the picture of her own terrific battle. Her "Yes!" had sent him to his death, yet to eternal life. Her "No !" would have prevented his making atonement, would have kept him chained to the desolate beach, eventually to die there unredeemed, a lunatic. For Ellen's coming was too late—too late. How glad was Hester that strength had been given her to utter that "Yes!" when the little word was the hardest of any to be said!

"Thank you, Hester ! Dear old pal! You understand."

It was as though Dudley stood there beside her and spoke once more. Her face was tilted upward and she seemed to wait expectantly, oblivious of the gulls returning now in twos and threes to their Throne high up behind her.

The pages of the Book of Memory turned over. She saw how the ship's grating carrying its human flotsam was being miraculously swept round the headland towards the floating mass of seaweed, for the water-devil seemed to have been satiated by Dudley's sacrifice and to have had mercy on the castaway. And then that one wild impulse to do the work "he" had essayed to do. How she had raced down to the little beach above her children's paddling pool then deep under water, but just then a calm back-water. How she had slipped out of her dress and clashed into the water to swim out to the grating, now inside the "race" from the Pontoon, and bring it ashore but fifty yards from the seaweed mass where Finlay, unable to swim, waded out to receive it and her.

The castaway still lived. Finlay's strength and slight knowledge of resuscitation, combined with grim determination to win, had assured the man's rescue from death. So "he" had not died in vain ; and, even whilst Hester Long cried a little, and her small body shook a little from her sobs, she experienced joy and thankfulness that to her had fallen the task of helping "him" along his dreadful road to the wonderful goal.

On her lap lay open the diary she had given "him", and which Ellen Dudley had returned to her from among his possessions. A hundred times she had read every word "he" had written. A hundred times she had felt "his" depressions, "his" exaltations, "his" fears, and "his" poor hopes. And there, seated above "his" beach, she read once again the words "he" had written on the fly-leaf:

"The day will come when I shall know that I cannot go on living. When I am dead, will the finder please return this book to Mrs. Hester Long, the finest woman I have ever known?"

And underneath:

"Hester—'The Moving Finger writes; and having writ, moves on: . . .'"

The sun was sinking when at last she rose to her feet to go, realizing that it was late. Edith knew where she was, and would go home with her boys and milk the cows for her. Edith would not come with her that day, nor did she wish ever again to visit that beach.

The small work-lined face, crowned by its wealth of light brown hair, shone with a glory when she said her au revoir to "his" beach. Standing at the edge of the bluff headland, gazing over the place where Arnold Dudley had died, gazing into the shining distance towards England, she was the embodiment of the Spirit of Empire. The gentle sea-wind played about her uncovered head, teased the hem of her white skirt.

Never will the Empire go down whilst it can produce its Hester Longs.

www.ingramcontent.com/pod-product-compliance
Lightning Source LLC
Chambersburg PA
CBHW030401020726
47493CB00003B/912